For centuries, stories of love have been told amongst our human race.

The handsome knight, who sets out on a grand adventure to rescue the princess in distress from a powerful evil. Always challenged but never defeated the knight rescues the damsel. With one kiss the two instantly fall in love, living happily ever after.

The young man, kind and genuine, who chases the woman of his dreams but can never obtain her. The woman pays no attention, dating awful men and unknowingly hurting the one she should truly be with. Then the young man finds a way to show the woman he was the one she was looking for all along. The two fall in love and live happily ever after.

Love is pure and innocent they say. Love cures all they say. There is one true love for us all they say. Love, love, love, the ultimate obtainment for the human race.

But.

Aren't there two sides to the same coin of love? Isn't there a tale............

A Tale of Twisted Love

Written by:

Maddison L. Beckley

Published by <u>The Heartbreak</u>, Spokane Washington.

<u>www.ataleoftwistedlove.com</u>

Book Cover Design: Ana Grigoriu

First Edition, Paperback Edition, 2015

<u>**Dedication**</u>

For the big dreamers of our world.

For the ones who come from nothing and turn it into something.

For those who put in countless hours of hard work to make their goals become realities.

Lastly, for the fans and readers of my work now. Because without you I would be nothing. Thank you & remember...

Fear nothing to accomplish anything,

Maddison L. Beckley

Table of Contents

Prologue
The Man of Darkness

The clock had just reached the early A.M. hours of night as a young woman with midnight black hair sat comfortably in her home. She read a romantic novel by a dimly lit lamp in a dark house. The cold wind was howling outside, scraping tree branches across the glass of a nearby window.

The young woman was engrossed in a story of love, barely taking notice to the sounds outside. Only the sounds of romantic words rang in her mind. She smiled with each passing page, fantasizing that the man in the book would someday appear to her, sweeping her off her feet as he had the woman in the story.

Meanwhile, a man stood inside the darkness of the woman's home, peering onto her as she read. He was one with the darkness. A shadow of sorts, not to be noticed by even the keenest of eye or sharpest of mind. Like a spider patiently waiting for a fly to be ensnared in its web, he stood, waiting. The waiting game had taken place for hours, he was patient, stalking the corridors of the woman's house and setting his webbed traps in place for her.

For you see the man of darkness was not waiting to sweep the black haired woman up in romantic bliss as the woman had envisioning while reading. No, this kind of man was a sort of grim reaper, a man of monsters and evil, a true American horror.

A cup of warm tea had been cooling beside the woman as it had every night she read. The tea was one of the woman's favorite drinks before bed, it had special ingredients to relax the body and put her restless mind at ease.

The woman blew on the tea and took a sip. Deeming it cool enough to drink she began to consume the warm liquid poison with each turned page.

As she did the man's teeth began to glow in the darkness, smiling as he knew his time to strike was near. This hadn't been the first night of watching the woman from afar and from it he had discovered a pattern in her routine of books and tea at the late hours of night. Tonight, the man shrouded in darkness meant to take advantage. The fly was about to be tangled in the unsuspecting web.

The packets of tea had been tampered with by the man of darkness. He had put his own special ingredients inside the remaining tea bags. A deadly powder that would stop a human's heart, killing them in a matter of minutes.

A death of a broken heart some would say.

As the woman sipped more and more of the tea, a sensation of tingle and drowsiness overcame her. She thought nothing of effects, thinking that the normal tea was finally kicking in, making her become sleepy like it always had before.

She finished the last ounces of the tea, setting the cup down while continuing to read.

Slowly but surely the effects that the man in darkness had added engulfed the woman's mind and body. Suddenly the woman felt nauseous and began to worry that something was wrong. She stood up looking for her phone to dial 911.

As she stood, she felt weak. Her phone was nowhere in sight. The woman panicked, rapidly looking around for her phone, but it was too late. Time had run out.

The man stepped out of the darkness revealing himself to the woman. She stood in horror at the dark figure, but she could not scream or move. She was nearly paralyzed.

Instead the woman became dizzy, losing her balance and fell to the hard wood floor with a *THUD*. At that moment the man swiftly made his way toward the dying woman. She tried to claw at him in defense, grazing his neck with her nails, but the strength to fight was leaving her. A moment passed and the woman could no longer move. She felt her life drifting away and the man of darkness became nothing but a blur.

The poison in the tea had nearly taken its last toll.

Wide eyed the woman lay lifeless on the floor as the man of darkness picked her up in his arms, slinging her limp body over his shoulder. He carried the woman down a flight of stairs and placed her on the bottom step.

The woman with midnight black hair caught one last glimpse of the dark figure as she lay on the bottom stair poisoned and dying. *This is not my man of romance,* she thought in her last moments. The seconds passed and the blackness finally took her.

Hours passed as the man of darkness covered the downstairs room in the woman's home with thick clear overspray protective sheeting. He had to be methodical and patient in his work. Any slip-ups would be fatal. Once the room was completed and the wrap covered every inch and crevice of the room, he dropped the woman's body in the middle of the floor.

As the man stepped back, he gazed upon what he had accomplished. Viewing the plastic covered room as a painter would a blank canvas. He grinned with satisfaction, his work of art was about to begin.

But as the next step came, the man became nervous with anticipation. Although he had researched for countless hours and seen how to perform the task, it was one thing to watch and another to do. This wasn't the first life he had taken, but this would be the first time he dare claim the prize he had sought after for so long.

Reaching down beside him the man of darkness unzipped a black bag he had brought. The inside of the bag reveled various shapes and sizes of stainless steel knives. The silver of the blades sparkled in the darkness of the night as the man peered inside. Lit only by a sliver of the moon that crept through a nearby window.

The man of darkness decided on a smaller knife, picking it up with his gloved hand. The feeling of touch was unfamiliar to him as he had never used these knives before. Uncertainty and curiosity filled within the man as he stared at the silver blade. With a gentle swing of the knife through the air he posed as a conductor of murder while exhaling his nervous breath, now ready to begin.

His attention shifted to the lifeless corpse as he prepared what he had set out to do. Setting the steel knife on the plastic covered floor, he ripped off the woman's blouse. Buttons came undone as he did, rolling to the floor.

Underneath the shirt revealed a black lace bra. The man of darkness unhooked the back of the claps and threw the bra aside, leaving only the snow white skin of the woman's upper body exposed. He carefully examined the woman's chest and reached for a black sharpie from within the black bag. The sharpie skated across the woman's skin with subtle movement and careful placement to the precise spots that he had practiced so many times before.

One last time the man of darkness examined the woman's chest, this time from afar. Now looking at the black marks drawn, he nodded in satisfaction of his work.

Again reaching for the small steel knife the man of darkness took off one of his gloves to gently feel the steel across the skin of his hand. The blade was sharp to the touch and ready to feed on the winter flesh of the dead woman.

While the steel grazed the skin a dark calling came from inside the man's head, whispering for him to claim the prize he so desperately sought after. *Take it,* the voice said over and over in his mind.

With one last deep breathe to calm the last of his nerves the man of darkness drove the sharp steel blade of the knife into the woman's chest. Blood oozed from the wound, leaking to the clear plastic wrap canvas.

The howling wind once heard outside the house halted. Leaving only one sound left to be heard inside the darkness of the house. A knife slowly sawing into the woman's soft snow-white flesh.

They did this to you, whispered the darkness, *they did this to you.* And all the while the dark whispers hissed, the man of darkness sliced away, claiming his prize.

Chapter One
The Terrors at Night

Red and blue neon lights pierced through the pitch-black November night. As the shrieking of sirens became louder so too did the fear. It was the fourth time the killer had stuck.

A bone chilling wind blew throughout the nameless city as police arrived to their destination in a rural neighborhood.

People had begun to gather outside of one of the houses, each looking to catch a glimpse of the terror that had taken place inside. A once seemingly peaceful house had now turned to horror.

As the crowd of people grew in size, outside a policeman stepped in and began directing the crowd to move back. The officer then began to set up a yellow-taped perimeter reading *"DO NOT CROSS"* in big bold letters.

Most of the police had already arrived on the scene when an all-black Crown Victorian with dark tinted windows and cleaned rims pulled up. The car distinguished itself from the rest of the police vehicles. Out stepped a tall scraggly haired man with weary eyes and a long grey overcoat. His name was Detective Paul Fisher.

Paul observed the scene and growing crowd at hand. He sensed an uneasy feeling amongst the people, which were in large part silent and wide-eyed. *Who could blame them,* Paul thought. He knew fear had gradually risen amongst the public since the killer had first struck almost three months ago.

The police had been stifled in their search for what had been now dubbed by the media as the "Heartbreak Killer". The name was birthed from the specific way in which the killer slain the victims. All of those that were found had died of cardiac arrest brought on by what was later determined as an overdose from anti-depressant pills. In an essence breaking their hearts.

The Heartbreak Killer was an elusive one. Killing throughout the city, which was out of the norm for most serial killers who frequently stuck to a specific area. This tactic made the public extremely fearful, expecting that anyone of them could be next. Not only was the killer regionally unbiased, but also unbiased about the class of people. Striking in seemingly peaceful and upscale neighborhood one night and poorer lower class residents the next. On this specific cold November night the body found happened to fall in the peachy upscale category.

Up to this point there was only one pattern that had been established by the police. The Heartbreak Killer took a strict fancy to women.

All of the Heartbreak Killer's victims had been as such, however, the type was a diverse range of females. Blond hair, blue eyes, age 25, and petite. Black hair, brown eyes, age 45, and big boned.

The most significant problem facing the police in finding the killer now was that whenever the killer attacked a victim there were no witnesses. Nor had there been a lick of evidence left behind. No DNA, no cryptic messages, no murder weapons, nothing.

In an era of high tech resources the killer still eluded, indeed a skilled tactician in the craft of murder.

Detective Paul Fisher stepped under the yellow tape towards the house when a fellow officer spotted him and called out in his direction.

"It's been a long time since I have seen that face," said the officer in a playful voice.

"I wish it had been a little bit longer of a vacation. This looks nothing like the beach." Paul replied coldly. "Let's take a look at this victim."

"Yes sir Detective Fisher," said the officer snapping back into a more professional manner. "Follow me."

As Paul walked into the house, he sensed a certain evil afoot. Almost as if the killer was watching him, waiting to pounce at any moment. *The killer wouldn't be that foolish, too smart for such a move,* thought Paul and his paranoia subsided. *It has just been awhile.*

While Paul followed the officer to the body found in the house his mind drifted back to how he was assigned to the case.

The captain of the police force had called him a couple of weeks back.

"Fisher," the Captain had said in his usual stern and commanding voice. "No one has been able to sniff a whiff of this damn Heartbreak Killer. I know you're going through some shit, but the public is terrified. You're the best man I have in homicide and I need you."

Paul objected to the Captains request for days. He had lost his wife to breast cancer nearly a year ago and the death had taken Paul to a dark place, blaming the insurance company for his wife's death.

"We won't pay for any more testing," said the insurance man over the phone. "She hasn't responded to the regular treatments we are accustom to paying for, therefore we won't be wasting any more money on unproven methods of treatment."

"Waste money?" Paul screamed. "How is there any waste when it comes to a human life?"

"I am sorry Mr. Fisher but we have done what we consider to be enough. Anything else will have to come from you now." And the insurance man hung up the phone.

A couple of months later and Paul's wife passed away.

Struck with depression, anger, and guilt that he couldn't afford any more treatment, Paul took to the bottle. His life became consumed by alcohol and his work suffered. Afterward Paul became a liability, too emotionally pained to function in the real world. Finally seeing the signs, the Captain put Paul on leave from work until his life got back on track.

Days turned into weeks and weeks turned into months. Paul was slowly being consumed by darkness, only thinking of his daughter Alexis's safety did he agree to help on the Heartbreak Killer case. Paul had heard through the news, that the killer fancied single women and his daughter fit the profile.

Alexis was the last person Paul cherished and loved in his life so he set out to track down a mad killer. It was just enough motivation to propel him from his dark depression.

Paul, forgetting for a brief moment what he was now doing, snapped back into reality from his dark memories.

Now in the room of the victim a bit of horror overtook Paul's face as he scanned the room his fellow officer had guided him to. He hadn't seen death in quite some time.

The downstairs walls of the room were pale white and the floor was filled with light brown wood boards. In the center of the room lie the Heartbreak Killers work, a woman limp and cold. She looked to be 5'6 or 7 with a skinny build and her skin was fair as most people were during the winter season. Along with the body, she had long black hair that went to the middle part of her back. The victim had been undressed and only her underwear remained, black with lace.

Scattered around the woman's body were cherry colored red rose pedals. *It's like the killer has made a bed of the rose pedals for the victim to rest on,* thought Paul as he continued to scan the room from the bottom rung of the stairs.

Slowly, Paul stepped forward for a closer look, but just as he flattened the first rose pedal with his foot Paul noticed something strange on the woman's exposed chest.

"Have you seen this yet?" Paul inquired.

"What are you talking about?" The officer replied as he came to the side of Paul.

"Look at her chest. Are those stitches?"

The two men went closer and bent over the body to inspect. Some sort of black stitching appeared to be present in-between the woman's breast. Running an inch below the victim's collarbone and continued down between the breasts, ended midway down the stomach.

This sight puzzled Paul as he remembered in briefing that the killer had only drugged his victims with an overdose of pills, never making any other marks on the bodies. *Is this a different killer,* pondered Paul? *The flowers and the stitches aren't the norm of the Heartbreak Killer.*

"This is unusual," piped the officer. "I have seen every victim the Heartbreak Killer has left and never has there been any marks on the bodies".

"So this is out of the norm then?" Paul asked, reaffirming his suspension. "I was thinking that just now."

"Yes, this elaborate set up with the flower pedals and this stitching is definitely out of the norm for the Heartbreak Killer." Replied the officer, who now sounded just as puzzled as Paul.

"The killer…" Paul began but was interrupted by the officer.

"What is that on your shoulder Detective? Is that blood?" Said the officer stepping closer to examine.

"What are you talking about?" Said Paul, who took a glance at his right shoulder. Immediately Paul spotted a dark blotch that had begun to seep into his grey overcoat. He reached for the spot with his pointer finer and took a swipe. Putting his finger up to his face the blotch appeared red and thick. *What is this?*

Before either of the men could get another word out something dripped on the side of Paul's face. His whole body froze in a paralyzed state as he put a hand on his cheek. Fearful of the occurrence Paul looked up at the ceiling.

"Oh my god." Paul said, raising his voice as he saw the source of the dripping.

A giant blood red heart had been drawn above the victim's body. *This isn't a normal heart*, Paul recognized gazing at the drawing.

The red heart was broken and split down the middle as if it had been torn in half with one side flipped upside down. In the direct center of the broken hearts space was an object pinned to the ceiling.

"Is that a human heart in the center?" Paul gasped and pointed upward. *What is this monstrosity?*

Inside the middle of the blood painted heart was a pinned heart, still oozing with fresh blood it had once pumped.

Another droplet of blood fell from the human heart, splashing onto Paul's nose. He was still frozen in horror of the terror presented to him on this night. *It's like the killer is displaying his own twisted art for an audience of police.* Paul snapped out of his frozen state and stepped back to the staircase, almost gasping in shock at the sight, not fully realizing what he was witnessing.

As Paul reached the stairs, he surveyed around the full crime scene again. Countless droplets of blood had been disguised within the color flower pedals around the body. Paul became somewhat shell shocked now seeing what truly lay in front of him.

An art gallery of death and horror, created and signed with a killer's signature. *The Heartbreak Killer,* thought Paul.

Without a word Paul turned away from the gruesome scene and made his way out of the downstairs room and headed back to the outside of the house.

"Detective?" The officer called out to Paul with confusion. But the detective gave no reply.

As Paul reached the door to the front yard, cameras began to flash at him and loud voices rang. The media had arrived, hungry for news of heartbreak. The flashes of light blinded Paul and he stumbled out the front door. *I am not ready for this, not now.*

A swarm of reporters and various media sources surrounded Paul as he tried to get to his car. Within the barrage of bright lights and loud noises Paul heard one reporter yell out "Who is the victim? Is this the work of the Heartbreak Killer?" Paul pushed the media aside; he was in no mood to answer any questions for them. *This news will only spread the fear of the public,* Paul thought as he made his way through the reporters.

Reaching his car Paul unlocked the door, opened it, and jumped into his driver seat. Still gathering his thoughts, he started the car. Paul took a deep breath and everything became clear. *The stitching, the blood drawn symbol, the heart. The killer had removed the woman's heart.* His mind raced at the idea. *Why now, why a symbol left with rose pedals?*

With the media buzzing around Paul's car he came to a realization to his question and shifted the car into drive. *The Heartbreak Killer is changing into a new kind of monster. His confidence is growing.*

Chapter Two
Into the Mind of Darkness

What are people's inner most desires? What has them up for countless sleepless nights, laying in the darkness of their rooms? Do they restlessly ponder how to obtain a particular desire or object that can never quite be grasped?

I had often wondered with this train of thought as I pictured my own desire, but part of me knew the answer to my own questions of others.

Countless times I have heard these other people's stories and their deep desire to obtain something out of grasp as I sat across the desk and listened. Some people came to my office speaking to me of their loveless lives, seeking to obtain some sort of love again as they feared the curse of being alone forever. Others came to me figuring that an increase in money would answer for their lack of happiness. Whatever the problem was, humans always desired something they didn't have that they felt would complete them.

At least these people could feel some sort of emotion or have a realistic plan to cure their dysfunctional lives. *How could I obtain what I desired?* There was only one item that would cure me, make me human again, and finally bury the darkness that surrounded my sleepless nights.

I pondered this very conundrum now as I stood peering into a glass casing on a sleek black pedestal. Inside the glass casing held my desire, my dream, and my hope for a better life. A symbol of what I thought was missing inside me.

For you see my inner most desire was to feel emotions, be human, to reclaim my missing heart. *Who am I? How can I become the man I once was?*

Inside the glass lay a piece of a human heart, still moist with the blood that had been circulating through it the night before when I had extracted it from its owner.

As I stood gazing at this sort of trophy I had claimed, I was taken back to my past memories. *Where had I lost my ability to feel? The man I once was.*

I was an extremely successful therapist, yet all the countless books and articles I had read on emotional dysfunction and serial killers gave me no answers to the where and how of my inflictions. Instead, books only told me how a serial killers mind worked or how it was created. Usually the cause stated some sort of tragic event in one's life that caused them to become a social outcast or maybe even a deviant at a younger age who expanded into the realms of psychopath and killer as they grew older.

That was never me.

My life had been from my standards, normal as a child. Neither my father nor my mother had psychologically abused me nor had I been physically or sexually abused. Really the worst thing that had ever happened to me in my youthful years was that my father had never believed in me or at the very least acted like he did. He would say "Perry you will never get your degree" or "Perry you will never earn enough money with that degree."

Yet even after my father's negative doubts, I had indeed received that degree, a PHD in cognitive psychology.

Surely, that little verbal abuse wasn't enough to make me into the soulless, human less, dark surrounding killer I had now become. Even with all those disbeliefs my father had in me, he never broke me.

There was only one true emotional scarring I could recall. That was the heartbreak I suffered from women and love.

They did this to you, hissed the dark monster at the thought.

Although I was a shell of my former self now, I still remembered the care I once had for other people. *Maybe that is why I broke, I cared too much.*

My genuine care for others had sparked my interest in becoming a therapist in the first place. I had seen the evils of the world. Some of the evils had distinct faces like me, while others were masked and hidden from the public perception. As I grew older and saw these evils I realized the importance in helping innocent people stray away from the traps evil ones set. I wanted to be the light in the darkness.

That was a long time ago though, I thought still staring at the bloody heart. Now I had become the evil I once swore to fight off. I had become the darkness. People had broken me. *Mostly the women I had loved, who took advantage of my kindness and loyalty.*

"Women," I scoffed aloud, then laughing manically to an empty room. "Men always receive the bad rap in relationships while women glide by on a free pass in our society." *Were they really any different than men? Women cheat, lie, and use their beauty to manipulate. Maybe all humans are cursed to be this way to each other.*

For whatever reason, I took relationships very hard when I was in my early twenties. Sitting in my room after a break up crying, not eating, not moving. Once, I thought love was pure and beautiful but after the many emotional scaring's I learned the evils of women and love.

They deserve to pay for what they did to you, whispered the dark monster inside me.

I continued to stare, like a child into the window of a toy store at my trophy. Gazing at my desire, my missing happiness.

It had taken me countless weeks of books, videos, and practice on various pieces of meat and fruit before I had been ready to take a plunge at this piece of heart.

At first, I was satisfied with killing my victim without leaving a trace. Each death calming the call of my dark monster. But after the third woman, the monster called for more, and I wanted what those in my past had somehow stolen from me, my heart.

They did this to you, rumbled my dark monster once more

The idea of taking a piece of heart had come to fruition a couple of weeks after I had turned the news on and saw them dub me the Heartbreak Killer. A fitting name I had said aloud at the time. I was in a sense heartbroken, as mine hadn't been working for years. Now I was doomed to live out my life as an emotionless creature. Also adding to my infamous name was the fact I used anti-depressant medication to kill my victims.

I am so clever, I thought smirking at my genius. "Ironic how I used the very drug that is supposed to cure heartbreak as a weapon to stop the person's actual heart. Therefore dooming them to cardiac arrest and breaking their heart." I smugly boasted to my new found trophy.

Another moment passed and I became bored of my new piece of heart. I had been staring at it for nearly an hour now. Carefully, I picked up the glass case holding my precious trophy and placed it in my safe behind the wall where my bed rested. *I can't leave this out, it would be too foolish.*

After I had securely placed the bloody heart back into the safe and locked it I ventured to the living room and then outside to the balcony.

I lived atop a thirty-story apartment complex in a penthouse that was located in the heart of the downtown city. I wonder if people would have thought in their wildest dreams that the Heartbreak Killer was overlooking the city he killed in. All from the comfort of his home.

"I am sure if they knew…" I said pausing. "Well if they knew where I lived I would be in prison." I began to chuckle at my foolish thinking.

While I stood on the balcony, I could see the sun rising up over the city. It was then that I realized I had been out almost all night preforming a long heart removal operation on a patient. *Well it was more of a fighting victim than a willing patient.*

As the sun rose higher, you could start to distinguish the city I overlooked. Large skyscrapers stood around me in a various arrangement. Some buildings stood in the distance and others were adjacent to my view, but none were close enough or tall enough to block my view.

To the left of my balcony you could see a mall, a library, and the city hall. To the right you could see the ocean water about 10 blocks away. I enjoyed the ocean and it was one of my favorite sites to see when I was younger. Although I had grown accustom to the sight of it now, it was still pleasant to gaze upon. Especially when the ocean breeze would rise to my balcony and hit my face with a salty cool slap.

The season was much too cold for the ocean though. In fact it was much too cold to be outside. *At least for my liking.*

As I returned to the warmth of my living room I had a sudden urge for coffee. I hadn't slept at all in the night so the coffee effects would help me to wake up before I had to go to the office.

I reached for my music player on a nearby coffee table that stood in my living room and ventured to the kitchen.

Arriving to the kitchen, I plugged the player into a docket that connected to speakers surrounding the entirety of my house. *What am I in the mood for?* I thought as I skimmed though my selection of artists. *Mozart*, I finally concluded.

There were three types of music I was fond of, classical, jazz, and 80's. I enjoyed Mozart the most in the classical realm. Regarding jazz, I preferred either Miles Davis or David Brubeck, a tossup really. However, my favorite jazz song was Sing Sing Sing by Benny Goodman. *The greatest jazz track of all time.* As for 80's music I had no preference, the music of that time spoke to my soul. *Well, the emptiness where it once resided.*

Picking the Turkish March Piano Sonata NO. 11 by Mozart, I began to make coffee from a newly purchased maker. *What a lovely and cheery song. It really sets the mood right after the success of the strenuous heart surgery.*

After placing a slick black coffee cup under the maker, I pressed the flashing button to start the process. I decided to depart to the bathroom while the coffee poured into my cup. I hadn't looked at myself at all since the late night stalk.

I had always been devilishly handsome or at least that's what women had told me. *Women lie,* hissed the dark monster. *Why believe anything they speak of.*

Speaking of looks, I stood at an intimidating 6'4. However, I was not overly bulky, more on the slender side if anything. When I was a teenager my mother would say I looked like a child from Africa and needed to eat more if I planned to be healthy. *How incredibly stereotypical mother*, as I thought back. No doubt I was thin though, and even now into my mid-thirties I hadn't put on much bulk.

Staring into the bathroom mirror, I noticed a small cut on my neck. "She cut me." I said rather shocked. *Not to worry.* I always had taken extra precautions to clean under my victim's nails, no matter how sure I was about not leaving a trace. *You can never be too careful in the business of serial killing.*

I brushed the back of my hand across the side of my face still looking at the cut in the bathroom mirror. Always clean-shaven, as I was never a fan of beards. They made me itch uncomfortably whenever I had grown one out. Plus, I believed in carrying a professional look and facial hair wasn't a part of that category for me.

My lips were fairly thin and lacked much lusciousness. I didn't much care for the sight of them but what was lacking there was made up for in my eyes and nose.

I personally loved my nose. It had a perfect base and length, never being too wide or too pointed. A crowning achievement in the face world I would say.

My eyes were tight and slanted with piercing forest green irises. They had the power to look into ones soul, either melting your heart or terrifying your bones. I knew how to give the look of each at will, using them to my advantage in seduction or horror.

To top off my devilishly good looks was thick black hair. My hair was as black as death, which paired nicely with my black soul. I used various styles for my hair, some days I felt it would be nice to slick it back with some gel for a more professional look. Other days I preferred to part my hair in the middle to give me a sort of wealthy prep look. *Today… let's make it a messy slick back. More appropriate for work.*

After I set my hair in a suitable style I made my way back to the kitchen for my cup of coffee. *By now it has to be cool enough to drink.*

Mozart was still peacefully playing in the background as I grabbed the black mug. The smell of freshly brewed coffee had always woken me up when I hadn't slept much the night before. I inhaled the hot fumes through my perfectly proportioned nose. *Ah, sweet vanilla… Now the news.*

I always fancied seeing what the news had cooked up on me the morning after I had slain someone. I was the talk of the town these days, the infamous Heartbreak Killer terrorizing a peaceful city. Pausing the music in the kitchen, I carried my coffee into the living room.

When I reached the living room I searched for the remote, finding it wedged between the couch cushion. The TV was already on the Channel 28 News as I turned it on. *There she is, the queen bitch herself.*

Channel 28 News had especially taken a liking to my killings and sequentially ran with the story. It was they who first dubbed me the Heartbreak Killer. The station was notorious for broadcasting as much of the graphic violence from my killings as they could get their hands on. Not only that but Channel 28 News would also try to pry interviews from the sobbing family member even when they pleaded for the privacy to be left alone. They were as ruthless as any media outlet in America and at the head of the vicious snake was the masked evil herself, the bitch of Channel 28 News as I preferred to call her.

Terry Connor, the true evil in this world.

I had met Terry once when I opened up my new psychiatric firm years ago. She was ruthless even then and from what I could see, all Terry cared about was her career and her news rating, nothing else.

Rating, all the media cares about.

Now, Terry Connor was the cities sex symbol and beloved by the public. I always wondered how many dicks she had to suck to get into the position she was in now. Terry was that type of woman though. Manipulating men with sex and destroying anyone that stood in her path to fame. She was fueled by the greed and ambition inside her.

In many ways, Terry was emotionless like me. The one difference was, I wanted to feel again, she seemed to be content living without emotions.

As shrouded as I was in darkness, I considered there to be nothing eviler than media. The media is a secretive evil, one many people don't realize is right in front of them every day. They consistently rot your mind with their agendas and make money off of other peoples miseries. *All because the consumer watches. People love to see the dirty laundry of others.* I have seen the evils of the media as they attack weeping widows with hounding interview questions instead of trying to comfort them like human beings. And at their worst, the media can control how the public thinks with their own spin on things, painting the picture their way. Even if that picture is a deceitful lie.

All for the sake of ratings. Disgusting

The media has even spread my name into fame. The Heartbreak Killer, a real life serial killer. Even if I was infamous and hated, I was now known. All thanks to the media. *Why would they do such a thing? Because I sell and spread the fear to the innocent consumer.*

Making me known to the public had caused people to be horrified to walk the dark streets of the city at night. I was now a living boogieman who terrorized the city. *The media doesn't care though, as long as I sell they will spread the fear.*

I often fantasized of what it would have been like if the news decided to label me as a vigilante instead of a monster. Painting my killings as a necessity for the greater good. They could have easily done it too and they have before. *But that doesn't sell like my fear.* News stations glorify our countries military, who go to other countries and slaughter their civilians, military or not. *Aren't they just like me, cold-blooded killers?* Yet, they are portrayed as glorified heroes, brave and honorable. And I am the monster, a distraction to the masked other evils of this world.

Surely I am a monster. I don't question that, but my body count is four. What was theirs?

What was the body count of the police force that has shot and killed countless unarmed civilians, later dubbed as criminals by media? How about our American government who waged wars on innocent countries with innocent people? The nuclear bomb we dropped on Hiroshima for what cause? It's a necessity to keep us safe preaches the media and heads of state but the Heartbreak Killer isn't. No, he is a monster.

Why? Maybe all those women deserved to meet their death as the others.

I may have a mind full of darkness but I see far worse in this world than I. The world is twisted into a sick darkness that people are now blind to and I am just a distraction for the greater evils to roam freely and hide in plain sight.

I hate the fucking media.

The TV spoke up.

"Breaking news today, the Heartbreak Killer has struck again." Terry Connor said pretentiously through the TV. "Last night police received multiple complaints of loud music coming from a nearby neighborhood home. As the police arrived on the scene, they discovered the body of Becca Parsons, a 27-year-old Caucasian woman, dead inside her home."

Always have to signify the race to make people care more or less, I thought as I watched intensively.

"Police further investigated the crime scene and confirmed that this was the work of the Heartbreak Killer. Detective Paul Fisher declined to speak to the media involving the detail of this murder, however. But as Channel 28 News has come to learn, the killer is believed to have left a mark behind."

I smirked hearing the news of my new found symbol. I have always believed that you should take pride in your work. *Even if mine was highly illegal.*

Once I had discovered my crowning name I began to think of a way to stir the media up and give them a show. Although, I wasn't sure if murdering women was considered a show. Never the less, I was a cocky showman at empty heart, applying the belief to my dark art.

I have to give the fearful fans what they wanted.

After my third victim I came to the conclusion to make such a mark. A broken heart with the right side flipped upside down to symbolize what I thought of love. *Dark, twisted, and broken.*

Personally, I thought it was brilliantly crafted. Even if I doubted the media or police were wise enough to decipher the symbolism I was presenting them. Regardless, I had gained enough confidence in my new found work and decided to take my killing ways up a notch.

I pondered how to draw my heart while I was carefully doing open-heart surgery last night. While I was slicing I decided against the use of the victim's blood and instead to use some blood red paint I had purchased before the execution.

Using the woman's blood is too vile and messy, I thought at the time. Not to mention it left the door open to unnecessary mess-ups. Red paint had serviced nicely and would fool the police, at least until they had taken the substance in for testing.

"Although we have no word on what the symbol is, it is clear the killer has become more confident in their work," said Terry Connor.

"Truly terrifying, Terry." The anchorman who was working beside Connor said.

"Yes indeed, I just pray the police can find the person responsible before anyone else gets hurt." Terry replied.

No you don't you fake bitch, you love all of this. It's making your ratings skyrocket. I was disgusted by her fake smile and emotionless sympathy for these people.

"In other news, Detective Paul Fisher is back with the police force. Detective Fisher had previously been on a leave of absence starting in January after his wife had passed away from breast cancer. The chief of police has confirmed with us that Detective Fisher will now be heading the case of the Heartbreak Killer."

The chef of police appeared on the TV in front of a large crowd of media.

"I know how panicked the city is at this moment," said the chief of police in a stern and commanding voice. "These are dark times, but I have full confidence in our police force to track down this killer and bring whoever is responsible to justice. Detective Fisher will now be heading the case. He is one of the finest and most tenured detectives we have. There is no doubt in my mind that he will find this Heartbreak Killer."

Detective Paul Fisher, I thought with intrigue. *Would this be my worthy adversary? The hero to my villain, like so many truly grand stories had.* I began to wonder if this could be the man to bring me down.

The Detective seemed fitting as any while he addressed the TV and crowd with weary eyes and messy brown hair. *Troubled over lost love ones like me, yet still fighting the darkness instead of becoming it. Something that I haven't been able to do.*

He is no match for you, mocked the darkness in my mind.

I pressed the power off of the TV on the remote and went to refill my coffee cup still in thought.

While the coffee maker refilled the cup I went to my music player knowing the perfect song to play for the moment.

"Welcome to the Jungle, Detective Fisher." I said pressing the play button. The music echoed through the spacious penthouse as I ventured to my room to get dressed properly for work. *Let us see if you have what it takes to bring down the infamous Heartbreak Killer.*

Chapter Three
Alone

Detective Paul Fisher sat at his desk at the police station inside his old office.

Paul was rummaging through evidence, scanning over case files, and reading old news articles. Anything he thought would help lead him closer to the killer.

The Detective had been up all night after being at the crime scene, avoiding going home. Home was where all his pain and misery resided. An empty house with no one to greet him or curl up next to him in the cold bed.

The sun was dimly shinning now in the cold of a November morning, and officers were making their way to the police station for another days work. Paul welcomed the sound of people around as he had been sitting in silence for quite some time.

There has to be something here, thought Paul, still looking through the mess of papers while chewing on the end of a pen. Paul was fully caught up on the case but like the others before him, found nothing that could break it open.

"Detective Fisher," interrupted a man in a white lab coat, who had poked his head into Paul's office. "We have the lab results on the blood work from the ceiling."

Hopefully the killer left some of his own DNA in it, thought Paul. He rose up from his desk and headed toward the lab with the man in white. His legs tingled as he walked, they had fallen asleep from sitting.

"What do you have for me?" Paul said as he reached the inside of the lab. "Hopefully some good news about that blood painted heart."

"Well Detective, this sample you gave me…" The white coated man paused.

Instantly Paul knew he would not like the man's response.

"This blood," continued the man. "Well it isn't blood at all Detective."

"What do you mean it isn't blood?" Paul said with a frustrated tone.

"I mean exactly that, Detective Fisher. This sample you gave me isn't blood at all, its paint."

"Paint, what the hell do you mean?"

"Just what I said, Detective. I'm sorry."

Paul's mind was fatigued from his sleepless night and hadn't fully grasped the meaning behind what the man was saying to him. *He sounds like a damn fool. Somehow he had to of made a mistake. Paint? That can't be right.*

"The sample contained a lot of lead bases in it. The characteristics of any cheap paint you would find at a department store. The color and texture may resemble a blood like substance from afar but it's just paint if you examine closer." Explained the white coated man.

"Were there any other traces?" Implored Paul.

"I'm afraid not Detective. I couldn't even tell you a specific store that sells it. The paint is that generic."

"Thanks anyways," said Paul with disappointment. *This is going to be a tougher case than I anticipated*, he thought as he turned to walk back to his office.

Paul had been a part of hundreds of homicide cases throughout his career. The crimes were typically committed by buffoons, who left

DNA samples in every corner of the crime scene. Semen, blood, hair, or fingerprints always turned up at some point, especially for a repeat offender. *This one is different. Smarter than most of the people I've dealt with. The killer knows how to clean up after the crime without mistakes.*

"Paul get in here." Said a voice from inside a room behind him.

Paul recognized the deep irritated voice. *The Captain,* he thought before turning around.

The Captain was an older man. His skin was aging, his hair was grey mixed with some white while gradually receding, and his eyes were hollowed from seeing too much in one life.

As a man the Captain was tough but fair to his employees. Paul respected him and felt he had a good standing relationship with his boss.

"Close the door behind you and sit down." Said the Captain as Paul entered.

"Captain I don't have…" Started Paul.

"Save your breath Detective, I already heard the results of that blood work. Or should I say paint work? This is about you Paul. I know you haven't taken the death of your wife well over the past year. It's not easy to lose a loved one, especially when it's a death too soon…" The Captain paused for a moment. "Paul, I called you in on this job because you're the best man for it. Hell, you're the smartest detective we have on the force and we need you. This city is in a fear induced panic and only our most equipped men will find this slippery killer."

"You can thank the media for that," said Paul. "They have taken this story and spread it like a wild fire. It's no wonder these people are scared. You turn on the news or look at a paper and all you see is the Heartbreak Killer story."

"More of a reason why you need to get yourself together. The media has always taken fear and spread it throughout the public, no matter the story. Fear sells and people want to feel safe at night. A serial killer is a big story anyways, but let's keep this one within our city. I could only imagine the media frenzy if this story goes national."

"I would love nothing more than to find the killer but this one is different Captain. This killer doesn't make the mistakes like the regular criminal. He is smarter than most of the people I'm accustom to dealing with."

"Is the great Paul Fisher admitting defeat on his first day back?" Mocked the Captain. "I remember a time when you proclaimed you could solve any case. You were so gung-ho and determined to make this world better before the tragedy. Where is that Paul at?"

"He died with his wife. He died when he learned that people chose to let others die, even when they have the means to do things that can save lives. All because of their greed and corrupt systems. I feel like a damn hypocrite to say that this Heartbreak Killer is any worse than the men at the insurance company? They both kill innocent people."

"I know the pain Paul, but you have a chance to make amends for your loss. That view is hard to see in your darkness now. Regardless of how you feel about your wife's death you can't change what happened. But you can change who lives or dies at the hand of this killer."

"Don't you think I want to?" Exploded Paul. "I have a daughter out there who fits the profile. She is the only thing I have left and that's the only reason I came back, to protect her. I just don't know if I have it in me anymore Captain. My life has been destroyed. All I have done since her death is sit at home, drinking to forget." Paul bounced up from his seat and pounded the Captains desk, knocking over papers from the force and vibration of his action. "I can't deal with the pain of her death and the only thing that keeps me numb from it is the alcohol."

"Sit your ass down Fisher," roared the Captain.

Paul realized his emotions had gotten out of hand.

"Do you think you're the only person in this world that's lost someone? Answer me!"

"No," Paul replied trying to grip his emotions.

"Good, now get your shit together before I have your ass demoted to a traffic officer. Like I said before your outburst Paul, you have a chance to make amends for your wife by saving the innocent women of our city. I believe in you. If I didn't your ass would still be locked inside your house inebriated from a bottle. You're one of the smartest men I know and a great detective. The people need you now more than ever. Be the hero that saves this city and get your life back together."

"Okay Captain, I'll get it together."

"You're damn right you will Fisher. Now go home and get some sleep, I know you've been here all night. We can talk about the case tomorrow."

"Yes Sir," Paul spouted sheepishly as he walked out of the Captain's office. *He's right. I can't do anything to save my wife now, but I can save the people of the city. I have been a child, sulking and sipping my bottle of booze while I waste away. She wouldn't have wanted that. No matter how hard it is to deal with the feelings inside.*

Paul exited the police station and made for his car.

As he entered the car his cell phone began to buzz inside his pocket. He pulled his phone out and saw it was his daughter, Alexis.

"Hey hunny, what's up? Is everything okay?" Said Paul as he answered.

"Hi Dad, everything is fine. I just haven't heard from you in weeks and I got a bit worried about you. So I called to check up on you. I know how lonely you are without Mom." Alexis said in her usual sweet and innocent tone.

"Yeah sweetheart, I'm okay. I actually started up on a new case so I have been pretty busy and haven't gotten a chance to call you."

"I heard about that on the news this morning. They said you're heading the Heartbreak Killer case. Are you sure you're ready for that Dad? It's been less than a year."

"Your mother would have wanted me to get back to work. I can't mope around for the rest of my life. Plus, this gives me a chance to keep busy and think less about your mother."

"Still, I worry about you Dad. I know how hard this has been on you. But you're probably right. It's just, this is a huge case, and it's all over the news. I'm kind of scared Dad. The killer targets women and I feel like I could be next sometimes."

"Don't talk like that Alexis, you have nothing to worry about. I'm going to find the killer before anyone else gets hurts, I promise. You know your old man is still a great detective."

"I know Dad. How many cases have you solved again?" Teased Alexis.

"I lost count, hundreds though." Paul said with a smirk.

"I am just being paranoid. It's hard not to be when the story is all over the place. I was thinking about coming over tomorrow to check up on you, maybe hang out like old times. Would that be okay?"

"Of course sweetheart, how about we go out to dinner first?"

"Sounds great Dad. I will call you tomorrow okay? Take care of yourself please. If you get to lonely you can always call me."

"Okay, you to hunny." Paul said clicking off the phone.

Alexis had always been close with Paul. She was Paul's only child and he loved her to death. He did everything with her when she was a kid. Alexis was daddies little girl. But since the death of his wife and her mother, they had grown apart.

She is the last good thing I have in my life, thought Paul, as he started to drive away from the station. *I won't let you get hurt too.*

As Paul pulled up to his driveway he hesitated to get out of the car. Instead he stared out at his lonely house. Paul feared coming home every time now. *It isn't home without you here.*

Memories haunted Paul's mind every time he stepped foot inside his house. At one point the comfort of home was a place Paul couldn't wait to get to after work. His wife would always be waiting for him with a hot meal and a smile after a tough day of job.

"How was your day hubby," she would say to Paul as he walked through the door.

"Work was long babe, sometimes I think I should just quit." Paul would say whenever he had a rough day.

"But Paul, how can you be my superhero if you quit fighting the bad guys." She would playfully respond. "Superman wouldn't quit just because the job of saving the world was too hard, and I don't think

Louis Lane would like it much if he did either. She finds a man in uniform sexy just like me."

She always knew what to say to Paul when he had been run ragged. He loved her for that.

But those days were gone. Now Paul came home to cold silence. What was once his safe haven had morphed into a dark and miserable prison cell. *A prison of my memories,* thought Paul finally exited the car.

As Paul opened the door to his dark and empty house, a flicker of hope jolted through him that he would see his wife standing there again. That he had just been in a long nightmare and when he awoke she would be alive and well.

But it wasn't a nightmare, it was the reality of Paul's life now. He was living the nightmare and his dreams were the only escape left.

Once Paul was inside, he went to the kitchen to look for something to cook. He hadn't eaten since the day before and his stomach was growling.

Rummaging through the pantry and fridge Paul noticed a picture on the wall beside him. It was of him and his wife. They were smiling for the picture while Paul had wrapped both of his arms around her. They were much younger in it, but they were happy and in love. The future seemed so bright for them then.

"I miss you so much." Said Paul still hoping his wife would answer his lonely plea. "How am I supposed to go on without you?"

There was still no answer and Paul's appetite began to sour as his heart started to ache. *All those memories.*

Instead of food, Paul reached for a bottle of gin. He slumped to the cold hard floor of the kitchen and started to weep in the darkness. Paul pulled the bottle cap off the gin and began to chug, trying to dull the everlasting pain; he endured as fast as he could. But nothing could dull these pains for long and Paul fell to his side, his face stuck to the tile.

I am alone, he thought.

Chapter Four
A Spider and a Fly

Blah, blah, blah is all I heard as I sat in my office chair.

I was currently listening to a client express to me that their life was so dreadful that they were unable to function properly in society.

Personally, I was too lost inside my own dark and emotionless self to care about my clients problems anymore. This feeling had been lingering with me for some time now. *I have to be the worst therapist ever,* I thought as the blah's rang in my head.

Once I had been caring of the people who stepped into my office, seeking my therapeutic advice. But without my emotions, how could I even relate to these emotional creatures. They were a different species than me, I was envious.

"How do I fix my problem Dr. Nelson?" Said the woman in my office. "I have been sad for so long. I feel so hopeless and alone, like a dark cloud has been hovering over my head and won't leave."

Have you tried the method of serial killing? Wishing I could repeat what I was thinking to see the reaction. *It has been my method for dealing with my hovering cloud of darkness for some time now.*

"Well, Mrs. La Bella, it sounds like you could be suffering from Dysthymia, which is a mild form of depression that lasts more days than not for over two years". I responded. "You could also have a more serious type of depression that would take a certain type of medication to improve your underwhelming mood. However, I won't know for sure until you come in for a few more sessions and take some tests."

"Anything that will take this sadness away doctor," she replied somberly.

I could kill you, Mrs. La Bella. Surely that would take away your sadness... Damn, I should be nominated for therapist of the year. This could be a cutting edge technique for stopping depression, by murder.

"I will try my best to help you feel better Mrs. La Bella, but for now all I can do in our first session is listen to your story and jot down some notes on therapeutic improvements we can implement in the future. I am going to give you some papers to fill out every night for the next week. Just answer the questions honestly after each day and bring them back to me during our next scheduled session. Also, try exercising during the week and write down if it has any positive effects on your mood."

"Thank you Dr. Nelson, I will see you next week." Said Mrs. La Bella standing up, grabbing the papers, and exiting my office.

I sat back in my chair and sighed relief. She was my last client for the week, thankfully. I had almost reached a breaking point during the countless clients and their crazed emotions. Half of me was surprised I hadn't reached over the desk and killed one of them after hearing the numerous sob stories of failing marriages, anxiety disorders, and sociopathic tendencies.

Maybe you should have...therapist of the year, said my dark monster. *I am thirsty for new blood.*

I was jealous that these humans could feel emotions as I sat across from them, empty and dark. *Who am I kidding, I can't feel jealousy.*

Regardless of the urge, I would never be so stupid to kill a client. Doing so would leave a pattern, easily being traced back to me. I was far too aware to let that pattern happen. No, I looked elsewhere for my targets.

Sometimes it took me weeks to find the right person. I was extremely methodical when I stalked my prey. Patience was the key to success in my hobby of murder. At least if I wanted to stay away from lethal injections, and I surely did.

Even now, as miserable as I was, I still had the instinct to survive. *It must be human nature to survive, but why? A truly comical notion.*

I began to gather my belongings from the office and turned off the light before I locked the door. As I reached the outset of my office, the sun was setting in the horizon, casting a large shadow on the parking lot. *A perfect time for me to stalk.*

It had almost been a week since my last gush of blood. There hadn't been time in my schedule to start looking for my next victim.

As the months had passed since I killed my first woman, I had found a routine that worked. When stalking, I would find a place to park my car downtown and begin to walk around the city.

The downtown area was a killer's paradise for stalking prey. Always densely populated with diverse groups of people, especially on the weekends. These advantages allowed me to blend in seamlessly, a stalkers ideal situation.

While I walked around, the main objective was to survey for potential victims. The type of person I searched for only had to match a broad criteria. Woman, mid- twenties or older, and alone. After I set my eyes on a profile match I would follow her at a distance, observing her actions to see if I could move onto the next step.

Stalking women had worried me at first, but with a bit of practice I realized just how easy it was. Humans aren't as aware of their surroundings as you or I would think.

What was amazing to me, is how many details you can dissect away from a person by following them around from afar. I came to see the people I followed acted the most like themselves when they thought they were alone with no one watching. Masks come undone, showing their purest forms. *But they weren't alone, someone is always watching. I was watching.*

For instance, I discovered that the woman with midnight black hair was sleeping with three different men. A slut when no one was watching, her mask was removed. She seemed to feel no remorse from my viewpoint. She even had a boyfriend who seemed to treat her in a nice manner when they were together. His love for her blinded him from the truth though. *It is a sad and cruel world we live in.* Seeing those disgusting acts from the woman with midnight black hair gave me all the ammunition I needed for inflict my wrath.

Darkness began to creep upon the city as I arrived downtown. Only street lights and towering buildings with scattered lights lit the area. *People naturally fear the dark, so they made lights to feel safe. They are never safe, the man of darkness lurks.* I parked my car and descended into the dark night.

The night air was brisk and the wind piercing as I paved my way through the city. I wore on a black wool jacket over a red sweater, with a black scarf, and black leather gloves. *Black clothing blends well with the night.* I was never a fan of the winter season, especially when snow began to fall. So naturally I over dressed to counteract my hatred of the bitter cold.

As I crept closer to the heart of downtown, I began to scan for potential victims. At this time of night most people started traveling in packs, going from bar to bar, becoming intoxicated and foolish. So I had to stay sharp as I discard any large groups passing them by without a single glance. I was searching for someone who was still shopping and not interested in going out with friends. Women rarely drink alone, anyway.

Across the street, I spotted a woman who was carrying a couple of shopping bags around her arm as she come out of a local clothing store. I began to follow her at a distance. She was walking very casually so it was easy to keep up with her.

A man came up to the woman and I paused for a moment, pretending to look at something on the ground.

The two people kissed and began to walk together.

Damn, that won't do. I'll check inside a store.

There was a shoe store a block ahead of where I had stopped. When I walked inside the store, I began to half-heartedly browse for shoes. As I surveyed the room, I noticed a woman in her late twenties browsing the women shoe shelves alone.

She was tall for a woman, standing around 5'8 or so, with honey blond hair hanging just past her shoulders. She seemed right, but I could only see the back of her head from my vantage point so I decided to get a better view.

I casually walked behind her, pretending to pay no attention and instead browse the selection of shoes she was positioned in front of. I began to fiddle through the various styles of shoes while peeking to my right at the woman. She was still shuffling through her own side

of the shoe shelve. *Still no face,* I thought, so I decided to strike up a brief conversation with her.

"Excuse me." I said as nicely and friendly as I could muster. The woman shyly turned to me with a startled look in on her face.

As I laid eyes on her face I was abruptly taken aback by her beauty.

The woman had ocean blue eyes that exerted an innocent quality. Her lips were luscious, her skin pale and pure as a porcelain doll. *Whoa,* I thought staring at her. *When was the last time I found a woman pretty?*

She still is a woman, my darkness reminded me. *They are all liars on the inside.*

I snapped out of my gaze. *Focus.*

"Sorry, I know this is a strange question but I'm shopping for my girlfriend's birthday next week and she really wanted a new pair of shoes." I said with a forced smile. "I have no idea what I am doing though. Could you help me out?"

The woman's face softened with a smile. Her teeth were white and sparkling. "Aw, how sweet of you. I wish I had a man in my life who would buy me some shoes. Of course I will help you. What size is she?" Said the woman sweetly.

"Um." I paused to look at the section I was in. *Size Seven.* "Well, of course, she is a size Seven. Aren't we in the section?"

"Just checking, you could have just been over here to get a little better look at me." The woman said with an innocent giggle. "You know some men are like that."

I forced out a fake laugh. *Some men like me, but I'm not planning on hitting on you like those men. I want your heart sweet girl.*

"Oh no, not me, I'm just a clueless man in need of a woman's assistance." I responded as passively as I could manage.

"Perfect, let's see what I can do. What kind of shoes do you have in mind?"

A fly never sees a spider's web until it's entangled within. She has bought my fake charm like a beautiful fool.

"Well, to be honest, I don't have a clue. My girlfriend never asked for a specific pair, she just hinted at it. I'm a bit over whelmed. This is the fifth store I have been to."

"You poor thing, that's so sweet that you're going to all this trouble. She must be a very special woman to you."

"Yeah, she really is. I want the present to be perfect for her."

"Hmm, does she like to dress up and go out? You can't go wrong with a pair of heels. I don't think a woman can have too many of those."

"Heels could work, but there are so many different styles. I could never make a decision on which was the right pair."

"I'm sure she will love whatever pair you get her, just because she knows you took the time to get them for her. At least that's how I would feel if it was me."

The honey blond haired woman then began to scan the shelves. "What about this pair?" She said, lifting up a pair of sparkling grey heels that had a closed end tip.

Those are quite nice, but I think my fictional girlfriend wants something different.

"I think she mentioned something about preferring open end heels more than closed end ones" I quickly responded.

"Okay, what about this pair." Said the woman, lifting up a pair of slick gold heels with straps that I assumed went around your ankle.

I like this one, whispered the dark monster. *She is perfect for our collection, innocent and sweet.*

"I like those… but I don't like them enough. Ah, this is frustrating, I think I will have to come back a different day after I think it over some more. I just don't have the heart for this much disappointment."

"Are you sure? I don't mind helping you."

"It's okay, you did a great job. Thanks for your input and I promise I will take it into consideration when I finally buy a pair."

With that I gave the honey blond haired woman another false smile and walked out of the store.

You can only talk to someone about shoes for so long before you lose your mind. How do women spend hours upon hours shopping for them? I am already nauseous from five minutes of looking at them. No matter, I got what I needed and she is the perfect prospect.

I briskly walked across the street to a coffee shop that was perfectly adjacent from the shoe store.

There was a quietness inside the coffee shop as I walked in, with only a couple ordering from the counter. I checked my watch it was 7:15. *Not too late,* I thought, sitting down by the window to watch the door patiently.

The last required step in my first stalk was to follow the potential target to her car so I could snap a picture of the license plate.

As I sat, I began reflecting on the woman and the strange feeling that struck me about her beauty. *She is so innocent looking. Everything I wasn't. Why did her beauty strike me so?*

Finally, the honey blond haired woman appeared from the shoe store carrying a bag. *I wonder if she bought one of the pairs she showed me.* I stood up and checked my watch. *7:24, women always make you wait around for them.* Before I exited the coffee shop I made sure that the woman had walked past me. As soon as she did I began my venture out of the door.

The woman was walking at a blistering pace, making it difficult for me to follow. When this was the case I had to be sharp to avoid being spotted. If she did see me I would have to start the process over.

Who am I kidding, I won't be seen. I'm the Heartbreak Killer.

I started my prowl by walking on the other side of the street, about 20 feet behind the woman. *So far so good.* She hadn't a clue that I was following her but the streets were empty so I didn't have much coverage if the woman decided to turn around or cross to my side of the street.

A group of five people were coming up ahead of me as I blistered my paced. I managed to get right behind them and blend myself in. However, I quickly noticed that I was exceedingly taller than all of the group. *I will be spotted immediately,* I thought.

My only advantage now was the darkness of night, but the lighting from the shops and street lights eliminated any hope to hide my face. *This is going to be trouble.*

Then the honey blond haired woman came to an abrupt halt in front of a local Italian restaurant. As she did, I broke from the group and ducked behind a nearby light pole. I peeked out to see if I had been spotted. *Nope, I'm safe… for now.*

As I continued to peek around from my position, I noticed a large sign that read "Freddy's Authentic Italian" in bright red neon letters above the restaurant the woman was now standing in front of. Accompanied with the bright neon lettering was a cartoonish Italian man with a large black mustache, giving a wide grin. *Subtle, that must be Italian Freddy,* I thought as I shivered behind the pole.

The woman reached into her pocket and pulled out a phone. As she did I recognized a chance to cross onto her side of the street. There was an alley beside the restaurant only thirty feet from where she was standing. If I could duck into it while she was on her phone I would be in a much better position

As the woman put the phone up to her ear I made my move across the street. First checking to make sure there were no cars coming, I jetted across, intently staring at the woman to make sure I wasn't seen.

I quickly arrived to the other side. *She is still on the phone. There is no way I was spotted.* I then scampered into the dark alley way and poked my head out just enough to catch a glimpse of the woman.

A moment passed and then another woman appeared, giving my woman with honey blond hair a hug. They expressed their pleasantries and went inside the Italian restaurant.

God Damn it, this woman is going to make me wait even longer? She better be worth it.

She is, the heart is pure, the dark monster reminded me.

I pondered what my next move would be while I leaned against the brick wall of the alley. Waiting outside was out of the question. My body was already frozen and doing so for an hour or two more would surely give me a cold.

I peered around both corners of the alley to view my surroundings and judge if there was another store I could wait inside.

To my left, next to the restaurant, was a street light and an adjacent parking lot. *Damn nothing.* To my right, across the street, were abandoned buildings for rent. All of which were likely locked. *Damn, Damn, Damn.* I was running out of options.

Going inside of the restaurant would be extremely risky. *Can I maneuver this one,* I thought. A chilly breeze glided past me, making me grasp at my coat and chest. *This is too risky. But there is just something about this one.*

You know you want this Perry, whispered my dark monster. *Her heart is the pure. The Heartbreak Killer fears nothing.*

"Fuck it," I said under my breath and walked towards the doors of the restaurant.

Before I entered I tried peering into the windows, but the type of glass obscured my view, making it impossible to see the true definitions of the people inside. *What's a little risk without big reward,* I thought and I decided to go in blind. *Hopefully she isn't close to the entrance.*

As I entered, I quickly glanced around to see if I could get a view of the woman. *Nothing.* Instead, the restaurant greeted me with the sounds of some sort of smooth jazz music, smells of garlic bread, and a young woman with dirty blond hair.

"Welcome to Freddy's," she said to me in an upbeat and peppy tone. "How many for you tonight, sir?"

"Uh… sorry I think I'm going to sit at the bar. Do I just seat myself?" I said to the greeter still paranoid and glancing around.

"Yes of course." Responded the dirty blond greeter. "It's to your right, sir."

"Oh, thank you." I replied coldly.

Before entering, I surveyed the bar to make sure the woman and her friend did not have the same idea as me. The design of the bar was old-fashioned set with an oak wood counter, old hang pictures, and dim lighting. *Nope all clear,* I thought as I made my round.

The good news for me was that the bar had a perfect view of the front entrance of the restaurant. I would be sure to see anyone leave if I was aware.

I found a wobbly wooden bar stool at the farthest end of the oak counter. There were two other men sitting in stools as well but neither obstructed my vision of the entrance. I had to be extremely attentive to catch a glimpse of the honey blond haired woman.

As I sat on the stool, a tall and husky bartender asked me what I wanted to drink.

"Can I get a gin martini with as many olives as you can put in it?" I responded as my stomach growling with hunger.

"Would you like that dirty?" Said the bartender.

"Sure, thanks." I said quickly, to be distracted.

While I waited, I again noticed the smooth jazz playing over the noise of people conversing. *What the hell is up with this music?* To me it seemed out of place with the Italian theme. *Maybe I'm being as stereotypical as Freddy the Italian outside.*

My drink was placed in front of me, where I was resting my hands on the counter. *Three olives, I said as many as you could put fast man... Damn Perry.*

"Are you hungry, Sir?" The bartender asked as he placed my drink down.

"No thank you, just the drink for now." I said.

The bartender gave me a head nod and walked over to another customer. I needed to be prepared to leave at a seconds notice so food was out of the question. I sipped on my martini and ate one of the olives. The taste of the drink was a tad stronger than I was accustom to but I would never complain about more alcohol. *Especially not at the price it cost for one martini.*

Glancing at my watch, the time read 8:02. Ten minutes had passed since I had sat at the bar. *Should I risk looking around to make sure she is still here? She had to be*, it had only been twenty minutes since the woman with honey blond hair and her friend had arrived and I assumed it would take them another forty-five minutes to order and eat. *If they were efficient.* Women together wouldn't be, they liked gossip among other things.

Another ten minutes passed and the bartender asked if I wanted another drink. I said yes so he wouldn't wonder why I was sitting on one drink for such a long period of time. I gulped the remainder of my first drink and ate the last olive. Patience was a virtue I had to have while I stalked, but for some reason I was losing mine with each passing moment.

Another drink was placed in front of me, this time with one olive. *What a dick, does he want a tip?* Just as the thought came to my mind I spotted the woman and her friend walking to the front door. My eyes widened like a lion spotting his gazelle. *Game time.*

Both women stopped for a moment to gossip at the entrance. Then the friend went to the greeters' desk and grabbed a peppermint. I watched intently, waiting to make my move. The two women exchanged a hug and the honey blond beauty exited out of the front door while the other one headed for the bathroom straight ahead of where I sat.

Without another thought I bolted.

When I appeared outside, I saw the honey blond haired woman crossing the street to my left just 30 feet away. She was walking at a reduced pace so I easily kept up with her. I followed her for three blocks, at what I assumed was at a safe distance.

Then the woman turned a corner block and disappeared from my sight. Immediately I picked up the pace when I recognized that she had entered a parking lot. This was the one and only chance I had to get a picture of her plate before she was aware of me.

I put up the hood of my jacket and took out my phone, I was ready.

As I turned the corner the woman was opening the trunk of her midsized car, placing her shopping bags inside. Quickly, I turned back around so I wasn't spotted. There I waited silently, listening for the loud slam of the trunk being shut.

Come on... ... Come on....... Thud. Taking one last gulp of air I sprang into action. *Now!*

The backlights of the car had just flashed red in the darkness. Swiftly, I swooped by as the white lights to back up made their presence known. Steadying my hand, I snapped a picture of the plate number with one graceful movement. My phone exerted a bright flash as I took a picture and I darted away.

The woman had seen the bright flash and opened her car door.

I began to sprint.

"Hello?" I faintly heard the woman say out into the darkness, but it was too late. I had blended into the night, as the man of darkness should.

A fly never sees the spider's web, I thought with a grin.

Chapter 5
Crossing the T

Although Paul loved his daughter, the sight of seeing her was sometime too painful to bare. Alexis resembled his wife in more ways than one and that reminded Paul far too often of what he had lost. Her hair was golden blond, her eyes a beautiful ocean blue, and her face sweet and innocent. All the qualities of his lost wife.

For Paul, those resemblance were enough to overwhelm his fragile psyche.

The Detective sat across the table from his daughter now, drinking a cup of coffee at a shop. Paul had planned for dinner but without much head way on the Heartbreak Killer case, he was needed at the station. Time was of the essence as the city increasingly became more on edge with each passing day the killer walked free.

"Dad you look terrible." Alexis finally spouted out across the coffee table. "Have you been sleeping?"

Paul was looking down at his coffee, trying to avoid a glance at Alexis while he regained emotional composure from thoughts of his wife.

"No sweetheart, this case has put a lot of pressure on me." Said Paul, partially lying. He hadn't been sleeping, but it wasn't from the pressures of the case. That dilemma had been on the back shelf in his mind, while his wife's memories still haunted the front.

"Well as long as it's not about mom I can sleep a bit easier. But if it is, you can talk to me about it Dad. You're not the only one struggling."

"And you can come to me too. I'm still your father and I am here to listen to your problems. I'm doing fine though." Paul lied again. "The case has me too busy to think about anything else anyway."

"I bet Dad. My friends and I have all been talking about it. The killer is all that the news talks about these days. It's like they want us to be scared."

"Are you?" Asked Paul.

"Am I what? Scared? Yeah a little bit. I mean the killer has been out there for months and still, no one has a clue to what this person even looks like. For all I know the Heartbreak Killer could be sitting right over there." Alexis pointed to a man walking past the window of the coffee shop.

"You don't need to worry Alexis. The killer is too smart to go after the detective's daughter."

"Too smart? That's not reassuring at all. I feel like that makes me the perfect target." Alexis snapped back.

She may be right, but I can't fill her head with that fear, thought Paul. "If you think you need some protection to feel safe I can probably arrange a police car to sit outside of your house at nights."

"I'm probably being paranoid. It's hard now being alone in that house without Barry there. Especially when you know a killer is out there."

Barry, I never liked him. He was Alexis ex fiancé, who months ago, had been caught cheating by her. Paul had hated Barry before that though. He was cocky and arrogant, thinking he entitled and above the rules because of his big shot lawyer status. *What did she even see in him,* Paul thought while he pictured Barry.

Regardless, Paul knew all too well about the loneliness of an empty home.

"I understand hunny, just let me know if you want someone to watch your house. I can tell the Captain that you think you have spotted someone suspicious snooping around the outside of your house. He will allow me to send someone."

"Thanks Dad, I will let you know." Alexis said with some relief.

Paul was finally able to look up at his daughter. *My beautiful girl,* He thought. *I will keep you safe from the killers of the world.* Paul gave Alexis a fatherly grin and the two sat for a few more minutes in silence, sipping their coffee.

"I have to get going hunny." Paul finally said. "I am the person who has to catch this scary man. How can I do that if I sit and sip coffee all day?"

Alexis smiled at her father's joke and they both stood up, exchanging a warm felt hug.

"Love you Dad, be safe." Alexis said in the embrace.

"Love you too, hunny." And with that Paul left the coffee shop.

Paul arrived at the station before the majority of his coworkers had gotten back from their lunch break. Sometimes he preferred working when the office was empty, letting him concentrate with more efficiency.

As Paul reached his office, he began to think of where to go next. Since there were no new killings or evidence, he was condemned to rehash old papers and files. Paul reached for the different cases, hoping to find something to advance his search. *Maybe I missed a pattern.*

Paul began scanning over the most recent file, reading bits and pieces, and searching for something he could sink his teeth into.

Becca Parsons. Black hair, green eyes, Caucasian, 27, single. Profession, nursing assistant. Cause of death, heart failure due to an overdose of anti- depressant pills inside her home on November 13th. Discovered a piece of heart was removed post-mortem as well as the first sighting of the killers marking, a twisted and broken blood red heart.

Paul turned to the next file and read.

Sarah Jenson. Brown hair, brown eyes, Caucasian, 29, boyfriend. Profession, bartender. Cause of death, heart failure due to overdose of anti-depressants inside her home on October 23rd.

Next case.

Jenna Perkins. Brown hair, blue eyes, Caucasian, 36, single. Profession, waitress. Cause of death, heart failure due to overdose of anti-depressants inside her home on October 2nd.

Last one.

Kayla Sullivan. Blond hair, blue eyes, Caucasian, married with no kids. Profession, manager of a retail sales store. Found dead by her husband from an overdose of anti-depressants at her home on September 17th. Was first considered to be a suicide, but after multiple bodies were found it was deemed the first murder victim of the Heartbreak Killer.

Three distinctions stood out to Paul after he finished scanning the files. One was the race of women, which were all Caucasian. This was common practice for most serial killers however, as they stuck to people within their own race. This pointed in Paul's mind, to the killer being white. But some of this speculation had been established before Paul had taken the case.

Knowing the race wasn't much help either, 78 percent of the city was Caucasian. That would only narrow the search from 1.2 million people in the city to roughly 936 thousand people, basically leading to nothing of a lead.

The second distinction was that the killer used anti-depressants to kill the victim. *How did the killer manage that? Especially in the privacy of every victim home. There was no sign of forced injection on the bodies nor cuts, scrapes, bruises, or rope marks either, which would indicate some sort of struggle and force.*

"Hmmmm," Paul murmured as he thought.

Did the victims unknowingly take these pills? Maybe the victims knew this killer beforehand? All assumptions though as Paul's mind raced through scenarios. None of which led him any closer to finding the killer. *It may be worth looking into, however, to see if there was anyone new around the victims around the times of the deaths.*

The last distinction worried Paul. The killer seemed to take a life every two to three weeks. This meant Paul was running out of time and options before the next body would appeared. *I have to find something soon.*

Officers had begun to file into the station now, raising the noise level considerably. Paul's concentration began to teeter. *A good time to step out into the field,* Paul thought, grabbing his over coat.

Before he exited the office, Paul saw one of the sergeants walk by his office. "Sergeant," shouted Paul. The sergeant poked his head inside Paul's office. "Will you have one of your officers run through the phone numbers of the victim's parents and significant others of the

Heartbreak Killers case." Continued Paul. "See if they knew of or saw any new people in the victim's lives around the time of the murder."

"Will do Detective," replied the Sergeant.

"Oh and sergeant, if any of the people in questioning have information, will you tell your officer direct their number onto my desk so I can get in touch with them."

The sergeant nodded and turned his attention away from Paul, leaving him alone.

Time to make some headway, thought Paul as he picked up each of the four files and headed for his car.

Paul's mind drifted as he drove. The radio in Paul's car played an unfamiliar melody as his drove and his mind began to drift. As if in a trance, Paul began to day dream of the Heartbreak Killer.

Who is the Heartbreak Killer? What drove a person to such evil ways? What if he had been like me? Someone who had lost his loved one and was driven to madness by the pain. What if I am seeing my future of madness through this living mirror? Ironic and a bit symbolic, a man who kills by breaking hearts is being pursued by a man whose heart has been shattered and left in darkness. Who is the Heartbreak Killer?

The bulk of the transient thought receded as Paul pulled up to the most recent victim's house. Still though, one question resided deep within him. *What if we are similar?* The thought sent a shiver down Paul's spine and he quickly exited the car

A grey sky covered in dark clouds and swirling wind unpleasantly greeted the detective. The sight screamed of potential storms to come.

Only yellow tape marking the front doorway was left to signify the crime scene that had taken place just a week ago. *Luckily the crowd*

of media and civilians didn't stay, thought Paul as he made the rounds to the neighbor's houses.

Each neighbor Paul visited proved to be frivolous. None of those who answered the door seemed to have any new knowledge or leads that could be of use. Instead, the people inquired Paul about the Heartbreak Killer and if he was close to capturing the person responsible. Each time, Paul politely told them that the case was confidential and then walked to the next house.

After an hour of questioning, Paul decided to go back inside the house of horror he had exited so abruptly before.

Walking inside the home Paul sensed the same evil that had lurked on the night of the murder. It was as if the stench of death could never rid the walls. *Some clue has to reside here, I never had the proper chance to investigate.*

Paul went back down to the basement where the scene of the crime had occurred.

The woman's body had been taken away but the rose pedals and blood red painted heart still remained. Paul went in for a closer look at the painted heart that had taken him aback before. *So mysterious, what are you trying to say to us,* Paul thought. *Is your heart broken so these women pay for what they did?* Suddenly Paul reached for his heart as he thought, somehow feeling the killers pain. *Maybe my heart resembles this broken and twisted symbol.*

A moment passed and Paul shook off the thoughts of his broken heart. He then examined the room to see if anything had been missed by the forensics team, but nothing caught his eye or seemed to be out of the norm.

Paul ascended back upstairs and into the living room.

There was something that caught Paul's eye as he surveyed the room. *A lone cup mat.*

The mat stood out to Paul because of the way the living room was set. Everything was perfectly in place and clean, all except for the stray mat sitting on the coffee table next to a single sofa chair. *Why would someone who keeps a living room so clean leave out a cup mat?*

Paul went to the chair and table to get a closer look.

Maybe I am grasping at straws, thought Paul glancing over the cup mat. *People are forgetful.*

Getting on one knee, Paul examined around the coffee table and chair. As his vision descended to the floor level Paul spotted an object underneath the chair. He grasped at where it lie and pulled it out from under. *A book,* Paul realized as he held it up to his face.

The cover of the book featured a muscular and half shirtless man holding a black haired and petite figured woman in his arms. Behind the couple was a sunset shaped as a heart. *True Love* the title read.

She was reading and then for some reason, dropped the book... Because of the killer. There must have been a cup on the mat but the killer took it and forgot about the book. Why take the cup though?

Paul stood up from the ground and headed for the kitchen. He rummaged through the fridge in search of a lead. Some orange juice sat idle in the door compartment and Paul pulled it out, opened the top as he did. Nothing seemed to smell unusual in the juice but Paul set it on the counter anyways. *I need to take this to the lab.*

Searching through the fridge a bit more, Paul discovered a carton of milk and took a whiff. The scent had soured so he scanned for the expiration date. *Expired, still I need to take it.* Paul placed the milk next to the orange juice.

No other liquids were held inside the fridge so Paul closed the door and continued to the cabinets.

The first cabinet Paul opened reveled a box of tea. He picked up the package but the remains were empty. Paul then glanced over the box and noticed a bright warning label on the side. *May cause drowsiness* the warning read. Like a lightning rod the answer came to him.

"Of course," Paul murmured.

The tea, the Heartbreak Killer poisoned the tea bags. The woman would have thought that the first onset of effects were just from the tea so she would have never thought to dial 911 and before she knew it she would have been inebriated. The killer had to do was watch and wait.

Paul's phone began to vibrate in his pocket.

"Hello." Paul said still in deep thought, barely paying attention.

"Detective, I think we found the Heartbreak Killer." Said an unfamiliar voice. "Someone just called it in. Heard a woman screaming and saw a man running." Said a voice.

Paul's eyes widened, "Give me the coordinates, I'll be right there." He dropping the box of tea and sprinted to his car. Forgetting about what he had just learned.

Chapter Six
A Honey Blond Surprise

"Perry, I love you but… I'm still young. I need to have some me time before I get serious with you." Said a faceless woman.

"I stayed for you like you asked. I even moved colleges for you. Now you start up college and you're leaving me so you can find you?" Perry said, almost in tears.

"I am so sorry Perry, you'll be okay though." Said the woman with a twisted smile.

"No don't leave, please don't leave." Said Perry, racing towards the woman as she walked away. The faster Perry ran the farther the woman became. "Come back." Perry pleaded. "How can do this to someone you love."

But Perry's plea wasn't heard. The woman had disappeared into a sea of blackness, leaving him alone. Perry fell to his knees in sorrow disbelief as the same sea of blackness swallowed him.

Then in a flash the dark sea dispelled, leaving Perry inside an enclosed white room. He looked for a door or exit but there was no escape. Perry was trapped and pleaded for the faceless woman to help him escape, but there was no answer. Only silence in the white room.

All Perry was left with to do was curl up on the floor and weep as the thoughts of the hurtful women flashed in his mind. "Why, why, why. I thought love lasted forever." Perry whimpered. As each passing tear dripped to the floor it became red like blood, staining the pale white floor of the room. Soon the floor was filled with blood as the tears seeped from Perry for what seemed to be an eternity. Then the blood tears began to dry, becoming a black oozing tar and suddenly the white room was covered in black stains. Leaving what was once white forever stained with filth.

I thought love lasted forever…

Gasping for air I awoke to an ice cold sweat. Both my pillows and sheets had been drenched from what I assumed to have been hours of terrible and nightmarish filled dreams. It felt as if I had been drenched by a bucket of ice water.

The faceless woman constantly haunted my dreams, turning them to horrid nightmares for as long as the darkness had surrounded me. She was an ever reminding symbol of my creators, the ones who had turned me from Perry to monster. Those memories inside my dreams, of the women who had hurt me always lingered. A relentless reminder of the why and how of the person I was created to be. *I always end up in that black stained room,* I thought, getting up from my sweat-soaked bed.

The clock on my nightstand read 3:27 in the morning, but there wasn't a tired bone in my body now. I decided to do some research on my new victim, the honey blond beauty at the shoe store.

Getting a person's plate was chore in its own right, but that information was only the tip of the iceberg in regards to my serial killing blueprint. *You see, what good was a license plate number without a way to access the information?*

Before I started to terrorize the city as the *"Heartbreak Killer"*, I had to depict my plan. One option was to call one of my old friends in college, who had taken up a government job that gave him access to people's information. I thought about using him for help on license plate information, but how could I trust anyone else?

In my business it would have led a trail for the police to follow and now that my killing spree was gaining media steam, my old friend as well as the police could have easily connected the dots back to me.

"Hey Perry, I went back to all those plates you asked for and... Well, they were all registered to the victims in the Heartbreak Killer. Is there anything you want to tell me?"

"Nope, just a weird coincidence. How crazy is it, that they had all hit my car before they died." I imagined saying in the fake scenario of hypothetical possibilities.

No, that would never do. Serial killing was meant to be a solo hobby.

The next idea I had was to relentlessly stalk my victim until they lead me to their home. However, I wasn't particularly fond of that part of my game of spider and fly. Even my most recent encounter with the honey blond haired woman had tested my physical and mental health, and that had only been a few hours. *Too strenuous.*

Hell, I scoffed at the idea of me following around a potential victim for countless hours after I had obtained the plate number. Maybe the woman wouldn't have even gone home that night, instead going to a boyfriend's house for a sleep over of sorts. Then I would be forced into waiting in my car, freezing, and contemplating giving up my dream of poisoning her with my elixir of death. *No, no, no this way would not do.*

So what was a lazy serial killer left to do with his first two ideas put to waste? Well, I had one advantage that most would envy. I was extremely sharp witted.

Before I even started down the dark path I had taken, I took my brain and fed it the knowledge of computers and how they operated.

Also how the internet worked, how websites were made, and most importantly, how to hack with flawless success.

Yes, once I had learned that my other ideas had huge risks involved, I decided to learn how to hack computers and the systems inside the digital world.

The skill to obtain hacking knowledge was no easy task, however. It took me quite a bit of time to master the technique and hone it in on places like the police department or the DMV. But after many thousands of hours of relentless practice I learned how to hack a system.

Hacking was just the skill I needed to obtain to have access to license plate information. Once I was inside the system the rest was cake, I simply typed in the plate number and presto, everything I needed came up. Address, Name, Date of birth, and even criminal records. All I did then was write down information and poof, I was out of the system. I was a mere spider peering into the large home of private information, never to be seen or heard, so long as I was quick.

As easy as I make it sound there was a risk that came along with hacking. If I was ever discovered inside a system, someone could trace me to where I was accessing the internet connection from. I countered this by using public connections.

There was one in particular, close by my apartment. A service station that I enjoyed using. All I had to do was purchase something there and I would receive the password for the day, gaining access to the internet.

The service station was only one of many places I went. You see, I was a bit paranoid about being caught so I took no chances by using a plethora of different access points. The downtown library was one of those places that was of easy internet access for me. In dire crises I could even use the lobby of my apartment complex, but the old adage is you shouldn't shit were you eat.

I picked up my laptop from the desk in the study, put it inside my black leather satchel, and made my way to the elevator. *Time to feed on your prey Perry,* crackled my darkness as I made my exit.

The hall was silent outside of my apartment as I pressed the button pointing down on the elevator. I waited patiently and was met with a *ding* as the elevator reached my floor. When the door opened a group of young people greeted. They smelled of liquor and were obnoxiously laughing from what I assumed was a night of heavy drinking.

One group member was holding up another as they stumbled out of the elevator and past me. *Too much fun for that one. I remember when I was young and care free. Now I'm cursed by my dark monster and can't care.* I stepped inside the elevator and it greeted me with the same tacky music it always had. *Fuck, I hate this music,* I thought while I pressed the lobby floor.

Finally, I reached the lobby and made my way for the door.

"Can't sleep again Mr. Nelson?" The usual grave shift door man said to me.

"Nope, I had a dreadful nightmare. I need to take a stroll to calm my mind" I responded in a courteous manner. The door man smiled and opened the way out. I enjoy seeing the man for whatever unknown reason. *I wonder if he believes my constant nightmare stories,* I thought, making my way out onto the sidewalk.

The weather was freezing outside of my apartment lobby. A chilly November wind had graced the city for weeks. *Even if I was not a welcome host to it.*

Downtown was a ghost town at this time of night but it was always a pleasant sight for me to see the emptiness of the city. The only sight or sound now was the sizzling of hot steam coming from the various manholes. In a way, the darkness of night had always called to me, always easing my pain-filled mind. *Maybe that is why it consumed me.*

When I reached the service station, I stationed myself on a couch by the fire place. I loved the warmth the fire provided after a chilly walk. After I unpacked my laptop, I made my way toward the counter.

"Can I get a black cup of coffee?" I said to the man behind the counter.

"What size would you like?" He asked back.

"A venti sounds good to me. Will you leave a little room for some cream?"

The man nodded and went to make the coffee. I waited only a brief moment before the coffee was presented before me.

"Would you like our WIFI password sir?" The coffee man said while handing me the coffee.

"Yes, thank you." I responded.

The man wrote the password on my receipt and handed it to me with a grin. *I should give him a tip,* I thought. Before returning to my place by the fire, I placed a dollar in the tip jar, picked up a cream, and then made my way toward the couch.

As soon as I sat, I began my hacking routine while I sipped on the coffee, which burned my lips. *Feed me Perry,* implored my darkness as I began rapidly typing on my keyboard.

Within a few minutes I was inside the DMV system.

I reached for my phone to glance at the pictures I had taken from the night before. Scanning the number, I began to type the license plate onto the search bar. *Yes, feed your darkness, who is this woman? I want her heart.*

The information appeared to me as if it had been spotlighted. Like a bug, the laminating words on my computer screen drew me in. Alexis Fisher, blond hair, blue eyes, 5'9, age 28, address 3137 E. Brooks St.

Fisher… Where have I heard that name before? My eyes widened, and as if a lightbulb had just appeared above my head I knew. *Paul Fisher, the detective on my case? Is this his daughter? It couldn't be that perfectly arranged… Could it?*

Immediately I went to a search engine and typed in the name Paul Fisher. I hadn't checked into him as I had first intended when I saw him heading the case.

I clicked on the first link that appeared, a bio page of Paul Fisher. His profile picture was of him and his wife, smiling, with a beach and palm trees in the background. *An old Honeymoon picture I reckon. She passed away recently I remembered from the news report.*

I clicked on a section labeled *about.*

Paul Fisher, date of birth March 13th, 1972. I scrolled past some useless information, looking to find a relative section. *Alexis Fisher, Alexis Fisher, Alexis Fisher,* was humming in my mind… *Bingo. Relatives, Daughter, Alexis Fisher,* I read across the screen.

I clicked on the hyperlinked profile name.

It's her, the honey blond haired beauty, the daughter of Paul Fisher. I was suddenly struck with a state of disbelief as I leaned back into the couch, still pondering the information I had just received.

Can I even go through with killing the detective's daughter?

Yessss, hissed my dark monster within. *Kill the girl, show the people that the heartbreak touches every soul. Spread your terror Perry.*

A dangerous thought and proposition, but part of me was enticed.

Imagine the news frenzy if the Heartbreak Killer slay the daughter of the man whose job it was to bring me down. The city would be forever engulfed into fear induced chaos. No one would feel safe again. I would be forever infamous.

The cockiness of my personality wanted to do the kill and so did my dark monster, still whispering to me. He was only satisfied with blood and death.

However, is it the smartest idea for me to do something of that magnitude? Surely I would never make it out alive and if I did, the pursuit would be relentless after a death of that proportion.

I gazed upon the picture of Alexis Fisher once more. Depicting her every which way.

In the picture Alexis was standing in a blue dress and black heels. Her smile was white as pearls and straight as arrows. *Just as I remembered.* Her blue eyes were almost hypnotizing to me as I stared into them. *Blue like the ocean.* Her skin was of a porcelain doll, fair and soft. *Surely to be burned if the sun set on its mighty rays upon it.* Lastly, the gold tint of her blond hair. *The color made it seem as if a taste may be sweet like honey.*

She is beautiful, she looks so pure and innocent. Men must fall for her left and right.

Alexis's mesmerizing beauty was strange to me. I couldn't remember the last time I had viewed a woman as such. My darkness had left me indifferent to the look of women for so long. All I saw now was flesh and bones, nothing else. But her beauty pierced through my darkness in a way.

I couldn't decide on what I wanted. My mind was in the middle of a tug of war. *To do or not to do,* I thought, remaking the famous Hamlet quote in my mind.

Still sitting back against the comfort of the couch, I sipped my coffee, and stared into the fire.

The beauty of Alexis began to fade into the darkness of my mind, just as the faceless woman in my dream had. The ever-consuming darkness never stops, he is the gluttonous monster who is never full.

Kill her, the monster whispered to me, once again inflicting my mind with its evil poisons.

Maybe there was a time I could resist the deathly call but my body was too stained with blackness now.

I packed my things into the satchel and left the coffee shop.

The sun was peaking above the city as I stood outside but I couldn't see the light. The darkness of my mind clouded all. I had made my choice to be the monster, the man of darkness, the Heartbreak Killer, long ago.

I threw my coffee into a nearby trash bin and began to make my way home. With each step, my dark thoughts expanded and my plan hatched.

The sun was almost as clear as day when I reached my building but soon everyone would see the morning as I had during the walk back. Dark shades or misery.

The cold November wind still howled and swirled through the nameless city, and my dark monster howled in pleasure. He knew it was almost time to feast.

Alexis Fisher, you are mine.

Chapter 7
The Killer Manual

This was my biggest kill to date. The preparation had to be strenuous and precise.

With the four victims before I usually spent a few days studying their movements, their habits, and their routines. The detective's daughter would be different, another animal all together. I had to plan for novel circumstances.

Detective Fisher could have professed concern about me killing women that were in the same category as his daughter. That kind of worry could lead to various police personnel lurking around Alexis's house, trying to keep her safe at the Detectives personal request.

Along with that thought, Alexis herself could be an adequate opponent compared to the others, being a daughter of a policeman. Detective Fisher could have educated her to be more aware of surroundings or how to defend against potential intruders. She was beautiful but I couldn't be deceived by looks, they are not always what they appear. *I learned that the hard way.*

When preparing for any kill I had to obtain multiple items. The first item on my list was enough anti-depressant pills to stop my victim's heart from beating. This was the easiest step for me. I had at least three patients a day that were suffering from some sort of depression. All I had to do was skim off four or five pills from their prescriptions I wrote them.

To this day, my patients were unaware of the disappearance of their pills. I just assumed that they were complete idiots, but what did I know, they were all depressed and dealing with some serious life problems.

Regularly, patients on anti-depressants received a refill once or twice every month, so the timing was a bit tricky. But I had mastered the timing and within a week or two I could collect enough pills for my victim.

Once I accumulated enough of the pills, I had to carefully crush them into a powder that would be soluble in liquid. The powders consistency was key, the victim had to be unaware that they were consuming it. Where the powder was placed depended on the habits of the victim themselves. Always something they consumed on a daily basis.

The second step in my killer's manual was to find the materials I needed for an extraction of a piece of the victim's heart.

I had patiently practiced this step in my house for months, trying to find the right material that would prevent any left behind evidence. The first couple practice attempt in particular were an utter disaster. Unknowingly, I had purchased a thin type of plastic covering and after I had squirted ketchup over it, the covering ripped through and spilt. Ketchup consequently spilt to the floor. *Lesson learned rook, thicker covering.*

Anything dealing with blood in particular was a messy matter. Always spraying, oozing, and leaking all over. As I cut through the midnight colored hair woman, the blood tried to squirm into every corner. Luckily, I had practiced and was ready for such an event.

What a glorious night of darkness, hissed my dark monster.

After I had my overspray protective sheeting, I moved onto cleaning products.

I could go to any local department store for these items. The key for me was to switch up the store I went to each time. *See the pattern? First the internet now this.*

The one thing that amazed me when I started this was that I could find almost everything I needed to pull off a murder at a local department store. Sometimes when I went into the store I sarcastically thought to ask an attendant if they could lead me to the "how to clean up murder" isle. Seriously, the store had it all, scrubbing brushes, oxidized bleach, rubber gloves, and heavy duty trash bags. *Everything I needed.*

Once I had the pills and murder inventory stocked, the last step was simply being comfortable enough to go through with the kill. This variable depended on me and how easy the victim made it to pick up on their tendencies.

How do you pick up on the tendencies of the people you stalk? By watching the victim, and I discovered a way to do that without being close. Cameras.

The brilliance of it all was that I only needed to get inside my victims house once before the kill to place my microscopic spy cameras inside the privacy of their home. Afterward, I could sit back and watch them from the comfort of my own home. The best part? None of the women suspected a damn thing, being themselves and reveling everything to me while no one was watching. *But I was watching.*

I set out on this very task after work, under the cover of the night sky.

As I drove in silence, I began to mentally prepare for my task. *I have to be as sharp as ever,* I thought as I tapped my fingers on the steering wheel of the car while I drove. *Am I nervous?*

With only five blocks to go before I reached Alexis's home, I veered off the road and parked in the neighborhood.

The first thing I noticed as I parked my car were the street lighting around me. *This is going to be a problem,* I thought. I would have to improvise now and be a bit more careful where I lurked.

As I walked towards the destination, I began to think. *What if Detective Fisher is waiting for me, setting a trap? No, he wouldn't dare think I would attack his daughter. Or would he? Why am I paranoid?* I stopped for a deep breath, needing to focus all my diverted attention onto the task at hand. *Get it together, Perry.*

Once I was a block away from Alexis's house, I rehashed my strategy.

Do I want to walk by the house first or find a way to get in through the back?

Looking around at my surroundings, I noticed that most of the houses had tall wood fencing scaling around the back yards. I would be forced to hop fences, risking a dog barking in the back yard or worse, a person seeing me. *No, I need to go by the front of the house first... I will jog by, that will work.*

I went back to my car and changed into some tight black leggings, black shorts, black hoodie, and my college alumni colored beanie. *Good thing I always packed for multiple circumstances.* Once I was fully changed, I took off jogging.

An ice cold rain began to fall upon me as I ventured back to the corner block I had stopped on. *Here we go,* I thought as I rounded onto Alexis's street.

Making my way past a few houses I checked my phone, her house was coming up on my left, two down. When I came up to it I began to scan and take mental notes. *Dark colored base, white trim, two or three stories, large windows on the right side of the house, lights on inside, tree in the yard, dimly lit in front.*

Turning away from the house, I made a look for her car on the road. Instead, I noticed there was a police car parked on the opposite side of the road. *OH SHIT.*

I kept jogging as if I hadn't noticed anything alarming. Once I passed the police car, I quickly made my way up another road.

Once I was out of the police cars view I stopped and took a deep breath, putting my hands to my knees. *The Detective is worried,* I thought. *He must not have any leads on me. Good, but bad too, this makes things difficult.* I had never done my dance so close to the men and women who wanted to bring me to justice. *I need to reexamine my approach.*

I sat motionless in my car for hours, drenched from the cold rain. My mind was churning like a finely tuned machine. *What do I do?* I had my lack of heart set on killing Alexis, but was it arrogant of me to believe I could take on a challenge of this magnitude? *Do I even care?*

After a long and deep thought, drowsiness over took me, and soon I lulled to sleep.

The white and black stained room appeared to me again in my dreams. *Is there a way to clean the dark mess or was it forever stained,*

I began to wonder as I sat alone in the room. Suddenly, black tar began to ooze from the creases of the white walls. *Kill the woman,* hissed a voice from inside the walls.

I was woken by the sound of a passing car. My body was encumbered with the cold that had forced its way inside the car, freezing my damp clothing and bringing me to shivers.

I turned the car on to try and warm up.

While the heat flowed, the dark monster inside me began to pollute my mind, reminding me of why I had become this way. Reminding me of my empty heart. *Kill Alexis, regardless of the risks.* I had nothing to lose. I was barely alive, a walking shadow of darkness.

With the cover of the night sky still there to hide me and the rain pattering on the ground to distort the sound of footsteps, I made my way to Alexis's house once more. *I need to go through the back this time,* I thought running in the darkness.

Within minutes, I found the house that shared a fence with Alexis's backyard and made my way towards it. I was careful not to be seen as I did, sulking in the darkest corners of the neighborhood that presided over me.

Quick and quite, I moved into position by the neighbor's fence. Glimpsing over the large wood fence, I checked for any danger. *Looks clear,* I thought

With one forceful hop, I was over the fence, landing on the other side without a sound. Once I surveyed the yard for danger, I sprinted to the back side of the fence as fast as I could.

Again, I peeked over to scan for any sign of trouble before I jumped over. The path looked clear to me but it was hard to tell in the pitch black of night. *Hopefully this isn't a trap, be ready to run.*

I made my leap into Alexis Fisher's backyard and landed into the wet grass below.

From what I could make out the yard was spacious, with various trees and bushes scattered throughout. I located some blanketed bushes to hide behind and gather my thoughts for the next step.

As I crouched behind the bushes I let out an exhale of misty air. *So far so good. Now, I need to get inside.* Pulling out my phone I checked the time. *2:43,* the bright screen read.

While staring over the bushes I fidgeting with a damp leaf as I prepared my next move. I could faintly make out the outline of the house from where I was crouching, but there were no lights on inside that could show a true definition. Then I spotted a stairwell that appeared to lead up to an old-fashioned door. *That's how I get inside.*

I surveyed the house once more for potential dangers. Nothing seemed threatening but I knew as well as any that the darkness can mask anything. I closed my eyes to listen but only the sound of the rain falling to the earth came to my ears. In one swift motion I made hast towards the stairwell.

Once I reached the bottom rung, I ducked down to the side. With a closer examination I could see that the stairs were old and run down, made of splintered wood and peeling paint. After I caught my breath, I began to creep up, step by step, trying not to cause a single sound on the wooden boards.

A light flashed onto me as I reached the top of the stairs. *THE POLICE WERE WAITING!* Without hesitation, I bolted down the stairs and raced towards the fence.

But before I flung myself over the fence, I came to a halt. *Why is there no shouting after me?* I turned back towards the house and crouched in the bushes. *It was just a sensory light I triggered,* I thought, spotting the light hanging by the doorway.

I took another deep misty breath and relief overtook me. *Just a light... Hopefully the light nor me racing down the steps woke Alexis.*

The sensory light shut off minutes later and the yard was covered in darkness once more. *This time I need to be quick in opening the door when I am up there.* I pulled out a lock pick from my pocket and again ventured for the door.

As before, the sensory light sprang to life when I reached the top of the stairs. Instinctually I paused; *a man of darkness should never be in the light.* However, I quickly found my purpose and went towards the door.

The door itself was a maroon painted wood with a copper tint handle. In the middle of the door there was an old fashion octagon glass stained window.

Picking the lock took me only a matter of seconds, but before I opened the door, I mentally prepared. I always had a fear that an alarm would trigger and shriek at me, warning everyone around that I had entered. Tonight was no different as I turned the copper handle to go inside. Luckily, no shrieking alarms were there to greet me, only the silent darkness from inside the house. *Into the darkness I go,* I thought as I made my way inside and quietly closed the door behind me.

The inside of Alexis's house was pitch black once the door was closed. My eyes had not adjusted to the darkness since they had been pierced from the bright sensory light outside. So I waited, couching down until I could make out the surroundings.

Adrenaline began to flow though my body and heightened my senses as I realized the magnitude of the moment. After another moment of waiting my eyes adjusted and I could see the layout of the house. Contrary to the outside of her house, which appeared old fashion to me, the inside was quite modern from what I could vaguely make out.

There was art on the walls, which seemed to be of the same outrageous expense I had paid for in my own home. The floors had been redone to a nice walnut stained wood and the furniture was brown and black leather. All placed side by side with black wooded coffee tables and elegant lamps. Everything inside was complimented by scattered nick knack items from exotic locations. *This style is comfortable to me*, I thought and calming overcame me. The threat of being caught inside Alexis's home subsided and my adrenaline drained. *It's almost like we have the same taste.*

I kept quiet and made sure to cover my tracks as I continued throughout the house. A kitchen came into view from the right side. The lighting was dimly lit by a hanging lamp above a steel oven and stove. As a whole, it was a spacious kitchen, with a rectangle counter top island in the middle of charcoal colored tile flooring. A steel double door fridge stood next to a sink that seemed to be made out of stone. *She has grand taste, I'll give her that,* I thought before moving my attention away.

A stairwell to the left of the kitchen lead downward and straight ahead was a dark hallway. I could see what appeared to be four doors that led with the length of the hallway. *She probably sleeps up in one of them,* I thought, deciding to make my way down the hall of doors.

The walls were covered with various sized framed pictures. I noticed that one of the pictures was of Detective Fisher, Alexis, and a woman I didn't recognize. *It must be her late mother. She has similar*

beauty to Alexis. In the picture they were all smiling for a photographer behind a set background. *The classic family portrait.*

Another picture hung next to the Fisher family that caught my eye. It was of Alexis and a man of similar age to me. He stood taller than Alexis by six or seven inches, with short brown hair and a well-trimmed beard. Next to him, Alexis was holding out her hand with a sparkling ring on her left ring finger. *She had been engaged, but when I had met her she said she was single. Was she lying to me too? ... Or maybe the relationship didn't work out.*

I came to the first door that was located on the right of the hall. I twisted the handle with gentle touch. Inside the room was a bathroom with an old-fashioned tub that hadn't been framed to the walls.

Three doors to go. She has to be in one of these. I closed the door and made my way further up the hall.

The next door was on the left of the hall. Turning the handle, I was met with a loud creaking noise that made me cringe. *Be quiet, Perry.* Inside this room lay filled with clutter. From what I could make out the walls were white with assorted dark splotches. In the center of the room, amongst the clutter, I noticed a partially made baby carriage. *I wonder if she had been planning for a child with her fiancé in the picture.* Along with the crib, other various items had been either taken down, left on the floor, or crammed inside still opened cardboard boxes

Two doors remained as I reached the end of the dark hallway, both paralleled each other. I decided to reach for the right sided one and again the sound of the knob creaked as I turned. To me the noise sounded like a screeching train had just gone through the house. *It's all in my head,* I thought, realizing it was more circumstance than anything.

Peeking through a slit in the door, I laid my eyes upon Alexis, the honey blond haired beauty. She was lying in her bed fast asleep. I froze as I gazed upon her. She reminded me of a princess waiting for a prince to kiss her, waking her from an enchanted sleep.

However, tonight the prince wasn't staring at Alexis, only the man of darkness and his kiss of death.

Still, seeing Alexis was unsettling to me for some reason. I wasn't used to a woman in that light of innocence and beauty. *Why does she have that affect?*

My darkness put an end to the thought, calling out to me.

Kill her now, in such a vulnerable state of sleep. Slice her throat and rip a piece of her heart out for your collection. I want to feed one the pureness of her soul, Perry.

As tempting the call was, I had too much restraint for such a foolish action. Anyways, it was only a matter of time now, I could wait. *A work of art like this takes time. Surely to be my most recognizable. It mustn't be rushed.*

I took one more glance at the honey blond haired beauty wrapped comfortably in her blankets and then closed the door. It was time to find a spot to hide until she leaves.

I thought for a moment on where to go. *Which is the least likely spot she would look... The garage.* I headed back down the hallway and to the right, down the stairs.

When I reached the inside of the garage, I was met with more darkness. There were no windows or cracks to hint even the smallest shimmer of light in.

I flicked on the light switch once the door closed behind me. The garage was snug with Alexis's red four door parked in the middle. Along with it there were quite a few boxes and old furniture scattered around on the other side. *An adequate hiding spot*, I decided. There I positioned myself in the cover of old and useless things, waiting for her to leave.

As I waited for the hours to pass my mind began to drift away with questions.

Why am I drawn to the beauty of Alexis? Was it the purity she seemed to exert? Even when I met her at the shoe store she seemed so innocent. The opposite of someone like me. I am dark, evil, and stained with bloodlust. Maybe that is why she calls to me. Could Alexis bring hope for a cure to my cold black heart?

She is just a woman, responded my dark monster. *She is just like all the others. Remember, the ones who broke you and turned you into the monster you are now. Isn't that why you kill women, Perry?*

Yes, women have been treated as the innocents in a relationship. Yet I have seen them just as dark and evil as men. They tortured my soul to oblivion but maybe one can be different. Maybe one can save me by showing me the light again. Showing me there is hope for love in this world.

You're a killer Perry, there is no going back. Your monster has been set loose, it's too late. Women made you into this, they deserve to pay at your hand now.

But I don't want to be this way....

KILL HER PERRY, RIP HER HEART OUT JUST LIKE THE WOMEN DID TO YOU, screamed the darkness.

Before I could respond I heard the sound of rustling above me. *It must be morning.* I checked my phone, *7:31 am.* Another hour passed between the noises but Alexis was still inside. My patience was waning as the weight of being awake for twenty-four hours dawned upon me. Then, I heard the sound of thumping becoming louder and louder. *She is coming down the stairs,* I thought.

I sat motionless in silence. The door opened and the sound of the garage door raising rang. Then a nearby box began to shuffle. *No go away, I can't kill you this way*, I thought, grasping at my knife and holding my breath.

Kill her Perry.

The sound of a car door slammed shut and the engine roared. After a moment, the garage door made its way back down with a grinding screech.

I was in the clear to move about the house freely.

Bit by bit, room by room, I methodically placed my tiny surveillance cameras in rooms of importance. The kitchen, the bedroom, the living room, all the places I deemed appropriate.

The cameras were expensive items to purchase but well worth the money. They were no bigger than the tip of my pointer finger and stuck to almost any surface I placed them on. It was safe to say you would really have to be searching for one to spot it. *Hence, why women are dead and I roam free.*

I had almost finished up with the house tour and camera placing bonanza when the garage door rumbled. *What was she gone for 20 minutes?* Adrenaline shot through me again. I had no time to think, I needed to leave in a matter of seconds or else I would be trapped.

Bolting for the back door just as the garage had stopped rattling, I flung it open. The sound of the garage closing could be heard as well as the faint noise of the downstairs door opening behind me. *Flee, Perry, flee.*

I closed the door as quietly as I could manage, and without thinking, I launched off the deck onto the hard earth with a rumbling tumble. *Ouch,* I thought, springing to my feet and hustling to the bushes that I had hid behind before.

Ducking behind the bushes, I rapidly peeked through the branches to see if Alexis had seen or heard me. She was visible in a window, but she wasn't looking out. Instead, she had her phone on her shoulder and seemed to be washing her hands in the kitchen.

I waited for her to leave my sight. With the fence was only a couple feet behind me, I needed just a second or two before I was out of her yard.

Alexis exited from the window and I sprang into action. Running and hopping the back fence. Landing to the ground again, I made my way through the neighbor's yard and towards my car.

My pace was frenetic. *I can't be spotted,* was the only thought racing through my mind.

Once I reached the street in front of the neighbor's house I immediately stopped running to catch my breath. Glancing around, I didn't sense I had been spotted, so I wiped the sweat from my brow and strolled the rest of my way to the car.

I am safe, I thought. *The Heartbreak Killer is never seen.*

Chapter 8
The Bitch of Channel 28 News

I run this tiny, pathetic, excuse of a city. Every man wants to fuck me and every woman hates me for being what they aren't, a famous god damn sex symbol. What I say goes and everyone listens, no matter what bullshit I spew to them.

Terry Connor had just hung up the phone with a senior news executive who ran a nationally broadcast news station.

"We are looking for a new woman co-anchor for our station." Said the executive. "Your reporting and ratings are phenomenal and you're just the kind of spark we need to get the viewer's attention again. If you keep this trend up we will be pushing hard to give you the upcoming opening. We just need to see a little more before we are comfortable giving you the position. Maybe break a big story or something?"

This was music to Terry's ears. *I have wanted to be the face of the nation since I started my career, not of some silly city.*

Terry had been pushing to the top from a very young age, by manipulating the men of power above her with her astonishing good looks. Flirting and even sleeping with some who proved to be more difficult to persuade were all fair game to her. Terry had an unquenchable thirst to get to the top and nothing stood in her way. *Men are easy, all you need to do is flash sex and they will give you anything.*

Women were a different animal, but Terry had learned to handle them as well, by spreading nasty rumors and lies about her competing rivals. If that failed, Terry knew that at the very least she would outwork the other women by only focusing on her career and substituting her social life. *Nothing matters but getting to the top.*

Over time Terry's methods had proved fruitful, single handedly bring the once joked about Channel 28 News Station to the now power house of the city.

Male viewers tuned in for her beauty. Terry had brown hair that was freshly trimmed and pampered every week, brown almond eyes that screamed sexual innuendo, and perfectly tan toned skin that glowed even in the cold winters. But what set Terry's appearance off was her body. Plump breasts, long legs, and skinny waist.

A popular magazine had even proclaimed Terry one of the top 100 sexiest women alive as her rise and fame grew.

Terry wasn't just popular with men, however. Young women who aspired to one day be as pretty as her also tuned in. They obsessed about what new clothing Terry was wearing, or to see how she had styled her hair and makeup that day. All to get tips on how to become more beautiful and keep up with the fashion trends that Terry was so in tune with.

Even older women viewed in just too mock Terry with their jealousy. Regardless of the reasons why the public viewed her news channel mattered little to Terry. Just that they did view. *Ratings get you to the top.*

The ticket to the national news job is the Heartbreak Killer, Terry thought. Ratings had tripled since she first broke the story months ago. Everyone seemed to be intrigued by the killer and Terry herself had given the name to the once unknown assailant.

Terry Conner's ruthless pursuit of story on the Heartbreak Killer was unmatched by any rivaling news stations in the city. She made sure to be the first one to the scene and then to the TV broadcast. Showing any and everything that would stir the viewer's emotions, blood, violence, death, and crying spouses or parents of the victims. Nothing was foul play to Terry. *That's why I'm getting this job offer. I will take it to places others won't.*

Terry's phone rang again.

"Miss Connors, we just picked up on a call to 911 about someone fleeing the scene of a screaming woman's home." Said a soft spoken man on the other end. "Police think it's the Heartbreak Killer. If we leave now I think we will get there before anyone else does."

"Perfect, I'll be ready in ten, be here in nine." Terry snapped back.

"Yes Miss Connor," and the phone clicked.

A white news van labeled, Channel 28 News Team, screeched up to Terry Connor's estate eleven minutes later. Terry was already outside waiting with a fierce scowl.

"You're late," Terry shouted as she ripped the news van door open.

"I… I'm sorry Miss Connors." Cowered a young man with a large camera in his lap. "We got stuck in traffic."

"I don't want your pathetic excuses. If we don't break this story first… Let's just say you won't like what happens next." Said Terry, still shouting as she slammed the door behind her. "Now punch it jack ass."

The van blasted off the pavement, sending smoke into the air as the rubber wheels burned.

"Listen here," demanded Terry to the small crew in the news van. "I want as much drama as I can get. That means people crying, blood flying, even a dead body if we can find a shot. Whatever it takes to really shove this Heartbreak Killer story into the public's face. This story is a ratings monster and Channel 28 News needs to be at the top of it all. You hear me?"

The crew nodded attentively.

They are a bunch of damn retards. I could say anything to them and they would nod their heads in agreement, pathetic.

Police cars suddenly raced by the van, their neon lights flashing through the darkness of the night.

"Follow behind them as fast as you can." Said Terry.

"But Miss Conner," pleaded the driver.

"Why are you talking? I said punch it."

The van began to accelerate and tail behind the racing police cars.

"We are going too fast." The driver said with fear in his eyes.

"Stop being a little girl." Terry said looking at the odometer which read, *104.* "Keep on that cops ass."

The driver made a glance over to Terry with his eyes wide, brows raised, and mouth open.

"Watch the road." Terry said with a point of her sharp finger.

The van bobbed and weaved through the traffic at a blistering pace. All of the Channel 28 News crew watched in terror of the maneuvering, holding their breaths and tightening their seatbelts. Within moments, the crew arrived to a scene of cop cars and a gathering small crowd of people, all huddled together on a street in front of the neighborhood house.

"Get back, get the fuck back." Yelled an officer as he tried to set a perimeter around the growing crowd.

The news van screeched to a halt and Terry flew out of the door, along with a camera man, attempting to keep up with her pace.

"You better keep up. We need to get a shot of the body inside this house." Terry yelled behind her to the camera man.

The officer shouting out directions spotted Terry Connor sprinting to the house and ran after her.

"Whoa, where the hell do you think you're going?" Said the officer blocking the entry to the door of the house.

"Get out of my way. Do you know who I am?" Said Terry trying to push the officer out of the way.

"Yeah I know who you are, that bitch of Channel 28 News. I don't like you, so get the fuck out of the way before I restrain you for trying to obstruct a crime scene."

"This bitch shits on peasants like you. I'll get something out." Terry said shoving the officer as she walked away. "You're a nobody, not even worth my breath."

I'll get my story. This crowd should give me something... Right there.

Terry Connor charged for the crowd of people, ready to spread more of her fear of the Heartbreak Killer onto the city.

Chapter 9
The Game Changer

I was glued to the computer in my study. In front of me sat four monitors, each showing me a different room and camera in Alexis Fishers home. *There is something different about her,* I managed to think each time I viewed her. This time she was making pasta in her kitchen for dinner. *But I can't put my finger on what.*

Regardless, the time had almost come for me to strike and take a new piece of heart. *Alexis Fisher, whatever it is won't save you from the wrath of my dark monster. From the wrath of the Heartbreak Killer. You're mine.*

I had been patiently watching Alexis for hours a day now, for two consecutive weeks since my visit to her home. Once I even followed her around the city, discovering that she worked at a local book store. *I can't completely despise a woman that likes to read.*

I wonder if she read the one where the killer comes to extract a piece of the woman's heart, whispered my dark monster at the thought.

If she hasn't yet, she will soon.

The countless hours of surveillance on Alexis had led me to what I needed to complete my murder, her routines and actions. I had set a plan in place.

Five out of the seven days of the week Alexis made a full pot of coffee in the morning and a half pot when she came home from her day at work. With the discovery of her fondness for coffee I could easily plant my deathly powder. *Humans fall to slaves of their routines.*

Tonight was the last night I lay at bay, for tomorrow I would strike Alexis Fisher down and rain even more terror onto the city. The thought of what Terry Connor and all the other news outlets would say once the detectives daughter was dead pleased me and made my darkness swirl into chaotic motion in my mind.

After an hour more of watching Alexis, I grew weary and headed for bed. I needed to be well rested for the task at hand, it was the biggest one to date. *The game changer.*

My sleep was filled with nothing but empty darkness. A usually occurrence in the years following my dark monster's birth, especially when the time was near for a kill. The darkness that shrouds my mind dreams only of black nothings and white horror rooms. The endless cycle that haunted me.

I awoke to a cloudy and windy dawn, ready to feast on the heart and blood of the pure Alexis Fisher. My dark monster was relentless and hungry as ever before. *Kill the pure woman Alexis Fisher, Perry,* it called all morning. *Let me feast on the blood and death.*

The morning was spent crushing pills to dust and filling the remains into vials. As I crushed, I watched the last living day of Alexis Fisher. Watching her drink coffee, eat her breakfast, and get herself ready for work. I found it strange to watch a person on the day they die. Never knowing that the looming death was just around the corner. *I play a god of sorts, watching from above, knowing when their time is.*

As soon as Alexis left the house, I would make my move to place the powdered poison. I would have approximately eight hours to plant it inside her coffee maker before she came home. Then all I had to do was watch and wait for her to start drinking. Slowly but surely Alexis would consume the entire pot and be doomed to death, presenting me with the heart my monster craved. *Blood, death, revenge*, the monster whispered as I continued to crush and watch the honey blond haired beauty.

Alexis left for work a brief thirty minutes later, and as soon as I was satisfied with the texture of the powdered poison, I departed for her home. *Let's get this done as quickly as possible,* I thought.

I had some coverage from the grey cloudy sky but not nearly as much as I needed to blend into as the night hours would provide me. In a perfect world I would have waited for darkness to make my move but Alexis could easily arrive any time after her usually eight hour shift, making it too risky to be inside after that window of time.

The plan to get inside was similar to the night visit. Drive by the house to see if the police were still around. *Check.* Park a few blocks away. *Check.* Sneak into the back yard through the opposite neighbor's house. *Check.* Everything went smoothly for me, even with the lack of coverage, I seamlessly snuck into Alexis's back door as before.

Once inside of Alexis's house, I immediately headed for her coffee pot. *The less time inside here the better,* I thought as I made my way into the modern kitchen with grey stoned floors. From there I spotted the pot I had viewed from my hidden camera. *Bingo.*

All I needed to do now was plant the powder at the bottom of the glass pot and it would dissolve into the coffee at the set brewing time. I glanced at the coffee makers scheduled brew, *5:30. Too perfect, only six hours away and it will be done before she ever arrives.*

With the last of the pot finished, as was accustom for Alexis to do after work, she would be doomed to unknowing death of cardiac arrest.

I reached inside my pocket for the vile. Pulling it out I peered into the glass, gazing at white contraption of doom and smiled. My darkness crackled manically inside my head, feeling the time was near to feast on blood and death.

Without another wasted second, I yanked the black stopper from the vile and dumped the containments into the coffee pot. *Yesssss, the spider has strung his web of entrapment,* bellowed my dark monster, smitten with what I had done. *Now we wait and feast.*

Wait indeed, I headed for the back door. But before I hid behind the bushes, I reached for my blade hidden inside my coat and cut the cables on the back of the sensory light. *This way when I make my way back up I won't be spotted.* With a quick and precise flick of the wrist, the cords severed from the sharp blade and I ran down the stairs, hiding behind the bushes of Alexis Fishers backyard. *Now I wait.*

I lay still for quite some time. My darkness began to ooze itself throughout my body in preparation to feed. It always possessed the most power right before a kill, right when the scent of death was strongest. Little by little the black rotting ooze dribbled through my body. First covering my mind, then my lungs, and finally my extremities.

The place where my heart once resided was left for the end as the black ooze pooled around and festered, then hardening itself into a black coal shaped heart that felt nothing.

All of the killing had turned me into less of a man and more into the monster I now was. My once good-natured soul shattered a little more and left me more consumed in the darkness

As I lay helpless to the process at hand, I stared at the dark grey sky and flipped through the twisted tale of Perry Nelson. The images and sounds of the women who had wronged me rapidly moved throughout my mind and festered inside the pit of my stomach. With each passing tale I became more enraged and vengeful inside. I think those heart-wrenching images were what my dark monster wanted me to see. The darkness wanted me to hate the world and make those who wronged me pay.

Out from all of the haze my darkness had created came a light, and when I snapped from my pain filled trance it was dark outside. A single light had come on from inside Alexis Fishers home. *She is finally home*, I thought as I looked through the bushes into the window and then to my watch. *6:14, a bit late. No matter, now I wait for her to start drinking the coffee and slowly she will be mine.*

I turned to my phone and activated the cameras from it. There I could see Alexis's belongings sitting by the stairwell, but she was nowhere in sight. I looked up from the phone to see another light flicker on from what I guessed was her room. *She must be changing.*

Turning my attention back onto the cameras, I finally saw Alexis appear from the hallway and as she walked to the kitchen. She went to the fridge to get something, putting it into the microwave, and then continued for the coffee pot. *Yessssss, the fly is buzzing into the web,* hissed my monster. Indeed she was, filling her cup up with freshly brewed coffee on my screen. The moment was near, Alexis only needed two or three cups before she was cast away into the depths of death.

I stood up in the darkness of night. Lightning flashed in the sky above as I did, followed by the boom of thunder. *Perfect,* I thought. *A fitting setting for a serial killer.*

My dark monster began to wildly dance inside me. I reached for the knife still held inside my coat pocket while I watched the cameras on my phone. The cool steel of the blade was a welcomed kiss to my monster, which percolated at the feel. *Kill, blood, revenge, take what is ours. Kill the detective's daughter and rain the fear of the Heartbreak Killer.*

Before I stepped toward the house a cool rain drop hit my face. I looked up and another flash of lightning lit the sky ablaze. When the thunder rumbled again so too did the fall of rain, pounding the earth. I began to pace towards the house and with each passing step my dark monster raged and raged. At this point I was no man, but instead, a living monster. Nothing could save Alexis Fisher from my wrath now.

Stationing myself under the stairs of Alexis back porch, I checked the phone for her position. She sat on her living room couch sipping the brewed coffee, dying. I zoomed in on the camera in the kitchen. The pot was still too full for the effects to come into play, so I decided to wait outside a bit longer.

While I did, I listened to the sounds of the environment. The rain and howling wind were trying to cleanse the earth of its dirty residue. Yet here I stood, the monster amongst it all, and no amount of rain could clean my broken soul.

It is time to kill, pronounced the monster sensing as a wild beast does. I checked my phone and saw that Alexis was heading for the pot of coffee, pouring more into her cup. *Her senses will be dulled after this one, becoming drowsy. A perfect time to blend into the shadows of her home. Then, thinking the coffee isn't working she will go for the last cup and meet her end. Time to hide in the shadows of her home, Perry.*

With a moment or two passing, Alexis made a motion to the downstairs basement. Now was my chance to reach the inside confinements of her home. I raced up the stairs all the while staring at my phone to make sure the coast was clear. Swift and quiet, the man of darkness never makes a noise.

I turned the copper knob of the maroon colored door and crept inside without more than a click of the door latching behind. *Now to find the shadow to hide and peer onto the victim as she dies.* Alexis was nowhere near the back door so I was safe to make my move. Spotting a dinner table shrouded by shadows I ducked underneath. From there, it was a clear view to the living room where Alexis Fisher sat and sipped on her coffee. I lay without movement or heavy breath. One with the darkness.

The taste of this beauties heart will be sweeter than all the rest, cackled the monster in my mind.

From my vantage point I saw Alexis appeared from the downstairs with tears in her eyes. She flopped onto the couch and began to weep to herself. *Why is she crying,* I thought.

Who cares, tears are the least of her problems, countered the dark monster. *Focus on the task at hand.*

"I am alone," Alexis said just loud enough for me to hear from my hideout. She then stared out into space with her teary eyes. The sight took me for surprise as I had never seen a woman cry like this before.

The only person I have seen cry like this was me, when I was alone and hurt. Alexis's eyes gleamed ocean blue through her salty tears. *She's beautiful, even when she cries.*

But ugly inside like all the rest. Waiting to feed on men like you used to be. Kill her Perry, cackled the monster

Alexis reached for the poisoned coffee cup and began to drink and wipe her tears away. Within seconds, she had pulled out her phone to make a call.

I focused my hearing onto what she was saying.

"Hey," Alexis said, taking a pause. "You know just having one of those nights." She took another sip of the coffee, slowly draining it away as she talked. The conversation went on from the other end but I couldn't make out who she was talking to.

"Yeah, it's just hard to be alone some nights. I never thought at my age I would be sitting here with no one in my life." Alexis said again to the other person on the line. "No, I don't want to go back to him at all, that's the thing. But it still hurts sometimes, knowing what happened and then I see something that reminds me of the pain and I break down a little bit."

She must be talking about that man in the picture. The ex-fiancé, I thought lying stiff and still under the table. *I know that pain.*

But does she know the pain that it caused you? Why don't you show her? Look, the coffee is almost finished, whispered the dark monster. *One more down and she will be lifeless and ours for the taking. Kill her Perry and let me feast on her blood.*

"It's like my heart is cracked and it bleeds little by little with each passing day. I just want it to stop, I want to be able to trust someone again." Said Alexis.

Her heart bleeds? Is she like me, heartbroken, I thought.

"Hopefully your right. I just need to find a nice guy. One that isn't like the rest."

I'm not like the rest.

"Thanks for talking to me, I was a complete mess a second ago. I'm getting kind of sleepy though and I feel a bit dizzy. I'm going to try to drink some more coffee to wake up and get some reading done to take my mind off everything." Alexis said with a flashing grin. "Okay you too, bye."

With that, Alexis put down the phone and finished her last gulp of coffee. She then stood up and headed for the kitchen.

After that, my view was blocked by a wall so I couldn't see what Alexis was doing, but I assumed she was filling up her cup with more coffee.

Yesss, she will be dead any moment now and we can feast on her lifeless corpse, the dark monster hissed.

Moments later, Alexis came back into my view with steam rising from her coffee mug. A loud rumble of thunder could be felt though the house as she sat down on the living room couch. The rain outside began to fall harder than before, pounding the windows and roof.

Alexis sat her coffee mug down to cool and I could sense the time was near.

Reach for your steel Perry and let's make our presence felt. She is growing weak and weary now. Kill the detective's daughter. Kill her and spread your terror through the city. The monster began laughing inside my mind and I felt its black ooze flood through me once more. I reached for my steel blade, ready to strike down my prey.

Alexis put the mug to her lip and I was ready to spring to my feet. The dark monster was wild and feral inside me, howling into my mind and presenting me with all the painful memories I had endured. But before Alexis sipped her doom she stared out to the storm and said something softly.

"Please get me over this heartbreak," and a single tear fell from the honey blond haired beauty, splashing onto the wood floor.

And just like the flashes of lightning that could be seen outside, the words and beauty of Alexis Fisher impaled my dark monster. A flicker of life was shot into me and for the first time since I had been the killer, my blackened heart thumped in my chest. *Bubump. What is this,* I thought clutching the knife in one hand and pressing the other to my chest.

KILL HER PERRY, screamed the monster.

No Perry, the emotions shouted back.

I lay stunned in the darkness of Alexis Fisher's home, not knowing if I should kill or save her. *The silver blade or the flicker of emotion.* A battle of good verse evil raged inside me.

Chapter 10
Run and Chase

BREAKING NEWS, interrupted a headline across the TV's of the nameless American city.

"We now take you live to Terry Connor for this emergency report." Shouted the TV to anyone watching.

Terry stood in front of the camera. A man behind the camera counted her down with his hand. Three fingers, two fingers, one. The red light came on and the audience awaited the news.

"I am on the scene in this local neighborhood, where police have set a perimeter that spans some 10 blocks." Terry said to her new TV audience. "Police have informed me that they are in pursuit with who they believe to be the Heartbreak Killer. All residents are to be on high alert as this Killer is extremely dangerous."

Terry then spotted a woman from the neighborhood and hustled towards her with the camera following.

"Excuse me ma'am do you have any information to tell Channel 28 News." Shouted Terry Conner, pointing a microphone into her face.

The woman was old, wide eyed, and looked as if she had seen a ghost when the camera reached her.

"I... I... I heard screaming in the house behind us." The woman stuttered. "She was a young blond haired woman... and then a shadowy figure ran out across the yard and into mine."

"Did you get a look at this man?" Demanded Terry, now, almost pressing the microphone to the woman's face.

"Nnnnnn no," the woman hoarsely responded "He disappeared and I went to check on the woman… ssssssso much."

"So much what?" Said Terry, practically force feeding the microphone down the woman's throat.

"Bbbblood… everywhere." Said the old woman begging to weep, while the camera zoomed onto her tears.

After the shot was filled, Terry turned the camera back onto herself. "You heard it here first on Channel 28 News. The Heartbreak Killer has struck in the city once more. Presumably killing a young blond haired woman in cold blood, tonight."

Meanwhile, Detective Fisher followed the shadow man through the neighborhood.

Dogs were barking, sounding the alarm to the whereabouts of the killer's location.

"I need all available officers to my location." Paul shouted into his personal hand held radio.

Paul had just arrived to the scene when he spotted a man running through yards and hopping fences. When he saw this, Paul immediately exited out of his car door and chased after the man. He had been chasing him for two blocks now.

The killer spotted Paul as soon as he had stopped the car. The screech of rubber tires to the coarse pavement gave away his position. Paul was having trouble keeping up the pace of the shadow man. Each step lead to his breath becoming heavier, while sweat profusely dripped out of Paul Fishers pores.

"I'm in pursuit of the suspect on foot. He is running on through the neighborhood on foot. Be on high alert, the suspect is extremely dangerous and could be armed."

Paul hopped over a wood fence and into a yard after the killer. When Paul hit the ground of the yard, another dog barked to his left and lights flickered on from two separate houses. Paul sprinted towards the sounds and lights, hopping fence after fence.

A woman had come outside of one of the houses with its lights on and Paul called out to her. "Which way did that person go?"

"We heard someone climb the fence into the front yard. My husband is out there looking, now."

Without another moment's hesitation Paul went for the street.

Someone yelled in Paul's direction.

"He went that way." The husband said pointing up the street.

Paul spotted the killer just forty yards away in one of the streetlights. Catching his second wind with a pump of adrenaline, Paul sprinted after.

The killer had reached a four way stop, and without a glance, ran across the intersection.

Suddenly, a police car flew by. Spotting Paul, the car came to a screeching halt. "Detective Fisher get in." A fellow officer called out. Paul jumped into the car, pointing in the direction of the killer and the officer took off driving.

"Do you see him?" Said Paul.

"Yeah, running across the street as I was coming by. But I didn't catch a glimpse of the face." Said the officer.

Paul stuck his hand out the window to shine the spotlight in search of the killer. "Right there," said Paul as the light shone on the position of the killer.

"I see him," the officer snapped back.

The police car bolted after the killer as he made a B-line for another fence and climbed over. The officer and Paul made another screeching halt and raced out of the car doors.

Both men sprinted to the fence and jumped into the back yard. The other side of the fence was too dark to detect the shadow man, so the officer and Paul both reached for their flashlights and guns, each shining their light through separate parts of the darkness.

"Quiet," whispered Paul as he listened for the sound of footsteps or heavy breathing.

A loud rustling sounded out into the night and both men pointed their flashlights to the direction of the sound. The lights reached just in time to see a large man with dark hair dropping to the other side of the back fence.

"GO," shouted Paul as he sprinted towards the fence. When he reached the other side, the neighborhood had been left behind Paul. Now, a spacious forest of pine trees towered over the two men. Leaving no trace of the elusive man.

"Spread out," Paul ordered to the officer as he reached for his hand held radio.

"This is Detective Fisher. I have followed the suspect into the woods. I need immediate assistance." The accompanying officer had distanced himself some ten yards away from Paul as he finished the call. Both men still had their flashlights and guns readily in hand, while inching farther and farther into the monstrous depths of trees.

Only a faint moonlight gave its way through the stormy sky and onto forest. The crunching of twigs could be heard as Paul carefully made his way through. *Bumbump bumbump,* his heart pounded as his light guided the way.

Paul lost sight of the other officer now and was on edge, ready to jump at the slightest of noises. *Bumbump bubump.* Paul heard the snap of a branch break in the darkness and pointed the flashlight towards the sound. *Nothing is there,* he thought, taking a deep breath.

Thunder began to rumble in the sky. *A storm is coming,* thought Paul and cold wind picked up, blowing the tree branches and swirling pine needles on the forest ground.

Bumbump bumbump, Paul's heart pounded as he rested his back against a pine tree, trying to catch his breath and regain his nerves. *The killer has to be close.* He peeked over the tree to view the forest, and slowly began to move again.

Then, a *bang* whistled through the dark, followed by an agonizing scream. Paul raced towards the sounds. *Bumbump bumbump.* He saw a light near the ground and went for a closer look.

The accompanying officer laid on the ground, gaging in a pool of blood.

"Officer down. Officer down." Shouted Paul into his radio.

As Paul came to the officer's side, he shined a light that revealed what appeared to be a stab wound in the officer's chest. Blood was profusely spitting from his flesh.

"Put pressure on it." Said Paul, guiding the officer's hand to the wound. "Did you see where he went?" But the officer could only muster a faint point while gaging on blood as he tried to talk. "Save your words, I will find him."

Before standing up, Paul noticed the officer's gun was missing. He felt for it through the thicket of pine needles but came up with nothing.

BANG, a shot flew past Paul, feeling the wind of the bullet pass his face. He raced for a tree, ducking behind it as another shot was fired, hitting a tree and exploding pieces of the bark and wood alike.

Bumbump bumbump, raced Paul's heart as he hid behind the tree.

With a deep breath, Paul pointed his gun and flashlight into the open forest and fired a shot into the dark. While he did, Paul made a run at another tree.

Two shot were exchanged back at Paul when he made his move. One hitting a tree in front of him while the other sailed by him without notice. Diving to the ground, Paul rolled behind another tree. *Bumbump bumbump bumbump. Four shots fired four more left.*

Paul took another deep breath, trying to calm his nerves and relax his pounding heart. He then turned off his flashlight and listened for sounds of footsteps or heavy breathing in the darkened forest.

Branches began to crack just ahead of Paul, followed by lightning streaking through the cloudy sky, and then the rumble of thunder. Paul peeked over one side of the tree but could see nothing of distinction. *Wait for it,* he thought.

Again, lightning scurried across the sky, giving a flash of light to the forest. Paul spotted the killer moving up some twenty yards from his position and ducked back behind the tree. *I'll wait for the lightning to make my move.*

More movement could be heard ahead, the sounds were getting closer to Paul's position. *Bumbump bumbump bumbump,* his heart beat as thunder rattled the sky.

Wait for it, wait for it, Paul thought as more sweat poured from his body and dripped to the forest floor. A flash of lightning lit the forest again and Paul was ready. He pointed his gun into the open forest and

fired into the area he had just heard noise from, but the killer was nowhere in sight and the bullet made contact with a tree, sounding a cracking echo.

Thunder again followed the lightning and this time with its massive bellow came a heavy rain.

Paul attempted to listen for noises once more, but it was useless now with the droplets of water pounding the ground. *Where is this killer?* Taking another deep breath and closing his eyes Paul attempted to block out the sound of rain and focus all his power on the sound of the ground.

Crunch...BUMBUMP... CRUnch... BUMbump... CRUNCH... bumbump...

The flashlight flicked on and his gun pointed out. *NOW!* Paul rolled off the bark of tree into the open forest, and like a deer in the headlights the killer was spotted wide eyed by Paul's light.

The killer fired a shot but Paul was too quick, diving out of the way and rolling to his feet. *BANG BANG,* blasted Paul's gun.

Smoke rose and the killer fell to his feet, dropping the gun in a yell of pain.

"Freeze mother fucker." Paul yelled as he made his way over to the killer. The flashlight exposed the suspected killer to be a younger man with greasy black hair. Two bullets from Paul's gun had pierced the man in the shoulder and ribs. The man made a move towards a knife as Paul moved closer. This move had already been anticipated by Paul and he stomped his foot onto the killers arm.

A howl was let out by the man and he dropped the knife as a bone could be heard crunching under the force of Paul's foot.

Quickly reaching for handcuffs, Paul restrained the man who was still yelling out in pain.

"I have the suspect in custody. He is wounded and I need immediate medical attention." Paul said triumphantly through the speaker of his radio.

Soon dogs could be heard barking along with people shouting. Then dozens of flashlights began to light up the once dark forest, all descending onto Paul's position.

"Over here," Paul shouted waving his flashlight in the air. "I have him right here. I have the Heartbreak Killer."

Chapter 11
Metamorphosis

Years ago, if someone would have told me that a cold hearted killer could be birthed because of countless and cruel heartbreaks I would have told you it's utterly impossible.

As I studied psychology in college, nothing was ever mentioned in the books about such an event accruing. Instead, psychology books stated lack of proper brain function or empathy as the main reason a killer would emerge amongst us. Another theory may state that traumatic events accruing in the first couple of years of a human's life would cause a killer to come about.

But can one measure your soul? How damaged your heart is? Who's to say that a heart doesn't have a breaking point in a psychological sense, leaving you forever in eternal darkness? Theories often change and replaced by new ideas.

A killer birthed from a broken heart? Preposterous. Yet here I was, the Heartbreak Killer, a monster from a broken heart.

Once I was a happy young man, full of life, ready to set out into the world and help the people who desperately needed it. My mother had instilled those things into me at a young age. But she had never informed me that all the bad in this world could indeed consume me too, turning me into the exact evil I wanted to prevent.

Every person struggles with certain evils in this world. One with an addiction to drugs, never able to break free of the illustrious call. Another may struggle with poverty, which puts you at a disadvantage in our cold world. Whatever the struggle, evils lurk in every corner, attempting to prey on the innocent and devour them into a darkness forever.

For me, I struggled with love as a young man. I find it funny that love isn't talked about in this world as an evil, but in the end the evils of love are what took me to the darkness. Twisted love games came and went and when they were finally through with me I was changed into a monster.

Who is truly evil? Who are the monsters of our world? Do you ever wonder like I do?

A monster is always painted as the face of evil. The boogeyman who hides in your closet or the serial killer who stalks in your city. These are the faces of evil that the media pushes into the public's minds as evil, the things you should fear at night.

I thought differently being that monster.

Who was the creator of such an evil thing as I?

Wasn't I merely the creation of our cruel world? I didn't choose to become a killer, quite the contrary, I set out to help this world. Someone else had created the Heartbreak Killer, and in that crime weren't they the ones who should be talked about as the true evils of our world? *The master behind the puppet. The Dr. Frankenstein to his created monster.*

I can't tell you how or why countless heartbreaks had left me cold and dark inside. But what I can tell you, is that after those wounds I sat in my room for days, which turned into weeks, and then into months. All I did was cry at the cold world and its evils that preyed on my heart and soul. *Similar to what I had witnessed from Alexis Fisher while I hid inside her home.* But when my transformation was finally complete, and the last piece of heart had broken, I had morphed into the Heartbreak Killer.

Afterwards I tried to deny what I had become. Seeking help from others, ingesting pills to prevent my darkness, just hoping I could change back to the old me. The feelings never came back though, and after years of denial I let the darkness in, deciding to embrace the monster the world had created. At least with my embracement of darkness I could have my revenge on the many creators.

The Heartbreak Killer went to slay Alexis Fisher, to feed the darkness once more and inflict revenge onto his creators. But as he peered onto her for the last time in the shadows of her home, weeping beautiful and painful tears, something else spoke to him. Another voice, a flicker of tiny emotion, a thump of his black heart.

For the first time in over eight years the dark monster inside had a rival. That rival told me no, that Alexis could bring me back, and for half a second my ice cold heart grew warm with a beat. A beat produced from Alexis Fisher as I gazed upon her wallowing in her own despair and heartbreak. All the while the dark monster was screaming to end her life. Let her sip the last of her poisoned coffee and meet the steel blade.

What was the man of darkness and the media anointed Heartbreak Killer to do? Kill and be the darkness or listen to the pronounced no that sprang about from the flicker of emotion.

My knife gripped tight while I hid under the table of Alexis Fishers home. She had just let down a tear from her ocean blue eyes.

KILL HER, screamed the monster.

NO, I finally screamed back, and instead of slaying Alexis Fisher that night I saved her. In a flash, she stood up and walked to the bathroom. *My one chance,* I realized and I made my first attempt to be a good human being in a near decade.

NOOOOO, screamed the blood lusting dark monster, trying his hardest to stop me.

I ran to the coffee mug that was sitting on the table, knocking over the poisoned filled liquid that would have ended Alexis Fishers life. Then I jetted to the coffee pot in the kitchen and emptied the remains into the sink. *She won't remember how much there was, anyways. Her memory will be faded at the dose of powder she consumed.* And before Alexis appeared from the bathroom I ran from the home. Terrified of the unknown emotion that had flicked through me.

But as I ran away, for one glorious moment, I was Perry Nelson, not the dark Heartbreak Killer.

Now back at my home all I could think of was, *could she be my savior, my antidote, my hope?* I wanted to believe it true. I wanted to believe that I could change back and feel more of those emotional flickers. *But could I trust another woman? After all they have done to me?*

On the outside Alexis appeared to be pure, innocent, and beautiful.

Everything I wasn't. That was why she called to my emotions, but how could the same thing that created me be my savior?

I was lost in these types of thoughts as I laid inside my room for days after. *Could I be changing back? Back to Perry of old?*

All the while my darkness tried to convince me to go back and finish the job. *Women are what made you into this Perry,* it said. *Why would you think she is any different? She deserves to have her heart ripped from her chest just like they did to you. Take it from her Perry, you are the Heartbreak Killer now.*

But the other voice countered something new.

She can save you, Perry. Turn you back into the man you once were. She made you feel by giving you a heartbeat. Isn't it worth a try, to see if she can truly be the woman you use to search for before the darkness overtook you?

The two voices raged battle inside my head, each jockeying for control

Hate her, stalk her, and make her blood pour to the floor, said the dark monster.

Love her, pursue her, and make her change you back, said the strange new voice.

KILL.

LOVE.

Kill.

LOVE.

Ki…

LOVE.

… The darkness was silenced inside my head, if just for a moment.

Finally, after days of debate I had my answer. *It's worth a try, isn't it? Even if I have forgotten how to assert myself into someone's life as a welcomed entity and not the unwanted killer.*

The next day I set out for my newest stalk. A stalk for someone's metaphorical heart. *A killer to man, I hope.*

The plan was to show up at Alexis's work and surprisingly bump into her.

I was nervous in the morning leading up to the accidental bump in.

Should I dress more casual with jeans, a t-shirt, and some sneakers or should I go more upscale with a suit and tie. What do women even want now?

After much debate about what to wear, I decided on a solid black collared shirt, dark blue jeans, and a grey peacock coat.

Or maybe I should dress in a white collared shirt... Yes I am feeling a bit whiter today... It's just a woman Perry, weren't you good at this once?

Sometime after I had picked an outfit, I found myself in the bathroom debating how to style my hair. "You're becoming a pussy," I finally declared to my reflection in the mirror.

Where is this heartless killer you claimed to be? Worrying about your hair now? Come on.

I left my hair in its normal and neatly slicked back state. Taking one last look at myself, I declared satisfaction and made my way to the bookstore where Alexis worked.

When I reached the parking lot of the bookstore another wave of nervous doubt crept through me. I had been a killer wearing the mask of a normal person for so long. *Wearing a mask is always easier than being yourself,* I thought. As the emotionless Heartbreak Killer, I could care less of what people thought of me, but I wasn't him on this cold November day. I was Perry Nelson, a man who cared about what Alexis thought of him.

Do I even know how to talk to her? It all seemed silly to me to worry. When I had seen Alexis at the shoe store I was natural and charming. Now, I felt as if I may faint at the slightest sight of her. "Fuck these new feelings," I said in my car as I prepared to venture inside the store.

You can do this, Perry. If it doesn't work out you can always kill her... Thanks reassuring mind. Let's do this.

The inside of the bookstore was massive. Rows and rows of books with labels for anyone's heart desire towered in every corner. Couches and chairs were placed amongst the shelves to sit in and read. In the back of the store there was a children's section with a large tree made of paper, surrounded by colored chairs and tables to sit in. There was even a small coffee shop located to the right entrance of the store.

Damn, I thought the art of reading was dying? Regardless, I was thoroughly impressed with the spectacle.

Alexis was nowhere in sight as I looked around, so I ventured my way through the bookstore. As I walked around, I casually attempted to overpower my urge to run out of the building in fear of her seeing me.

There was something surreal and haunting about being in the same building as Alexis, knowing that nights before I was in her house waiting to kill her. *Life is full of surprises,* I thought as I found my way into a section and pretended to skim the books. While I skimmed, I heard someone say something in my direction.

"Hey, aren't you the shoe guy?" Said a sweet voice behind me.

I spun around, and there stood Alexis in the isle with a pearl white smile.

"What? Who?" I said petrified.

"Remember me? You asked me to help you pick out a pair of shoes for your girlfriend?"

"My girlf... Oh right, uh yeah it is you." I said trying to recover my wits. "What a coincidence."

"How did she like them? Did you take my advice on the heels?" Alexis said as her eyes gleamed ocean blue.

"Oh, you know what? We actually broke up. She..." I paused. *Jeez Perry get a hold of yourself.* "She cheated on me actually. I found out right before her birthday. I never had a chance to give her the present."

"How horrible! The same thing happened to me with my ex fiancé. Well the cheating part."

So she is single. Good.

"It was horrible. I was really shaken up, so I decided to get a new book to fill up my time."

"Ah I see. Well you came to the right place then." Alexis said with a giggle. "So you enjoy the thrill of killers and murder then?"

What? How does she know? Did she see me? Is this a set up?

"Um what?" I murmured.

"I said you must enjoy killers and murder, you're in the thriller section silly." Alexis said pointing to the section label.

I am? I turned to look, and sure enough I had managed to stumble into the thriller section.

"Of course I am. Ha, why else would I be in this section." I said trying to laugh off the panic. *Smooth Perry, you're really playing it cool.*

"Well do you need some help finding something? I enjoy thrillers too, I find serial killers fascinating."

...You do? Maybe this is meant to be, I thought.

"Yeah that would be nice, thank you. I promise I'm not always in need of so much assistance." I said exerting out a nervous laugh. Alexis smiled and laughed with me.

Alexis guided me through the bookshelves and I nodded, trying to act interested, but I wasn't really listening. I was under a love spell from her beauty, wanting the moment to last forever.

We laughed and smiled our way through the shelves of thrillers and little by little my heart began to beat. *Bubump.* By the end, Alexis had recommended one of her favorite thrillers. I picked it up off the shelf, telling her I wanted to purchase this recommendation.

Seemingly pleased I had picked out her selection this time, Alexis took me to the register to ring me up.

"I am really sorry about your break up." Alexis said as she was putting the book into the plastic bag. "I know exactly how you feel. Cheating is never easy to deal with."

I don't even know how I feel, I thought.

"It's okay, I know everything happens for a reason." *Wow what a cheesy line, I'm horrible at this.* I gave Alexis a bashful smile, snatching my book from her, and began to walk away in shame. *What are you doing? Go back, go back. Finish the deal, Perry.*

Somehow, I managed to stop myself before the exit. As I turned back around, time seemed to slow down, and the bold words came pouring out from me. "Hey, would you like to go out sometime?"

What am I saying? She is going to deny my. I should have killed her. I'm an emotionless human, I don't know how to talk to women

"I would love to." Alexis replied with another pearl white smile. "I almost thought you were going to walk out of here without asking, actually." Alexis reached for a pen and jotted down something on a notepad. "Here is my number, call me."

"I will," I said with an unknown and dumbfounded facial expression.

Grabbing the paper in as cool of a fashion as I could muster, I began to walk for the exit.

Alexis shouted out to me right before I departed.

"Hey stranger, my name is Alexis, might be important to know when you call."

I turned back around again and shouted. "My name is Perry, Perry Nelson," and scurried out of the store.

I am Perry Nelson. Nice to meet you Alexis Fisher, I thought as I stared at the number and smiled. *Bubump bubump.*

Chapter 12
Fleeting Feelings

For the first time since his wife died, Paul Fisher awoke to happiness. He had arrested the Heartbreak Killer in the night.

The city was safe, his daughter was safe, and Paul would now be considered a hero. Finally, a new chapter in his life was starting. A positive break in a miserable year.

Eager for the new day Paul readied himself for work, putting on his usual loose fitting collared shirt that was left untucked from a pair of light blue jeans. *Time to see what the news is saying about the arrest,* thought Paul when he finished dressing.

First Paul went to the kitchen for a cup of black coffee. Then he sat on the couch in the living room and turned on the TV. The top story ran across the screen in bold, *MAN IN HEARTBREAK CASE ARRESTED.* Paul smiled at the headline. *Maybe I wasn't as washed up as I thought.*

After a few more minutes of TV, Paul finished his coffee and went to brush his teeth. Afterward he departed out to his car to take off for work.

The air outside of Paul's home was crisp and cold. Snow had begun to fall and stick to the ground. *The first snow of the year,* Paul thought as he made his way inside his black Crown Victorian. *A bit contrary to the mood of the city today I think.* While the car defrosted from the cold Paul went back inside for a coat, almost forgetting one in his cheery mood.

As Paul drove, he recapped the nights chase with the Heartbreak Killer. The moment had been quite nerve racking in those woods, but after the man with black hair had been taken to holding, Paul felt a great sense of relief. *All I need now is a confession about the other women from that sick psychopath and he is finished.*

A swarm of media stood outside the station as Paul arrived. *They are like mosquitos waiting to feed on blood.* As Paul parked, the swarm surrounded his car, making it difficult for him to get out and inside the station.

"Is it true that you have apprehended the Heartbreak Killer?" One man shouted to Paul.

"Detective Fisher, has the suspect confessed to the killings of the deceased women?" Another woman said, putting a microphone to Paul's face.

Paul paid no attention to the media, keeping silent as he pushed his way through the frenzy. *They aren't getting answers from me, not until I question this man.* Once he reached the inside of the station, Paul made his way towards the holding cells and was met by two officers guarding the cell.

"Is he in there?" Paul said.

"He was transferred to the interrogation room about twenty-five minutes ago. The Captain wanted me to tell you to go there when you got in." Said one of the officers.

"Thanks," said Paul, and he made his way to the interrogation room.

When Paul reached the interrogation area, he noticed the Captain was accompanied by a few officers. All the men were intently watching from the other side of a one way mirror as an interrogator was questioning the man with black hair.

"Fisher you're late," said the Captain as Paul entered through the door.

"Has he said anything yet?" Asked Paul.

"Well he's a killer alright. He has admitted to the murder of that blond haired woman last night, but he won't say much more in regards to the other women. Maybe you should go in there and see if he changes his tune?"

"Okay Captain. Any word on the health of the officer that was stabbed last night?"

"Critical condition was the last report this morning. He lost a lot of blood. However, the doctors said it's a good sign he made it through the night."

"I'm glad to hear it. That could have easily been me getting stabbed."

"Well thankfully it wasn't. I need you to worry about getting this man to confess to the other killings or else we may be looking at the wrong suspect."

Paul took the Captains words with another glance and headed inside the interrogation room.

Inside, the suspect sat opposite a table from the interrogator. The room was grey with nothing on the walls besides the blackened one way mirror. A chillness was also felt inside the room. Paul took a disliking too the feel but as any detective knew, the more uncomfortable a room was, the more likely someone was to rattle and confess.

Without looking the interrogator waved Paul over to a chair next to him. He was an older man with a fading hairline of brown and sprinkled white hair. He had on a pair of rectangular shaped lenses with a gold framing as well as crow's feet that had started to develop around his eyes.

Still without any eye contact the interrogator spoke. "You must be Detective Fisher, you're late. I had to begin without you. I assume the Captain filled you in on our little chat with Mr...?" The interrogator stopped speaking to look at the suspect with a cold dead stare.

"Mr. Minks. Carson Minks," the suspect stuttered.

The suspects arm had been placed into a cast from where Paul had broken it the night before. Accompanying the cast, were dark bags underneath his hazel eyes and white bandages that could be seen poking out of the man's bloodied collared shirt.

"Mr. Minks has confessed to killing the woman last night but seems to have no idea about the other four women." The interrogator continued. "Now, either Mr. Minks is innocent of the other murders or he has accrued serious memory loss at the most convenient time. Regardless, I think we should try to jog Mr. Mink's memory before we deem him of anything. Maybe some of those lost memories will come back after some convincing, Detective."

Paul was still standing while giving Minks a sharp look on top of a stoic face. "Look Mr. Minks, the way I see it you have two options." Started Paul. "The first is you confess that you murdered the four other women and I tell the judge to let you rot in prison for the rest of your life, or you can do this the hard way, and I will request that the judge gives you the death sentence once you are found guilty on all accounts."

Hearing this made Carson Minks squirm in his chair. "I already told him, I didn't do it. You have the wrong man."

He wants to play hardball, well let's play.

"I know you're lying. You know how I know that? Said Paul.

"No, how?" Said Minks.

"Because I have evidence from each of the separate murders that pin you to all of the women's deaths." Lied Paul. "Why the heart Minks? Did some girl break your heart and you couldn't bear that pain of rejection? So you had to take it out on innocent women?"

"Detective, I didn't do it." Pleaded Minks. "I swear."

"You admitted to us that you killed the woman last night. How am I supposed to believe that you didn't kill the rest when there has been a killer on the loose? Do you think I believe it's all some big coincidence? Mr. Minks you realize you stabbed an officer last night? If he dies… Well, you don't have a prayer. You might as well take the deal I'm giving you right now before things change. Just tell me you killed those women."

"I… Listen, I know it looks bad, but I didn't kill those other women. I'm not that other killer."

"Who's the other killer?" Paul said with curiosity.

"You think I'm that Heartbreak Killer, right? The one that the news has been talking about. Well, I'm not, I just copied him or tried too, but I guess I wasn't as good at it."

"You copied him?" The interrogator and Paul said simultaneously.

"I got the idea from him, from the killer. He showed me a way to deal with my broken heart. Gave me an outlet." Minks said with tears in his eyes.

The pit of Paul's stomach began to churn as the words came out.

Is the Heartbreak Killer becoming a symbol for some people? I thought the media was just spreading fear to those in the city, but it's even worse than that. To some twisted people the Heartbreak Killer seems righteous. I was so set on finding the killer I took this lead with blind ambition, but of course this man isn't the Heartbreak Killer. This man here is sloppy and drew attention to himself. The Heartbreak Killer is precise and wouldn't have confronted the woman head on without poisoning her first.

Paul's face began to turn white as he realized he had been blind by his own fierce determination to finding the killer.

Mr. Minks took notice to Paul's reaction of his confession and began to laugh manically.

The interrogator seemed baffled on what had transpired, looking back and forth between the two men. "Detective are you okay?" He said to Paul.

"I… I need some air." Said Paul, quickly exited the room. The Captain was waiting for him on the other side.

"What is it Fisher?" The Captain demanded.

"He's not the man." Said Paul.

"What… How do you know?"

"Captain its worse than we thought. This man is just a copycat killer, a bad one too. The real Heartbreak Killer is still out there inspiring people who are desperate. That man in there, he thinks that the Heartbreak Killer is doing a good thing. Slaying women because they deserve it. So he took the idea the killer presented him and tried it for himself"

"How do you know all this with certainty?" Said the Captain with a bewildered stare.

"I didn't get a chance to tell you because I was called in, but I found out how the Heartbreak Killer is getting to the women without any struggle. There is poison in their drinks, something each of the women would have consumed almost every day. It didn't even cross my mind until now, but the Heartbreak Killer would have never killed a woman with a weapon, he's too smart for that. That Carson Minks is sloppy, too sloppy to be the killer we're after."

"Fuck Fisher, how could you..." The Captain shouted. "Never mind that, we need to figure out what to do next. Paul this is bad, everyone woke up today feeling safer. If this mad man is still loose the city isn't safe. Even worse, if the media catches wind about this we will be torn to bits. You for being too emotionally incompetent to get the right man because of your dead wife and me for putting an old, washed up, and depressed detective on the case in the first place. That's the headline for us, Paul."

"I made a mistake, but I have been busting my ass for this case. I just caught a murderer for god sake. I was in a fucking gunfight, risking my life for this case. Don't call me incompetent." Steamed Paul.

"I don't think you are Paul, but the media will. They don't care about anything other than good ratings and dramatic stories. That bitch Terry Connor will turn this story into a publicity nightmare for both of us if she finds out. I don't want to see you again until you have a strong lead on another suspect. I'll keep this under wraps for as long as I can, but you better find this fucking Heartbreak Killer before we both get fired."

After those words, Paul stormed out from the room. Upset at himself more than anything, he charged towards an aluminum garbage can. Paul kicked it once, denting the side, and then again, knocking the can over. With a thud, trash littered the hallway as the lid rolled off onto the floor.

As the anger of disappointment boiled, Paul leaned against a nearby wall, trying to regain control of his emotions while staring out a snowy window. *I'm in over my head. I really am just a drunk washed up detective. I'm not stable enough for this case,* he thought. *I was wrong, this is perfect weather for the bitter cold reality that faces me and my city.*

Paul's Fishers happiness from the morning sank into the piles of falling snow in the city. Again, he was greeted with the unwanted feelings that had weighed on him since his wife passed. *I can't do this,* he thought still staring upon the pale white snow.

Chapter 13
The Black & White Date Night

Life can change in the blink of an eye.

I had found this saying to ring true during my tenure as therapist. One day a person can feel on top of the world, the next day a tragedy strikes and they are in my office sobbing, begging to be medicated. I have lived in darkness for so long, but things were beginning to change for me. My darkness had been quieted and now emotions flickered inside me. It gave me hope that I may be changing.

My life began to take on its usual routine. The one thing that stood different for me now, was instead of scouring for my next target I was hoping to find my heart and soul. Instead of taking a heart from someone I needed to win one, and only one person had that power to turn the switch, Alexis Fisher.

After I received Alexis's number at the bookstore, I began to play the waiting game, much like I would with my stalking. *I can't be too anxious or I will ruin the whole thing.* I had decided to wait three days to call. *One day was desperate, two was what they expected, and three was when I would strike,* I thought beforehand.

Naturally, I had no idea what I was doing as I dialed the number, but I remembered reading once about this technique of waiting to call women. So three days it was. The call was, well let's say it was just good enough. The jump from a killer to smooth talking man was drastic. I was rusty and nervous, repeating my words dozens of times and adding unneeded um's and uh's throughout.

While I talked to Alexis, my mind began to associate back to the time of my first kill. I was clumsy and made mistakes that I only learned to correct with practice, but it was good enough and in the end, I killed the woman. At the end of the phone call, Alexis said yes to my proposal of going on a date. Flicker, flicker, the emotion of happy flashed through my body when I heard the word yes come out. *At least I think the feeling was happy, it had been so long.*

I set the date for the following day, at seven p.m. I was taking her to a high scale restaurant in the downtown area. It was one of my favorites, serving overpriced meals, expensive wine, and hosting egotistical customers and entitled waiters alike. *My type of crowd. Even if my emotions had a pulse, I was still a luxurious and high class man.*

My women seducing skills may be rusty, but I could always over compensate with my abundance of money. Women like money right? Who am I kidding, I was still a nervous boy. Maybe I should just do what was easy for me now and kill her.

Yessss kill her, whispered my dark monster in agreement.

The feeling of nervousness had overcome me when I went to get Alexis's number. *That was scary enough.* But the looming anticipation of a pending date made the number seem like a grain of sand next to a bolder.

Just kill her Perry, wouldn't that be easier than these useless nervous emotions?

My darkness had a point. Emotions were strange and awful at times.

The night before the date consisted of mostly sleepless tossing and turning in my bed as I anticipated all of the horrible mistakes I could make during it. When I finally drifted off to sleep I was haunted by the white and black room. This time the room was less stained with the black oozing tar. *Peculiar*, I had thought in my dream as I looked upon it. When I awoke, it was snowing outside. *A bad omen to start the big day. I hate snow.*

I decided to spend the whole day getting ready for my date with Alexis. *I need to be perfect to mask my faults.* The first step in my quest for perfection was picking out my outfit. I began skimming through my closet, passing on each item. When I reached the end without a match that satisfied me, I decided to go and purchase a new one. *I may be an emotionless being but I always loved material fashion.*

There was a place on the other side of the city I always fancied to go. The retail store had the best suits and tailors around.

When I arrived at the suit store, it took me some time to find something that caught my eye, something I thought would impress Alexis. *These new feelings are turning me into an idiot*, was crossing my mind as I browsed the many racks of suits.

At the pinnacle of my search I stood in the mirror with a navy blue blazer and matching slacks, paired with a white collared shirt, gold plated cufflinks, and a silk tie as red as a woman's lipstick. *Damn it looks good.*

"I'll take it," I proclaimed to the tailor.

I still had a few hours to kill before I was set to meet Alexis so I decided it was best to clean myself up as when I arrived back to my home. Turning to an MP3 dock, I plugged in my music. *What do I want to listen to*, I thought as I scrolled through the play list. I settled on some cool jazz. *Because I need to be as cool as possible tonight.*

Sounds of David Brubeck and Miles Davis rang through the house as I showered and cleaned up. When I finished, I began to shave my stubble. I was almost through with the shave when the blade nicked into my neck. *Damn that stings,* I thought as reached at the small wound. Assessing the damage, I realized the cut was no larger than a centimeter in length, but the sight of it unsettled my nerves even more. *Hey Perry why do you have that cut on your neck? Are you a serial killer? Dad*!

Stop being paranoid you can barely tell.

After I deemed myself ready, I stood in front of a mirror one last time to make sure everything was perfect. The suit fit snug to my body and the red lipstick tie popped with the navy blue blazer. I pulled on each cuff of dress shirt, made sure my hair was set, and proclaimed to my mirror self "damn you look good."

I checked my watch, there was still an hour before the meeting time, but my mind was anxious with nervous anticipation. So I decided to make my way out early and wait.

The snow had stopped falling from the sky, but the outside ground had held its sloppy remains. *A surprisingly pleasant and peaceful scene*, I thought strolling to the restaurant. The whiteness of the snow reminded me of Alexis's fair skin. *Pure and beautiful.* Along with the snow, Christmas lights were being hung around the tall buildings of the city as December was upon us. The sight of the colorful lights and white snow put rest to my nerves and I exhaled a sigh of relief. *Things are more beautiful now that I am feeling again.*

I arrived at the restaurant with forty-five minutes to spare. A thin man with a thick moustache greeted me at the door, taking my overcoat, and seating me at my table. The table itself was covered in a red velvet cloth and in the middle was a small oil candle burning in the dim lighting with a scent of vanilla and pine.

Around the restaurant walls were old paintings, scattered and placed in various corners and walls. Most of the paintings featured European scenery and landmarks that complimented with the restaurants Italian theme.

A woman in a red glowing dress sat on a stage in the back of the restaurant playing a slow and soothing melody on her violin. The stage overlooked a small dance floor for people feeling so bold. *More like the intoxicated,* I thought. It was customary for local musicians to play at night here and it was one of the reasons I had such a fancy for the restaurant in the first place. *Not many people appreciate live music while they eat anymore.*

All together the restaurant scene seemed to be a proper setting for a romantic date. *Sure as hell better than that Freddy's place. But what do I know, I was killing women a month ago, now I am... dating? I know nothing of romance.*

While I waited for Alexis, I ordered the most expensive bottle of red wine they had. Personally, I wasn't a big wine drinker, but I felt most women had a taste for it. Minutes later the waiter brought the bottle to me in a bucket of ice with two glasses.

"Will that be all, sir?" Asked the waiter.

"Actually, can you get me a gin martini? The wine is for my date." I said

"Of course sir, I will be right back with it."

As the time reduced before our date my nerves began to increase again. I checked my watch every chance I could in anticipation of Alexis's arrival. Trying to regain my composer, I began to drink the martini. Each sip seemed to dull the anxiety. *Why am I so nervous, it's just a woman? A beautiful pure woman.*

As unlikely as it seemed now, I had been such a womanizer before I went to the darkness. Now it felt as if I was going out on a date for the first time. In a weird sense it was, I felt as if I was being reborn and in that feeling I was having trouble coming to grips with the flickers of my once extinct emotions. *Maybe it's natural to feel this way.*

The woman in red finished playing her violin number and stood, taking a bow to the crowded restaurant. People gave a warm round of applause and she smiled before exiting the stage.

A quartet of jazz musicians followed. Each member holding different brass instruments along with one drum set and another went to a piano that was always onstage. *At least I'll have some jazz, maybe it will be a cool kind to calm my nerves.*

I finished the last of my drink, eating the olive at the bottom, and checked my watch again. *Ten minutes until our meeting time.*

The quartet began to play a calming and familiar melody to me. *Take Five, how ironic I need to take five this instance. Get a grip Perry.* As the melody played, I saw her. Alexis had walked up the stairs into the main part of the restaurant.

I froze in my seat, stunned as a cold sweat broke from my body. *Run away, go back to the comfort of murder,* my mind pleaded, but my body was petrified.

Alexis Fisher had spotted me, giving a smile and wave. *Too late, I'm caught. This was a horrible idea.*

Time slowed as she walked towards me and the mere seconds seemed to last for an eternity. No longer could the music the quartet be heard as I stared at Alexis's beauty. She wore a tight snow-white dress that let off a sparkle in the candle light as she moved. Her heels matched the color of her dress perfectly. Around her neck hung a white pearl necklace and her honey blond hair had been straightened down with a curl at the end, bouncing with each elegant step. *She is an angel, sent here to save me.*

I am not sure if my jaw had dropped to the table at that point, but she laughed and called out my name as she reached the table.

"Hello Perry," Alexis said with a sparkling smile.

I was still in a shocked state but managed to reply what I thought were "Hello" and "Alexis." I then stood up to shake her hand and she laughed at my gesture.

"I didn't know this was a business meeting where we shake hands. Didn't you ask me on a date?" Alexis said.

"I…" *Idiot, Idiot, Idiot.* "I'm sorry, I just, I… I haven't been out on a date in a while, and you look… well you look amazing." *Stupid, Stupid, Stupid.*

"Why thank you," Alexis said still flashing me her sparkling white smile. "I haven't been out in a while either so don't worry. I'm a bit nervous to be totally honest."

"Here let me get that chair for you." I said pulling the chair out for her. *Nice recovery from your nightmare start.*

"A gentleman already, but it looks like you started this party without me."

"What?" I said, confused as I sat back down.

"Your martini glass is empty."

"Oh, right. Yeah I arrived here a bit early and decided to have a drink. But look, I bought us some wine so feel free to start." I reached for the bottle of wine, uncorking it, and poured some into her glass.

Alexis took a sip as soon as I handed her the drink and I began to stare at her every movement in a trance like state. *I am out of my league,* I thought.

"Are you going to pour yourself one? I don't think it would be polite of you to have me drink alone." Alexis said, interrupting my thoughts.

"Oh, of course not, sorry." I poured a glass and took a sip. The taste was bitter and made me cringe. *This is why I don't drink wine.* Alexis didn't seem to notice my face, instead asking me about the restaurant, saying she had never been inside before. "Yeah it's upscale. I personally enjoy the live musicians that play here so I come around a lot."

"I see… So tell me about yourself Mr. Perry. I feel like you're a stranger still. I mean you come to my bookstore and don't even want to tell me your name after you get my number. It was all very mysterious."

"I am truly sorry, I told you I haven't done all of this in quite a while. What do you want to know?"

"I don't know… Anything, what do you do?"

"Well I have my PHD. in cognitive psychology and I opened my own clinic almost 10 years ago. Really, I just treat patients with therapy and medication. I guess that's a simplistic summary."

"Hmmm, so you like helping people?" Said Alexis.

"Yeah you could say that." *Or you could say I use too, when I was a normal person.*

"Interesting, so are you good at reading people? Can you read my mind right now? I may need to be careful around you." Alexis said with a quick smile.

"Well, I may know a bit about how people process things and how to pick up on certain nuances they may have, but no mind reading unfortunately." *Jeez I need to loosen up.*

"If you don't mind me asking, since you are experienced in the field, what do you think about this Heartbreak Killer? What would make a person so cruel? Kind of random but it's all around the news these days."

I was taken aback by the question. No one had asked me about myself before. *She sees me as cruel. I am cruel, but she wouldn't understand what made me the way I am.* I didn't know how to respond so instead sipped at my wine, attempting to think of a response.

The dark monster whispered as I thought. *See Perry, you can't live a normal life. Women think you're cruel, a monster. They're right, be the killer and ditch this pathetic act.*

I am trying to though. If she can make me feel again, maybe I have hope.

She will never see the real you, only the mask you put on for her. You are a monster. There is no going back.

I can try. I have to try.

"Is everything okay?" Said Alexis. "I didn't mean to put you on the spot, I was just curious on what a psychologist's view would be about a serial killer. I guess as a woman I get scared."

See Perry you scare her. Why not show her the real you, kill her.

"No, it's okay, it's just no one has ever asked me my opinion on the killer." I finally responded.

"I can see you are a little uneasy about the question so let's drop it. I don't want to ruin the date over a stupid question. Anyways, did you hear the police think they caught the person?"

"Caught who?" I said.

"The Heartbreak Killer, it's been on the news all week."

It has? Who did they catch? Surely not the right person, I thought.

"No I didn't hear anything about that. I have been busy all day… What have they been saying?"

"Nothing really except the police have someone in custody, and they think it's the killer."

That imposter, whispered the dark monster in my mind. *We need to show the world you are alive and well. Here is your chance, kill her. The detectives daughter, make him pay for his false proclaims.*

No. I don't want to.

Yes you do Perry. Women are evil, they deserve your wrath. She is no different.

I began to break out into a cold sweat as the darkness called to me. "Will you excuse me for a second?" I blurted out.

"Um yeah, are you sure everything is okay?" Alexis said with an eyebrow raised.

"Yeah, I just need to use the restroom."

I quickly turned for the bathroom. Once inside, I made sure I was alone and locked the door behind me. I went to the sink and splashed some water onto my face. *Get a hold of yourself Perry, you're blowing this. Who cares about the Heartbreak Killer right now?*

You do, because you are him, replied the dark monster.

I looked at myself in the mirror while water dripped from my face. *Stop pretending you can change, you are the Heartbreak Killer.*

No, I can change, she proved it.

Then why do you still hear my voice? Why do you care that someone else is posing as you? Alexis has you tricked, just like all the other women before her. She is nothing special. She will lead you to your demise.

You're wrong. I never wanted to be the Heartbreak Killer. I want to be Perry.

HA, did you want to be Perry when you decided to slaughter those women. Cut their hearts out. Make trophies of mangled human flesh. You're a monster and monsters don't change back once they are created.

I can change, I feel again. Alexis proved there is hope for me.

You will never change. She is poisoning your mind with falsities. Kill her, embrace what you are.

Get out of my head, leave me alone.

I am apart of you Perry, I will never leave. I am the darkness that was created. Embrace me.

LEAVE ME ALONE!

"Get out," I screamed into the mirror as I grabbed at my hair. "You aren't in control of me. Leave!" I pounded the sink with my fists. "I can change back."

The darkness became silent and I took a deep breath, looking at myself in the mirror again. A cold sweat had broken out again and my hair had been put out of place. I splashed more cool water on my face and reached for a towel to dry it. Fixing my stray hairs and taking another deep breath, I looked at my mirror self. "You can do this, you can be Perry. Perry is charming and confident. Go show her."

When I made it back to the table Alexis awaited me with a stern face. "Are you sure you're alright?" She said to me. "Is there something wrong with me or what I said? I feel like you don't want to be here."

"Of course I do, it's nothing like that. As I said before, it's just been forever since I have been out on a date. You are as beautiful as anyone I have ever seen and honestly, I was nervous and needed to regroup. I know it sounds silly but it's true."

"That's not silly at all. I like that you're nervous, Perry. Honestly, it's one of the reasons I said yes to going out with you. My ex fiancé was a cocky asshole and I wanted someone who seemed sweet and genuine. You being nervous just shows me that you're real."

"Well that's good… I guess? I promise you though, my nerves have passed, so let's start over. Hello, my name is Perry Nelson. I have a PHD. in cognitive psychology, and I think the Heartbreak Killer is an asshole who should be locked up for the rest of their life."

Alexis broke from her serious stare with a laughed. "Well hello again Mr. Nelson. I am Alexis Fisher, I work at a bookstore, and I also think that the Heartbreak Killer is an asshole."

From that moment on the night was wonderful. We talked about anything and everything that came to our minds. Alexis impressed me with her intelligence. She wasn't just a beauty, she had a brain as well, revealing to me she was going to college for an education degree and explained that it was her desire to teach people.

"I've always had a desire to be around the youth and shape them with my knowledge. I think that is more fulfilling than making a lot of money." Alexis said with a deep passion as she spoke.

Coincidently, I told her about my desire to help people and how I had just been lucky enough to be successful in the work I loved. "It wasn't about the money for me either." I responded.

As the wine bottle began to drain, more personal feelings began to arise between us. We each took turns talking about our failed relationships and how we had been hurt by the people we cared about.

"Men are pigs. All they care about is sex, and once you give them what they want they get bored." Said Alexis.

"Women think they want the nice guys, but when you give them everything they think they want they get bored." I said to counter.

We began to laugh at the debate, realizing we were both angry with the opposite sex.

I also learned about Alexis's mother and her fight with breast cancer. How the insurance company had refused to do all they could. How her father was struggling to deal with the emotions of it all. Even how Alexis was struggling to deal with the death, but had to be strong because her dad was such a mess. *Detective Fisher and I have more in common than I could have imagined. We both have had our hearts torn out,* I thought as Alexis told her story.

The drinks had reached me and I began to feel drunk. My mind wondered. *Is it normal to talk about such things on a first date? Maybe we are both drunk? Maybe we are both crazy? Maybe we were are both heartbroken killers? ... Wow I am drunk.*

Alexis grabbed my hand. "Enough sad talk, let's dance." Her eyes gleaming ocean blue as she spoke.

"Dance?" I said surprised. My attention directed over to the dance floor. People had found their liquid courage and begun to make their way over.   All dancing to an upbeat swing tune the quartet was playing.

"Yes, dance. Don't tell me you can't dance a bit Mr. Nelson. You should know a lady likes to dance when she's out."

Thankfully for me, I could dance quite well for a tall and lanky man. But I doubted my coordination in a drunken state. Never the less I made a nod in agreement to Alexis's proposal and she pulled my arm towards the dance floor.

Once we reached the floor, Alexis began to dance in a silly fashion, shaking her hips from side to side. Alexis smiled at me and her ocean blue eyes sparkled. She seemed unaware of anything else, only the music that flowed through the air. I watched her silly dance for a moment more and began to chuckle.

"What's so funny?" Alexis asked me.

"You have no rhythm." I said with a stupid grin.

"Oh, is that so? Well I don't see you moving at all. Show me what you got dance master."

Without a second thought, my drunken instincts took over. I grabbed Alexis's hands and we began to move with the beat. I twirled her around, pulling her in and out to the music.

Then the music switched to a slower pace and we began to waltz from side to side with our hands interlocking. I led and Alexis followed. After a minute or so of the routine, I let go of her hands and began to move my feet to the music. *This wine has put a fire to my feet. I am on right now.*

Alexis began to giggle now as she watched me dance. "Wow, you have some moves. I'm impressed."

"I think it's more from the wine than anything, but thanks." I said.

After a moment more, Alexis and I went back to our hand being locked and I spun her around a few more times.

Alexis was the most beautiful woman I had ever set my eyes on. We were as in sync as any two drunken people could be. My feelings began to flutter as we finished out the song.

When the song ended, everyone stopped their dance to clap for the quartet. The men took a bow and announced they would play one more song. A smooth and slow paced rhythm hummed through the air, allowing the love birds to nestle up close and dance slow.

I nervously looked at Alexis. She glanced at me and then down to the floor, inching closer to my side. It took all of my liquid courage to grab her waist and pull her into my chest. I took a deep breath and we began to rock back and forth, side to side, to the sweet melody.

I could feel her breast press up against mine as she laid her head on my shoulder. Electricity shot throughout my body, butterflies fluttered inside my stomach, and feelings poured into my dark heart. *Bubump bubump.* I was alive for the first time since I had become a man of darkness. *I can change, I told you. Monsters can change,* I thought to myself.

When the song ended, Alexis looked up at me. "That was nice, it's been too long since I have been with someone that danced like a gentlemen." She whispered to me.

"I enjoyed it too." I whispered back "Let me pay for the bill and we can go."

I left money on the table for the wine and we made our way to the doors. Grabbing our coats from the check out, I placed hers around her shoulders and continued to open the door for the both of us.

Outside, falling snow and chilly winds met us. But as cold as I should have been, I felt warmth inside and the breeze was refreshing to my face.

"Thanks for a wonderful evening." Alexis said. "I wasn't sure how it was going to go at the start, but things turned out to be very pleasant."

"I had a great time as well. Sorry again for the start." I said with a bit of shame.

"You made up for it. Usually first dates are full of boring introductions, but we actually talked about things that mattered. Most of the time men don't feel comfortable talking about things like that. I just hope it wasn't too much for you." Alexis said.

"Not at all. I'm glad I was able to learn more about you. I know from my line of work that life isn't all roses and sunshine."

"It defiantly isn't." Said Alexis with a brief pause. "Well, I guess this is goodbye then."

"Yeah I guess so, hopefully we can do this again."

"Hopefully," Alexis said with another sparkling smile. Her ocean blue eyes pierced into mine and she stepped a little closer to me, latching onto my arm. *What does this mean, does she want me to kiss her?*

I wasn't feeling so bold now. The liquid courage had run its course so I gave her a hug instead, said my goodbye, and began to walk away.

What are you doing? She wanted you to kiss her! You can easily murder women but you chicken out on a kiss. I stopped for a moment, my back still turned to Alexis. "Come on Perry," I murmured under my frosty breath "You can do this."

I turned around to Alexis waving for a cab. I paced back, hoping I would reach her before she got inside one. A cab pulled up and she opened the door. I was still ten feet away and Alexis hadn't noticed me, ducking inside the cab door.

"Wait," I called out to her

"Yes?" Alexis responded, poking her head out of the cab window.

"You forgot this," I said and my instincts took over. I leaned into the cab window and closed my eyes to kiss her.

When our lips touched, the electric feel jolted throughout my body. Her lips were luscious and soft to the touch of mine. They tasted of the sweet honey her hair appeared to resemble. The feeling was explosive, something I had never dreamed to feel again. My heart thumped against my chest as I pulled away.

I stared at her, dumbstruck with emotional novelty. Alexis's face had become dazed too. *Oh no she hated it. I shouldn't have trusted my instincts, I am a killer not a lover.*

"Wow," she said softly.

"I'm so sorry, I thought…" I said with no real response.

"Sorry for what?" Alexis implored. "It's what I wanted. A truly perfect way to end the night."

"Perfect?" I said confused.

"You really are clueless with women huh, Perry Nelson." Alexis said with a feminine giggle. "Call me okay?" She rolled the cab window up and waved a goodbye to me.

She isn't wrong, I thought standing alone as the cab drove away. One thing was for certain in my mind though, I wanted to see Alexis again.

I walked home in a happy state. The feeling of the kiss still lingered throughout my body and some part of me already missed Alexis, even if it had been only moments without her.

When I reached the comfort of my home, I went to my room to change out of my date outfit and into something comfortable. As I changed, I noticed my glass trophy case sitting outside of its safe haven. The lone and dried piece of heart sat inside.

With one swift stroke, my mood became cold. I realized that even if I could become human again, my monster still sat inside me, caged and waiting to strike. *What would it take for my darkness to come out in front of Alexis?* The thought alone was startling to me.

As much as I wanted to triumph over my dark monster, I knew how fragile I really was. The dread that any little misstep could lead to Alexis Fisher's heart inside the glass cage was sobering. *I don't want her heart that way. That would mean I failed.* I turned away from my trophy, disgusted by my past actions.

After I changed, I went to the TV in the living room to try to get my mind off of my monstrous deeds and thoughts.

BREAKING NEWS: MAN IN HEARTBREAK CASE HAS BEEN ARRESTED, read across the bottom of the TV screen in big red block letters. I had forgotten about Alexis's mention of the Heartbreak Killers capture earlier in the night. *Who is this man pretending to be me? Claiming my name*, I thought with more disgust.

As I watched more of the story unfold in front of me I become infuriated.

How could they accuse this man of being me? So sloppy, so foolish. How could Detective Fisher even think this man was me? Maybe he isn't the adversary I had anticipated. Maybe he is a fool like the rest.

Rage began to build as the smug Terry Connor sat in on the news, gloating of the police accomplishments and mocking me with her every word. "The Heartbreak Killer thought he could escape the law untouched. The Heartbreak Killer was sorely mistaken. He thought he was clever and smart, well he will be facing the death penalty soon enough." Terry boasted as the news rolled along.

She is sorely mistaken. All she is doing is provoking the real Heartbreak Killer.

Imitating someone could be charming to some but to me it was insulting. My reputation was being tarnished by every word Terry spewed.

My dark monster returned as Terry bashed my name. *I told you Perry, you're still the Heartbreak Killer. Stop your charade of being a man with feelings. Deep down you only care about one thing and that's the revenge of the Heartbreak Killer.*

I use to care about him, but now I know I can be someone else. I shouldn't care. Terry is just an idiot like all the other media.

Then why do you become enraged as you watch the news. This should be good for Perry. Perry could start fresh knowing someone else will take the fall, but you don't want that. You want them to know that you are still lurking. Your arrogance has always been prevalent inside you just as I am.

You're right.

Of course I am Perry. Let's show them. Let's spill some more blood and put the fear of the Heartbreak Killer back into the people who think they are safe now. Expose the lies of the police and news alike. Show Detective Fisher what a fatal error he has made and kill his daughter.

No, it won't be her.

Then who, whispered the dark monster.

I looked on at the coverage of the news. Terry Connor continued to spew the poison and falsities to everyone watching in the city. "Justice will always prevail Heartbreak Killer. Now the city will watch you die and everyone will cheer with joy that an evil monster is put down."

I gritted my teeth and clenched my fists. *I will feed you darkness, but only with an evil worse than me. This is your last hour.*

Chapter 14
The Bitch of Channel 28 News Pt. 2

"I need everyone in this room to pull their heads out of their incompetent asses and find me something on this nameless suspect." Terry Conner screamed to a room full of fellow news staff members. "The police have declined to comment on who this person is and I need something new to report on about the Heartbreak Killer." She paused, looking at her staff still sitting. "Do you not understand English? Go now, time is money."

The staff exited in a scurry, fearful of Terry Connor's wrath. *I work with idiots. If I wasn't running this station we would all be out of jobs,* Terry thought. She had been without a good lead on who the suspect was for two weeks now, and the police had ducked every question Terry had asked them. *I'm growing impatient with everyone's bullshit.*

Terry waited to exit the room last, going for the door outside. She leaned up against the bricks wall of the Channel 28 News building, reached into her purse, and pulled out a pack of cigarettes. Terry continued to light one with a lighter in her other hand. *The police are up to something. Why else would they keep all the information to themselves about the person they have in their custody,* Terry thought as she inhaled the smoke. *No matter, I will get the story I want out. This killer will get the crucifixion from me and my audience will eat it up, they love this story.*

The cigarette in Terry's mouth had dwindled to its end and she dropped it to the ground. Reaching back into her purse for perfume, she sprayed herself profusely to rid the smell of the toxins she had exhaled.

When Terry felt ready to be seen by people, she opened the door of the news station and walked to the area where most of her researchers were.

"Who has something I can report on tonight that will give us some sort of ratings." Said Terry.

The workers stared at her blankly. No one dared to say a word.

"You better give me a good story or so help me god someone is getting fired in this room. We go on in one hour, there better be something on my dressing room desk in thirty minutes."

Terry left the team to hustle for a story and headed for her private dressing room.

The inside of Terry's dressing room was filled with white leather couches for guest and people of interest, a large black wood coffee table with magazines of fashion, celebrities, and anything else that interested Terry at the time. She had also demanded a fifty-inch flat screen TV be hung on the wall where she liked to watch herself the night before, critiquing any miscues that may have happened the night before. The finishing touches to the room were the walls, which were painted Terry's favorite color, lavender.

As usual when Terry entered her dressing room, the desk was piled with overflowing mail from fans and creepy men alike. She despised reading fan mail so instead Terry hired an assistant to impersonate her while reading and replying to a select few letters.

Next to the mail there was always a freshly stocked bouquet of flowers in a china glass vase. Today, yellow lilies greeted Terry. *At least those are nice to look at,* she thought as she sat in her chair in front of a vast mirror.

Things had not always been this way for Terry. She started out as a weather girl in a small town of 25,000 people when she was fresh out of college. As time went by, and her career became more established, Terry managed to move away to the city and co-host the early slot of the news. After three years of flirting, lying, sucking, and fucking, she made it to the prime time slot at five and Terry's fame soon skyrocketed. With the fame came more money and a bigger dressing room, catered to her liking. *It was all worth it,* Terry thought when she had first entered the new dressing room. But now, Terry's ego had grown and she wanted more, a national stage.

This Heartbreak Killer story is my rise to the top, Terry thought when she first broke the story. It hadn't spread to the national news yet, but it would eventually. She had to be at the tip of the spear that drove the story to every home in America. After everything was said and done, every national news station would know the name Terry Connor as the woman who broke the massive Heartbreak Story. After that kind of break there would be no doubt she would get offered the national job. *The story is a ratings monster and one of the biggest I've seen in decades,* Terry thought.

"Make-up, now," Terry demanded out to her assistant as she looked at herself in the mirror. "You are one hot bitch," she said to herself. "Every man in America wants to fuck you, and every women envies you, wanting to be you."

A young girl rushed over with a bag of make-up and began to powder Terry's face to cover any blemishes. The girl then continued to put mascara on Terry's eyelashes and add a tiny bit of black eye shadow to make Terry's almond brown eyes pop on TV.

As the assistant anxiously did Terry's make up, Terry herself began to do her hair. She usually kept it straight and down for TV. *I look best this way,* Terry thought as she did.

Before Terry finished getting ready, there was an abrupt knock on the dressing room door. "What," Terry screamed to the noise. *They know I hate being disturbed before my show.*

"I'm sorry for bothering you Miss Connor, but there is a call for you." A woman's voice cowered from the other side of the door.

"You know damn well I don't take calls before my show. Are you too dumb to remember these simple rules?"

"I'm… I'm sorry Miss Connor… I know you don't take calls… but."

"But what? You're an idiot?" Terry asked, interrupting the woman.

"It's about the Heartbreak Killer. A man called and has something on the identity of the suspect the police have in custody. I told him you don't take calls now, but he will only talk to you and said if you didn't come now he won't call back."

"Well it better be worth my damn time to interrupt me just before I go on. I'll be right there, tell this man to wait."

Terry stood up from her chair and stormed outside of her room.

The cowering woman was standing directly outside with a phone in her hands. Terry glared at the woman and snatched the phone from her quivering hands.

"Get the hell out of here before I ruin your career." Snapped Terry, and the woman scampered away as fast as she could.

"Hello, this is Terry Connor speaking. Do you have something for me about the Heartbreak Killer or are you just another creepy fan calling me?" The phone was silent for a moment but Terry heard the faint exhale from the person on the other line. "Listen creep I told you..." Terry started to say.

"I have something to tell you." Said a man with a deep toned voice. "I know who the Heartbreak Killer is."

"Ha, do you know how many callers I've had proclaiming this? Even if you did, why would you go out of your way to call and tell me?"

"Because I know how bad you need and want the information. I know what it will do to your career if you break the story and I will give it to you, but it will cost you."

"Cost me what?" Said Terry not buying into the scam the man was selling.

"I know you're skeptical, I would be too. People must call in everyday with tips about the Heartbreak Killer like you said."

"Yes they do, so why should I believe you?"

"Because I am the man's therapist... My offer is this, meet me for dinner. I find you wildly attractive and we will see where it goes from there. When the night is over, if I'm satisfied with your company, I will give you my clients name. I'm risking my therapist-patient confidentiality by telling you this information so I have to be sure I receive the... the right offer" Said the deep voiced man with a chuckle.

Terry did not doubt the man found her beautiful. Many times before, men had called her with similar offers. Most had been vile and disgusting men with nothing news worthy, so Terry was good at weeding out the liars. However, other men had real news worthy material and were lonely enough to sell their stories for a beautiful women's time, a woman like Terry Connor.

"Do you think you are the first man to offer me something like this?" Terry said, becoming irritated. "Do you realize how many creepy men call me with fake news stories just trying to convince me to go on a date with them? Do you really think that some story will convince me just because you proclaim you have the information? Talk is cheap, I am going to hang up the phone now."

"You didn't let me finish, Terry." Said the man in a stern and confidence tone, now. "I will give you my name and you can look up my credentials for yourself. I promise you, I'm not one of those creepy men you speak of."

"I'm listening," said Terry. *He is slicker than most of these fools,* she thought.

"I want you to know however, if you so much as breathe a word of this conversation to anyone or present anything on the news before I give you the name, I will give this information to another news station. Maybe that young girl on Channel 2's News station. Imagine her career spike after breaking something like that."

This pushed a button inside Terry. *Everyman in America wants to fuck you, do whatever it takes to get to the top.*

"Okay mystery man, I will keep this a secret between you and I." Said Terry changing her voice into a flirty tone.

He can't resist me, I'm the sex symbol of the city. Why else would he call me first?

"You have yourself a deal. I will go on this date with you as long as your name checks out."

"Good," said the man in a charming manner. "I do believe we have meet before Terry. In fact, you covered my psychiatric clinic when it first opened. Of course you weren't as established back then."

He has some balls to degrade me by bring up my past, I'll give him that, Terry thought after the man finished his sentence.

"I do believe I remember our meeting." Lied Terry. "I was just getting my career started then. But it been a long time and I don't remember your name."

"My name is Perry, Perry Nelson. Let's say dinner Thursday, eight o'clock at the Italian House. I'm looking forward to seeing the beautiful Miss Connor in person again."

The phone line clicked.

Terry set the phone back on its resting dock and dug out her own cell phone. She reached a browser and typed, *"Perry Nelson Psychiatrics",* into the search bar and clicked on the first link that came up. A picture of a man with black slicked hair and piercing green eyes appeared. Underneath the picture read *Dr. Nelson, PhD, Clinical Psychiatrics.*

Terry continued to scroll down to the bio. *He was telling the truth,* thought Terry as she read through the man's bio. She scrolled back to top with the picture. *Well at least this one is attractive, young, and wealthy.*

Terry let out a cynical laugh at the events that had just transpired and walked back to her dressing room. *All I have to do is flash sex and this Dr. Nelson will sing the tune to a national news job. Men are all the same, stupid and easy. Terry Connor always gets what she wants.*

Chapter 15
A Mirror of Resemblance

The police department had confirmed Carson Minks admissions. The man had killed his ex-girlfriend after getting the idea from the Heartbreak Killer. Mr. Minks was just as he had said, a copycat killer.

After the sobering news, Paul had wondered to a nearby bar, attempting to cope with his mistakes. The media had swarmed him once again as he left the police station, asking question after question. But Paul barely took noticed of them. He was inside his own head, still wondering if he had it in him to be the good and functioning detective he once was.

She isn't here to save you this time, Paul. She would have given me back the strength and confidence. I'm alone now, Paul thought of his wife as a bartender poured him a shot of whiskey on the rocks.

I'm going to lose this case if I don't find the killer soon. The media has insured that. Once a case like this gets put on the news, it starts a wildfire with the public, and soon that fire will burn everyone involved until the problem is resolved. It will only be a matter of days before another body shows up and the public discovers the dirty little secret we are now hiding.

The bartender set a glass cup in front of Paul and went to tend on a group of women who had entered the bar. Paul took a sip, tasting the sting of the whisky on his tongue, and the burn that followed in his belly. The drink warmed his chilly and depressed body from the cold outside.

As Paul sipped, his mind recalled a fascination with serial killers and sociopaths as a young man in college. He had learned about how killer's minds worked in psychology classes and the history of those convicted killers in criminal law classes. Paul had always pondered why these people turned into monsters. He despised the monsters, seeing them as an evil that made the world a worse place, a fearful place. *I want to stop them,* Paul use to think in class. *I want to stop them from hurting others.*

The answer to the question of why had never been closer to Paul, now, as he sat at the bar.

The killer is quite interesting though, Paul thought as his mind shifted to the Heartbreak Killer. *Was your mother cruel to you? Did she beat you and call you ugly? Did you never meet her impossible expectations? Did the women you loved break your heart to many times, turning you into a woman hater? Or maybe you lost your loved one like me, and couldn't deal with the pain. Leaving you with the knowledge of how dark our world is. Deciding to join it instead of fight. Maybe I'm becoming you, the next Heartbreak Killer. Who are you? What drives you to be the monster?*

Paul's cell phone began to vibrate in his pocket, breaking his deep thoughts. He checked the I.D., *Daughter* read across the screen.

"Hello my beautiful daughter." Answered Paul, trying to sound as cheery as possible.

"Hi Dad, I just saw the news at work. Is it true? You caught the Heartbreak Killer." Said Alexis on the other line.

"We don't know for sure hunny, but I hope so. I have to keep my daughter safe."

"I heard that an officer was stabbed too. Are you okay Dad? You didn't get hurt did you?"

"No Alexis, I am perfectly fine. You shouldn't worry about me, it would take more than some killer to take down your old man."

"I know Dad."

"Listen hunny, I can't really talk about the case anymore. You know its police protocol."

"Okay, I just wanted to make sure you were doing fine. I actually called to tell you some good news anyways."

"Good news?" Paul said with curiosity.

"Well I hope so at least. I met a guy, he asked me out to dinner. We are going out tomorrow. I'm really excited but a little nervous to."

"That's great Alexis." Paul said trying to disguise his discomfort with the news.

"I know how you get with guys Dad, but you shouldn't worry. I'm twenty-seven, I know what I am doing." Alexis said with irritation.

"I know Alexis, it's just… you know how many scumbag guys are out there. Even Barry turned out to be one."

"Yeah, Barry was one, and you know how hard it was for me to get over him. You should be happy I'm out and dating again."

"I don't think a father is ever happy when his daughter dates, no matter how old you get."

"I'm happy dad, that's what should matter to you. After Barry, I wanted nothing to do with men but I'm finally ready I think. The guy seems really nice. He is actually kind of shy and clumsy, but I think that may be a good thing. The confident ones are usually the scumbags."

"I'm happy for you hunny, but Alexis you have to be careful. You can never be too sure with anyone. Will you call me when you get home from the date so I know you're safe? You know your dad worries about his little girl."

"I know you do Dad, probably a little too much. Plus I'm not a little girl anymore."

"You will always be little to me. So give me that call?"

"Okay Dad, if it will make you feel better."

"It will, love you." Said Paul with a smirk.

"I love you to." Said Alexis before clicking the phone off.

Paul placed his phone back in the pocket of his jeans and ordered another drink. *That guy better be nice or I will break his legs. No one hurts my daughter.*

When Barry had cheated on Alexis, Paul went to his house and told him if he ever talked to his daughter again he would be sorry. *In hindsight that would have been a mistake to hurt Barry, he is a lawyer and would have sued me silly.* Paul laughed at the idea of punching Barry in his face. *It would have been worth it,* he decided. *That smooth talking punk. He was always scared of me.*

Luckily for both men, Barry had been silent since Paul's threats as far as he was aware.

The bar began to fill as Paul sipped on his new whiskey. The one he was in had a reputation as a police bar. Most of the officers at his precinct would come in after a hard day on the job. *God knows we need it.*

Paul's attention shifted onto a woman that had just walked in. She sat next to him on a stool and ordered a drink. Paul glanced over at her, trying to be subtle.

The woman had long tan legs left uncovered by a short blue dress. Her hair was long, straight, and dark brown. Her nose was large, pointing outward, along with think dark lips.

She hadn't noticed Paul's gaze as she tried to catch the bartender's eyes for a drink.

As soon she ordered and the drink was placed in front of her she gave Paul a glance and smiled at him shyly. Paul smiled back with an awkward drunk grin and then turned towards a TV. *Is she into me,* thought Paul, taking another gulp of whiskey.

Paul hadn't been with another woman since his wife. He was in no sort of mood to find a new woman either, but the combination of alcohol and bad news had made Paul loose, horny, and desperate for comfort. *I should say something, but what?* Paul felt shy and rusty to the thought of talking to the woman, but the feeling of buzzing alcohol compensated for his worries.

"Hey, I'm Paul." He finally blurted out.

"Why hello, my name Chelsey." She replied with a feminine tone.

Paul put his hand out for a shake. The woman laughed at the gesture putting her hand out to meet his.

"Nice to meet you. Do you come to this bar regular?" Said Paul.

"Every once in a while. I'm not much of a drinker, but sometimes I need to blow off some steam. I work a few blocks away so it's a convenient spot for me to come too."

"Blowing off steam from a shitty day at work, am I right?"

The woman laughed again and nodded in agreement.

Alcohol consumed Paul as he continued to converse with the woman and the stress of his life seemed to fade. He babbled on and

on, half-unaware of his words. But the woman seemed to enjoy his company and the alcohol made Paul seem more confident than he was.

After a few more drinks and flirting, Paul had convinced the woman to come back to his place to finish off the night.

The drive home was a blur to Paul and in what seemed to be seconds, he was at his house with the woman by his side.

The two drunk lovers began kissing as soon as they reached the door way. Paul's body had taken over as his mind was polluted with drunken lust. Soon the two began ripping each other's clothes off and revealing their hidden flesh.

What was her name again, Paul thought as the clothing flew.

"Where is the bedroom?" The woman whispered in Paul's ear.

"This way," said Paul, cupping the woman's hand as he guiding her to the bedroom.

Paul plopped on top of the bed and removed his underwear, while the woman stood, fumbling with her last remaining clothing. Paul's drunken lust was giddy with anticipation and finally the woman removed the last of her garments, revealing her tan tint body in full.

She was a thick woman with a strong and athletic build. Her breasts were small but perky, with little pink pointed nipples and her hips were wide and round in shape.

The sight of her flesh made Paul's blood pump rapidly.

"How do I look?" Questioned the woman.

"Amazing," responded Paul.

The woman smiled at his answer and dimmed the light before lying in bed with Paul. As she did, she began to kiss him on his neck and ears while rubbing his cock with her hand.

Before the pleasure could engulf him, Paul noticed a picture of his wife out of the corner of his eye on the nearby nightstand. Abruptly, his drunken lust calmed and his mind become clear and sober. *What am I doing,* Paul realized.

Paul turned away from the drunken woman in bed and positioned himself at the edge of the bed.

"What's wrong?" Said the woman with a look of confusion.

"I can't do this." Said Paul, deflecting the woman's advances away from him as he sat.

"Why? Is it me? Did I do something wrong?" Said the woman.

"No, it's nothing you did. I just can't do this."

"Are you married or something?" Demanded the woman.

"Something," Paul said in a somber tone.

"Just my luck, picking up a man who's married. Why are you out picking up someone if you have a wife? It's not fair to women like me who are just looking for a nice guy."

"Get out… Now." Said Paul in a fierce tone.

"Okay, sorry, you don't have to be an asshole." Said the woman, quickly putting her under garments back on.

"Here take some money for a cab." Said Paul, searching for his wallet as the woman gathered the last of her things.

"I don't need your money." Said the woman. "You're a dick, bye." And with that, she left Paul alone in his room. A loud slam of the front door could be heard moments after, and he was finally alone in his house as he had been for so many months.

Paul began to rehash back to the thoughts he once had sitting at the bar.

I'm so lost in this dark world. Was that you too, Heartbreak? Trying to fill your emptiness with the company of strange women. Finding it doesn't satisfy the sting of lost love.

Paul stood up, naked and cold, and went to a large hanging mirror in his room. "Who are you?" Said Paul in the mirror. "What have you become?"

The symbol of the red broken and twisted heart began to burn in Paul's mind as he stared at his naked reflection. Suddenly, the Heartbreak Killers symbol appeared on the glass of the mirror and red liquid that had once been painted at the crime scene trailed downward on the mirror. Paul clutched at his aching heart while imagining what was real and fake.

Maybe we aren't as different as I had wanted to believe, Heartbreak. Us cops and monsters.

Chapter 16
A Womanly Perspective

It was strange for a man like Perry to have my attention. He was an outlier in my dating world. I'm attracted to a confident and outgoing man. But Perry seemed as though he needed an instruction manual to dating and a bottle of liquid courage to be competent around a woman.

Usually, the lack of confidence on a first date would have been a deal breaker for me. Pair that with how poorly the night had started out, I was skeptical I would be interested sitting at the table and waiting for him. Perry seemed so awkward at first, he couldn't even make a proper conversation with me, stuttering and then sitting in awkward silence. It was all so strange.

As nervous as I had been to go out with someone new, Perry made me seem like a regular on the dating scene. *What was he doing in that bathroom, anyways?* I had almost left when he made me sit there for ten minutes alone, but I am glad I hadn't. He came back a new man, and although I could still see his little uncertainties around me, I grew to find it cute and charming. *What a dancer too, even if he was lanky, he danced with grace.*

I needed someone different in my life though, so maybe it was a perfect match at the perfect time.

Barry was the type of man I usually look for but what attracted me to him turned out to hurt me in the end. Barry was such a great talker, I mean he did it for a living as a lawyer, but he had been so smooth with me. I came to realize though, that Barry was smooth and confident around me because he didn't care about my feelings. *He was a liar, a cheater, a man without real feelings.*

When I found out Barry had cheated on me while we were engaged I was devastated. I had believed all his lies for years.

"I love you," Barry would tell me or, "you're the only one I need in my life." He would say these words with a false smile and I believed it all. In the end, all of his talk was bullshit. If I was the judge and he was the lawyer, he would have been selling me on a relationship that was guilty.

After all the heartache of our relationship ending, I vowed to find someone different then Barry. To many times I had come across lying men in my young life, willing to say anything I wanted to hear to get into my bed.

That's why Perry had my attention now. He was handsome sure, tall with black hair and a good sense of fashion, but he was not smooth. I think that if anything, his clunkiness showed how true his intensions were with me. *He cares,* I thought.

Perry wanted the date to go well and make a good impression on me. With that kind of pressure it made him nervous and awkward. That was his charm to me. Men like Barry could be smooth because they never truly cared about making a good impression on me.

And that kiss Perry gave me was magical.

After I had arrived home from our first date all I wanted was for Perry to call. The anticipation of that next time he asked me out lingered deep within my mind. *I wonder if a man like Perry will play games with me. Maybe all men are born to make us wait on them.* I was being selfish though. Perry was probably too nervous to even call me again.

He will become confident around me, just give it time.

However long the wait, it was refreshing to have my mind on another man.

Barry had been constantly calling me, pleading with me to take him back. The longer I stayed alone the harder it would be to say no. *Being alone is not something I'm fond of.* Women fear being alone once they reach a certain age. *What's wrong with me,* I imagined the women thinking, *my looks are only downhill from here. That's all men care about right? I'll never get married now. I'll never find love.* Maybe being alone was just one of my deep fears, but I liked to pretend that I wasn't abnormal.

Perry finally called me two days after our first date. I couldn't have been happier when I answered, hearing his voice on the other end. He asked me if I wanted to attend a Christmas play with him and I graciously said yes.

I hadn't learned much about Perry yet, but from what I did pick up on, he enjoyed things that most people would consider higher class. The men in my past life never asked me to such events as a play. So the feeling was something new and exciting. I was thrilled to step out of my comfort zone.

When the day of our date came about, butterflies fluttered around inside my stomach. *How does a man so awkward, manage to make me feel so nervous,* I thought as I was getting ready for the night.

Men had always found me desirable, but I had never let my blessed looks go to my head. Nor had I used them to manipulate people as some of my girlfriends did. I was raised to know there are far more important things in life than how you appeared. However, being humble didn't mean I wouldn't pull out all the stops to impress Perry tonight.

Picking out an outfit was the hardest decision of my day leading up to the date. *I want his jaw to drop at the sight of me,* I thought browsing through the selections of clothes in my closet.

I must have shuffled through my closet five times and tried on half of my outfits before I settled on one. I wasn't sure what fit into the category of play attire, but I was sure Perry would be sharply dressed. *He's worn something dressy every time I've seen him I think.* I decided on a medium length indigo dress with black heels. *Black always contrasts my fair skin but it seems to fit right for tonight. I hope he likes it.*

The night quickly came after and when I reached the theater, Perry was waiting outside. He smiled and waved me over when he noticed I had arrived.

Perry was dressed sharp just like he always seemed to be. This time he had on black slacks with a royal blue blazer over a white collar shirt and a skinny black tie. *I wonder if he only owns suits,* I thought as I walked towards him. *Maybe I will find out if he ever invites me over. Either way he looks handsome.*

"You look stunning," Perry said as I reached him.

"Thank you, you're sweet." I said back. "I wasn't sure what to wear to a play."

"Are you sure? The outfit looks perfect to me, especially the black heels."

"Thank you," I said with a shy smile. *He likes my outfit and more confident tonight too… Good.* "What play are we even seeing?"

"A Christmas Carol. I read somewhere that it was good and I thought you may enjoy doing something with a holiday theme."

"I think that was a good assumption."

"Good, shall we then?" Said Perry reaching out to take my hand.

As Perry led the way to our seats, he politely opened any door that stood in front of us, allowing me to pass through first. The gesture made me smile and he continued to build upon the second part of our first date.

"Do you want anything to eat?" Said Perry as we sat down in the theater.

"No thank you, but maybe something to drink." I said.

"What would you like?"

"I don't care, surprise me." I said with a genuine smile.

Perry gave me a nod and went off, leaving me in the theater chair. Time seemed to drag by as I waited for him to return. I surveyed the crowd and saw older men in sharp suits accompanied by women with extravagant dresses and furs. There was also a large assortment of egregiously large hats worn by both sexes. *This is high class fashion? A bit ridiculous,* I thought.

Perry made his way back to the seats right as the lights dimmed and the play began. He placed a bag of popcorn on the ground and then presented me with a bottle of apple juice.

"Hope you don't mind apple juice." He whispered in my ear as he sat down, handing me the juice.

"No that's perfectly fine." I lied. *I did say surprise me though, Alexis.*

"Good," Perry said with a grin.

At least he can feel like he did a good job.

I began to get anxious as the play went on, finding myself desperately wanting Perry to hold my hand, or even have him put his arm around me. *Maybe we are too old for that kind of nonsense.* Nevertheless, with each passing moment my anxiety rose. Perry's touch was calling to me, yet, he hadn't even so much as glanced at me since the play stated. I wanted to feel that same spark I had when he kissed me.

I have to get his attention. Maybe if I move my hand around some he will get the hint. I began to wrestle with my hands, but Perry wouldn't look away from the play. *It's just a play, Perry. Look at me, your date, please.*

After my first failed attempt to grab his attention, I decided to reach for the popcorn that Perry was holding. As I reached into the bag, I brushed my hand against his. *Come on take the hint.*

Perry finally glanced over and his forest green eyes pierced though the dim theater lights. *He has beautiful eyes,* I realized.

"Do you want the popcorn?" He whispered in my ear.

No I don't want the popcorn, I want your hand. Come on, no man can be this oblivious... Although, it took him a few minutes to catch onto that kiss...

"No, this is enough." I said showing him the pieces of popcorn in my hand. I stuffed the handful into my mouth but one of the kernel missed, dropping into my lap.

"Here, you missed one." Said Perry politely. He picked the lone piece off my black dress and put it near my mouth with his fingertips.

Does he want me to eat it off his hand or grab it? Ah, I don't want to be too desperate, he could be freaked out.

I reach out with my hand and grabbed the piece of popcorn from his, tossing it into my mouth and smiling at him.

"Thanks, I promise I'm usually more graceful than this." I said after.

"Oh I don't doubt that. I saw your moves on the dance floor the other night." Said Perry as he made a goofy gesture in his chair, which hardly resembled any of my dancing.

"Jerk," I said sarcastically "You better quit teasing me. My moves were better than yours." I said doing my own goofy imitation.

Perry laughed at the gesture.

"Shhh," someone hissed at us in the dim theater.

Perry and I made a glance at each other and smiled, turning our attention back to the play.

Hold my hand and I'll be satisfied. He practically forced me to be loud. I gave another quick glance at Perry and he met my eyes with his. I quickly turned my head back to the play. *This game is killing me, just do it, Perry. I want you to. Maybe it's this arm rest, it always gets in the way of hand holding. That must be why he hasn't made his move. Make it, make it, make it.*

Perry's hand lifted the arm bar up and scooted toward me.

Yes almost there come on. I could see Perry hesitate and he became restless and fidgety. *I'm waiting, come on, put your arm over me.* I could barely contain myself; the anticipation had built up too high.

Perry then lifted his arm up and gently placed it over my shoulder.

Finally, yes. Not the hand but I'll take it.

I gave Perry a smiled, scooting into the side of his chest and rested my head there. *This is all I ever wanted silly man.*

As I watched the play, the warmth of Perry's body too mine was comfortable and relaxing. Something felt right being beside him. *He is like my own personal heater on these cold winter nights.*

When the play finished and the lights brightened the room, the audience clapped as the actors came to the stage to take a bow. Perry and I left before the crowd with his arm still around me.

Outside of the theater, we waited together on the cold December night as Perry waved on a cab for me.

"I had a great time again, Perry." I said grinning. "Believe it or not this was my first play."

"Really? Well I hope you enjoyed it. I thought it was well done." Said Perry.

"Yes it was enjoyable." *Now kiss me,* I thought.

A cab pulled up to us before Perry could, and instead he opened the door for me.

"Next time I get to pick the date." I said gracefully inching toward Perry's chest and gazing into his forest green eyes. "It's only fair since you choose the first two."

"Next time?" Said Perry seemingly shocked at the notion. "So there will be a next time?"

"Yes, I hope so." *You tall idiot, now kiss me.*

"Me too." Perry said with a bashful grin.

Perry didn't hesitate this time, leaning down to me.

I closed my eyes and leaned into the kiss.

This time our embrace filled kiss wasn't just a peck. Perry gave me one, then two, then three long kisses. His lips weren't thick or luscious but they were warm and moist to the touch.

The butterflies from earlier in the day returned, fluttering inside my stomach and chest as our lips locked. Our touch of bodies warmed away the cold December night, and my heart beat inside me like a drum.

Perry pulled away from me and I opened my eyes, gazing into his mysterious forest green eyes once more.

"Goodnight," said Perry with an awkward half smile. "I will call you tomorrow, okay?"

"Sounds good Mr. Perry Nelson. Don't keep a lady waiting." I responded as I hopped into the cab. He closed the door behind me, giving me a wave through the window.

Wow that was everything I could imagine. He is such a sweet guy, I thought as the cab drove away.

I blissfully thought about Perry and the date the rest of the ride home.

When the cab pulled up to my driveway, I noticed a car that resembled Barry's parked in the street. *That can't be his. Not after such a great night. No.*

I stepped out of the cab and saw Barry sitting on the steps to my doorway. *No I don't want to deal with this now.*

"Alexis, I..." Said Barry, standing up as I walked toward my house.

"Why are you here? If my Dad knew... He told you to stay away from me." I said with anger.

"I know, but I had to see you."

"Why? Did it not work out with you and one of your sluts, Barry? I have nothing to say or hear from you." I said pushing him aside as I walked up to my door.

"Listen, I know I messed up, and I'm so sorry. Cheating on you was a mistake and now all I can think about is how big of a mistake it was. I want to make thing right between us again. I had to come and show you that I care about you."

"Well, I don't Barry. You cheated on me, while we were engaged no less. I was in love with you and you broke my heart. I can't take that back. I could never trust you again."

"Let me try to show you I can change." Pleaded Barry. "I know I can, I miss you Lexi."

I unlocked the door, opening it, and stepped inside. Barry tried to grab at my arm as I did, but I pushed him off and turned back around to him.

"People don't change, Barry. You're a lying, cheating, pig, and that's what you will always be. Now leave me alone or I'll call my Dad"

"Plea…" Barry tried to get out but I interrupted him.

"Oh, by the way, I met someone and I think I like him. In fact, I was just out with him. He is a gentlemen and someone I could see myself with. The opposite of you really."

Barry's jaw dropped at the words and with that, I slammed the door in his lying face, locking the door behind me.

I breathed a sigh of relief as a put my back on the door.

Did I just say I liked Perry, I suddenly realized. *I guess I do… I really do.*

Chapter 17
Manipulation Games

How does a killer catch his prey?

The dominate predators of our world all have their own unique advantages. Spiders have nearly invisible webs, hawks have keen eyesight, and sharks have their massive size and scent for blood. *But what advantage did I have on my prey?*

Terry Conner was no fool. She undoubtedly used appearance to her advantage. Maybe even the allure of sex to trap men, getting her way with a simple spread of the legs. Of course I assumed that's how Terry rose to the top of the city anyways. Becoming as famous as she was, Terry knew how to use her given talents as advantages over people.

I never hated Terry for those reasons though. In fact, I applauded her for using her advantages. No, in my eyes she was a creator of evil. The same creators that had birthed me, the Heartbreak Killer, and I had a burning desire to stop these creators from birthing any new evils.

Along with Terry's apathetic personality, she worked for one of the evilest things in the world, the media. What does media care about? One thing, and one thing only, ratings. The media will spew anything out for people to watch and Terry was the perfect one to spew.

How much of what I saw from them was even reality? I doubted much. *They love to spew their lying filth.*

Even as the media mocked me, proclaiming I had been caught, it was all a lie to get a story out and entice people's interest. I was tired

of all of the bullshit. *Time to make the media pay. I will get the truth out.* I had reached my breaking point.

What can a killer use to his advantage? To ensnare a beast like harlot beast like Terry. Well, it was quite simple to me. I could use my psychological expertise to manipulate her. And the best manipulation? Find a person's biggest strength and use it against them for their undoing.

Terry's strong ambitions to find out who the killer was by name drove her. I knew that she would go to great lengths to acquire that information. It would be a rating boost for the ages, and could make a career. *The first person to break it would win a grand prize,* I assumed.

But that alone was not enough. I also needed to play a role that Terry assumed of all men. The role of a man who thought Terry was undeniably attractive. The role of a horny man who wants sex. *That's what Terry is used to.*

Sure, my assumption was an educated shot in the dark. I had no hard evidence that Terry was such the woman I had painted in my mind, but I was smart. I could read people like books. I had to for my profession.

Yes, ambitious Terry Connor thought she was coming to meet Perry Nelson, the lonely, horny, and information worthy man. When in fact I was not such a man, only one wearing the mask she expected. I was using my advantage. Manipulation games.

No Terry, you're not meeting the man I have painted for you. You're meeting the Heartbreak Killer tonight, and I will stop your press coverage for good.

I sat at the Italian house, sipping on a martini and chewing on a breadstick. *Patient as a spider, waiting on my victim to come into my web of lies and manipulation.*

I was early for the date as usual. Terry hadn't arrived yet, but I was almost certain she would. *The information I have is to scintillating to pass up.*

Alexis had wanted to go out tonight but I had made up a lie to extract my vengeful plan.

"I have to work late, tonight." I said to her over the phone.

"But Perry, I had our date all planned out." Said Alexis, trying to rebuttal.

"It will have to wait for another day." I reluctantly said as things had been going well for us, but this needed to be done.

I may have been ever so slightly feeling again but the dark monster inside me was prevalent and waiting to feed. Seeing the lies spread about the so called Heartbreak Killer's capture on the news rejuvenated the darkness in me. Even when I thought I could suppress it for Alexis, I was proven to be foolish. The dark monster still haunted my heart and soul as much as I wanted it vanquished.

This has to be the last time. My future is with Alexis, I thought before I went to meet Terry. *I can't be both the Heartbreak Killer and Perry. There can only be one.*

Just then, Terry Connor walked inside the doors of the Italian House. *There she is, that evil bitch. I knew she couldn't resist my juicy information.*

Someone shouted out at Terry as she walked further inside the restaurant.

"Look its Terry Connors." Said a blubbering man. People turned to look and Terry smiled, waving at them.

What an egotistical bitch, so fake. How are these people so blind?

I had just begun to stand from my seat and wave Terry over, but she recognized me before I had the chance.

"Mr. Perry Nelson I presume?" Said Terry as she walked up to me. *Time to play the role.*

"Aw yes, and you are the beautiful Terry Connor. I didn't know if you were going to show up." I said in a charming manner. *Yes I did.*

"Well your credentials checked out and I thought, why not. If you really have the information you say you do then it's worth the trip. Plus a free meal."

"I'm certain you will be more than pleased, but first I need to be satisfied on my end of our deal. This kind of information could get me into a lot of trouble. Fired even. So what do you say, let's eat?"

"You will be more than satisfied Mr. Nelson." Said Terry with a flash of a fake smile as she touched my arm. *Her ambitions have no limits. Just as I hoped, sexual seduction.*

I quickly examined Terry as she was sitting down. She was in a low cut, skin tight, red dress. Her breast were practically popping out of the dress and jiggled with any tiny movement. Terry's hair was neat and tightly put back in a sort of pony tail as well. *They do say the devil wears red. She may very well be.*

Truth be told, though, if I had been a normal man I may have found Terry sexy, wanting to fuck her. At least I assumed sex is what she thought I wanted for this information.

The only question in my mind was would Terry bite on the sex? She had to or this night would be a failure. *I need to have her alone in a private setting. She will bite, her ambition will stop at nothing,* I assured myself. *I just need to play my cards right.*

"So, what made you come to me?" Said Terry now sitting comfortably in her chair. "Surely you had a reason. You could have contacted the police with your information. Isn't that in your legal right as a psychiatrist?"

"It is, but I felt that I could use this to my advantage and still do my civil duty as a therapist." I responded.

"Ah, a man of ambition, I had hoped for as much. I too am a person of ambition so let's get right to the point then Mr. Nelson. What do you truly want from me for this information?"

"A good time with a beautiful woman. I haven't been out in sometime, and I find you wildly attractive." I said with a grin.

"Stop the bullshit, Perry." Said Terry with venom in her words. "We both know what you really want. So why even put on this charade? Do you think I am naive to the desires of men like yourself? All any man wants is sex. You find me attractive and you want to fuck me, which is all this is."

"I honestly don't have the faintest idea what you're talking about Miss Connor." I responded in a coy fashion.

"Oh, I'm sorry, are you the one man on this planet who isn't out for sex?" Terry snapped back.

"Is that so hard to believe?" I said again in a coy tone.

"Do you think you're the first man to come into my life that has some information or some position for me? You're not, and you won't be the last. I know what you really want. Now, do you think I would actually do something like that? You must, if you would be as bold as to call me with this offensive offer."

Yes, I actually think you're an ambitious slut who will fuck any man to get you to the top, I thought with a juvenile grin.

"Well you're here now aren't you? I also know what kind of break this would be for the story and what it would do for your career." I snapped back. I was sick of her bitchy tone and face. *She doesn't want me to play games then let's go at it Connor. Two twisted evils bent against each other.* "So maybe, in fact, you should fuck me if you want this information."

Terry wasn't amused with my tone and scowled at my words.

"Calling me with some offer that may or may not be true, and thinking someone of my stature would bite is farfetched." Said Terry with a scoffing laugh. She then put her purse on the table and began to rummage through it until she found a cigarette, and placed it in her mouth with a light.

Terry took a few puffs of the toxins before she continued.

"I'm sure you are aware Perry, I am a celebrity in this tiny city. I can pull out this cigarette and smoke it without anyone saying a word to me. I can do what I want, when I want. I've earned that right. So who are you to me?"

She thinks she can play the power card on me, HA.

"Well Terry, maybe I was mistaken, you don't need this story for your career. Maybe you are happy being the face of Channel 28 News, but I always thought that you could go bigger. I was mistaken, I thought you had ambitions. Like I said on the phone, I can always give this to that pretty young news girl over at that other station."

I stood up pretending as if to leave.

"Ha, sit down," Terry said with a devilish and twisted smile. "You know Perry, you have some balls on you. Most men will fold like paper at my words. I'm a strong woman that most men quiver at. Being strong willed, I can see your strength as well. I thought maybe I could come in here and boss you around, but I see now, you won't be over powered or outwitted."

Terry reached across the table and stroked my arm with her cold hand.

Yes, your ambition blinds you, come into my web Terry Connor.

"Sorry I came at you so harshly. You know men sometimes think they can push us women around." Terry continued, still stroking her hand on me. "So what do you say, let's eat, have some drinks, and see where the night takes us."

"That's all I wanted in the first place. We will both help each other tonight." I said with another fake smile. "I promise, I am a gentleman."

"Yes, I can see that now, a handsome one as well." Terry said back with a fake smile of her own.

Two evils covered with fake masks smiling at each other, disgusting. If only she knew what was under my mask.

"So we have a deal then?" I implored.

"Yes, I think we do…but Perry." Terry said, her face turning stern and wicked.

"Yes Terry?" I said.

"If it so happens that you are lying or are trying to trick me about this information… I will have no choice but to make up a story about an obsessive therapist who stalked me. Constantly leaving me voice mails and harassing me at my house and work. Maybe even tried to forcibly have sex with me. I can see the story now, Dr. Nelson loses license after being found guilty in rape case against Channel 28 sweetheart."

I laughed, and this time I wasn't faking. *She is everything I had imagined. But now all your cards are on the table and I still have one left. It's quite the joker.*

"Oh don't you worry, I wouldn't dream of lying to Miss Terry Connor. So long as I am satisfied."

"Like I said, you will be more than satisfied. Who else can brag about going out with Terry Conner?" Her foot ascended onto my crouch and Terry began to sway up and down.

I bet half of the city if they offered you money you slut, I thought, nearly cringing at her touch.

"Now buy me a drink and let's enjoy the night." Said Terry, again grinning devilishly.

We both sat drinking for the next hour. Each talking about nonsense, both filling the others ears with lies, bullshit, and pretentious notions. I pretended to consume my drinks, but instead, dumped them into my water glass when she wasn't looking.

I needed a clear mind for my task, but I could surely act as if I was drunk, so I did. The act would make Terry feel more in control and comfortable. Hell, I wouldn't be surprised if she was doing the same thing to me. We were both as fake and manipulative as could be.

"Why don't we get out of here Mr. Nelson?" Suggested Terry. "Finish the night at my house. You can tell me about this Heartbreak Killer there. After we get more acquainted of course."

"I like the sound of that." I said back.

"Did you drive here? I don't think I can drive back after all of the drinks." Terry said with a slur.

"Why yes I did, I can take us back to your place if that's okay?"

"Ah sounds like a wonderful idea Mr. Nelson. I knew you were a gentlemen."

As we stood up, Terry put her arm in-between mine and struggled to walk by my side. I guided us out of the restaurant and to my parked car, opening the door for her.

"I love the leather seats." Said Terry as I entered the car from the driver side. She then began to rub her whole body on the seat.

"I do as well, they are easy to clean." *Clean up your blood when I slit your chest open and see if you even have a heart.*

I started the car and proceeded to leave the parking lot.

"Can we listen to some music?" Asked Terry as she again began to rub my resting arm. "You know, set the mood a bit."

"Of course," I said pushing the power button and turning the volume on the dial up.

A song had just finished on the 80's station and was followed by Don Henley's "Dirty Laundry". *How fitting of a song,* I thought

"Have you heard this song before, Terry?" I inquired.

"No I haven't, but it's not very mood setting." Terry said back.

"Oh, I think it very much is so." I said with a sharp smile as I put my hand on her thigh and gave a hard squeeze.

"Oh you like to be rough Mr. Nelson? I like." Said Terry biting her lip.

"You have no idea Miss Connor." I said grasping harder and turning the dial up with my free hand. "Now show me where you live. I can't wait to get more acquainted."

"Okay, right this way." Said Terry pointing in a dark direction.

We drove out into the night with the song blasting in the car.

It's time to take out my dirty laundry, I thought listening to the music and smiling while gripping the wheel.

Chapter 18
Stop the Press...

Terry lived outside of the densely populated inner city, on a large mountain side that overlooked the majority of the inhabitants. The community atop this mountain was gated and isolated from the less fortunate souls below. All the houses inside were massive and luxurious estates, with huge front yards and four door garages hiding expensive cars. *It pays well to be an evil bitch,* I thought as I arrived to the gates guarding the wealthy.

Terry's house was no exception to the others in the community. It had its own private gate that surrounded the perimeter. The driveway was a long and filled with loose gravel, leading to a white house with stone steps and towering white pillars in the entrance way. The front yard was spacious with neatly cut grass, hedges cut into various shapes and sizes, and a fountain that matched the all white house.

These doors have to be fifteen feet high, I thought as we walked to the front of the house. The doors were made from a maple brown wood with the engravings TC on each side, and accompanied with polished old fashion gold handles.

"Pretty impressive, huh? I guess it pays to be beautiful and famous?" Said Terry as we walked inside the massive doorway.

"It's pretty nice, a bit extravagant for my taste though. You live here alone?" I said.

"Yes I do, although I do have half of the men in the city wishing they could live here with me. I think this is more than you could have expected, is it not? And all for giving me a silly little name."

I ignored her pretentiousness.

"How about we keep this night going. I'm guessing you have something to drink?"

"Ah right to the point, I like that. Yes, through those doors to the right is the kitchen. You should see the bar once you're there. Help yourself while I get changed… into something more comfortable."

"Will do Miss Conner, don't be too long now." I said making my way in the direction Terry had pointed too.

As I walked, my darkness began to call out to me, sensing the contiguity of death at hand. This was in uncharted territory, however. I wasn't use to being an invited guest into the house of a victim, and the light in which I was exposed too was unsettling to me. *I am a man of darkness, I belong in the shadows.*

You don't need to drug Terry though, my dark monster whispered as I reached the bar. *You will easily over power her. No one can stop the Heartbreak Killer. No one can stop your darkness, not even an evil bitch like Terry. Let's see the fear in her eyes when she finds out the man she is looking for was right in front of her this whole time.*

I fiddled with the poison in my pocket as I made the drinks. It had been my plan from the start to poison Terry, but as I stood in the kitchen debating with my darkness, I felt an arrogance slip over me. *No she doesn't deserve the peaceful death of poison. Terry deserves something far worse. This is personal, I want her to suffer.*

When the thoughts settled, the drinks were left untouched from poison.

I emerged from the kitchen with two drinks in hand, and came back to the entrance of the house. Terry emerged from the top of the staircase that overlooked the doorway entrance shortly after. She wore nothing but black laced underwear and a matching black lace bra along with black heels.

"What do you say, Perry. Are you ready to start our business arrangement?" Said Terry looking down on me from the staircase.

"Yes I think I am ready for it." I said with a grave grin.

"Excellent."

Terry made her steps at a slow pace, as if she was modeling for me and letting me savor the moments of seeing her nearly naked.

Look at that ugly bitch, thinking she can sway you with sex, said my dark monster. *The Heartbreak Killer only wants one thing, the heart inside your chest.*

"I'm guessing this is everything you imagined it would be, Perry." Terry whispered in my ear as she reached me. She grabbed a drink out of my hands and took a sip. "Just remember, if you're lying to me, I'll ruin you." Terry then proceeded to lick my neck with her disgustingly dirty tongue and cupped my crotch with her free hand.

"Let me go to my car first. I forgot a condom." I said, trying to get away from her grasp.

"Ha, a condom? Why would you want one of those when you can fuck me without one? I assure you that I have my own methods of protection. I would never trust a man with such a task."

Because you're a dirty slut that would probably infect me, I thought. *That's if I was getting a condom and we were going to have sex. No, I need my knife to slit your throat.*

"I would feel more comfortable with one." I said again, deflecting her sexual advances.

"Whatever gets you off Mr. Nelson. Come upstairs once you get it, I'll be waiting in my room. You'll hear the music playing to guide you in my direction."

With that, Terry gave me a kiss on the cheek and pushed me aside, walking slowing back up the stairs.

My killing tools awaited me in the trunk of my car. Once Terry was out of sight I hustled too and began to rummage through the large quantity of items inside.

What do I need? I can't just walk into the bedroom with a knife, she could get away. No it has to subtle. I have to make sure I have her cornered before I strike. Once I located the set, I laid out my knives and picked up a small blade that could easily be hidden in my jacket pocket. *This one will have to do until I kill her,* I thought as I reached for a blade no bigger than pocketknife.

I heard the music Terry spoke of playing upstairs as I made my way back inside the house. I crept up the staircase that Terry had gone up before I exited. The hallway at the top was dark and lead down both directions. I continued to follow the sound of music to the end of the left hallway. At the end of it, there was a door slit open with a bit of light shining through.

This is it..., I thought clasped the steel end of the small knife inside my jacket. *Time to kill the Bitch of Channel 28 News.*

Slit her throat and let the blood flow. Tear this cold bitch's heart from her chest, beckoned the dark monster. *Show the city the Heartbreak Killer isn't locked up but instead alive and well. Spread the fear. Show the public that no one makes a fool of the Heartbreak Killer.*

I pushed the door open with a soft touch of my hand.

As the door opened, Terry was laying in the center of a large bed with her legs spread. The sheets below her were as red as blood, with black laced frill at the ends, and her initials sewn into the pillows. The lights were dim, only lit by burning lavender scented candles.

"Making me wait, Perry. Tisk, tisk, tisk." Said Terry in a promiscuous tone and she rose from the bed. "Don't be scared, I won't bite."

I had my hand inside my jacket pocket, clutching at the steel blade. The dark monster was ready to feast on her blood.

She is coming to you, do it, kill her. KILL HER, demanded the monster.

Terry was within feet of me and I could feel the darkness swirling inside me as it always had. I began to pull the knife from the pocketed sheath, but Terry grabbed my arm before I could reveal it completely.

"Get comfortable Perry, take off your jacket and clothes. Here, take this drink, we don't want cold feet now. I know it can be intimidating sleeping with a celebrity of my stature."

I was forced to let go of the knife as Terry peeled off my jacket. She then threw it behind her head, towards the bed. My eyes widened as the jacket flew. The knife dislodged out of the pocket, then skating on the hard wood, and resting underneath the bed frame. I looked to Terry, but she hadn't noticed.

"You seem tense, I'll help you undress." Terry said, loosening my tie and unbuttoned my shirt and throwing both clothing items behind her.

A new song began to play on the radio and Terry seemed to take notice.

"This is more to the mood wouldn't you say?" Said Terry starting to dance around me in a strange and sexual fashion. She slapped my ass with her hand and bit on my ear. "I want you to make me bleed. Fuck me until I can't walk." She whispered.

This bitch is crazier than me, I thought.

Terry appeared back in front of me, grasping at my belt, and un-notching the hinged latch. When she managed to unhook the latch, she pulled the belt from the loops of my pants and both items fell to the floor.

Terry then bent over, sticking her backside into my groin and began to gyrated around.

"Get on the bed." Terry said after a moment, grasping my wrist. She yanked me to the edge of the bed and pushed me flat on top. "Stay, I'll be right back." She said and exited the room.

I jolted up from the bed upon her exit. *This is my chance. I need that knife.*

I crouched down to search under the bed, but it was dark and hard to see anything of distinction. *Hurry, she will be here any moment.* I put my hand out to feel around, but it was useless, I couldn't feel the knife out. *Shit.* I stuck my head under the frame again and a flicker of light reflected off the steel and into my eye. *There it is, at the end of the left side of the bed, near that nightstand.*

I stood up again and raced toward the end of the bed.

"I told you to stay put Mr. Nelson." Said Terry from behind.

I froze. "Uh…" Is all I managed to get out.

"Get back on the bed you bad boy."

Terry shoved me onto the bed again. As I fell, I felt her grab at my wrist and then something cold and hard latched around it. *What the hell is she doing?* I heard a clicking noise and when Terry had stood up from me, she had handcuffed my left wrist to a post of the bed.

"What the hell are you doing?" I demanded.

"Now… You're going to tell me about this patient of yours. His name, where he lives, what he looks like, the works. And if you don't… I am going to hurt you." Said Terry with a wicked smile.

"You crazy bitch, what about our deal?"

"Fuck your deal. Do you really think I would sleep with someone like you? Some pathetic creep who thinks he can bribe women for sex? I can manipulate you men so easily. When sex is offered, you all lose your wits."

I shook and pulled at the handcuff, but nothing budged. I was stuck, a caged animal.

SHE DARE DEFIE YOU, screamed the dark monster inside me.

I let out a yell of rage and shook the cuff even more, trying to break free.

Terry went to her dresser drawer and pulled out a small razor blade.

I stopped struggling when I say the razor. *I underestimated her, my arrogance blinded me. I should have just poisoned her,* I thought.

"So, do you want to do this the easy way or the hard way Mr. Nelson?" Said Terry grazing the razor to the palm of her hand.

If I can just reach the knife. It's right below me.

"I want the hard way bitch." I said, spitting at her. I began to flail again, trying to break away. A deranged monster who had been chained. I was enraged that I had been bested. *No one bests me, I am the one who bests you.*

Get the knife Perry. Kill the evil bitch, demanded the monster.

"Whatever you want." Said Terry reaching for my leg.

I tried kicking her as she advanced, but I missed wide from doing any damage. Terry managed to pin my leg down just long enough and slashed me with the razor, cutting the back of my calf. *AHHH,* I thought, but I didn't let her hear my scream. My cut leg jerked away, managing to kick Terry in the face and she stumbled back.

"This can all be over if you just tell me and then you can be on your way." Said Terry with a smile that would send shivers to the bones. "It's not worth all this fuss. It's just a name, what can you do with it? Look, here is the key." She pulled the key from her black laced underwear, dangling it in front of me. "Just tell me and you're free."

I reached down to the floor with my right hand, desperately grasping under the bed for the knife. *Come on where is it.*

"You think you're going to find something to hit me with under there? Hahaha." Terry manically laughed. "I'm not stupid like you, I thought ahead. So tell me or I'll cut you until you bleed out."

Come on where is it. My hand went back and forth on the cold wood floor.

"You better cut me some place it hurts, because you're never getting this information from me." I roared.

"Maybe I'll cut you on your pretty little face. Leave some scars so you can always remember Terry Connor." She mocked.

Kill her Perry. Rip her heart out. She mocks you thinking you're trapped, we have one more card though. Find the knife.

"Come try me you bitch." I snarled.

Terry descended onto me.

I made one more stretch with my hand under the bed, patting frantically. *HERE,* I thought, feeling the steel knife in my hand. But

Terry swiped at me before I could strike, gashing my side, and this time I let out a grown as Terry stepped back once more.

"Tell me, now." Demanded Terry.

"That's all you've got, I couldn't even feel it. Come give me more." I mocked back, now grasping the blade in my hand under the bed.

"I have more for you hunny. You don't scare me, you're a pathetic, lonely, nothing. I am Terry Connor, I run this town and that's how it is. Men want to fuck me and women want to be me."

Terry made a swift move towards me with the razor blade, trying to gash my face.

NOW KILL HER, screamed the dark monster.

In one swift motion, I took the knife in my hand from under the bed and plunged it forward. The small steel blade pierced through Terry's belly, spilling a waterfall of blood to the floor.

I looked up at her face. Horror now filled her eyes as she tried to speak.

"It was yo…" Was all Terry managed to get out as blood gushed from her mouth as she tried to speak.

"Yes me. I'm the Heartbreak Killer you evil bitch." I said with a grin of death and darkness. "And one way or another, I said I was going to fuck you tonight." I roared with might.

I ripped the blade from Terry's gut and tossed it up into the air. I caught it again in my free hand, and within a blink of an eye with all of my force, I jammed the bloodied blade into the side of her neck.

Blood sprayed in all directions, covering the walls, the bed, the floor, and me. Terry flopped onto the floor next to me. Her eye twitched and then nothing more. *Good riddance you evil media spewing bitch.*

Terry Connor was finally canceled.

I felt around Terry's bloody body for the key, finding it in her lifeless hand. I unlocked myself and headed for my car, dripping in blood.

The darkness was feasting inside my mind all the while. Feasting on the blood bath of Terry's corpse.

I found my black bag inside the trunk and filled it with everything I needed to clean up the bloody scene. Once I had everything packed, I went back to the room.

What a mess, I thought surveying the room. *All because I didn't want to do it the easy way. I hope you're happy.*

Blood festered on the floor and splattered all the way to the top of the ceiling. Some of the blood on the ceiling was dripping back down to the floor, making a small puddle. The blood on the wall was gradually dribbling down as well. *What a beautiful scene. Too bad no one will see it.*

I dropped my black bag to the floor and put on my cleaning gloves. *Better get to work.*

First I placed a wide sheet of plastic wrap onto the floor. I grabbed Terry's dead body and dragged her onto the plastic sheeting. Then for hours I scrubbed the room with oxidized bleach, occasionally turning the lights off and scanning with a black light to see what stains still resided and needed to be cleaned over. When the stains had vanished, I snatched the sheets from the bed and wrapped them into some plastic, tucking the remains into the bag.

When I was satisfied with the work inside the room, I went to the hallway, the stairs, and any other place I may have dripped blood while I went to get my things. This was a faster clean, with only a few droplets scattered about the area.

When all the blood was cleaned to my liking, I turned my attention to Terry.

A clock read *1:34 a.m.* inside Terry's room. I had time but I needed to hurry. I took out a surgical blade and began cutting into Terry's chest. *Let's see if someone so evil even has a heart,* I thought, anxious to see.

Twenty minutes of cutting into her flesh, I reached the heart. Forcing my hand into the open wound, I grasped the heart and yanked it from Terry's chest. I almost expected the heart to be as black as coal, dried up, and shriveled. But to my surprise, as I held it to my eyes for examination, the heart seemed similar to the other woman's. *Maybe a heart can't be blacked by darkness.*

Before I finished, I took the knife and extracted a piece from the heart in my hand, putting the severed flesh into a plastic bag and sticking the remainder of it back into Terry's chest cavity.

Yes, the heart you desire. Isn't it beautiful, said my darkness, as I gazed at the piece of heart in the baggie.

I need to clean off, I thought after a moment of staring. I found a shower to rinse the blood from my body and face. The soap stung the wounds Terry had left me as I cleaned, making me wince in discomfort of pain.

Once I was clean and bandaged, I put on new clothes that I had brought, and made my way back to the room Terry's corpse resided in.

Looking around, I remembered that I had forgotten to take the cuffs and glasses that surely had my DNA on them. I grabbed both and stuffed them into my black bag. Before I left the room for good, I turned the light off one last time, scanning the room for any rouge spots of blood, but nothing was to be seen. *Good work Perry, a real pro.*

Turning the light back on I focused on Terry. "I'm not done with you yet... Not by a long shot." I wrapped her lifeless body up in plastic, making sure none of the blood leaked to the floor. "You're coming with me." I said and dragged the corpse through the hallway and down the stairs *Thump, Thump, Thump.*

Before I dragged the body outside, I backed my car to the steps leading to the front door. *It's probably good to carry a dead body the least amount of distance.* I dragged Terry the remaining distance and threw her lifeless body into the trunk, covering the remaining evidence with a large quilted blanket.

I rushed back inside for my other things while scanning for droplets of blood that may have leaked from the plastic. *All Clean.*

Taking one last glance at the inside of the house from the front door, I shouted out. "Goodbye Terry," and closed the fifteen foot wooden doors behind me.

I hopped in my car. *Wait I need one more thing,* I thought and ran back inside. I grabbed Terry's car keys off a nearby table at the entrance. "Fuck you Terry," I yelled again before slamming the doors.

I went off into the darkness with Terry Connor's corpse rattling in my trunk. A certain satisfaction overcame me while I drove. I had just ended a creator of evil, ridding the city of poison and despair for a time. *Even though they won't think of it that way. I will be labeled the bad guy, once more.*

"Last stop, Terry." I said, getting out of my car as I reached the final destination. I stared up at a large building in front of me for a moment and exhaled. *What a night.*

My watch read, *2:51 a.m.* Again, I peered upon the building standing in front of me, seeing the large white numbers two and eight placed on the top. *I have to hurry, it will be day time soon.*

I glanced around the area to make sure the coast was clear. *Good, time to show the city the Heartbreak Killer is free.*

Chapter 19
... *Breaking News*

The sky was colored grey from clouds and winter air as the dawn rose, revealing the atrocity for the public to see.

People from all floors of a large company building stared across the street. Flashing lights of police and medical alike had just arrived, drawing more attention as they parked their cars on the curbs of the street and attempting to make a blockade to secure the area. Civilians walking from all corners of the street blocks began to flock to the commotion.

As the curious masses gathered and realized what was afoot their faces began to sour, gazing onto a horrific sight.

"Get back, get back." Police yelled as they tried to set a perimeter between them and the growing crowd.

The faint sound of a helicopters propeller could be heard in the distance. Gradually, it became more distinct to the ears of everyone around the scene, *womp, womp womp*. When the helicopter reached the destination, it began to circle the building and a news woman and camera man positioned themselves for a clean shot above.

Other media outlets arrived seconds after.

Van after van, the media poured in. Some were local, others were from out of town. All of them began to set up around the perimeter, pushing people out of the way so they could capture a clean shot.

The mood around became a buzz with the murmurs from the crowd of what was transpiring.

"Breaking. Breaking. Breaking. Breaking. Breaking news." Various reporters shouted into the cameras as soon as they were in position.

"We are live at the Channel 28 News Station, where this morning was met with a horrific event." Continued one of the stations reporter.

The live cameras focused in on the scene at hand, broadcasting it to the masses.

A woman was chained by each limb to large white numbers, two and eight. Her body was painted in blood and her head hung down on her chest. The chest and stomach of the woman were carved open, reveling the inside contents of her mutilated body. Damaged organs dangled out of the cavity, lightly moving with the cold wind.

Men with ladders and bolt cutters made their way to the woman, trying to shake her free from the entrapment of bound chains. They rattled and pulled but the woman would not budge from her imprisonment. The men then cut into the bolts, trying to set the woman free.

All the while the media was rolling the footage as the events played out.

Each man stood in position as the chains began to break. Ready to catch the woman as she fell. Another clamp of a bolt and the body fell down, but the weight of the woman was underestimated, knocking over one of the men and falling down several stories of the Channel 28 News Station.

The crowd let out a gasp as the body plummeted and splatted to the snowy ground.

"We have just received this news." Announced a woman reporter as she heard the word through her earpiece. "The woman appears to be Ter…" But the woman could say no more, pacing off to the side, and pushing the camera away from her.

"The woman chained atop the building has been identified as local Channel 28's own, Terry Conner." Said another man to his viewers.

The mass of civilians huddled around the reporters heard the identification. Some gasped, some started crying, some passed the word to the back of the crowd, and one ran for a trash bin throwing up from the sight and news.

The buzz began to grow.

The news crew inside the helicopter zoomed their cameras off of Terry's mutilated body as they spotted red on the otherwise white snowy ground in front of the Channel 28 News building. The camera had picked up on what appeared to be a giant heart made up of red clothing with one side of the heart flipped upside down and broken off.

"It looks to be a fifty, no bigger than that. It's a broken heart, made up of what appears to me to be red clothing. One side of the heart seems to be flipped upside down." Said the woman in the helicopter to her viewers.

Word of the heart reached the ground and reporters began to spread the news to their viewers.

The buzz grew even more as everyone searched for a shot of this gigantic broken and twisted heart.

As the news passed within the crowd, each individual began to murmur "Heartbreak Killer, Heartbreak Killer, Heartbreak Killer." And the stench of fear rose in the crowd. The killer was still at large.

"He's back," said an old man to his wife as he watched the news from his home.

"Who is?" Asked his wife.

"The Heartbreak Killer. The police got the wrong man. He killed that Conner woman."

"Terry Conner? Isn't she that really sweet and beautiful one on the Channel 28 News Station? What kind of monster would want to hurt her?"

The story spread like wildfire as the media licked their chops on the titillating story. Spreading it from town to town, city to city, all across America. In hours, the story of the Heartbreak Killer had become national news and millions of new Americans were contaminated with fear. The headline "Heartbreak Killer murders news celebrity and sweetheart, Terry Connor."

"We are fucked Fisher." Said the Captain. "Not only does everyone in this city know we don't have the Heartbreak Killer, now the whole damn country does too. I just got a call from the head of the FBI, they are headed our way."

"Why would they come all this way for a couple of murders?" Said Paul sitting in a chair inside the Captains office.

"Because Fisher, no one gives two shits if some nobodies die. That happens all the time, but when a celebrity dies people all around freak out. Especially when it's a murder from an unknown serial killer who has the balls to leaves the spectacle for the public to see."

"She was a glorified news anchor, barely a celebrity. It's ridiculous, people are up in arms over some woman with nice tits and a pretty face who brought them their nightly news? But before, when four other women were found dead, we were handling our jobs admirably."

"Don't be naive Fisher, people are idiots. They view celebrities as some kind of demigods. Regardless of what kind of list celebrity Terry was, she got men hard from her beauty and women jealous of her success and looks. Just because she was a pain in our asses doesn't mean people thought of her as we did."

"So what now? Am I supposed to give up this case to some jerkoff FBI agent?"

"There is no other option, the Heartbreak Killer has become a national headline. They don't think we can do the job alone anymore."

"You expect me to just step down? I have been busting my ass trying to catch the killer. I risked my life to bring in Minks even if he wasn't the Heartbreak Killer."

"My hands are tied Paul. Those FBI agents will come in and take over, you can either help them or step down."

"Bullshit," said Paul and he stormed from the Captains office, slamming the door behind him.

"Get back here Fisher, that's an order... Fisher." Yelled the Captain through the walls.

Paul ignored the words, leaving the station in a rage.

"AHHHHH," Paul screamed inside his car, pounding and shaking his steering wheel with his hands. "You are ruining my life."

Midday brought in the FBI. Men in suits filed into the police station. Some were carrying bags, others carried boxes.

"Who's in charge here?" Said a woman dressed in a royal blue pants suit and black heels. The woman had caramel hair tied in a tightly knit ponytail behind her head. "I am FBI Agent Price, sent here to head the investigation on Heartbreak Killer case."

One of the men in the police station pointed toward the direction of the Captain's office. The FBI agent gave a nod and made her way in that direction.

"You must be the FBI agent." Said the Captain as Agent Price entered the room. "To be honest I was expecting a…"

"A man?" Said Agent Price.

"Yes a man, but it really makes no difference to me. I'm sure you're a fine agent. Agent…?"

"Agent Nina Price, and you must be the Captain of this precinct."

"Correct." Said the Captain reaching his hand out over the desk.

Agent Price politely met the handshake. "Just in case it does make a difference, you should know I finished in the top of my class, ahead of those men." Agent Price said in a sharp voice.

"I don't doubt it. With a case getting as big as this I am sure the federal government would send one of their best."

"All the men on this case seem incompetent of finding this Heartbreak Killer, anyways. It could use a woman's touch." Said Agent Price seemingly ignoring the Captains words. "What's it been now four women found dead inside their homes?"

"Five actually with Connor's this morning."

"Five women, hmm. I read this Connor's woman was quite popular around here. Even known nationally."

"Indeed, I'm sure the public was fond of her, but personally, Miss Connor wasn't respected around this station."

"Why is that?"

"Let's just say she was relentless to getting any story she could from us, basically harassing us for information. A real pain in the ass, but what can you do. It's the medias job to get stories out."

"Ha, the big bad police force terrorized by a journalist?" Said Agent Price, cracking a smile.

"Laugh all you want but Terry Connor was a different breed."

"A strong woman that didn't put up with the bullshit? She sounds like someone I could have befriended. But enough small talk, let's get to the killer. Debrief me on the details so I can get started."

"I only know some of the details, I think you're better off talking to Detective Fisher. He was heading this case before you came here."

"Well call him in." Demanded Agent Price.

"I would if he was here, but he left. He didn't take the news of you coming here well."

"I bet he will be less happy when he sees that a woman is taking over."

"I doubt much could make Paul Fisher more depressed than he already is."

"What to do you mean?"

"Well… Detective Fisher has been dealing with… Personal issues. I don't feel like I should go any further into it than that with some FBI agent I just met though. Just know that he has been in a darker place lately."

"Noted. Where can I find him?"

"That's a good question. I would check the bar down the block first and then his house. I'll give you the addresses."

"An alcoholic cop, how stereotypical. This should be a pleasant introduction." Said Agent Price with a sarcastic chuckle.

"Listen Agent Price, you may be an FBI agent but don't come into my precinct with your arrogance. I'll have you know Detective Fisher is a great detective and he was busting his ass before you got here."

"Sorry Captain, I didn't mean to offend you. I'm sure he is. It's just a cliché, an alcoholic cop. Lighten up a bit."

"I'm grinning from ear to ear, can't you tell?" Said the Captain with a cold stare.

"Yes I can tell this place is filled with the cheeriest of company. Where can my investigation team place our equipment?"

"I'll have some of my men clear some space for you."

"Very well then, I guess I will go track down Mr. Fisher now." Said Agent Price, sticking her hand out once more for a handshake. The Captain looked displeased, but obliged with the gesture.

Leaving the Captains office, Agent Price signaled one of the agents to come with her, leaving the rest to sort through boxes and find office space.

Agent Price checked the nearby bar first. A couple of men were inside having drinks and shooting pool. However, in her steadfast rush, Agent Price realized she had forgotten to ask about Detective Fishers appearance. So she had no choice but to announce herself.

"Is there a Detective Fisher here?" Said Nina Price. The men stared at her blankly and shrugged. "Nobody? Okay then."

Leaving the bar, Agent Price headed for the home address the Captain had given her.

She arrived expecting the house to be dreary and rundown due to the image the Captain had created for her about Detective Fisher. However, she was pleasantly surprised to see his house was well kept, with a new coat of paint on the trim and various trees and bushes in the yard all covered in snow.

"Wait here, I will just be a moment." Said Agent Price to the companioning agent as she exited the car.

Nina climbed the stairwell filled with ice and snow and gave a brief knock on the door. A minute passed and no one had answered the door. She knocked again, this time with more conviction. "Detective Fisher, I'm FBI Agent Price. I was sent here to help with the Heartbreak case."

A shadowy figure emerged through the opaque glass. The door swung open and out popped a man that Agent Price assumed was Detective Fisher.

He was taller than Nina, with straggly medium brown hair, and baggy eyes. The man had the appearance of someone who had just woken from a coma.

"What do you want?" Said the man with a gruff tone.

"Detective Fisher?" Asked Agent Price.

"Yeah and you must be the FBI Agent taking over my job." Said Paul.

"I am Agent Nina Price and I'm here to help so we can catch this killer before all of America fears for their lives. The Heartbreak Killer has not only become a threat to the people of this city but to people all over the country now."

"Help as in take all of the glory for yourself after I have been busting my ass and done a lot of the heavy lifting to catch the killer. I'm sorry, but I don't think I want to waste my time getting screwed over like you FBI agents love to do, every so often. Good luck though, you'll need it. This killer is as elusive as they come." Said Paul.

"Are you really going to be that prideful? You think I will take the credit for this? I am a fair woman, not some greedy and ambitious FBI agent. This has nothing to do with credit for me. I want the people of this country to feel safe, just like you."

"Oh is that so, then why did it take the death of some proclaimed celebrity to command your attention. You don't give a damn about the people, you give a damn about the recognition this case is receiving now. That's why you're here, to puff out your chest when the public is watching so you guys look like heroes."

"Detective, it has only just now come to our agencies attention. Plus, we only deal with high end national cases, not local. A couple of deaths are hardly worth the FBI's time, but when a story gets put into the spotlight with such brutality and then shown to the public we have to step in."

"I was unaware that the killer had gone national, but what do I know I'm incompetent, right. At least you FBI agents seem to think that's the case. That's why your here right? You think a police force can't handle the job of the quote on quote real cases."

"I am here because people caught wind of the death of Terry Connor, and it became a national story. Therefore on our radar. I don't know what it is with males and their pride. You can never just take some assistance, always wanting to do it the hard way. I promise you though; you will get just as much credit as I do if we catch the Heartbreak Killer."

"If… If we catch him Agent."

"I'm confident with the help of us and our resources, it's only a matter of time before we do."

Paul Fisher began to laugh. "You are so confident in yourself, huh. We will see just how confident you are after you look over the files. This isn't some run of the mill killer."

"Will you help me or not? I think this case can benefit both of us, and working together will only strengthen our efforts. Your Captain spoke highly of you and I don't doubt your abilities as a detective."

"I will think about it Agent…"

"Price." Said Nina.

"Agent Price. Be at the police station at nine a.m. sharp to discuss the case with me. Depending on how our meeting goes I may or may not continue to help in the investigation. I haven't decided yet."

"Great, I think you will find working with me to be a pleasant surprise." Said Agent Price reaching her hand out to Paul.

Paul looked down but did not shake Agent Prices hand.

"Well you didn't disappoint the Captains description of a pleasant man." Said Agent Price. Paul scowled at her remark and with that, Nina Price turned away, heading for the running car.

"Oh, Agent Price." Shouted Paul.

"Yes?" Said Nina Price turning just before she reached the car.

"Lock your doors and hold a gun tight tonight. I hear the Heartbreak Killer has a preference of tall women in ugly suits."

Chapter 20
Mysterious Gifts & Surprising Questions

A certain peace had overcome me with the death of Terry Connor at my hands. My darkness was silent and satisfied. Even better was the part of me that felt a sense of heroism for saving the unknowing city from such a poisonous and lying tongue. *She poisoned enough minds for one lifetime.*

However, my plan to show the city my twisted work proved to be a bit too fruitful. Not only had I been successful in letting the people know that I was alive and well, but now the nation was on notice.

Even though raising awareness with the people was what I set out to do, the notorious fame I had received wasn't as rewarding as I had anticipated. Instead, I found I wasn't as concerned with being the monster, basking in fame I once was. Alexis made sure of that, and the thoughts of her attempting to regain my human qualities were now at the forefront of mind. But even with darkness silenced for now, I had a concerning sense in the back of my mind that one day come it would come back and whisper the call of death into my ear.

Thoughts of Alexis often crept into my mind when we were apart, filling the space my dark monster had occupied. Her beauty, her wit, her pure and innocent personality. It was all so refreshing to be around, being the man of once complete darkness. *I wondered if she thinks of me, or is even interested in someone like me. I sure hoped as much.*

For our third date Alexis decided that she wanted to go ice-skating.

"Perry please, it will be fun, I promise." Alexis had begged over the phone.

I, on the other hand, was skeptical to the idea of ice-skating. I hadn't skated since I was a teenager and feared of falling all over the place. Further embarrassing myself in front of Alexis. *A fear of embarrassment, how new.*

"Perry it's the holiday season and ice skating is a tradition during the winter time. I promise I won't laugh if you fall." Alexis had said, and it was a valid point, so I agreed to go.

The skating had turned into a pleasant surprise for me.

The rink itself had quite a view in the heart of the downtown area. Surrounded by large buildings, all of which had windows filled with different colored Christmas lights. Inside the rink, were decorated stockings, wreaths, wrapped presents, and at one end towered a hundred foot Christmas tree. Decorated with lights, ornaments, and a shining star at the tip that could be seen from a mile away in any direction.

As for the skating, I found myself to be more graceful than I had anticipated. At first, I struggled to obtain my balance, even grabbing Alexis's arm once to stop me from falling. But after a few minutes with the blades on the ice I managed to catch my feet and glided with Alexis by my side. I felt carefree as I did, I was alive again.

I became a little too cocky with my movement after a while. Trying to accelerate after Alexis when she said she could beat me in a race. Soon after we took off I fell on my ass and rolled on the ice. Alexis attempted to cover her mouth to stop from giggling, but the laughter came pouring out. After I stood to my feet, I chased after her but she was too graceful on the skates, leaving me far behind her. *She looks like a beautiful figure skater performing in a crowd,* I thought as I chased behind.

When we grew weary of the skating, we decided to make our way to a little coffee house for hot chocolate to warm up.

There we talked and laughed together. Slowly I became more confident in my new found self. *She is really something else. Bubump,* my heart thumped in my chest as I gazed at Alexis from across the table. I hoped that with each flicker of these feelings a little less of the blackness would pollute around my heart.

When the date was over and we parted ways, all I could do was think of Alexis. I sat in my bed and daydreamed. *Maybe I should text her goodnight? No that's too desperate. I'll wait for her to text me. I really want to though. No, I shouldn't.*

After twenty minutes of waiting impatiently for a text to come I become discouraged. *Maybe she doesn't feel the same as I do,* I thought before I drifted off to sleep.

Again the white room haunted my dreams.

This time Alexis stood inside the room, greeting me with a smile. She had a brush in her hand, its bristles covered in white paint as her body glowed in a radiant light. I watched as Alexis began to paint the white room, further brightening the color.

"I came to help you paint." Alexis said to me after a moment.

"Paint what?" I said confused. "The walls are already white."

"No they aren't, look." Alexis said, pointing at the black tar oozing out of creases of the walls.

"That's impossible," I said in disbelief.

"Black is always the hardest to paint over Perry. Didn't you know that? It takes multiple coats before it's totally gone."

I stood watching in amazement. Little by little, stroke by stroke, Alexis managed to cover up some of the black tar with her white paintbrush. The task at hand appeared impossible to complete as a new blotch would appeared just as another was covered, but after a while she managed to cover up most of the blackness with the paint.

Turning back to me when the task was completed, Alexis gave me another smile and the steadfast glow she was emanating brightened and blinded my eyes. I yelled out to Alexis, fearing she had left me alone in the room like all the women before.

But out of the brightness Alexis's hand reached out to me, landing softly on my tense shoulder. Her face appeared inches away from mine, and her ocean blue eyes sparkling like sapphires.

Alexis preceded to whisper something into my ear but the words sounded of gibberish.

"What?" I whispered back, but before Alexis could respond the black oozing tar gushed out from the walls, flooding the room and attaching itself to my body. The blackness began to drag me to the floor, attempting to drown me with its filth. I screamed for help but instead I began to choke on the thick tar. *Alexis,* I thought as I drowned in the white and black room.

I shot up from my bed in another cold sweat. *It was just a dream.* I exhaled, slicking my damp hair back and wiping the sweat from my brow.

Soft light peeked through a slit in my blinds, landing on the wall safe where my heart trophy resided. I had just added a new member to the exclusive club of hearts, which now formed what would be a third of a human's heart.

What was she whispering to me? I began to wonder while I gazed at my safe door.

My phone buzzed on the nightstand and diverted my attention and train of thought. It was a text from Alexis, reading, *good morning*. My heart flickered as I read. *She thought of me*, I thought.

Another text came in from Alexis.

So I had this idea. Since we have gone out a few times I thought it would be fun to get you a Christmas present. If you're okay with that. I am in the full-fledged Christmas spirit!

A present? For me? I hadn't received one of those since I became an emotionally deprived monster. *Monsters didn't think about presents... Is it normal for people who have been out to exchange presents?* I had trouble comprehending the concept, but after a second or two, I remembered that I was the one who had no clue about how normal people acted to each other in a dating relationship.

I wrote back, *that sounds wonderful*, and waited for a reply.

Okay, replied Alexis and added, *if you aren't busy on Christmas Eve I'd like to give you it then.*

I am never busy on holidays, killers are known loners.

Perfect I don't have big plans, I replied.

Suddenly I realized what our agreement meant. *I can't possible come empty handed. What do women even want?* Thinking back to when I was normal, I tried to remember what kind of gift I would have purchased for my old girlfriends. Then it hit me, *women are impossible to shop for, even for men with a degree of competency for relationships. I'm doomed.*

Christmas Eve was only a few days away, so I made it my soul mission to find the perfect gift for the perfect woman.

Wasn't it only a month earlier I went out fake shoe shopping, pretending to have no idea what I was doing for a woman I wanted to kill? Now I was shopping for real, for this same woman, and I still didn't have a clue what to get... What the fuck.

An intensive shopping debate raged in my head as I searched for the perfect gift. *Shoes? No Perfume... No something else, maybe clothes. Cheap or expensive. It has to be perfect. I'm doomed.* The longer I debated, the more the thoughts began to drive me insane. *Just like the women had before.*

I was at my end as I departed from a fifth store empty handed. *There is nothing worthy of that beautiful woman. Time to head home.* But as if divine intervention had heard my inner struggles, a glimmer of ruby red light hit the corner of my eye.

A small jewelry store that I hadn't noticed before stood across the street. Inside the window was a silver necklace with a ruby red heart attached to the end. Intrigued, I made my way to get a closer look.

The rubies sparkled in front of me as I planted my face to the window. *It's perfect in so many different ways,* I thought, gazing at the jewelry piece.

The heart piece on the necklace had an eerie resemblance to the heart I drew for my victims. *The broken and twisted heart, but this one seems to be put back together. Could someone have seen the one below Terry and taken it for their own already?*

I decided to go inside the shop to inquire about the necklace. A single woman with white hair and wrinkled skin stood inside, greeting me with a yellow and crooked smile.

"Welcome young man." The woman said softly.

"I came in to see about that heart shaped necklace in the window." I said looking around the store. The inside was dreary, dirty, and so dimly lit, I wondered how anyone could see any of the jewelry without pressing their face to the glass as I had outside. *Not a very welcoming place,* I thought. Even more curious was the fact the inside was nothing but cluttered with junk and odd items. *What sort of place is this?*

"Ah, I see, very curious." Said the old woman. She stepped off something from behind the desk, and shrunk down a full foot.

"What's curious?" I responded.

The old woman did not answer. Instead, she ever so slowly limped her way to the necklace at the front of the window. I asked again but the woman continued to ignore me, holding the necklace up to my face.

As I gazed at the ruby heart, I became mesmerized and drifted back to the night I held a victims heart in my hand. I had gazed at that blood dripping heart with such fixation, such desire. *You are so lucky to feel, to have a heart,* I had thought to the dead woman with midnight black hair. I wanted nothing more than to have my own then.

The flash of memory disappeared, leaving me with the sight of the ruby red heart necklace I was now holding in the palm of my hand. *This represents something different than the other. Giving instead of taking, maybe I am changing back after all. Even if my heart is gone I can metaphorically give one to Alexis.*

"How much?" I asked the old woman.

"It's not for sale." She said, walking back to her desk.

"Not for sale? How could that be?"

"Some things can't be bought with money. Is that so hard to conceive?"

"What's the price then?"

"There is no price. Take the necklace, it's always been yours."

"I don't understand… What kind of store is this?"

"You mustn't worry Perry, the necklace is yours. Now be gone."

"How do you…" I began to say, but the old lady smiled her crooked teeth and turned away, heading to a room in the back of the store.

I looked back to the necklace in my hand. *What does she mean, always been mine? How does she know my name?* I called out to the woman once more but there was no answer, so I clenched the necklace in my fist and exited out of the store.

As I walked to my car, I wondered if what I had just experienced was even real or all just a dream. It all happened in such a bizarre flash. *What was with that woman?* Whatever her reasoning was for giving me the necklace, I had found the perfect gift for Alexis Fisher. Still, the thought of what had transpired lingered in haunting fashion.

Christmas Eve came abruptly after my bizarre experience. With it brought along anxiety to present Alexis with the now somewhat mysterious, ruby red heart necklace. Before I went to exchange gifts, I placed the necklace in a shoebox I had stored in the closet, and wrapped it up in a simple red paper with white bow on top.

Alexis informed me beforehand that she could only meet for thirty minutes or so because she and Detective Fisher were going to dinner. Stating it was some sort of tradition she had forgotten about. The task of gift shopping and dates with Alexis had me completely forget about Detective Fisher and his search for me. *I wonder how that is going after the whole Terry Connor incident.*

We arranged to meet at the service station where I had discovered Alexis's identity some time ago.

I sat in my usual seat by the fire and ordered a coffee as I waited. The service station had been dressed up with Christmas decorations since the last time I visited. Usually, I was numb to the Christmas spirit, but tonight it seemed more enjoyable to me. *Maybe it's because I have someone to share it with.*

Alexis arrived minutes after me with a rectangular box, wrapped in light blue wrapping paper with designs of smiling snowmen and snowflakes. Alexis herself wore large brown boots, black leggings, a white wool sweater, a black scarf, and a matching black beanie. *She looks beautiful as always.*

"Perry!" Alexis said when she saw me.

"Hey Alexis," I said with a smile.

"I'm so happy to see you."

"Me too." *I think? I'm still getting use to these feelings.* Alexis gave me a hug as I stood to greet her and then proceeded to sit down next to me on the couch by the fire.

"I'm sorry I can only stay for such a short time. I know I asked you to make plans with me, but I totally spaced about our family tradition of going out on Christmas Eve. Plus, my Dad isn't doing too well without my mom around. Especially now that it's the holidays."

"It's okay, I have some family things I have to go too as well." I lied.

"Well then it works out for both of us. Anyways, here is your present." Alexis said brimming with the same excitement she had at the door. "I hope you like it."

I looked down at the wrapped present, wondering what it could be.

"Well open it silly. I'm excited to see your reaction." Said Alexis.

I began to tear the snowman wrapping paper. When I reached the box, I stopped to look up at Alexis face. She was grinning from ear to ear and her eyes were sparkling ocean blue.

Opening the top of the box, I glanced inside. There, resided a pair of light brown dress shoes with black laces and tongue.

"I know how you like to dress nice and we met at a shoe store, so I thought it was a perfect gift." Said Alexis while I pulled one shoe out to examine it in the light. "They should be the right size, I remembered from when we went ice skating. Size thirteen, right?"

"Yeah that's my size." I said still looking at the shoe. *She noticed I dress nice. My size too. Wow.*

"Do you not like them?" Alexis asked.

"No, I do. I just didn't know…"

"Know what?"

"Nothing, I'm not use to getting gifts is all. They're perfect Alexis, thank you." My heart thumped inside my chest and I let free a smile. A real smile, I was happy. *I think? Is this happy?*

"I almost forgot, I brought you something as well." I said as I reached under the couch to where I had hid the present and placed it near her.

"You didn't." Said Alexis putting her hand to her lips. "Oh Perry, you didn't have too. That's so sweet." Her face turned flush, matching the red wrapping paper now resting on her lap. "What is it?" She said looking up at me.

"Open it, you'll see." I said.

Nervous thoughts crept in as I watched Alexis unwrap the present. *I'm doomed, she will hate it. I should have stuck to being a serial killer.* A droplet of sweat began to roll down my neck as Alexis finished unwrapping.

"You did not," She said interrupting my thoughts.

"What?" I responded hoarsely.

"Shoes, we both got each other shoes?"

"Shoes?" I said bewildered. *That's right I wrapped the necklace in a shoe box.* "Oh no look inside."

As Alexis did, more sweat dribbled down the back of my neck. Her mouth began to open and her eyes widened as she looked inside. *I knew it she hates it, I'm doomed.*

"Oh my god Perry." Alexis said still peeking into the box.

Even worse she figured out I'm the Heartbreak Killer. I'm an idiot, a heart necklace from a creepy mystery store? Only he would buy something like that. What a horrible gift. Run, Perry, run.

"I don't even know what to say, it's beautiful. I can't believe you would buy something like this for me." She continued.

I sat frozen to the seat of the couch. *It's a good gift? I did well?*

Alexis picked up the ruby red heart necklace and stared at it like I had the first time I held it in the store. I sat in silence, still not knowing if my gift was acceptable. Alexis took her gaze away from the necklace and set her eyes upon me. The ocean blue of her irises were sparkling even brighter than the rubies held in her hand. Alexis inched close to me on the couch and latched onto me with an embracing hug.

"It's more than I could have ever imagined. It's perfect. Thank you so much." She whispered in my ear, still latched onto me.

I exhaled hearing the words. *I didn't mess up.*

Another moment passed and her embrace softened. "I was going to wait to ask you, but, I think it's the right time now." Alexis whispered in my ear.

"Ask me what?" I finally managed to get out.

"I want you to come to my Dad's New Year's party with me as my date. His work throws one every year. It will be fun, I promise."

"His work?" I said almost choking on my own words.

"Yeah the police department. I told you he was a detective right? I want you to meet him…"

I heard nothing more. The room melted away with only the fire burning in my eyes. *I knew it, doomed.*

Chapter 21
Differences & Similarities, Hearts & Heartbreak

Who does this Nina Price think she is? Paul thought as he drove to the station. *Coming to my house and trying to reason with me after she takes over my case. I doubt I receive credit for anything. I know those FBI agents look down on us.*

Paul arrived fashionably late to the agreed nine o'clock meeting time. He had done it on purpose, wanting Agent Price to feel as uncomfortable as possible while she was here.

"Glad you could join us today, Detective." Said Agent Price as Paul strolled into the station room of agents and officers alike. "Any reason you're late?"

"Not in particular, I just dreaded seeing you this morning. I wanted to put it off for as long as I could." Said Paul with a chuckle.

Some of the officers joined Paul in laughter. Nina, however, was not in the slightest amused.

"Detective Fisher, a word." Agent Price said towards the laughing audience and the laughter came to a halt.

Paul followed a pacing Agent Price into an unoccupied office room.

"Do you think this is a joke, Detective? I can have your ass thrown off this case so fast…" Nina tried to whisper.

"No, not at all, but I think it's a joke you're here. I didn't need your help, nor did I ask for it." Said Paul.

"And I didn't ask for some whinny, unprofessional, washed up detective to make a mockery of this case. Get over your prideful ego, it's making you look like a jack ass from where I'm standing."

"Washed up?" Said Paul, raising his tone.

"You heard me, everyone has been saying it."

"And what's that Agent Price?"

"That you mope around all day and drown your problems into a bottle."

"How dare you act like you know what I have been through." Shouted Paul.

"Oh no? Then inform me Detective Fisher. What has you so emotionally distraught that you want to piss away your career over petty bullshit with me?"

"Why should I tell you anything after you walk in here expecting to take my case? I have busted my ass on this; the case is the only damn thing I have left to keep me sane."

"You're mistaken Paul. I don't see it that way at all, I told you that yesterday. The reality is, I need your help. I don't know this city like you do or even this case like you do. I'm late to the game and you're my best chance at getting caught up before someone else gets killed. I'm not trying to take this case away from you at all Paul, but I don't need another obstacle in my way. I know full well how hard you have been working and I know how hard this case is to solve. I have looked through the files and it's as difficult a case to solve as I have ever seen."

"Maybe I am being petty, Agent Price. I just have had a lot on my plate. I don't think it matters either way to you, but you're right. It's not about me or you. It's about the people who are out there scared to death of this killer. I've lost sight of that in this sandstorm I have been going through."

"Look, whatever you think of me or this situation, just erase it, and let's start fresh. I know you're a great detective, Paul. I was just trying to ruffle your feathers a bit and snap you into the reality we face now. I have no idea what you have been going through, but I do know that focusing on this case will help you cope with it. Who knows, maybe this case can open up the door to other career opportunities for you."

Paul took a deep breath and rubbed the stubble of his face.

"Okay Agent Price let's get to work. Let me take the floor first." Said Paul

"Sounds good Detective. Let's catch this Heartbreak Killer."

Paul felt some relief as he exited the room, and a bit of self-confidence overtook him that had been lacking since the Carson Minks arrest. *She is kind of right you know,* thought Paul as he entered the room with officers and agents alike.

"Okay listen up." Said Paul commanding the room. "As I'm sure all of you know by now, we are tasked with finding the Heartbreak Killer. For those of you who are new to the game this is what we know. The killer uses a poison made up of anti-depressants to paralyze his victims and I'm sure by the doses, bring them to a slow death. It's safe to assume that the victims have no knowledge of the consumption of the poison due to the nature of the bodies. No bruises, no cuts, no signs of being tied up or forced to consume."

Paul paused to glance at Agent Price. She nodded at him to continue on.

"This leads me to believe that the killer has to watch his targets carefully to track their everyday routines. I recently uncovered that the

killer placed poison in the tea of one of his victims, however, I believe the killer may place the poison in anything depending on the habit of his victim. Now, poison is known to be a woman's choice in weapon for killing a victim."

"However," intervened Agent Price. "The placement of the bodies found don't seem to be random but instead placed. This leads me to believe that they are being moved by the killer. Now, it would be extremely difficult for the average woman to accomplish such a feat each time. That educated guess, paired with the recent discovery of a piece of heart being extracted from the chest of the women, points closer to a male assailant. As women tend to avoid such brutal rituals even in murders."

"Yes, very good Agent Price. It's refreshing to see the FBI has a little brains to it." Said Paul. "Now I'm going to be honest with all of you here, this killer is elusive. He has yet to leave a single strand of evidence. He is careful, methodical, and extremely intelligent. He knows the ends around to covering tracks. Due to this, we have no other lead, so unless something turns up with the Connor body we are in the dark... Agent Price do you have anything else to add?"

"Why yes, thank you very much, Detective. As you all have been informed here, I'm sure, since the death of Terry Connor this case has become of national concern. The FBI has made bringing down the Heartbreak Killer one of its highest priorities. My fellow agents and I have been sent here to assist you in any way necessary. Detective Fisher will still head the charge of this case so if you stumble onto anything let him or I know. Leads, tips, new evidence, anything that can potentially help our cause. Any questions?"

The group of officers and agents alike groveled amongst themselves but ultimately stood without question.

"Okay then," Agent Price said again to the listening group. "Let's get to work and find this man." Agent Price then directed her attention to Paul. "Detective Fisher, may I have another word."

"What is it?" Said Paul as he reached Agent Price.

"Have you seen the lab work on Terry Connor's yet?"

"No I haven't, remember my tardiness earlier."

"How could I forget, it was more of a rhetorical question. Her toxins screening came back negative for any sort of anti-depressants."

"Hmmm," pondered Paul.

"Hmmm indeed. The only chemical in her system at the time of her death was alcohol, but the amount estimated wasn't even over the legal limit. Do you have any impressions as to why the killer would change his method?"

"Was a piece of her heart taken?" Asked Paul.

"Yes, the heart was tampered with and a piece was removed just like with the last woman."

"The only reasoning I can think of right now is the killer had a personal relationship with Terry and felt confident he could kill her without the poison."

"Even if that's true, it doesn't explain why he wouldn't simply drop something into a drink. Personally, it was one of two things. One he was rushed somehow or…"

"Or he wanted to do it in a more personal way." Paul interrupted.

"My thoughts exactly. From everything we have uncovered about the killer, he makes sure to take his time. I think you used the word methodical earlier. So I agree that he wanted to kill Miss. Connor in a personal and somewhat cocky way. But a way in which she would know it was him."

"He didn't like that Terry was spouting off about him being caught. He wanted to punish her for it, and show the city that he was back. What better way than kill the one preaching the loudest and string her up in front of her own station?"

"If that's the case than he accomplished his goal. The whole world is watching now. Soon everyone will know the name, Heartbreak Killer. Still, I'm not quite sure what to make of everything. Like you said, the killer is elusive and his ever growing methods are somewhat mysterious. I think we should take a look inside Terry's house."

"Maybe there is hope for us yet, Agent Price. I'll drive."

After a lengthy drive in silence and a frustrating wait to bypass through the gates, Paul and Agent Price had reached Terry's house.

I guess it paid to be an evil bitch, Paul thought as he gazed at the large estate.

"She lived a modest life style I can see." Said Agent Price.

"Yeah no kidding, I guess it really does pay to be famous." Said Paul.

The two knocked on the large oak door of Terry's home. There was no answer so Paul reached for the handle.

"It's unlocked. Do you think someone is here?" Said Paul.

Agent Price put a finger to her lips and continued with a nod to head in and Paul nodded back in agreement. The Detective and the Agent withdrew their guns simultaneously as they entered the house.

"You think we would be lucky enough to have the killer living here now." Said Agent Price with a sarcastic smile as they stood inside the dark entrance of the house.

"Are you always this sarcastic in the field?" Said Paul as he took in the full view of the home.

"Depends. Do you not like my jokes, Detective?"

"You just seemed like a hard ass earlier. All business at my house and then at the station. I didn't expect anything else."

"I think loosening the tension is good in the field. High stress can lead to mistakes."

"True, how about we search the first floor and see if there is anything out of place?"

Agent Price nodded and the two searched around, but neither could find anything unusual or out of place.

"Upstairs?" Suggested Agent Price and this time Paul nodded his head.

"Do you hear that?" Said Paul as the two made their way up the stairs.

"Music, from down the hall." Said Agent Price raising her gun.

Paul followed suit, raising his gun to the side of his face.

The music led them to a partially opened door at the end of dim hallway.

"On the count of three." Paul whispered as he reached the door. Agent Price nodded. "One… Two… Three."

They blasted into the room, both pointing their guns in opposite directions of the room. But no one was in sight inside.

"It's just the radio; someone forgot to turn it off." Said Paul pressing the power button off on the player.

"Do you see the bed?" Said Agent Price.

Paul turned around to look. "No sheets."

"This had to be where it happened." Said Agent Price, whisking her finger across the bare mattress.

"Look, the bed post, it's all scratched and worn down. You think she was handcuffed to it?"

"That or she was into some wild things in the bedroom." Said Agent Price with a giggle.

"Seriously?" Paul said with a raise of his right brow. *Who is this woman? She is completely different from earlier.*

"And I'm the hard ass, Detective? Let's get this called in, we need a full sweep on this house."

Paul and Agent Price continued to examine through the rest of the room as they waited for the forensics team to arrive. However, like the other rooms of the Heartbreak Killers victims, nothing was left behind or to be seen by the naked eye. The two were left with nothing to do but sit on the staircase and talk.

"Have you ever thought about what would drive someone to such evil acts, Detective?" Said Agent Price fiddling with her fingers.

"Of course, all the time." Said Paul. "I think every person in our field at one point or another has. After all we have seen, it's only natural.

"What has your conclusion been drawn to?"

"I don't think it's as black and white or as easily answered as people want. Someone could commit one crime for one set of reasons and another could do it for a completely different set entirely. It all depends on the person, I guess."

"Well, what about our case. What about the Heartbreak Killer?"

Paul sat silent for a moment. He had thought about the Heartbreak Killer so often and was scared of the conclusion that came into his mind the night he had stared naked into the mirror. *I think he is what anyone could become, maybe even me. A broken soul from this evil world.* Paul shook his head to get the thought out of his mind.

"I don't know." Said Paul.

Agent Price looked at Paul with discouragement. Immediately, Paul knew she hadn't bought the answer he gave.

"I was a young woman once, and I believed that I would find my true love. A love that I now know doesn't exists." Said Agent Price, now blankly staring out into the openness of the house. "When you grow up as a little girl you see the princess and her happily ever after ending with a prince. That idea of love stuck with me as I grew up, but sooner or later, you learn it's a feel good lie."

"I know what you mean." Said Paul. *I know all too well.*

"I thought I found my prince charming once. Everything was great. I was young, carefree, and in love. But they never showed you the ever after in those movies and book stories. The after the princess and prince fall in love." Agent Price paused, still staring out into the distance.

"What happened?" Said Paul trying to urge the conversation forward.

"I think something similar to what you're dealing with now, Detective. I have seen the face of someone who's lost their loved ones in a cruel way and can't deal with the realities of what love really is or has become. But why should I tell you what happened if you won't tell me."

"That's a fair point, maybe someday I will."

"I asked you about the Heartbreak Killer because I think in a way what he is showing us is right. The broken and twisted heart symbol, the removal of a piece of heart, the death. In its own twisted way that's what love really is. It has an evil side that few ever dare to speak of or even think about."

"I have reflected on myself during the case and worry if I may be on the path our killer took. I see more darkness than I use too. I see the love you are describing and it scares me. In a way pieces of my heart have been taken from me just like our victims."

"The older we get the more the pieces of our heart break off, leaving us more vulnerable to that darkness. I think our killer is the byproduct of what happens when you have nothing left to break off and only darkness remains inside your chest."

"I think you're right Agent. But we have to be the ones to know the darkness and chose to help those who still have been untouched by it. That's how I tell myself that I'll be different from the evils of the world, the Heartbreak Killer even. That's why we have to find him before his darkness spreads much farther and touches others like the man I arrested, Minks."

Detective Fisher and Agent Price both stared off into their space and their own thoughts and ideas. Different wonders of hearts and heartbreaks roamed through their minds.

"Are you ready to tell me what happened to your heart, Detective?" Agent Price finally said.

"Ladies first Agent Price."

Chapter 22
The Crazy Things we do for Love

Countless men and women alike have come to my office to preach that love can make you crazy. I had found it preposterous during my years of darkness, but I wondered now if there was some validity to their statements. Certainly I was crazy for what I was about to embark on.

The Heartbreak Killer attending an event held by the very people hell-bent on putting him away?

Yes ladies and gentlemen, I'm attending the Police Department's annual New Year's party.

When Alexis had asked me the question I was stunned. What could I possible say?

"Well Alexis I can't attend such an event."

"Why not Perry?" She would reply.

"Well I'm actually a killer, the Heartbreak Killer. I think that going would be a tad risky, don't you?"

I then imagined her face turning white as she soaked in the dread. Either fainting at the shock of the news or screaming bloody murder and having everyone in the coffee shop attack me, beating me to a pulp.

"Alexis I would like to come but I can't."

"Why is that Perry?"

"I don't feel that way about you to be honest."

I imagined her starting to cry, running out of the building in an emotional frenzy. People would stare at me with rude glares. Then having lied and ruining all hope for myself, I would return back to the evil Heartbreak Killer. Doomed forever.

In reality though, I said this.

"I would love to go." I said to Alexis. She was so excited by the answer, she had tackled me onto the couch and attacked me with a barrage of kisses on my cheek.

"I can't wait." Alexis said back, after the barrage. "My Dad will love you."

Yes, love me indeed. Love to put a bullet through my chest. Love to lock me up and have me rot. Love to see me lethally injected.

What could I say though? I wanted to be with Alexis. I wanted to be normal human being with feelings. Yet, after I agreed, I could only think of was how crazy I must be to do this for a woman. *Indeed past patients, the crazy things we do for love.*

As each day came and went the more I began to dread the looming event. *Police are trained to detect falsities*, I kept thinking. I wasn't confident I could simply fake my way through this one. They surely had a profile on me by now, both physical and psychological. Detective Fisher didn't seem to be an idiot by any means either. He would smell out the dark side in me no matter how deep it was locked inside of me.

After days of worry, New Year's Eve was upon me, staring at me like a set of cold steel prison bars. *I'm certainly doomed,* I thought.

Alexis had barely kept her excitement in as she sent me pictures of her dress, asking me what I was going to wear, and telling me she couldn't wait almost every day prior. I made an attempt to be excited, but the bars of prison kept staring.

Only a couple of hours away before I have to pick her up, get it together Perry. You can do this. I had to be on the top of my game. Nothing could slip, so I began to prepare.

Early in my preparation came the idea that I would be a walking irony. The Heartbreak Killer was dark and evil, red and black in the eyes of the public. So I would present myself in something light and pure, white and blue, to disguise myself into the crowd.

The final product, as I stood in the mirror, was ocean blue dress paints that matched Alexis's eyes and a plain but classic white dress shirt. I even matched a pocket square with the pants and my tie to further my cause. To top the outfit off I wore the light brown shoes Alexis had just bought for me. *A true testament to my insane devotion to her.*

Thereafter I decided to make a drink to take the edge off the looming night. As I drank, I turned the TV onto the news. *I wonder who is taking over for the late Terry Connor.*

However, I came to find out that Channel 28 News had shut down until further notice. *At least I could stop some of the poison from being spread.* I flipped through the channels until one caught my attention.

"As news of the murder of Terry Connor has spread through the country in the recent week, the FBI has sent one of their own to assist in the capture of the dubbed Heartbreak Killer."

Interesting, I thought.

"The FBI has issued a statement that the Heartbreak Killer has become a top priority."

I kill one C list celebrity and the nation starts to care? People really need to evaluate their priorities.

Never the less, this was an unexpected turn of events. I wasn't sure what to make of the news, but pressure would be added if an FBI agent was sniffing around at the New Year party. *I'll need to be keen on that. See if they possess any more of a threat to discovering my hidden identity.*

There wasn't any more time to dwell on the news, though. I had to pick up Alexis in less than an hour. I finished my drink, double checked my appearance, and made my way out.

Thoughts of what was to come filled my mind as I drove the snowy roads. Uncertainty was always a bit nerve racking but I needed to be sharp and have my mind focused on wearing a tight mask. Not only did I need to make a good impression on Detective Fisher as a potential suitor for his daughter, but to also not give him the slightest scent that I was a potential suspect in the case. *You can do this Perry. You're smarter than them. That's why they haven't found you yet... But this is the bee hive I'm about to venture too.* I turned on some soothing classical music and quieted my busy mind.

I arrived at Alexis's house just a few minutes before I was supposed to pick her up. It was the first time going back to the house since I had made my choice to spare her.

No police cars tonight, I reminisced as I walked to her door. I felt an eerie presence overcome me the closer I came. *This is a complete 180, walking to the front door.* When I reached the door I knocked twice and waited.

"Just a second." Yelled Alexis through the door. A minute or two passed before she came back. "Sorry for making you wait. I had to make sure everything was perfect." Alexis said as she opened the door to greet me.

"It's okay, I was early, anyways." I said back, noticing my breath in the cold. *You always look perfect to me Alexis.*

"How do I look?" Alexis said revealing her full dress in the doorway. She was in a black dress and red heels. Her honey blond hair was straight and down with a red bow to match the heels.

"You look great." I said. "I love black and red together."

"Me too, but we don't match very well." She said with a laugh. "That's okay, you still look handsome." Alexis gave me a kiss. "Do you notice anything?"

"Um," I said, trying to stall. *Notice what?*

"The necklace silly. That's why I wore this outfit, it matches so well with it."

Alexis pointed to her chest to showcase the ruby red heart necklace to me. It was beautiful on her and the red rubies glimmered in the light, matching perfectly with her outfit as she had suggested.

"Wow, it looks amazing on you." I said stunned by her beauty. *Bubump,* said my heart.

"Why thank you, Perry. Are you ready to go?"

"Yes I am." I lied.

Alexis grabbed her coat, then my resting arm, and we were off.

The drive was silent as thoughts whirled, leaving my mind to pep talk itself. *Let's do this Perry. You're going to do great.*

"You don't have anything to be nervous about." Alexis said. "My Dad may seem scary, being a detective and all, but if he sees what I see in you then I don't think there is anything to worry about."

What if he sees what a Detective is trained to sniff out, a killer?

"I'm not nervous." I responded.

"Why are you so quiet then?"

"I'm just thinking."

"Thinking about what?"

About how I'm about to walk into the one place someone like me should stay as far away from as possible. About how this may be my last night of freedom. About how beautiful you are and how crazy I am for you to be risking it all.

"About impressing your dad and his police friends." I said with a false grin, trying to throw her off my nervous scent.

"Just be you Perry and you will impress my father just fine. You have done a good job with me." Alexis said grinning back.

Myself? I don't even know myself yet. How can I possible do that?

"Plus," Alexis went on. "I'm a grown woman who can make her own choices. My Dad's opinion doesn't mean as much to me anymore. He disapproves of almost every guy, but that's just because he's my Dad. So just worry about treating me like you have been Mr. Nelson and you should be perfectly fine." Alexis's grin turned to a full fledge smile and she grabbed my hand and held it tight.

He would really disapprove of me if he finds out who I really am, I worried. But the warmth of Alexis's hand grasping onto mine did comfort me some. *Bubump,* my heart sang as I felt her soft skin. *Relax, you will do fine.*

The event was being held at a highly regarded hotel downtown called the Newport. The hotel was one of the oldest and most recognizable buildings the city had to offer. The epitome of my taste in all things luxurious and old fashioned. Though the Newport Hotel had been remodeled and upgraded throughout the years, it still kept to its classic and old fashion form.

The outside of the hotel was made of jaded marble and large white roman pillars. The entrance doors were outlined with gold trim and spotless glass. Even as breath taking as the outside appeared, in all my years driving by, I had never been inside. If ever I needed a silver lining to the bee hive I was embarking on, it was the opportunity to finally venture inside of this elegant beast and view what it had to offer.

Alexis and I arrived at the Newport just as the party was starting. A young valet dressed in a white collar shirt, similar to mine, and a jaded green vest came to greet us and take the car. My muscles were tight and I gripped at the wheel as I stared at the golden plated doors, knowing the fate I was about to embark on. Reluctantly, I handed my keys to the valet. *I guess it will be the last time I need a car anyhow. I don't get those in prison,* I thought dropping them into his hand

Before we exited, Alexis touched my leg and gave me some encouragement.

"You're going to do great. I'll be by your side the whole night. And just so you know, this means the world to me, you coming and all. Some men wouldn't dare after just a few dates. I think it shows your genuine character." Alexis said, giving me a kiss on the cheak for luck.

A man? Hardly. I think you mistake the genuine for the stupidity and craziness. The speech did help though, no matter the outcome. *You can do this Perry. Put on an act of your lifetime.*

With that, I exited the car, put my arm out for Alexis, and made my way into the unknown beehive that awaited me. *Bubump, bubump, bubump,* thumped my chest. I gulped at the crisp air as a door man opened the golden trimmed doors and in I went inside, fearing to never exit a free man.

The inside of the Newport Hotel was a marvel in its own. The jaded marble outside, now covered the floor we walked on. The walls were laced green and white with a tiny gold trim. The center of the lobby was vast and circular in shape, filled with large aquariums, a lounge, a bar, two restaurants, and one café with a small merchandising gift shop. There was an unfamiliar smell of vanilla mixed with restaurant food and some sort of unknown spices that floated the air inside as well.

As we reached the center, a calming classical piece of Mozart could be heard floating through the talks and noises of the people inside. It was a wonderful spectacle to behold and in a quick flash some comfort set in. *This is my kind of place not theirs. A home court advantage of sorts,* I realized

Alexis guided me through the lobby to an out of shape woman sitting behind a large white plastic table.

"Names?" Said the woman in a cranky tone as she looked down at the table.

"I'm Alexis Fisher, and this is my guest, Perry Nelson." Said Alexis as politely as she could.

The woman proceeded to put a list up to her face. "Ah, there you are Miss Fisher. Here are your wrist bands." Said the woman, now, with a more welcoming tone. She reached for two green wristbands and wrapped one on each of us. "You're also encouraged to write down your names on a name tag so people know who you are. It's a great way to meet new people."

Like I need anyone knowing my name, I thought as Alexis reach for a sharpie and name tag. *Maybe I should label mine Heartbreak Killer, that way I'll kill the anticipation of getting caught.*

"Here you go, I made yours for you." Alexis said as she placed the tag on my chest. "Look, I even drew you a red heart at the end so you could at least match my necklace. Plus you'll be less threatening with a heart; your face is so serious tonight."

I stared down at my nametag. In black sharpie my name, *Perry*, was written and at the end, a drawn red heart. *As much as I try to stay away it manages to find me.*

"Thank you." I said still looking at the death of me.

"Do you not like it? You can make a new one if you want."

"I love it." I lied to not hurt Alexis's feelings. *At least it's the real me.*

"Good, me too. Now let's start the New Year off right." Alexis said in an excited fashion.

If by right you mean behind bars, then yes. Maybe that would start the cities New Year off right.

Alexis clasped to my hand and pulled me towards a door behind the woman and her desk. We were met by two men that I assumed were police officers. We presented them with our wrist bands and they opened the doors. *Into the bee hive I go.*

Greeting us on the other side of the doors was a large ball room.

On one side there was tables, food, and a large bar. A scouring banner hung behind everything, reading *Happy New Years,* in bold golden sparkled blue letters. The other side of the room was filled with people standing and socializing. A dance floor was also present amongst the crowd, but it had yet to be touched by the plethora of people. Next to the dance floor was a stage with a band dressed in black and white tuxes. At that moment, the band was playing some sort of jazz, but it was hard to hear a tune over the volume of the crowd.

Damn how many people are here, I thought, staring at a room that appeared to be filled by five hundred people or more.

As Alexis and I ventured into the masses, I noticed the ceiling, which was scaling high above and covered by a masterful painting. Half of the painting was of a blue sky filled with clouds, a shining sun, and angels gracing down onto whoever stood below at the time. As you gradually panned to the right of the ceiling, the sky became darker with twinkling stars and pale crater moon. *Magnificent,* I thought.

Seconds after I scanned the room I realized I was now in a room full of police officers, elected officials, and countless others who would love to see me suffer. A sudden illness over took me and I assumed my face turned ghostly as a cold sweat broke out.

The moment was here and the tension was high. *You can do this Perry, take a breath.*

I attempted to listen to my own advice, but it was to no avail, so I decided a drink would do a more adequate job. "Alexis why don't you find a table and I'll get us something to drink." I said trying to shake the sick feeling.

"Okay, will you get me a glass of red wine please?" Alexis said, seemingly oblivious to the peril I was in.

"Of course," I said trying to get away unnoticed.

Alexis grabbed my arm before I made my way to the bar. "Perry, are you alright? You look like you've seen a ghost."

"I will be, I promise." I said. *At least I hope.*

As I walked through the crowd of people I couldn't help wonder how many of these men were assigned to my case. *If only they knew just how close they were to the man that had eluded them for months.*

Reaching the bar, I ordered my usual martini and Alexis's requested wine. I continued to people watch as the bartender made the drinks. They all seemed so human to me, talking, laughing, and hugging. This is why I was feared being here, I wasn't human enough to blend in.

Shaking off my doubts, I focused my attention onto the band playing to the still empty dance floor. It brought me back to my first date with Alexis. I had been such a mess then with my eternal battle, yet I managed to endure through it. *I was struggling even more with my darkness then,* I realized. A picture of Alexis and I dancing on the empty floor grazed through my mind. I smiled at the thought, and as if I had just taken medication, my anxiety floated away.

If I could do it then I can do it now. Most of the people here are much darker and twisted than Alexis ever was. If I could act well enough around her then there was no reason to worry.

The bartender handed me the drinks and I headed for the tables. I spotted Alexis at a table alone and she waved me over. *Look at her,* I thought. *I don't know how I managed to get to this point with her, but I'm glad I did.*

"Look at you." Alexis said as I reached the table. "A second ago you looked like you were going to throw up, now you're grinning."

Me grinning?

"You didn't go over there and take a bunch of shots did you?" Alexis went on with a tease. "I don't think meeting my Dad would end well if you were a drunk tonight of all nights."

"No, I just realized that there is nothing to worry about. I passed the hardest part in meeting you. If I can do that this will be a cake walk." I said.

"Oh cocky now are we? You are quite… What's the psychology term you therapists use for mood swings?"

"Bipolar?"

"Ah yes, bipolar. You are bipolar tonight, but I do like the confidence, keep it up."

If only you knew. I may be the newest case study on psychotic bipolar disorder. Human being to heartless killer now trying to turn back once more.

We both had a laugh at our playful jabs and made a cheers as I sat in a seat next to Alexis.

"To a good night and better New Year." I said. Alexis agreed with a shy smile and we clanged our glasses together, *ting.* We conversed of things that were unimportant but it made no difference, I was just happy to be by Alexis's side.

"Let's go find my Dad." Alexis said after our drinks were dry.

"Okay," I said with conviction. My nerves were all but gone now. I was ready to meet the man that was head fast on my case. *Someday you may bring me to justice. But it won't be tonight Detective Fisher.*

"Actually, stay here, I'll go look for him and then come and find you." Alexis said.

I tried to remember what Detective Fisher looked like as I waited. The first time I had seen him was months ago, right after I had cut out my first piece of heart. He had straggly brown hair and wore baggy eyes then on the TV. I remembered receiving the impression of a man who seemed to be struggling with his own demons, yet somehow managed to stay on the side of good. That impression alone gave me a certain respect for him.

Detective Fisher looked the part of a worthy advisory to me. Hopefully he lives up the picture I've painted in my head. The man to take me down needs to endure the pain I have to have a chance.

Alexis appeared into my sight, waving me over to her. I was ready for the moment.

"I found him, he's on the other side talking with some people. He said he would meet you though. Are you ready?" Alexis said as I reached her.

"As ever a man could be." I said with a sly smile.

Alexis pulled me through a sea of people. Together we had to bump and prod our way through. For minutes I saw no sight of the Detective, rapidly scanning from person to person. Then as if the sea of people had parted for me, there stood Detective Fisher in the distance. His back was turned towards me but I recognized the shaggy brown hair.

My focus dialed in, razor sharp, and for some odd reason the tune of the band rang in my ears. *The start of Moonlight Sonata,* recognizing the melody. The music came with every step toward Detective Fisher. *Dun dada dada, dun dada dada.* Motions slowed and time seemed to be put on pause. *Dun dada dada.* Louder and louder the song became, and as if mirroring my anticipation of the moment the song defined to an intensity that only I could hear. I became entranced by the happenings of the moment.

I was within feet of the detective when a familiar voice whispered to me, breaking the melody trance completely.

Kill him. The dark monster had woken from its long slumber. *Rip out his heart, spill his blood, and let me feast on our enemy.*

Bubump, bubump, bubump, my chest throbbed.

Out came another sound, not of mind or the melody, a soft voice from outside of my transfixion.

"Dad, this is Perry. The one I have been telling you about." Said Alexis.

Detective Fisher turned around to me. His brown eyes met mine, still worn and weary, but sterner and livelier than I had seen on the TV. He was clean shaven this time, looking worlds better than I remembered him. Detective Fisher reached out to shake my hand. His eyes still staring into mine as if he was studying me, taking mental notes, trying to peer into my soul and see what I really was.

I reached my hand out to meet his.

Kill him Perry, my darkness whispered again. *End this game of cat and mouse. There is only one winner in this. Make it you. Slit his throat, bleed him to the floor, and show him the true power of the Heartbreak Killer.*

Our hands grasped together.

Detective Fisher's shake was firm, his hands rough with callouses. The feeling of touch felt haunting and dark to me. My instincts kicked in.

I am touching my enemy, the man who wants to kill me. Why should I spare him? Only the strongest survive in the world we live in. Before I could act, something graced my shoulder.

"Perry?" Alexis said and my dark instincts faded as her ocean blue eyes pierced through to mine.

"What?" I said as everything came back to reality, letting go of the Detectives hand.

"This is my Dad, Paul Fisher."

I turned back to Detective Fisher and smiled.

"Nice to meet you, Mr. Fisher. I have heard so much about you. My name is Perry Nelson."

"Call me Paul." Said Detective Fisher still piercing into my eyes. "I have heard quite a bit about you as well. My daughter is quite impressed with you so I thought it's only right I meet such a recommended man."

What has he heard? Not enough I assume or we would be having a different conversation somewhere else.

"Well, your daughter is wonderful, and I am grateful to be invited to such a beautiful event." I responded.

The Detective smiled at the complement. "This is my boss." He said, taking his eye contact away from mine, and turning to an older man with greying hair. *"Captain Thomas."*

The Captain put out his hand and shook mine, giving me a polite head nod along with the shake.

Detective Fisher then turned to the other woman he was mingling with. She was almost as tall as the Detective, with brown hair presented straight and neatly tied back. Her nose was sharp, her lips thin, and her eyes tight with a coffee brown tint. The woman wore a bit of makeup and was still pretty, but I could tell she was beginning to lose her youthful beauty from aging.

"This is Agent Price. She is here with the FBI, here to assist with the Heartbreak case." Said Detective Fisher.

Agent Price reached out her hand for a shake as well. "My actual name is Nina, but Detective Fisher refuses to call me by it." She said to me.

So this is the Agent sent to find me, a woman. Hmmm I will have to keep my eye on her, she could be very dangerous.

"It's a pleasure to meet you both." I said to the group

"So Perry, what do you do for a living?" Said Detective Fisher.

"I am a therapist." I said back.

"Ah, interesting, so you have a talent to detect people's behaviors. Where do you practice at?" Said Detective Fisher.

"Perry has his own firm Dad. He is very successful at what he does." Said Alexis, looking at me with a starry-eyed smile.

"Impressive. What kind of people do you specialize in if you don't mind me asking?" Said Detective Fisher.

"No not at all, I specialize in cognitive therapy but I am well versed in psychoanalysis as well. Not so much the old Freudian work but a modern version. I work with adults mostly, helping them overcome different types of mental aliments such as depression or anxiety." I said.

"I only ask you because I am curious on what a therapists thoughts would be on the Heartbreak Killer. You must be interested in a person like that, so close to home and all." Detective Fisher was again staring into my eyes as he asked. It made me a bit uncomfortable, giving me the feeling I was being interrogated by him.

Be careful with your answer. He may suspect something.

"Well to be honest Detective, I'm not quite sure what I think of him. My work isn't specialized in the criminally insane or in psychopaths. So I would only be making an educated guess." I said. *Oh shit, I said him.*

"Why do you think it is a man? You did say him didn't you?" Said Detective Fisher with an eyebrow raised.

Think fast. Cover the scent.

"Yes I did Detective. Serial killers tend to prey on weaker targets, and since men have the physical advantage over an average built woman it would be an easier prediction." I said with a smirk. "Also statistically there are far more men who become serial killer due to their more aggressive nature."

"Hmm, an interesting take from a man of your position. I wonder…"

He suspects something look at the way he is stares at me.

"Dad, quit grilling him. Gosh you always do this." Alexis intervened. "He is just messing with you Perry."

Detective Fisher's serious stare broke out into laughter as he turned to Alexis. "I am sorry sweetheart, you know I can't help it sometimes." Then he turned to me. "Forgive me Perry, sometimes I get into interrogating Alexis's new boyfriends. It's just the law enforcement in me. I hope I didn't make you too uncomfortable."

"Oh no, not at all. I thought nothing of it." I said. *What an asshole.*

"Well Dad, I'm sure you have things to discuss with Agent Price and your boss so we will get out of your way. Come on Perry, let's go dance a bit before its midnight." Said Alexis.

"Okay sweetheart. It was nice to meet you Perry. I will see you again I'm sure." Said the Detective with a menacing smile.

"I'm sure." I said smiling back.

"You did great." Alexis said as we walked away. "For a moment I was worried. My Dad said hello and you froze up, but you recovered nicely. Just like with me."

"You really think so?" I said not sharing Alexis's confidence.

"Yes. He wouldn't have messed with you like that if he didn't think you were okay."

Or he got the impression of the Heartbreak Killer. Something seems amidst to me. He was staring at me for a long time.

But my mind was put to ease as Alexis and I danced to the sounds of the band. The more we swayed together the less the tension of meeting Detective Fisher became, and my bubbling dark monster was quiet once again.

"I'm sorry my Dad called you my boyfriend. I know we haven't really decided on any of that yet." Said Alexis into my ear as we swayed back and forth to the slow music.

To be honest Alexis that was the least of my concerns.

"I didn't mind it Alexis." I whispered in her ear.

"Well I know how some men act when they get involved in hard commitments. I don't want to ruin anything between us. Everything is running so smooth right now."

It is going great.

"Don't worry Alexis, I'm just glad to be here with you tonight, promise."

Alexis held me tighter after my response and said nothing more of it. I could feel her heart beating on my chest as she did. I wondered if she could feel mine. *Does a heart as dark and shattered even beat with normal rhythm?* One thing was sure in my mind, I did want to be Alexis's boyfriend more than anything. *She is the light to my darkness. The perfect complement. This night proves it.*

As midnight crept closer, people began to huddle around a large clock hanging in the rafters. Alexis and I stopped dancing and joined the crowd. Collectively everyone began counting down as the final ten seconds ticked down. When the clock struck midnight, everyone shouted Happy New Year to each other and either hugged, kissed, toasted, or did an assortment of the three.

I had forgotten the joy a new year brought the normal people in the world. *A new start on their mistakes in life. Maybe I can atone for mine as well.* While the crowd celebrated, Alexis kissed my lips.

"Happy New Year Perry, I couldn't have asked for a better date to spend it with." She said to me after the kiss. "You want to get out of here now? Before the traffic?"

"Sure," I said still enjoying the soft touch of her lips.

The drive home was quiet for both of us. Alexis must have been tired from the night but the silence had me wondering if I had done something wrong. *She is never this quiet, that's my job.* I wasn't used to social events and there different customs so it could have been entirely possible I forgot to do something. *I sure hope not.*

My overall thoughts of the night were positive though. I was relieved to be out a free and undiscovered man. But how could Alexis possible know that. I was supposed to be a normal man, not a killer trying to pose as one.

When I pulled up to Alexis's house and she said nothing, I finally spoke up. "Well I hope you had a good time. I know I did."

"I did Perry, thank you for everything. I know meeting someone's father can be nerve racking, but I was impressed. I knew you'd do an amazing job though."

You have no idea.

"Well goodnight and Happy New Year." I said. *Something is wrong, I've ruined the night. My stupid lack of emotions and human skills.*

Alexis opened the car door but hesitated to get out, instead staying seated. She seemed to want to say something.

"What?" I implored.

Alexis glanced at me. "It's nothing, I was just thinking about something, but never mind." She said stepping out of the car.

"Did I do something wrong?" I said confused by her hesitation.

"Do you want to come inside?" Alexis blurted out, putting her hands to her mouth as if shocked by the words.

"Come inside?" I said baffled by the words.

"Yeah you know… I think it's the right time." Alexis said looking away and biting her lip.

I don't know… The right time for what, I thought.

"No, I can tell you don't want to, forget it." Alexis snapped, giving me no chance to answer.

"No I will come in, let me park. What did you have in mind?" I said.

But as if lighting had stuck a metal pole, my brain jolted, and everything came to me at once. My eyes widened and my lips tightened as I realized the answer to my own question before she said another word.

Chapter 23
Perspectives Blurred: A Killer and a Beauty

My mind raced as the words came out. *What was I doing? Had I just invited Perry inside?* Yes I had, the words had poured out of me.

"Do you want to come inside?" I said to Perry.

The way he had handled himself during the New Year's party had me. Perry showed great confidence and composure with my Dad, who can be intimidating to some. *Check.* Better yet, he agreed to come with me in the first place. *Check.* In my experience, men will make any excuse to hold off meeting your parents. As if it was such a big commitment, nevertheless Perry had agreed. *Check, Check, Check.*

When I was with Barry he made ever excuse to hold off meeting my parents. When I was with Barry he acted like an ass in front of my Dad. When I was with Barry... Screw Barry, this just proves Perry is so much better.

Whatever the feeling I was enduring now, asking Perry to come inside was bold. He hadn't been very revealing with his emotions whenever we went out, so I could only guess at how he really felt. But he was so sweet, I couldn't contain my emotions any longer. I wanted Perry Nelson.

The funny thing about it all was Perry seemed clueless as to what I meant by coming in. *What did I have in mind? Was he a man?* But Perry had never been one to take hints, or be aggressive, so part of me felt I had to be more assertive.

Saying the words took a lot of courage. I had contemplated the whole car ride if I should ask him to come in or not. The contemplation

made me silent, so Perry probably thought that he had done something wrong. *I know I do when he is quiet, which is always.*

My heart raced as we walked to my door. Not only was it the first time Perry and I would have privacy, but the first time I had been with a man in private since Barry. The anticipation of potential things to come was nerve racking and thrilling. *It always is if you care about someone. It has to be perfect. What if he doesn't like my body?*

The what if's began to seep inside me…

…*Sex,* I thought. Of course that's what Alexis was asking me. That's what normal humans did when they were dating. *She wants to have sex… Right?* Sure, I was used to entering a woman's home and ripping off her shirt and bra. But I wasn't a welcomed guest then, and it was to plunge my knife into their chest, not to see what it revealed. *Not for pleasure. For my dark monster, my pain.*

Could I even feel pleasure? Did the idea of sex even arouse me? What if I couldn't perform? Whatever doubts crept into my mind, I was walking to Alexis's door as the thoughts raced.

The time to see how human I had become was rapidly approaching as Alexis opened her door to let me inside. *Coming in the back a killer. Coming in the front to have sex,* I thought as I entered.

The house was everything I had remembered since my last visit. Neat, modern, and to my fancy taste.

"Let's have a drink." Alexis suggested to me as we walked up the stairs and into the living room.

"A drink would be lovely." I said as I sat on a couch I had once viewed from underneath the dark shadows of the table. *Sex…* I thought. *Do I even remember how to do it? It's been what eight or nine years?* I was brought back to how Terry's half naked body had repulsed me when she had walked down the stairs. What if Alexis's does the same, or nothing at all? *This is what happens when you try to be normal, Perry.*

But how could Alexis repulse me? She was beautiful and she was the first woman I had thought about in that way since I had lost my feelings. *Everything will be fine, be natural. Natural? I'm barely human.* I took a gulp of air and slicked my hair back...

...I offered Perry a drink. Gosh, I needed one to swish the doubts away. The what if's and nerves intensified when we reached the inside of my house. *What if this is too soon? What if it ruins the relationship? What if this is all he wants from me?* It's all I could think about when I started to pour the vodka into glasses. *You're just nervous, it will be great. You like him and he's not like Barry, he won't hurt you.*

I put a bit of cranberry juice in the cups to mix with the alcohol and brought them out to Perry. He was sitting in what looked to be deep thought as I reached the living room. *Is he nervous too? Do men get nervous about sex? No men don't have the same fears we do.*

"Here you go." I said to him with a smile. *Now where should I sit, close or far?* I decided to sit right next to him. Perry greeted me with an awkward smile and I began to gulp the drink down. *Taking the edge off this kind of anticipation is natural. What should I say?*

"Perry..." I said almost choking on the liquid in my mouth.

"Yes," Perry said looking at me with his intimidating piercing green eyes.

"I..." I began to say. *Tell him how you feel, break the tension.* I took another gulp of my drink. "The way you have treated me... You're so sweet and how you met my Dad without hesitation when I asked. It's everything I could have hoped for."

I looked onto Perry's stern face as I said the words. I felt vulnerable, like I was already naked and showing my all to him…

…Alexis handed me a drink. She hesitated for a second before sitting down, choosing to sit right beside me. *Oh no, am I supposed to make the first move? What do I do? How do I do it?*

I sat in silence until she called my name. "Yes," I said. *Have I already screwed this up?*

Alexis seemed nervous as she spoke. She told me that I was everything she could have hoped for. *Why is she opening up to me? Could it be I am doing a better job than I had thought?* A warm rush of feeling shot throughout my body as she finished her words. Her ocean blue eyes pierced inside of my dark soul. *Someone as beautiful as Alexis could like someone like me?*

"Alexis," I said. "I thought I was cursed to be alone and miserable forever. But when I saw you I knew things could change." It was the most truthful thing I had proclaimed to her. The words were real, and it was the closest I'd been to being the old Perry that I could recall.

For the first time in a long time I didn't have to think or wear my mask, it felt almost human.

"You really feel that way?" Alexis said back to me.

Feel… Yes I do feel. I am alive.

"I really do." I responded and I went in for a kiss and Alexis met me half way.

Instincts took over, for some reason I wasn't afraid to fail anymore. *She is the one to save me from my dark monster.* As our lips met, my heart raced. I couldn't remember the last time it had felt like this. Not just one beat or two, but continuous pounding. The warmth of feelings inside me flowed like lava.

My hands began to grow minds of their own, grasping and holding Alexis's warm body close to mine. The whole of myself craved to feel her warmth, her skin, her body. There was no more thinking inside my twisted mind, only doing…

…The anticipation of Perry's next words made time feel as if a year had passed in-between. *Is he going to let me say how I feel and say nothing back?* He didn't though, without playing a game Perry told me the most he ever had. His sweet words were all I needed to close the deal. *Kiss me Perry Nelson,* as I heard the words.

Perry didn't need a hint for this. His words or mine seemed to release him of a heavy burden. Perry leaned in for a kiss and I met him half way. His lips were warm and luscious like I remembered. Hands gravitated to my hips, pulling me into Perry's body, moving like a blind man feeling around in an unknown place.

I wasn't used to this aggressive nature of Perry but it was a wonderful change. *His touch is magical,* I thought as we embraced. Suddenly, my emotions gave into a euphoric frenzy of lust and love and nothing else mattered but him.

We rolled onto the floor, spilling our drinks to the side. I laid on top of him and we kissed more and more. Our tongues and lips flailing like madness and my hands began to run themselves up and down his smooth face and thick black hair.

Perry's hands found my backside and he gave a hard squeeze. *Oh take me now*, I thought as I felt the force and passion behind the touch. I bit his lip to control myself as he squeezed me. The force of the bite didn't seem to bother him nor did I care. *I am ready. You makes me feel so wonderful.*

I pushed off Perry's chest to stand while he lay on the floor.

"Is everything okay?" Perry said to me. "Did I go too far?"

Not far enough.

"No, not at all." I said to Perry, who had a look of a young boy thought to be in trouble. I couldn't help but giggle at him. "Come with me."

Reaching my hand out to meet his, I pulled Perry up and led and to my bedroom…

…We rolled to the floor. Things become natural for me now, as if I had been doing this all my life. I placed my hands on Alexis's ass and gave a hard squeezed over her silky black dress. The feeling of touch was firm and plump; something I never dreamed would feel good to me. The blood inside me began to pump while I squeezed, and I could feel my heart still beating like a drum. All I wanted now was to feel her soft pale skin on mine.

Alexis began to bite at my lip and pierced into the skin. A taste of salty blood filled my mouth and tongue. I squeezed even harder as she bit down. We were a pair of wild animals, only our primal instincts remained. Then Alexis stood up from me and stared down.

Was I too much? I was just overcome with some ecstasy of new feeling. I couldn't control myself.

"Come with me." Alexis said, her eyes wide and blue as she peered down onto me.

She pulled me up and took me down the dark hallway I had once visited when I was only a stranger. Passing the pictures I had seen and the doors I had opened as Alexis slept unaware of the lurking monster inside her home.

Alexis led me to her bedroom door, opening it while giving me a devilishly wide-eyed stare. As I entered the room, I grabbed her waist and pulled her close to me. She began loosening my tie and unbuttoning my shirt.

Then in unison, we both stopped for a moment. Alexis peered into my eyes and stroked the back of her fingertips across my smooth face.

"Do you want to do this?" Alexis said as her ocean blue eyes gleamed in the half dark room.

"I wouldn't want to do this with anyone but you." I said, meaning it fully. She was the only person who could make me feel this way again. *You make me feel human,* I thought as Alexis kissed me.

"Lay on the bed." Alexis said to me, giving me a playful push towards it.

I fell to the soft sheets and then sat back up at the end of the bed, kicking off my shoes and loosening my tie. My hair sat messy and my shirt partially unbuttoned from Alexis's aggressive touch. As I undressed, I began to look at her still standing.

The room was dark, only lit by the moonlight peeking through a window. Alexis gave a shy smile and started to peel off her black dress, strap by strap. The action made me overcome with some sort of exciting anticipation as if I was a young boy about to receive a present. I waited to see what lay under the wrapping paper.

Alexis let both straps of her black dress fall to her sides, and with a little tug, the dress dropped to the floor. She stepped into the moonlight of the room revealing her half-naked self to me. My eyes widened at the sight. Alexis's skin was porcelain, pale white and pure like I had imagined her. She wore a navy blue laced thong with a pattern of flowers and a matching set bra. *She is an angel set to save me,* I thought as I stared still wide-eyed and grinning. In that moment,

I was in amazement of Alexis's figure. *But as every young boy and a wrapped present… I can't wait to see what lies underneath.*

"You're beautiful." I said to Alexis as she posed. She continued to smile shyly as I complimented her and began to step toward me with grace. Alexis stood on my feet and lightly fell on top of me, taking me to the bed with a barrage of sloppy kisses. I felt the warmth of her bare skin on me, breathing more life into me with each passing second.

My hands began again, this time cautiously feeling her new shown flesh. The skin felt of a soft cream to my touch. Smooth and warm. Gradually, I made my way down her back and reached the lace of her thong, brushing over the material. The feel was coarser than her skin but still appealed to my new found pleaser. Once more I grabbed her ass and pulled her up closer to the head of the bed space where I now occupied.

Alexis began to kiss down my neck as I gasped her every inch. Her tongue painted around my skin, leaving a wet and warm trail behind. I stopped grasping and dropped my hands back to the headboard as the pleasure of her touch consumed me. But as my hands banged against the hard wood post a flash back overtook my mind.

Suddenly, I was now on Terry's bed, handcuffed with the cold silver blade in my hand. I looked around to see where Alexis had gone, but all I saw was bloody walls and the body of Terry Conner dead on the floor. Then like an unwanted guest, my dark monster invaded my pleasured and peaceful mind.

Slit her throat and let the blood flow, the monster cackled.

The memory vanished and when I came to Alexis was on top of me staring with worry in her eyes. My warm feelings inside had soured and run cold. I stopped what I was doing in a panic as my darkness continued to make its presence known. *No this can't be happening…*

…My lustful emotions were humming for Perry as I led him into my dark bedroom. I wanted all of him.

Perry sat on the bed as his green eyes piercing through the darkness at me. I was ready to show my all to him as he stared at me in wonderment.

I slid my black dress straps down my shoulders. *I hope he likes what I have to offer,* I thought with uncertainty. Even if I had been called beautiful a million times before, I was always a bit nervous to be naked in front of a man for the first time. *The feelings I have towards Perry make it that much more.*

Men have always placed more of an importance on how you look than us women. They liked curves, large breasts, and hips. Yet somehow expected us to be thin with no excess fat or flab. The expectations to be perfect for what a man wanted seemed daunting and near impossible to obtain.

I don't even know what Perry likes, I realized while I was undressing. Was he going to disapprove of me and my body, leaving me feeling rejected? Or even worse sleep with me still but not be satisfied enough to stay around. *Time to find out.*

My black dress dropped to the ground and I gingerly stepped into the moonlight that shimmered through my window. *I hope it's enough,* I thought as Perry stared in judgment of my half exposed body.

Underneath my dress I had worn my best laced underwear and bra for him in case of such an event. Indigo with flower lace print. I wanted Perry to know that he was special so I gave him the best I had to offer. *Do men even notice or care of such things? No matter, it's good for my self-confidence.*

The vulnerability I had experienced before, of saying how I felt, had managed to find me again as Perry's eyes widened. *Hopefully he likes what he is seeing. You look beautiful he says,* but men lie to get what they want. *Barry had made sure I knew that troubling truth.*

The spotlight of the moon had burned doubts inside me long enough, so I stepped towards Perry, my skin eager to feel his touch. I stood inches from Perry's sitting self and began to kiss his lips once more. Taking him back to the bed and we embraced with lust. His hands were soft and ginger on my back as he discovered new areas of me and my fair skin. Perry was cautious in his movement, carefully whisking his fingers on the back of my skin for the first time. The slowness of touch made me tingle with goosebumps. His hands then rested to my hips, grasping at the revealed skin and pulling me up closer to him.

The touch reignited my lust and my self-conscious began to fade. I began to kiss down his neck and lick back up it. All I wanted was for Perry to feel like he made me feel. *Amazing and wanted.* But as I did he went cold and tightened up, letting go of me. I lifted up from his chest to view his face it was paled and nervous. *What did I do? Does he not find me attractive? Did my touch displease him?*

"What?" I said confused. "Is it me?" But Perry didn't respond, instead he gazed into space with a cold sweat. The silence made me feel unwanted and rejected, I was worried. "Perry is it me?" I said again trying to shake him into our reality.

"No," he finally responded.

"Then what?" I implored.

"Just nervous," Perry said wiping his brow of sweat.

"Why would you be nervous?" I asked beginning to feel nervous myself. Again Perry ignored my call, looking away and staring into the darkness. *What do I do or say?*

"Perry, I'm nervous too, but I know how I feel and that's all I need to know. I want this." I said, trying to reassure him.

I put my hand on the top of Perry's head to stroke his hair, trying to sooth him. He turned back to me and the greens of his eyes had turned darker and his pupils expanded. They appeared different to me, something I had never seen before. *What is it Perry? Talk to me.*

"I haven't done this in so long." Perry spoke up. "I just want it to be perfect and I'm scared I'll mess up. Mess up with everything."

"You won't, stop doubting yourself. All I care about is that I'm with you. Nothing else matters to me Perry... Look at me."

Perry had begun to gaze at the necklace he had given me. *What are you thinking mystery man, you never tell me. Am I supposed to guess at what is inside of you?* He finally looked up from the necklace and our eyes locked together again. The dark green irises relaxed and brightened, and Perry grabbed back hold of me with his fingers pressing into my skin.

"Thank you," Perry whispered in my ear. "For saving me."

Saving you, I thought, but I had no time to dwell as he began unhooking my bra...

...I tried to rid myself of darkness, but the combination of the wood headboard, laying on a bed, and a woman in underwear had triggered the monster back.

I thought you were gone, I said to the monster. *Aren't you satisfied with Terry? Let me be.*

Never. Kill her Perry, just like you did Terry. I want the blood of her pure body.

She isn't Terry. Alexis is the opposite of Terry. You aren't in control anymore. She doesn't deserve to die.

All women are evil you naive man. We already have learned this, so why beat the dead horse. Hurt her before she hurts you, Perry.

That's what we use to think but I don't anymore. You were just poisoning me. Blinding me and dulling my feelings.

I looked up at Alexis. She seemed concerned and frightened. Her lips moved but made no sound. Again Alexis's lips moved.

"Is it me Perry?" Her voice spoke.

No its not you Alexis, it's me. This monster, he won't leave me. He wants to take control of me and hurt you.

I had to turn away from her. The battle brewing in my mind was too much to bare. My dark monster was attacking like never before, thirsty from his long banishment. The veins in my body went cold and began to sweat as I stared into the darkness of her room.

I can beat you, I told the monster.

Then why do I still call to you Perry. Deep down you know I will always lurk, the monster cackled.

Not with her at my side. She is the key to beating you.

The key to another piece of heart to add to your trophy collection.

No to a heart inside me.

I felt the warm and soothing touch of Alexis to the top of my head as I battled. Her soft and pure hands trying to calm me of the beast. Even if I couldn't express it to her, the touch was helping. I heard Alexis's voice in the darkness of my mind, telling me of her feelings and her longing to be with me. *If only I could tell you what I was. Why*

I struggle with this. If only I knew how to keep my fleeting feelings all the time.

Enough power came to me to lie and say I was nervous about us and sex. But I was nervous about something far worse, the darkness that wanted to kill her as she laid on me. The monster was inches away from taking control. I was losing my grasp on sanity.

Alexis's voice entered my dark mind again with clear and light intensions. "Look at me." Her voice said. The words game me strength to battle back to her while the darkness was consuming my mind. I turned to her and saw the ruby heart necklace dangling in front of me as a sign.

That is what I want. A heart of my own. A heart to give Alexis. My heart.

That kind of heart isn't a reality. We both know the truth. The symbol we draw with our victims is. Twisted, broken, and cold. We are the real...

I looked up from the ruby necklace and locked with Alexis's ocean blue eyes. They shone through my dark thoughts and if some sort of magic the monster vanished. I returned to the state I had lost for a moment. *She saved me again.*

My arms wrapped around her body and I held her tight. I could feel her heart beat against me and mine began to steadily beat again. *She will always save me from the darkness.* The flow of warmth filled me again and my mind was clear of all the dark and evil thoughts. *Thank you, thank you,* I thought, wishing I could tell her why.

I began unhooking her bra. At first, the hooks gave me difficulties, struggling to find the latches. *I am not used to doing this with a live body.* But after a clumsy minute I managed to unclasp the latches to relieve the constraints that held in Alexis's secrets.

Alexis sat up on me and the bra fell to the bed. I stared aimlessly, mesmerized by her naked chest. Alexis's breasts were perky and round but not overly large. Her nipples were a brownish cream and pointed. *I probably look like a fool staring, but I can't stop looking, you are beautiful Alexis Fisher.* Alexis smiled as I stared. *A boy in a candy shop.*

"Your turn," Alexis said to me after a moment of basking. She took off my tie and unbuttoned the rest of my shirt, throwing both to the bedroom floor.

A single finger skated across my unclothed chest.

"What happened here?" Alexis said touching at my side.

My cut from Terry, I thought.

"Just a scar from falling when I was little."

Alexis gave the scar a kiss and then loosened my belt, pulling away my dress pants. When she was done, she came back to me with kisses from my belly to my lips. As I kissed her, we rolled around the sheeting and I managed to pin her to the bottom of the bed.

As I pinned Alexis my lips found their way onto her neck. Her soft skin tasted sweet and warm like honey. My hands went to her breasts for the first time as I tasted her flesh. They were soft but firm. I had forgotten the feeling of a breast in my hands. *How wonderful,* I thought as I gasped at her flabby soft flesh.

My mouth followed my hands onto Alexis's chest, kissing and licking her cream nipples. She let out a soft moan as I did and her legs began to move restlessly while she grasped my hair, giving it a tug.

"Are you ready?" Alexis whispered in my ear.

My heart was racing, my blood flowing, as she presented the question. *I am ready for anything with you…*

…Perry struggled unhooking my bra. I wasn't sure if he was still nervous or if he was just like most men, clueless when it came to a woman's garments.

My mind had relaxed after the uncertainty presented by Perry. I just wanted to experience this moment with him. *As long as he is fine so am I,* I thought as his hands helped to alleviate my worries and bring me excitement with each of his fuddled attempts. I waited with anticipation to show him even more of me, piece by piece he would see the real me.

Perry managed to unclasp the hooks and I sat up on his lying waist. *Here we go,* I thought, letting the bra fall to the bed.

The exposure set in as Perry's eyes darted at my breasts, examining each and every inch. I was never a large breasted woman, which personally I was glad about, but I knew men enjoyed them that way. *Just like mine the way they are.* After a second or two I decided it was time to level the clothing disparity. *He doesn't get to stare at me if he's clothed.*

I started to tear his layers off piece by piece, tossing them like trash to the floor. I didn't care what a man's body looked like much. I craved the experience and emotions involved more than anything, but I still enjoyed seeing what lie underneath. *We are all human aren't we? Seeing skin brings pleasure.*

Perry was lean, his stomach flat, and his chest mostly smooth with little hair. His body wasn't overly muscular but I could see definition in his chest, arms, and shoulders. *Lean but athletic. Nothing I can't work with.*

I grazed his chest with my hand. The touch of his skin was cold but smooth. Moving my finger down him, I came across a rough part of his skin. It felt like a scar but the darkness of the room made it hard to make out the true definition. Perry claimed to have obtained the gash as a young child, but I was skeptical about his response. I didn't have time to think on it however, as he grabbed me and flipped me on my back side all the while kissing my neck and caressing my breasts. *I like the dominance he is presenting.*

Perry's lips followed and he started to kiss my breasts with soft grace. The feeling of his wet tongue shot a tingle through my body and I squirmed with pleasure. I twisted my legs and I let out a quiet moan, and in that moment, I was ready for him to take me. I wanted our bodies to become one and slid my underwear off, telling him to do the same.

"Come to me," I said. *I want to gaze into your piercing green eyes.*

Perry did, staring directly down into my eyes. While I gazed, I spread out my legs for him. He looked around at my naked body, almost unsure of what to do next.

"Don't be scared." I encouraged.

"I'm not… Not anymore." Perry said. "You're just so beautiful. It's like I'm staring at an angel."

I blushed at the comment and my heart fluttered at the meaning of his words. *He thinks I'm special. Not just some other girl.* I pulled him into me. His flesh had warmed as he fell closer to me. His heart beat and so did mine, both in perfect sync. My hands grasped the biceps of his arms and he went inside of me…

… I nodded my head. *Yes I am ready.*

Alexis peeled her underwear off first and I followed suit, taking mine off in a flurry of excitement. I again gazed at her naked body in full view. The look of her was as if I was seeing a naked woman for the first time. *So soft and pure. Her body would rival any artists work, a masterpiece.*

I remembered the midnight black haired woman as I looked at Alexis now. When I had taken a piece of heart from her for the first time, I stared at that woman's naked body as a killer, as evil ready to steal away. But even in my hate and villainy, I was nervous. Nervous to plunge my steel into her body for the first time.

The same nervousness then had come back now as I marveled at Alexis's naked body. This time I wasn't staring at her as a killer but instead a wanting man, as Perry. The feeling of a virgin was upon me again, nervous to plunge my flesh inside her. *What if I can't?* But I couldn't wait any longer. Alexis spread her legs for me, asking me to come to her.

And just as I had with the midnight black haired woman, I dove in with uncertainty of myself and my abilities. *Can I do this? Can a monster turn back to a man and love?* I felt her flesh warm on mine, her heart beating as mine was too. We were in perfect unison. All the feelings I had been missing for a near decade came flooding back inside of me and I went inside her wet warm flesh while she squeezed my arms…

We made love to each other. We grasped each other's bodies, squeezing and scratching. We whisked our limbs across each other's warm skin with loving passion. We kissed and stared deep into each other's eyes.

Blue or green. Black or white. Good or evil. What did it all mean in this moment of love and passion? Who are we inside and why do we fear the other minds thoughts? In this moment, our perspectives blurred together and we were one in the moonlight. A killer and a beauty.

Chapter 24
Twisted Love Stories

For hours, the forensic team swept through Terry Connor's house. The end results weren't what Paul wanted to hear. Not a single drop of blood, not a fingerprint, nor a single strand of hair. Nothing.

"It was expected." Said Agent Price.

"Still, it doesn't make the news less disheartening." Said Paul. "Sorry for the pun, but it really is."

"Don't forget, we still have the actual crime scene to investigate Detective."

"Yeah, but what are the chances he leaves us anything? He knows how to cover his tracks."

"We only need one slip up. No one is perfect forever. He had to have rushed a bit doing it out in the open."

He may well be perfect. Sure is perfect at irritating me, thought Paul as they drove to the Channel 28 News building. A day had passed since Terry Connor's death and Paul had yet to view the crime scene.

A large crowd was standing outside the police perimeter when Paul and Agent Price arrived, making it difficult to get anywhere near the crime scene by car. When the two reached the police perimeter a swarm of news reporters surrounded them.

"Any breaks on the Heartbreak Killer case, Detective?" Said a man unfamiliar to Paul.

"Agent Price, is it true you have taken over the case? How long until you expect to find the Heartbreak Killer?" Said a woman reporter sticking a microphone into the face of Agent Price.

Paul shoved the mob of reporters aside and made his way closer to the crime scene.

"Detective Fisher," the Captain called out. "Agent Price." He waved the two over to him. "Glad to see you here, Fisher. I wasn't sure if I would again after you stormed out of my office yesterday."

"What the hell is going on here?" Said Paul as he and Agent Price crossed the yellow police tape to the Captain. "It's been a day since this all happened and there are still people and news reporters swarming around?"

"It's a damn circus is what it is. It's been like this all day and it's only going to get crazier with the national news arriving by the masses." Said the Captain.

"They are turning this into some kind of spectacle." Said Agent Price.

"Only in America, turning a killer into some sort of celebrity." Said Paul.

"You two as well." Said the Captain. "I have been getting calls all day from the media about setting up interviews with you two."

"What? Why?" Said Paul.

"Because this story has become massive. The public loves a hero and fears a villain, and that's what the media wants to sell to them." Said the Captain.

"That's sick. This isn't some sort of fictional pop culture, real people are being affected." Said Agent Price.

"That's just the reality of the world we live in." Said the Captain. "So the sooner you get this resolved the better. The media won't stop until the story is over or the ratings plummet... Did you guys find anything at the Connor house?"

"No, but he was there, I could sense it. Sheets were taken from Terry's bed and it looked as if the killer handcuffed her to a bed post before killing her." Said Paul.

"Disappointing to hear," said the Captain.

"What do we know about the crime scene at hand, Captain?" Said Agent Price trying to change the subject.

"Let's walk and talk, I'll show you." The Captain led them through the crime scene, stopping at massive stretch of red clothing sunk in white snow that covered the entirety of the news station property.

"Is this the hearted symbol I read about?" Said Agent Price in awe of the spectacle. "It's enormous."

"Yup, and we are still searching through the masses of it for anything useful for the case." Said the Captain. "It's safe to say the killer was really trying to prove a point."

"The killer saw the news that proclaimed he had been captured. He wanted to show everyone they were mistaken." Said Paul. *What are you proclaiming Heartbreak?*

"I agree. The killer isn't a mindless fool, he wanted people to see this. This whole scene and victim was calculated." Said Agent Price.

"Whatever the reasoning, it doesn't help us find the killer." Said the Captain. "The heart is made up…"

"Clothes," interrupted Paul as he further inspected a section of the pile, picking a piece up with his hand. *Terry's clothes,* Paul wondered.

"What is the red substance on the clothes?" Asked Agent Price.

"Our lab reports indicate that this is the same paint found at the last crime scene." Said the Captain. "The killer soaked every last piece in it."

"Detective, I think these are Terry's clothes." Said Agent Price, now examining a piece from the heart.

"I think so too." Paul said back to Agent Price. "Is there anything else we need to know before we start looking around, Captain?"

"Only that Terry's car is parked in the lot behind the news station. Some of the workers here told us that she had left early, so they weren't entirely sure why the car was back here. One person claimed that Terry had left because she found a break in the Heartbreak story. Take that as you want but we looked through the car and there was nothing of value."

"Thanks," said Paul, giving the Captain a nod. The Captain nodded back and left the two alone.

"Do you think the killer could have called Terry pretending to have a tip?" Said Agent Price.

"I'm not sure, but it would make sense. If these are Terry's clothes then he was surely at the house, but without any other evidence we can only guess. Hopefully something sticks." Said Paul, still examining the paint soaked clothes.

"Let's hope for some good luck then. Maybe the sheets are somewhere amongst the piles."

The Agent and Detective made their way around the heart made of clothing, looking for any sign of the sheets missing from Terry's bed. They came across dresses, shirts, pants, bras, and underwear, but no sign of the sheets. Only red painted clothing resided within.

"Let's take a look up on the roof where the body was hanging." Suggested Paul. *There is nothing here.* Agent Price agreed and they headed for the rooftop of Channel 28 News.

With Terry's body now removed, only blotches of bloodstains and pieces of what appeared to be the mutilated insides of Terry remained behind. The white numbers two and eight where she had hung from were smeared with dried blood as well and a small puddle of blood festered below, almost frozen from the cold outside. Steel chains were left behind to dangle, moving ever so lightly as a soft wind blew.

"Nothing," said Paul as he leaned against the large number two. He stared down at the broken heart seeing it in full view for the first time. "I told you."

Agent Price leaned next to Paul on the large number eight, looking down at the broken heart too. "We will find him. It's only a matter of time." She said.

"I don't want there to be another time."

"Me either, but time is the only thing we will have on our side right now."

The sun was setting behind the city while the two stood on the rooftop, still taking in the full work of the Heartbreak Killer. Dark shadows began to descend upon the broken and twisted red heart made of clothes. Slowly, the large crowd was thinning out and the media frenzy calming as they started to pack their equipment into vans.

Nothing for them either, Paul thought. *At least I can take solace in that.*

"How about that story, Detective." Said Agent Price.

"How about a drink instead?" Suggested Paul.

"I hear it's bad to enable alcoholics."

"I'm more of a social drinker."

"And I am the Heartbreak Killer." Jabbed Agent Price.

Paul couldn't help but laugh. *She does make the mood lighter. I can't fault her for that.*

"My hotel has a bar. We can go there, but only if you make a deal to tell me that story." Said Agent Price with a momentary pause. "Deal?"

"Deal." Paul said. *Company while drinking is better than none at all.*

The bar was empty when Paul and Agent Price arrived to the hotel. Agent Price requested a beer and went to find a spot to sit at while Paul was tasked with ordering the drinks. *That's a strange choice for a woman*, thought Paul as he waited at the bar counter. *First a hard ass, then a comedian, now a beer drinker? She is full of surprises.*

"Story time," Agent Price said as soon as Paul brought the drinks to the table.

"Why are you so interested in this story?" Demanded Paul as he sat.

"For one I enjoy stories. Secondly, I have always found it easier to bond with someone when you know something personal about them. Don't be so defensive, Detective."

"What's the point of bonding with me when you're only here until the case is over?"

"My reasoning is irrelevant, you made the deal. Are you not a man of your word, Detective?" Said Agent Price, giving Paul a nudge on the arm.

Paul gave her a blank stare. *She has you beat there, just tell her.* "Okay, I'll tell you, but let me drink this down first."

Agent Price listened with quiet intent as Paul explained his love story, his heartbreak, and the spiraling path to a certain darkness. The buried memories of his wife flooded back to Paul and with them came the tears of pain and sorrow. Paul did his best to fight them back but in the end the levy broke and the tears rolled through. Agent Price reached out and touched his arm.

"Sorry, it's the first time I have really talked about this with anyone." Said Paul wiping a tear from his cheek. "I know it's not pretty to see a grown man cry."

"You are perfectly fine. We're all humans with sensitive emotions. I for one don't get caught up in gender stereotypes that say a man can't cry." Said Agent Price still clutching to Paul's arm. "I mean look at me, I am a female FBI agent drinking a beer."

"You do have a way to lighten the mood, Agent Price." Paul said regaining his composer with a smile.

"Thanks for telling me Paul. I know how hard it was for you to let it out."

"I guess it's your turn now, Agent Price? Since we are sharing our twisted love stories and all."

"You're right; I did make that deal earlier with you at the Connor estate. Hmmm." Agent Price looked away in thought. "Anyway you will let me off the hook now?"

"Not a chance, remember we are bonding."

"Okay, Okay, you're right, I can't back out now." Nina paused for another moment and her face hardened.

"I thought I found true love with a man once. I'm sure I felt for him in the same way you do about your wife. Things were great for a long while and I was happy. I thought I had found my prince charming, the one I had always dreamed about as a little girl…"

Agent Price took a deep breath and looked at her drink.

"The warning signs were small at first. One time had pushed me when we had a big fight. The action terrified me because he was bigger and stronger than me. But I loved him, and I thought it was just in the heat of the moment, nothing more. Then things proceeded to get worse. One night he was so mad he hit me, once in the face and the other in the ribs. All because he was convinced I was cheating on him."

Paul sat in silence, listening and thinking. *What kind of man hits a woman? I would never, what a coward.*

"Tell me who, he demanded. I told him it was all in his head but he didn't believe me. I found out the reason why one night. He had been cheating on me all along and the guilt was eating him inside."

"That's awful." Paul intervened.

"Yeah it was, and I wish that was the end of my story." Said Agent Price with a false and deflecting smile. "I was so young and naive back then. I was weak, and I didn't want to lose what I thought was love of my life. So instead of seeing the alarming signs, I went into denial and stayed with him. We tried to work things out, and for a while I saw hope in our relationship becoming what I had seen before all the abuse, cheating, and lies."

Agent Price took another deep breath and continued.

"Then that night came. He claimed to be going out with his friends and came back late at night, drunk and in disarray. I had woken up from the sound of him knocking something over so I went out to see if he was okay. I remember his eyes the most; they were blank as if he wasn't even there. A walking ghost of himself. He said to me, I know your cheating on me again."

Reaching for her beer, Agent Price began to drink, almost empting the remains of the bottle before continuing.

"I felt sick to my stomach when I heard those words. My heart began to break inside as I realized I was reliving the same situation that had happened before. I told him to leave, get out, I screamed. But he wouldn't, he grabbed me, throwing me against the wall. I was barely conscious after the impact, only coming to when he was on top of me trying to rip off my clothes. I screamed and hit him, trying to find a way to break free."

Paul could see Agent Prices face become pale and colorless the deeper the story went and his stomach began to churn with disgust.

"He barely felt a thing as I hit him. The alcohol had dulled every sense he had. When I realized my fists weren't doing anything, I bit at his face, trying to tear off any piece of flesh I could just so he would get off of me. I managed to bite him hard enough and he wailed, rolling off me, and clutched his face in agony. I saw my chance and ran for the door, but he caught me before I could leave, hitting me in the back of the head. He then continued to pound me over and over again with his fists. It was in that moment I saw death grasping at me. I knew I couldn't over power him. He grasped at my throat and I started to lose sight and strength. For whatever reason though, it wasn't my time to go. Somehow, I noticed a kitchen knife out of the corner of my eye. I don't know how or when, but we had managed to stumble into the kitchen. With my last gasps, I grabbed that knife and stabbed at him until he let go of my throat."

Paul was stunned without words.

"The funny thing about it all was even after the police had investigated and cleared me of any crime, I was the one left ostracized by everyone around me. I received death threats from the parents and the friends of the man, and people never looked at me the same. Once the news spread, somehow I had become the villain for defending myself. People viewed me as a killer, a provoker, that it was my fault I was getting assaulted in the first place. So I left, promising myself I would never be that weak again. It was then that I realized the world wasn't a fairytale like the movies and books showed me as a girl. Instead, the world I lived in was a dark and fucked up place. Constantly scaring good-natured people and consuming them to darkness. The rest of the story you already know. Decided to become an FBI agent, finished tops in my class, now Agent Nina Price."

"How did you manage to overcome all of that?" Paul managed to say.

"Who says I have Paul? But now you know why I was so interested to hear your story, I've lived one myself."

"Twisted love stories." Said Paul, still processing all he had heard.

"And now our two twisted souls are put in charge of a case to hunt down the man who shows the world what we have seen and know about true love. Who knows Paul, maybe the Heartbreak Killer isn't so different for you and I."

"I wonder what his story is… If it pushed him into doing something like this then…"

"I think that's why we are both here now, to find out that very question. I know that's why I requested to come here at least. To find out just how a man comes to be the Heartbreak Killer."

"Another drink?" interrupted the bartender.

"No," said Paul. "I think I've had enough. We both have."

Chapter 25
Progression

Progression is what all therapists strive for. We are presented with a problem by the patient and our jobs are to make them progress through it in a healthy manner. Progression is what every human seeks in life, to be better than the current version of themselves.

The fat man wants to shed weight, tired of his current unattractive and lazy self, so he goes to a gym. He desires progression of weight loss, wanting to be an attractive and energetic person.

A woman wants to shake her depression; she has had enough with the gloomy cloud surrounding her mind. The weight of her ailment grounds her, making it hard to do the simplest of tasks. So she seeks medication or tactics to attack the depression, trying to progress to a happy way of life while shedding her old ways.

I am the Heartbreak Killer and I felt nothing. A man of ultimate darkness. So I went to seek out my way of recovery, trying to feel once more, and find my heart. *But how does such a man find that progression in his life?*

Do people ultimately find the progression they wanted and seek? No, many of my clients never came to fruition with their goals. Progression is hard you see, people rarely change in a drastic matter. I have found that to be true during my tenure as a therapist. Progression is the rare and elusive beast that many chase, but few capture.

I attempted to attack my darkness with violence and revenge on those who hurt me. Darkness and blood were my cure for pain, my

way to progress. I thought that taking what they had stolen from my heart, my feelings and me, would cure me and make me better than I had become. *But it never did.*

Instead, I spiraled downward and my darkness spoke more and more frequently inside my shrouded mind. *Will I ever feel again? Am I doomed to be an evil monster forever?*

No.

I captured the elusive beast. I was reborn into the man I use to be, Perry Nelson. Heartbreak gone, no more, quieted from a different method. Instead of taking as I had in my darkness, I finally gave. I gave myself even as the darkness latched to me, poisoning my mind to take once more. *No more darkness, no more.*

As I lay in Alexis's bed naked and sweating, my heart still racing, I began to feel like never before. *An ecstasy of feeling,* I thought.

Feelings had come to me in short bursts, sure, but only as quick flickers of light in an otherwise pitch-black night. This new feeling was constant and wonderful. Feelings of great longing to never leave Alexis's side resided in me now, taking a place in the home that once held my dark monster. I wanted to be around her always and forever now. Having feelings weren't just a hope for me now, it was a reality. *I can feel again.*

Was it love? I wasn't sure, the emotions were novice and unfamiliar still. But as her soft pale white flesh pressed to mine the feelings somehow managed to pierce inside my dark exterior and wound the dark monster. I had made my progression.

"Alexis?" I said as I had laid underneath the silk bed sheets. "I am ready."

"Ready for what?" Asked Alexis.

"Ready to be with you."

"As in a couple?"

"Yes."

She kissed me and cuddled up even closer as she heard the words. We were a couple. The lonely Heartbreak Killer no more.

I arrived to work the next day fresh and revived. I smiled to the secretary at the counter as I strolled by, even giving her a wave. "Good morning" I said to her. She looked at me with confusion.

"Good morning... Doctor Nelson..." She said back, nearly tongue tied.

When I reached my office, I stared at my degrees on the wall. *That is the man you wanted to be, now be him once more*. With a deep breath, Dr. Perry Nelson the man was once again sitting behind the desk in his office. I wanted to help my patient's progress again, as I had before my dark inflictions. *I want them to progress as I had now. Anything is possible if I can do it.*

The days flew by after my night with Alexis, and along with them, the feelings and emotions were still intact. I was happy and changed without a peep from the dark monster.

I constantly thought of Alexis when we were apart. I couldn't wait to see her next. She was intoxicating to me, and the more I was around her, the stronger my emotions became. I was becoming more human each day with her as my medication.

Going on dates with Alexis had been a sharp learning curve for me at the time. I had forgotten how to act somewhere along the dark pathway. *That first date was a near train wreck.* But little did I know, being in a committed relationship was an even sharper curve than dating. Alexis expected more from me now. No longer could I hide away for days and days trying to concur my inner darkness. Alexis counted on me for advice, for comfort, for support, and for love. She wanted to see more and more of me, but I didn't mind, because so did I.

Then the day finally came when Alexis wanted to come over to my place. I had been dreading the moment since we had become a real couple. She had inquired many times before, but I always put it off with excuses. "My place is messy, let's just go out." "I would rather go to your place." "I don't want to stay in."

Even though I was progressing, I wasn't completely cured. I still had dark secrets hidden inside my place, unwilling to part with them for good. The steel knives that I used to cut human flesh, hidden away in my closet. The pieces of heart I had collected inside a case, tucked behind my bedroom safe. My various clean up tools and products, spread throughout the house. *Why can't I just throw them all away?* Even with all of the feelings, I still wanted my reminders of the darkness around. *Why,* I wondered.

Finally, I caved, and agreed to Alexis's request to coming over. I had run out of excuses, and I feared that she might come to the conclusion that I was hiding something from her if I kept the game up much longer. *You are Perry. She will find them and you will be ruined forever, the progress gone.*

Before she arrived, I imagined her discovering the dark objects scattered throughout my house. *If she finds them what would she do? Nothing good I imagine.* I would surely be finished. *Maybe that is what someone like me deserves, getting so close but ultimately losing it all.*

A buzz came from my door. "Alexis?" I said as I answered.

"Of course, you did invite me over finally, didn't you?" Alexis said through the speaker in my place.

"I did indeed."

"Well buzz me in silly, its cold out here."

"Sorry," I said, quickly buzzing her in. *I guess it's time to see if this is really meant to be.*

I scanned around my place once more, making sure that everything was in order and safely tucked away. *Just keep her away from my room and things will be good.*

I had cooked a special dinner for the two of us tonight. It was all set up for her to walk in and see. The lights were dimmed, the table set with a red cloth and candles burning, and in the background a slow jazz played from my speakers. *If I am to go out, at least it will be in style.*

Knocking came from the door. *She is here. Oh fuck.* I paced to the door and opened it with raised eyebrows and a scared smile.

"Hello handsome boyfriend. Gosh, saying that doesn't get old does it?" Alexis said as I opened the door.

"It certainly doesn't." I said blocking the doorway with my hand.

"Well are you going to let me in? This is a big moment in our relationship, me coming to your house. You almost had me worried you were hiding something up here."

"Why would you think such a crazy thing? You know I'm awkward."

"I guess so, but you have gotten better. Now, let me in before I tackle you."

"How about we go out for dinner instead, what do you say?" I said in desperation. *Please agree,* I thought.

Alexis's eyebrows raised to the question. "Not a chance Perry, I want you all to myself tonight. Now let me in silly."

I moved aside. Alexis gave me a hug and kiss before she walked in.

Once Alexis was inside, she darted from place to place, looking around to see what my house had in store. After a moment or two, she looked back at me. "This is such a pretty place, Perry. Who knew we both had the same taste in furniture and decorations. I love all the artwork too. You were worried to have me over, why?"

"Because I worry about being perfect." I bashfully said.

"Well you shouldn't so much. Are you going to give me the grand tour of the rest of the house or whatever this setup is called?"

"A penthouse, and maybe after, I have a surprise for you."

I led Alexis to the decorated table and her face lit up with excitement.

"Aw you did all this for me, you're so sweet. How did I get so lucky?"

"Sit down and relax. The food is ready; I just need to grab it from the kitchen."

"You cooked too? You're spoiling me Perry Nelson."

"I told you I wanted things to be perfect when you came here." I said with a smile.

For dinner I had cooked up some salmon for the two of us. I had learned from our short time dating that Alexis wasn't fond of the red meats like me, so I had to sacrifice for her. I had asked her why once and she told me that the blood that came from cutting into the meat made her woozy. *If only she knew the blood I had seen while cutting.*

With the salmon, I had chosen the sides of asparagus and baked potato.

"You remembered that I don't like red meat?" Alexis said as I sat the plate in front of her. "Impressive."

"Not too bad eh?" I said. "Oh I forgot something, hold on."

I went back to the kitchen, grabbing the wine and glasses, and turned on the music. "Here you are," I said, presenting and pouring the wine into her glass. I seated myself and we began to eat.

When Alexis finished she asked me for the tour. For some reason she was eager to see each and every room. *Maybe she is here to spy on me for her Dad. Wow I'm paranoid. Just don't ask to see my bedroom.* With each room came a complement, whether it was the paintings in my living room, the large selves of books in my study, or the balcony view of the city.

"Are you saving the best for last?" Said Alexis as we looked down on the snowy city from the cold balcony.

"What do you mean?" I said fearing for the answer.

"Well, I want to see your room and you haven't shown me it yet. Every man's true colors lie within their room."

"It's a mess." I lied.

"Oh I don't buy that for a moment. You messy? Look at this place, you couldn't find a piece of dust in it. Come on show me. Please, please, please."

Alexis dragged me inside and I reluctantly lead her down the hallway to the end door where my room resided. As I turned the handle a worry broke over me. *Did I put everything away? What if there is a knife out in the open or a drop of blood that stained the floor?*

I opened the door and turned the light on, scanning before Alexis could get a peak in. Everything seemed in order as I presented it to her. "Well this is my room, nothing special." I said with a show of my hand.

Alexis walked in and began to search around. I followed suit and carefully looked around for anything out of place. The fear of her finding something was pounding inside of me. *The bad emotions come with the good I guess.* The thought of her stumbling onto anything made me want to vomit. *Let's get her out of here now.*

I turned to Alexis, she was stepping into my walk in closet. *The black bag of knives!* I raced to meet her, cutting her off before she entered. *I need to get her out of here. This is too risky.*

"So this is the closet of the well-dressed Perry Nelson. Where all the good fashion lies." Alexis said pushing me aside to strum through my dress shirts and pants.

"Yeah, but that's boring, they are just clothes." I said, following behind her.

"Perry don't you know anything? I am a woman, I love clothes." *You may not love what else is in here though.*

"How about we go and watch a movie in the living room. My room is boring." I pleaded while attempting to stay calm.

"What are you hiding from me, Perry?" Alexis said with a suspicious smile.

"Hiding? Nothing, I just want to cuddle up and watch a movie."

The black bag was tucked away on a high shelf at the end of my closet. In front of the bag were old shoeboxes, obstructing the view from anyone who walked inside. Even though I was confident Alexis couldn't reach that high up, I didn't want to stay around to find out.

"You want to cuddle? I'm not sure if you have ever suggested that to me. I'm always the one who begs you."

"Well tonight is your lucky night I guess."

"Hmm, you are being strange Mr. Nelson. Do you have dirty magazines lying around somewhere in here?"

Actually dirty knifes.

"No nothing like that, I just want to relax is all."

"It's okay if you do Perry, I don't mind, but now that you're with me I hope this is all you need." Alexis said, displaying herself with her hands. "I can get jealous, even if the girls are on pieces of paper. You don't want to see me jealous, Perry."

"I promise it's nothing like that."

"I know it isn't, I'm just teasing you. Now, show me the rest of the room and we can watch your movie."

One dark disaster evaded.

We went out of the closet and Alexis studied the rest of the room.

To me my room was plain. A king sized bed with black sheets. A wooden nightstand with a lamp and reading books on top. All surrounded by plain white walls. Hell, I didn't even have paintings up in my room, it was the only one without them. *Why is my room so dull*, I began to think while Alexis sat on my bed seemingly satisfied with the viewing. *Probably because I was dull and dead inside when I arranged it. Alexis was right about showing my true colors.*

"Are you ready to relax?" I implored once more.

"Well I thought I was, but then I noticed this safe behind your bed. What is inside there, Perry?" Alexis said while attempting to stand on the bed to take a closer look at the safe.

My eyes widened without an answer. *What do people usually keep in a safe? Money, valuables, pieces of human heart?*

"If you aren't going to tell me I may have to discover the combination myself." Continued Alexis, now pressing on the key pad.

I hurried over and grabbed her arm. "Come on Alexis, let's go watch a movie. There is nothing in there that you need to worry about." I said nearly losing my cool. *Do not guess the code, please do not let her guess the code.*

"You really don't want me to know, huh? Was this why you didn't want me to come here? Is there some sort of secret item behind this safe door?" Alexis said pulling away from me. "If you tell me right now I will stop."

"Alexis it's nothing, I promise. Will you please forget about it?"

Alexis stared into my eyes. I felt as if she was reading my mind as she did, reading the thing I didn't want her to read. *The remains of the Heartbreak Killer is hiding inside there.*

"Okay Perry," Alexis said, giving me a kiss on my lips. "I guess some things a man has to keep to himself."

"Are you okay with that?" I said, hoping I hadn't upset her.

"Yes I think I'm satisfied. I was hoping to find something incriminating so I could hold it against you, but I guess whatever is behind that wall will have to be a secret." Alexis said with a laugh. "Let's go cuddle up and watch that movie."

If she only knew how close she really was to that incrimination.

I left Alexis to pick out a movie while I sat on the couch to breathe a sigh of relief. The fear of her finding any dark secret had passed. *At least for now.*

"Has anyone told you that you have a lot of thrillers?" Alexis said thumbing through my DVDs selection. "What's this one about the blood splatter analysis killer guy? It looks interesting, is it any good?"

"Yes it's excellent, based off books actually." I said. "It's a TV show though." *One of my idols too.*

"Oh, well maybe some other time." Alexis searched a little longer and came up to one she liked, putting it in the player.

"What did you pick?" I said trying to get a peek at the case she was holding.

"It's nothing you need to worry about." Alexis said as she cuddled up to me and threw a nearby blanket over both of us.

I found the response amusing and put my arm over her. As the movie began to play, I could only focus on Alexis as she intently watched. *Look at how far I have come in so little time,* I thought. *This must be what a happy person feels like.*

When I finally looked up, I realized what she had selected. "Oh, you picked this one?" I said.

"Yeah, it's a classic and this adaptation is amazing." Alexis said staring at the TV.

"I didn't know you were a fan of his work."

"Of course, how could I not be? I work at a bookstore, Perry. He is the most iconic writer that ever lived, don't you think?"

"He's certainly up there." I said trying to think of someone better.

"Do you not like my choice?"

"No it's perfectly fine, I was just in the mood for something less tragic."

"It's not tragic, it's a love story silly." Said Alexis giving me a kiss on the cheek. "Do you have any popcorn? I enjoy some while I watch a movie."

"I think so, let me check."

As I stood up and walked to the kitchen, I could only think of one thing.

Tragic or love story, let's hope we have a better ending.

Chapter 26
Impediment

Slowly but surely Perry and I had become a committed couple.

Perry seemed to grow before my very eyes. He wasn't the awkward and unsure man I had witnessed on our first date. I couldn't quite point out what the reason was behind his growth was but I was happy to see Perry shining. *Maybe he just needed a woman like me to guide him.*

My feelings towards Perry grew as he did. I could start to see the potential for our relationship to have a bright future, but at the same time the magnitude of feelings were unsettling. *I'm falling in love with Perry but I'm scared to tell him. What if it's too soon?* The first I love you was always the scariest for me. *What if he doesn't love me back?* Doubts were raised, but still the feelings lingered inside me, just waiting to be released.

The feeling of love had begun to surface when we first made love, but began to overflow when Perry had let me come over to his place for the first time. I took his gesture as he was comfortable enough to let me in. *He trusts me,* I thought when I left his house or whatever he called it. *Didn't he say penthouse?*

But with all the love and trust building, I held a secret, a problem amongst the bliss. Barry had been harassing me with non-stop phone calls since his doorstep appearance, trying to convince me to take him back. I wanted nothing to do with him but this led to him knocking on my door unannounced. I feared he may become violent if he heard the news of Perry and I's official relationship title. Barry had become emotionally unstable and any sudden movement or change could lead to a rash decision on his part.

Within the dilemma there was uncertainty on my part. *What can I do?*

I was also afraid to tell Perry about my situation. *How would he react? He is so mysterious.* I didn't want the news to turn off Perry or stunt our relationships growth. Impeding growth was never good for a new couple.

Even with all the confusion on my part one thing stood certain, Perry was the one I wanted to be with. I just needed to find a way to maneuver the sticky situation. *I need to tell Perry soon. The longer I wait, the worse it will look. Barry has to be cut off, he is the weed trying to kill the growing plant.*

The thought was easier to process than set in motion, however. Every time I was with Perry I felt the words hanging in my throat, just waiting to escape, but every time I couldn't manage to get them out. With each failed attempt, the thought began to weigh and a heavy pressure began to build. A guilty burden resided within.

With Valentine's Day fast approaching, it was time to come clean to both men. I needed to stop the potential impediment that loomed.

Who should I tell first, I wondered while sitting at home. *Perry, he is the one I care about now.* How to tell Perry was a different story. *Most men resort to violence or anger in the face of controversy. No, Perry is sweet, he wouldn't. Would he?*

Instinctively, I reached for my phone to call him.

"Do you have time to meet up with me today?" I said to Perry as he answered the phone.

"Of course Alexis, what did you have in mind?" Perry said.

What I had in mind was a simple walk in a park. The weather had been clearing up, and with no sight of snow on the ground or chilly winds in the air, a walk sounded pleasant.

My heart fluttered at the sight of my handsome man standing by a bench in the park when I arrived. With the sudden flutter came a nervous anticipation with the news I carried to him. But the mix of feelings made me feel alive. Perry had that effect on me; he was so much different from other men. *I have to tell him.*

The longer we walked and talked the more the looming pressure built. Even though it was a strange feeling to feel guilty about something I had no control of, the thought made me sick to my stomach. *You can do this. Be strong, he will be understanding.*

"Perry," I managed to get out.

"What?" He said.

I turned to face Perry. He had a grin on from speaking about a patient he had helped at work. *What if this hurts him? What if he loses confidence? Or if he fears that I am cheating? No I can't. I need to tell Barry and get him out first. That way Perry knows I'm serious about us, that I care about him. This is my problem not his.*

"Never mind, I had a problem, but I think I solved it just walking here." I said with a smile. *I've changed my mind.*

"Okay Alexis, but you know I am pretty good with advice. It is my job you know."

"Oh, what is it you do again?"

"You know damn well." Perry said with a comically stern face.

Perry reached out at my sides to tickle me. I screamed with laughter and ran away, trying to escape from his playful attack. He chased me through the park, finally grabbing me by the waist and wrapping me in his arms. He gave me a kiss and then stared at me with his green piercing eyes. *I love you Perry Nelson, I never want to hurt you.*

We spent the rest of the daylight at the park and I forgot about Barry and the troubles that were pressing in my mind. It was easy to do with Perry by my side, he made me feel so special. *Being in love can cure all,* I thought while feeding some of the ducks that had come back early from their winter retreat.

As the sun was setting and the darkness descended upon us, Perry pushed me on the swing. *A perfect way to end a perfect day with Perry,* I thought, feeling of a young schoolgirl.

"It's getting chilly, would you like to come back to my place? I'll cook for you." I said while I went back and forth on the swing.

"That sounds like a good plan." Said Perry giving me another push.

When it was too dark to see anymore, Perry and I made our way back to my house. As I drove with Perry following behind me, the urge to tell him my loving feelings flooded back to me. *I want to tell him how I feel. How much I care. He is so great.* I decided that tonight would be the night to tell him, I love you. *And Barry adios, a good compromise.*

With the decision made, the possible ways to proclaim the words raced through my mind. As each thought passed I became jittery with anticipation. *I am going to do it, I really am.* I just hoped he loved me too. *He will...He does.*

I pulled up to my house before Perry. He had been stopped by a traffic light as I was driving. This gave me a chance to make sure my house was tidy upon his arrival. As I opened my car door to hurry inside, I heard a voice in the darkness.

"Where have you been?" Said the voice.

"Hello?" I called out, but before another word was uttered, I realized who had said it. Barry stepped out of the shadows.

"You have been ignoring me Alexis. I don't think that is anyway to treat your fiancé."

I began to break out in a cold sweat. *Perry will be here any moment. What do I do?*

"Barry…" I said. "You need to leave right now. I don't want to see you."

"Aw I don't buy that for a minute Lexi." Barry said, inching closer to me.

Barry grabbed me by my arm but I managing to elude his grip and back away. I could smell the scent of alcohol on his breath as I scooted back.

"Barry you're drunk, leave now or I will call my dad. You are way out of line showing up here uninvited. I've had enough of it and you." I said raising my voice.

"This game is getting old Alexis. We both know that you're just trying to hurt me like I did to you. Going out with strange men and telling me you like them, it's all a lie. Some sick revenge game you're playing."

"No it's not. I was going to tell you that I'm officially seeing someone else now and we are never going to get back together. I don't want you in my life Barry."

"That's a sick joke, Lexi." Barry scoffed, attempting to get closer to me.

"It's not a joke Barry, get it through your thick skull, we are through." I said inching backwards.

"Ha, who is this man? I bet he isn't half the man I am. You're making a huge mistake Alexis."

"Leave Barry," I said as threatening as I could muster. *Perry will be here any moment.*

"Is he on his way here? Oh this should be great, I can't wait to see this pathetic fool. I'll show him who the better man is."

"No Barry, please, just leave."

But it was already too late. I could see Perry's headlights piercing through the darkness of my street. *What am I going to do, this isn't how it is supposed to happen.*

"Is this him? Oh this is wonderful. I'll show you what a pathetic loser this guy really is." Said Barry walking towards Perry's car.

"Barry stop." I said running to him and grabbing at his arm. It was a useless attempt and Barry pushed me aside with ease. "Don't do anything Barry, please, just leave." I pleaded.

Perry stepped out of the car. He had spotted Barry walking towards him.

"Alexis?" Perry called out. "What's going on?"

"So this is the guy that's trying to get in the way of us, Alexis." Said Barry looking back at me.

"Perry come inside and we will talk. He is being an asshole like he has always been." I said as strong as I could.

"Perry, huh? So you really think Alexis wants to be with you? She doesn't. She is just trying to make me jealous with a stupid game." Said Barry, now directing his attention to Perry.

"Perry it's not true. I promise just come inside and I will tell you all about it." I said. "I swear Perry."

Perry listened to my plea and stepped past Barry, ignoring his jeers of emasculation. "Tell me what Alexis?" Perry said, walking closer to me.

"That she is using you." Barry interrupted, following behind Perry.

"No Perry, he is lying, he is trying to get under your skin." I said beginning to weep as the moment became a living nightmare. *You liar, this isn't supposed to happen. Perry just come inside. I should have told you at the park.* "Please Perry, don't listen to him." I said trying to gaze into his piercing green eyes.

Perry stood between Barry and me. I could see the doubt on his face, as if he was stuck in the middle of two worlds.

"Alexis, I can't believe you would even think this tool would make me jealous." Said Barry, scoffing once more. "I'll just pretend this never happened and we can get back on track."

I continued to look at Perry, his face had become stern and cold. *Please Perry just come inside. I care about you not him, I love you. Just let me tell you I love you.* Perry met my eyes in silence. He gave me a gentle head nod and smile before turning to Barry.

"You know Barry, I heard how you treat women." Said Perry in a calm voice. "And I must say, your reputation didn't do you justice. You are by far the most pathetic, slimy, scumbag I have ever laid my eyes on. Why don't you leave before someone gets hurt?"

With that, Perry turned back towards me and grabbed my side, ready to walk inside. I was relieved and let out a smile. *Good Perry, believe me.* I wiped my tears. *Everything is going to be alright.*

"You pussy," screamed Barry from behind us.

But before I could see what had happened, Perry had been taken to the ground.

"No," I wailed. "Stop!" Tears began to fall once more.

Perry managed to free himself from Barry's attack. "Are you done? No one needs to get hurt, walk away Barry." Said Perry standing up.

"You aren't going to hurt me." Said Barry, also standing up.

I ran to Perry's side and grabbed his arm. "Come with me, you don't need to do this." I begged. *Please be the better man, come inside.*

"I know I don't." Said Perry. "Let's go."

As we turned, Barry snarled in disbelief that Perry hadn't taken his bait. Then I heard footsteps pound the ground, and the next thing I knew Perry began to stumble, knocking me to the ground. I fell to the pavement scraping my elbow and clunking my head.

When I looked up, the blurry figure of Perry was towering over me, wiping blood from the side of his lip. He looked at his fingers, and I saw blood dripping from them.

I looked to Barry and he stood with a stomach churning grinning. *He just punched Perry,* I realized.

Perry glanced away from his bloody fingers and onto me as I still lay on the ground cut and bloodied. The sight of me made Perry's piercing eyes widened and turn black, his fists clenched, his jaw tighten, and his lips curl.

"No Perry, no I don't want this." I screamed as I recognized his body language. But he stopped hearing my pleading words. "Nooooo."

Perry directed all of his attention to Barry. His face turned devilish and cold as ice.

"Let's go." Said Barry putting his fists up. Perry said nothing as he advanced onto him.

Barry swung again at Perry face, missing him by a wide margin. Perry reached out and grabbed Barry by the throat, giving him a squeeze and then throwing him to the ground.

I began to weep uncontrollably as the dreaded nightmare continued.

Barry tried to hit Perry as he laying on the pavement but the shots were easily deflected by Perry. With his two hands, Perry savagely clutched Barry's head and began bashing it on the ground. Barry let out howls of pain and screams as Perry continued bashing and rubbing the back of Barry's skull onto the asphalt.

"Stop, Perry, stop." I shrieked, stunned of the monstrosity accruing. Perry had turned to a crazed animal as he attacked Barry, and I knew he couldn't hear my pleas anymore.

When Perry was done bashing, he began to inflict punches to Barry's face. Blood began to fly and stain the black asphalt. Barry continued to scream in agony as he attempted to stop Perry's vicious blows. But it was no use, Perry easily overpowered him as a lion would a gazelle.

I was horrified by Perry's violent actions. *This is not the Perry I know, please stop, and come inside. I love you,* I thought still lying on the ground. *Let me just tell you, I love you.* He didn't stop though. Perry had turned into a monster without sense or sympathy, only blood and violence. *What have I done?* I was petrified

Lights in windows and porches began to flash on around the neighborhood. People had heard the screams and yells in the night. Now all looked onto the horror that had manifested itself on this night.

I managed to pick myself up off the ground and raced to Perry, trying to yank at him. With all my might I pulled his shoulders. Barry

wasn't even attempting to block the blows now. His body had taken enough, laying lifeless in a pool of his own blood. Perry must have felt my tug because he shoved me to the ground, not even noticing that it was me at his side. *Who is this man?*

The gazing eyes of the neighborhood had made their way outside now and I began to cry, scared of the escalating moment. *What is happening, why, why, why.*

Perry stopped his fists as he heard my cry behind him. He began aimlessly staring at his bloody fists, at the people in the windows and porches staring, at Barry. Bloody and cowering as if he had no idea where he was or had gone, Perry's eyes returned to the piercing green I was used to seeing as he looked back to me. The craze seemed to have left him and Perry stood off the beaten Barry, attempting to walk to me.

I slapped Perry's hand away in fear as he tried to help me up. I was confused and scared of what had happened. *Who is this man? Look what he has done.* As I slapped his help away, Perry looked onto me with confusion and hurt.

"Let's go inside Alexis, please." Perry implored.

"You're going to pay for this." Croaked Barry while he choked and spit on blood, still lying on the asphalt. "I'm a fucking lawyer. You're going to go away for attempted murder. You fucking monster, I told you Lexi."

Before another word was spoken, police lights flashed in the dark night. Perry turned to the red and blue neon as police officers ran from their cars, tackling and pinning him to the ground with handcuffs. They dragged Perry away from me and he stared back with the same look of hurt and betrayal on his face.

The officers threw Perry into the car. I stood up and tried to call to him but no words came as I saw Barry still lying on the ground barely conscious. The instinct to help a dying man came, and instead of running to Perry, I went to Barry without thought of my action. I tried desperately to help him as he looked to be chocking in a pool of his own blood. *What am I doing?* I thought after a moment of reaching him. *This is your fault,* I realized.

My eyes darted up and saw Perry's piercing green eyes glued to me through the glass of the police car window. He stared dumbstruck and betrayed by my actions.

"No, it's not…." I screamed at Perry running towards the car. But it was too late, he had looked away and the police car drove away. Perry couldn't hear my call nor did he want to. My actions had seemed guilty of everything Barry had proclaimed.

"Perry." I screamed reaching out to the emptiness of night.

My tears dripped to the bloody ground of the living nightmare. *But I love you Perry Nelson. I just wanted to tell you that I love you.*

Chapter 27
The Final Decision

I had lost control of myself and my actions. *Put away like a feral animal*. But what hurt worse was the feeling of being betrayed.

I sat in my cold dark cell staring blankly at a yellow stained wall. *Is this the end of my redemption, my progress?* How could I possibly fix the mess that had ensued hours ago? Did I even want to?

Barry had enraged me. All his taunts and assault on me. *That cocky curly haired prick.* But the last straw was seeing Alexis lying on the ground with her scrapped skin and teary eyes. *I couldn't let him do that to her.*

My dark monster and killer instincts engulfed me at that very sight of Alexis wounded and in pain. I had lost control again, and when I finally heard Alexis's pleas to stop, it was too late. I had beaten Barry to a pulp, and in those actions, I revealed my darkness to Alexis. She knew what I was truly capable of now. The dark monster I had sealed away in the dungeon had escaped.

Now I was in my own dungeon. *Maybe this was where I belonged all along. I am too unstable to be a human. I am too damaged. My darkness will always come back.*

Part of me welcomed being locked away. The betrayal I felt resided deep within me, stinging my every thought. *Why did she slap my hand away? Was she just fearful to see my inner monster? I could understand that, but why did she go to Barry instead of me?*

I saw Alexis run to Barry's side while I was being dragged away. *Why didn't she try to save me?* Maybe Barry had a grain of truth to his insults. *Is Alexis just using me? Was she just like so many women before? No it can't be true.*

Yessss, hissed my dark monster.

Go away, I said back.

All I could do was sit in my hurt thoughts, but with each one, I was taken back to the same questions. *Can I trust Alexis? Is she who I thought she was? Can I even be what I wanted? Will I ever be free of my dark monster?*

While these questions raced, and the battles of yes or no brewed, I became angry. I howled in the darkness, pounding my fists against the cold stained walls. *How could she do this to me? How are all women so cruel?*

After I could pound no more and my energy was zapped, I curled into a ball of exhaustion and fell asleep on the cold concrete floor of my cell.

Dreams eluded my sleep, and I awoke to the sound of a door creaking open with increasingly loud footsteps that followed. I sat up looking around, hoping that I had dreamed the events of the night passed. But to my dismay I was still locked away.

A shaded figure appeared in front of my cell door window. I wiped my weary eyes, trying to make out what I was seeing, but the light prohibited my sight. The figure unlocked my cell and stepped inside, staring down on my beaten body.

"So you finally did what I've dreamt about all these years." The figure said to me.

I stood up sharply. As I did, the light shone its rays onto the shadowed figured. There stood Detective Paul Fisher.

"Let's get you out of here, Perry." He said with a gentle smile.

"What did you mean?" I responded with confusion.

"What I mean is, I despise Barry and I dreamt about beating him senseless ever since he hurt my daughter. If you hadn't been there when he showed up this could have been me in this cell. I told him if he ever showed up again I would do what you did."

"Oh," I responded coldly. "Why are you even here?"

"Because Alexis asked me to help you."

"Surprising. She seemed to care about Barry more than me last night."

"That's between you and her, but I do know she really cares about you. She called me sobbing last night, and if I know my daughter like I think I do, she wouldn't ever go back to Barry."

I stood silent, eye to eye with my adversary not knowing what to say or do. *How can you know your daughter if you don't even know the man you are searching for is right in front of you?*

I reached for the side of my face for the first time since the fight. It was covered in scraps and my lip was now swollen and sore from Barry's punches.

"I'm not here to tell you I know what's going on between you two. But I know my little girl wanted my help to get you out. So whatever you're thinking just try to take it easy on her." Said Detective Fisher. "Let's get you of here now. She's waiting out there.

Without a response I followed Detective Fisher from my cell. My mind was to disorganized and fatigued to process so I followed as a drone. He led me to a room with Alexis sitting on a long wooden bench. When she saw me coming out I could see remorse in her eyes. They were bloodshot and baggy. She looked to be a mess of sorts. *A beautiful betraying mess.*

I wasn't ready to face her though. I knew that as I saw her now, my mind had yet to decipher how I felt. *Is this just the reality of any relationship? Or is she just another wicked woman that will undoubtedly break my heart.*

I turned my head away from her gaze as I walked past her with Detective Fisher.

"Here you go." Said Detective Fisher as he handed me my belongings. "Take it easy on her if you can, huh. If not for her, you could still be in there. She is a good girl, Perry."

"Thanks," I managed to say before walking away.

"Perry… I…" Said Alexis struggling to speak as I turned around.

I looked at her with blank expression. "I don't want to talk."

"Perry it wasn't what you thought."

"What I thought was that you cared about me. But what I saw was you going to Barry as I was getting carried away. Everything has made me feel differently."

"Barry was lying there, I thought he was dying, it was a reaction. You… You scared me. The whole moment did, but I'm here for you now. It wasn't your fault. Barry started it; he is the one who should be here."

"The thing is, I don't want you here with me right now." I said, walking past Alexis. "I want to be alone. That's what I am used to, anyways. You can go back to Barry just as you did last night."

"Perry, no, that's not what I want. Perry I wanted to tell you…"

Alexis's voice faded as I walked out of the police doors. The doors shut behind and I heard or saw nothing more of her.

Long ago I morphed from Perry to Heartbreak Killer as I sat in my room alone and isolated. In that time I grew to hate the world, to hate the life I had received, to hate all the people who had hurt me. That is when my darkness birthed, taking all my love away. *What would happen now? Where do I go from here? Who do I become?*

In the ensuing weeks, I once again returned to the isolation of my home. Each day presented new struggles within myself as I battled my doubts, my darkness, myself. *What is it that I truly want? What is it that I can truly be?* Long periods of time passed and I still had no answers for myself. *Black or white, dark or light, Perry or Heartbreak, trust or disbelief, feelings or emptiness, Alexis or alone.*

Alexis tried to reach me during my battle with calls and texts, but I ignored it all. *She will betray you,* my darkness would whisper at a single instinct to pick up or respond. *Women will always betray you. That is why they must die.*

One night my weary and battled mind was met with the dreams of the black and white room. Alexis was already scrubbing the black tar from the enclosed white walls as I arrived. She was smiling as the same bright light surrounded her as before. *She is beautiful,* I thought as I watched her scrub, *but is she what I thought or something I imagined?* Again, Alexis came to my ear and whispered a foreign tongue.

"What?" I said to her, still not understanding the strange tongue of words.

Alexis whispered once more. "I love you," she said with a gentle touch of my shoulder.

"How do I know you do?" I said.

"Look into your heart. You will find your answer."

Alexis disappeared and the black and white room dissolved into emptiness.

I awoke on the floor of my room with my heart pounding. *I haven't been able to look into my heart for so long. How could I ever know the answer?*

The morning sun shone its warm rays through my window and casted onto the glass trophy case sitting on its mantle. The pieces of human heart were fully lit by the pressing light and illuminated a certain presence to me. *Look into my heart,* I thought staring at the case. *Is this the heart Alexis spoke of in my dream?*

As I stared, emotions stirred inside of me. With each flurry of emotion came one of my victim's faces, invading my mind. The pit of my stomach churned as I realized the emotional horrors I had caused for them and their families. *I was wrong, this was not who I want to be,* I realized. *The monster has to be put to rest.*

The victim's faces blurred in my mind and formed the picture of Alexis. Our memories together flooded. The first date, the first kiss, the gifts exchanged, the New Year's night, and the love we made. *I love you she said in the dream...*

And you love her Perry, said a soft voice that hadn't spoken to me since the night in Alexis's home. *Believe in your feelings. Believe in love and you will be set free of your darkness.*

I touched my chest still thinking of Alexis. *Bubump, bubump, bubump.*

What do they say? Asked the voice.

I don't know...

Close your eyes and feel.

I listened, shutting my eyes to see inside my mind. I saw Alexis, I saw our future together, the chance to be happy. *I am happy with her... I'm in love Alexis.*

Then that is your answer, said the soft voice.

But what if she hurts me. What if she is using me?

Love hurts all Perry, but does that make it evil? You must overcome the doubts and pains, even in your darkest times. Kill the darkness and become free.

I opened my eyes to the glass trophy case still gleaming in the morning light. My dark reflection looked back to me. *All those innocent people. What have I done?*

"It's over you fucking monster." I screamed, standing from the floor. I paced to the glass case, staring down to it one last time. "I don't need you anymore." I said to the pieces of human heart. "I'm sorry, so sorry for all I've done to you innocent people. I was wrong."

With all my anger I lifted up the case and threw it to the ground, smashing it to oblivion. Glass fractioned in every direction and the pieces of human heart rolled to the ground. *I was wrong so very wrong.*

I hurried to my closet, throwing aside shoe boxes until I reached the black bag of murder knifes. I picked up the bag and flung it into the pile of shattered glass and pieces of heart. *I am through with you Heartbreak, I never want to see you again.*

The first feeling of what I thought was love overcame me as I saw the remains of the Heartbreak Killer destroyed on the floor.

Alexis... I need to tell her how I feel. I started to sing and dance through my closet as I dressed. The feeling was indescribable. *I love you, I love you, I love you,* I thought and rushed to the store.

Surely Alexis was wondering why I hadn't been talking to her. I needed to say sorry for everything. Even if she didn't understand at least she would know I cared and that I loved her. Nothing else mattered but my feelings for her.

As I drove to Alexis's house I prepared my speech. Everything had to be right, I had to communicate and make her understand why. *Understand why I have been distant. Tell her my story of heartbreak and then we will be together forever. Nothing will stop us then.*

A red light stopped me in my race and I had a chance to breathe and fester in the magnitude of emotion. I stared up at the sun and then to the people walking around the city. The world appeared beautiful to me in that moment.

Out of the corner of my eye I spotted a woman with honey blond hair and fair skin accompanied with a man. My loving heart sunk at the sight. *That can't be Alexis. No my eyes are deceiving me.*

The light flashed green and a car honked at me while I stared. *Just go to her house,* I thought, but something made me turn to get a better look. *Just to be safe, it's not her.*

I spotted the two across the street from where I was driving, but they were walking away from me, not letting me see a clear face. I maneuvered around the street blocks, bobbing and weaving in between traffic and streets until I was positioned to drive head on with the man and woman. With brief hesitation, I pushed forward to see.

My loving heart sunk even further. *This can't be,* it was Alexis and the man she was with was Barry. They were walking side by side, smiling and laughing together as I drove by unnoticed. *NO, NO, NO. She loves me, she said in the dream. My heart told me I love her. She said Barry was lying. This can't be true. She isn't like the others.*

I turned around to follow them. *He is forcing her to be with her, blackmail, anything.* I couldn't take the reality I was seeing. *There has to be another reason.* Alexis opened the passenger door of a strange red sports car and I parked beside a meter behind them to wait. When the car took off so did I, trailing behind them at a safe distance. *There has to be some reason for this. She said he was a liar. The dream. My loving feelings. No.*

I followed them for miles. My mind placed denial in me, this wasn't how the story ended for us. *How could I be too late? It's only been a few weeks. She didn't move on that fast. She told me Barry was a scumbag. This is all just an illusion I am seeing.*

The red sports car lead me to a suburb, parking itself in a driveway a few blocks within. I drove by the house and parked a few houses ahead. *My eyes are playing tricks on me that wasn't even Alexis.* I looked in my car mirror to see who stepped out, but they remained inside the car.

I exited my car and hid behind a bush in a neighboring houses front yard. I peeked over but still no one came out of the red sports car.

Then I spotted something else, *Alexis's car.* Parked right outside of the house they were currently parked in. *It really is her, how could she.*

The doors opened to the red sports car. Alexis came out and Barry followed on the other side. *Don't go inside, leave, please you are different, you have to be.*

Barry put his arm around Alexis's waist. She looked down at his hand and back up with a faint smile. They walked to the door and Barry proceeded to open it for her. Alexis stopped at the entrance. *Don't go inside Alexis, please.*

She gazed around for a moment and then said something to Barry. He put his hand on her shoulder and said something back, but I couldn't make out the words. After a moment of exchanged talking, they went inside and the door closed behind them.

No Alexis, I love you. You said you loved me, to listen to my heart.

The loving heart began to ache and throb inside me. I grabbed at my chest with a feeling of death. The heart was burning and breaking at the very sights I had witnessed.

"Ahhhhhhhhhh," I wailed out as I fell backwards on the grass lawn.

I lay stunned for an eternity and a single drop of foreign liquid eked from my eye. The bumping love I felt hours ago had come to a halt. *My heart,* I thought and the dark monster whispered kill.

Chapter 28
A Heart Sunken Farewell

Weeks had past and the Heartbreak case was cold. All Detective Fisher and Agent Price could do now was wait and hope that the killer made a mistake.

Having something new to report on made no difference to the ravage media however. All still starving for any shred news on the killer. They harassed Paul at his home, when he left for work, at the police station when he arrived for work, and even when he came home late at night a few would lurk about. A never ending assault for news.

But with no new murders to report on and Paul staying silent, the media began to fabricate their own stories. Some headlines read, *Connors and Heartbreak secret lovers?* Others, *Connors breaks heart of killer, leads him to murder.*

"Why the hell are they still here?" Said Paul as he arrived at the police station. "It has been weeks since the Connor murder and we have nothing to give them."

"I know the attack is tiresome, but the story receives ratings. Until that stops, the media will continue to make up their own stories and bombard our personal lives, trying to get any morsel of detail." Said Agent Price sipping coffee in her temporary office.

"Idiotic… Any chance there is a break in the case?" Said Paul sitting down beside her.

"Not even a little one. I don't know where the Heartbreak Killer is, but he is obviously satisfied with his work. Maybe he found God and changed his sinful ways?"

"Nice joke, killers don't just change one day."

The Captain knocked on the already open door, peeking his head inside the room as he did. "Please tell me you have something today."

"Unfortunately no, it's still ice cold." Said Agent Price.

"The Chief of Police is on my ass about this case. He says this case is making the whole police force look incompetent to the public." Said the Captain.

"Well what would you have us do?" Said Paul. "Maybe we should make up some leaked lead like the media has been doing. People seem to enjoy getting fed fictional stories."

"Very funny Detective, I'll have you know the Chief is talking about having your ass if this case doesn't get cleaned up. He thinks that due to your recent history, you're not mentally fit to be heading a huge case like this." Said the Captain

"He was the one who asked for me in the first place, he knew my recent history."

"Have you seen the papers today?" Said the Captain.

"No, I'm trying to stay away from the media these days. It's getting to be quite a chore to do so though." Snickered Paul.

The Captain threw down a paper he had been holding onto the nearby desk. Paul and Agent Price both looked down to view it. The headline read, *A Heartbreak from Inside: The Reason Detective Fisher can't Crack the Case.*

"What's this shit?" Said Paul.

"Well the gest of it is that the media seems to think you're too emotionally unstable to deal with the case." Said the Captain.

"Is this story why the Chief is changing his tone all of a sudden? Because of some stupid reports?" Said Paul. "How can anyone believe this shit?" Paul began to read aloud.

"As the killer roams free, so too does Detective Fishers emotional psyche. Unable to deal with the death of his wife, Detective Paul Fisher has been seen by multiple sources drowning his sorrows with alcohol and sex. One woman reported that Detective Fisher invited her over after drinks, only to lose his temper because of his late wife, sending the woman away with drunken rage. If a man in charge of finding the dubbed Heartbreak Killer can't get over his own heartbreak, how is he expected to find the ultimate of heartbreaks?"

"How are they allowed to print this bullshit?" Paul demanded.

"Paul, let's be real. We both know you have been heavily drinking. Hell, the first time I came to you your whole house reeked of booze." Said the Captain.

"I have grown beyond that now. It's been weeks since my last drink." Said Paul.

"I agree," piped in Agent Price still reading the article. "Paul has been a new man since I have been here."

"It doesn't matter what I see or believe. What matters is the public and media's perception and expectations of us." Said the Captain.

"How long do we have before the Chief calls me off?" Said Paul.

"A week, maybe two if I pull some strings." Said the Captain.

"A week?" Roared Paul.

"How can the Chief of Police expect us to accomplish anything if there are no leads?" Demanded Agent Price.

"It's out of my hands Agent." Said the Captain, turning to walk away.

Paul and Agent Price sat in silence after hearing the grim news.

Paul put his hands on his head. *How can they do this to me? Question my character and the competency of my work? I thought Terry Connors was a ruthless reporter.*

"Screw them." Said Agent Price, breaking the silence between them. "I know how hard we are working on this case. If they don't think you are competent then they don't know a damn thing. I use to think you were what they wrote in the papers when I first came here. Drunk and too emotional to function, but you've proved me wrong every day since then."

"Thanks Agent Price... Where do we go from here?" Said Paul.

"We go have fun... Show me the town." Said Agent Price with snarky smile.

"Are you serious? My job is on the line and you say let's go have fun?" Said Paul bewildered.

"Yeah, we need a break from all this. It's been weeks of us busting our asses and we have nothing to show for. Let's run through everything we have right now and if nothing new shows up we go out. What do you say?"

"How are you an FBI agent again?" Said Paul with a little smile. *She always cheers me up somehow.*

"Because I'm pretty, have tits, and men fantasize about me naked." Agent Price said smiling too. "At least men think that's how, anyways. Not even close to the reality. Remember, I was highest in my class in almost every imaginable category?"

"True, you did, but I think it's those tits you were talking about that put you over the top."

"Oh fuck you Paul Fisher." Said Agent Price playfully throwing the newspaper at him. Together the two laughed and forgot about the impending deadline that awaited them as they began to search the files once more.

After an hour of scouring through the same old work he had seen countless times before, Paul decided Agent Fisher was right. "Alright I'm tired of this; let's go out on the town."

"Really? I didn't think a hard ass like you would take up my offer of fun." Said Agent Price.

"Well this hard ass is going to change his mind in about one second so..." Said Paul.

"Sorry, sorry, someone isn't in the mood for my teasing I see. Okay, let me go get ready. Pick me up in an hour?"

"Why do you need to get ready?" Paul said with a stern face.

"I don't need to explain myself to you." Agent Price said sarcastically, but realized Paul was in no joking mood. "Just pick me up in an hour okay?"

"Whatever you say princess."

While Agent Price was away, Paul continued to hammer himself with useless case file information. All of which lead him down the same road. *We have nothing on this guy, if he doesn't commit another crime he will be off scot free.*

Disappointed, Paul headed for his office to see if he had anything decent to wear out. His usual get up of jeans, a button up, and an over coat were usually sufficient for Paul, but somehow Agent Price had sunk into his head. *If she is going to get ready I should at least try,* thought Paul as he rummaged through his desk drawers and office locker.

Paul managed to find a still packaged black dress shirt hidden away in one of his desk drawers. Paul stared at the packaged shirt for a moment and realized why it was hidden away. *She bought this shirt for me on my birthday before she died. The last gift I ever received from her.* Paul had taken the shirt out of his house because the sight of it made him weep and reminisce of his wife every time he looked to it. He had forgotten all about the shirt when he hid it away in one of his office drawers months ago.

As Paul held the shirt now, happy thoughts and memories of his wife flooded in. Paul smiled down at the black dress shirt as he remembered receiving the gift. *I can't wear this with another woman though,* thought Paul. But as if his wife had heard his thought, an answer sailed across his mind. *Wear the shirt Paul*, the strange thought said. *She bought it for just such an occasion… Your right, she did.*

Taking it as a sign, Paul put on the black dress shirt while he looked in the mirror. "Not too bad." Paul said aloud, and with that he took off to have a night of fun with Agent Price.

A storm of media stood outside of Agent Price's hotel as Paul arrived. Cameras began to flash at the sight of Agent Price exiting the premise. Somehow the media had found their way to the hotel and began badgering Agent Price as she walked to meet Paul.

"Hurry, get in." Paul said to Agent Price out of his car window and she began to push the cameras and media members out of the way.

"Detective, is it true what they say about you and your emotional state?" Yelled a reporter who had spotted Paul.

Another followed suit.

"Detective are you and Agent Price seeing each other now? What about your wife? What does this mean for the Heartbreak case?"

Agent Price jumped into the passenger car door and Paul raced away.

"What was all that about?" Paul asked as he drove.

"The media seems to think we are dating?" Said Agent Price. "At least that's the yelling I picked up on from the crowd."

"I heard it too. I guess they will reach for anything, huh."

"Who cares, screw 'em. Let's have a good time tonight. Where are we going?"

"You said you wanted to see the city, right?" Said Paul.

"Yes I think I said something of that nature." Agent Price responded.

"Well that's where we are going."

Paul knew of a spot on the mountainside where you could park your car and see the entire city. He knew the area from his earlier police days, when youthful teens would make their way up in the summer time to drink and fool around. It was the perfect place to meet the Agent's request.

"Well what do you think?" Said Paul as they pulled up to the edge of the cliff and parked.

"I think you took my words very literal." Said Agent Price with a giggle.

"Hey, you asked and I delivered."

"Deliver indeed, it's really beautiful. I was only teasing, Detective"

Agent Price and Paul exited the car together and sat on the hood, viewing the scenery of the city in full, below. The sun was setting and many of the large downtown buildings had started to illuminate from within, giving a lively feeling from the view above. To the right stretched the salty blue ocean scaling millions of miles beyond the sight of mortal eye.

"From up here you could never tell the city is buzzing with media and killers alike." Said Agent Price. "It all looks so peaceful and calm."

"The farther you step back the less you really see." Said Paul.

"Indeed… Nice shirt by the way. I don't think I've ever seen you attempt to dress up. Not even at the New Year's party we attended."

"Thanks, I don't know what came over me. I guess you saying you were getting ready inspired me to dress up a bit."

"Well that was thoughtful of you, Detective."

"Oh, I almost forgot, I brought us something to drink." Said Paul, jumping off the hood of the care and heading to the back seat. Paul rummaged for a moment before he pulled out a brown bag with a bottle of vodka inside. Paul handed the bag to Agent Price who was still sitting enjoying the scenery.

"Detective, I thought you were done drinking? Said Agent Price. "Remember, the tabloids today?"

"I'm just giving the people what they want. Plus, we are on a break from work so shut up and drink." Said Paul adjusting himself on the hood of the car again.

"But isn't drinking in public illegal officer?" Agent Price said with a continued smirk.

Paul let out a hard laugh and Agent Price followed as they passed the bottle back and forth, each taking a small swig and wincing at the harsh taste. All the while, the sun continued to set in front of them and the city was almost covered by darkness and bright city lights.

"Can I ask you something without you being offended?" Said Agent Price.

"Yeah sure." Said Paul.

"Do you ever think about getting back out there since your... your wife died." Said Agent Price.

Hmmm, thought Paul, *I never really have.*

"No I can't say I have. Honestly, I don't think I can take another heartbreak like the one I've been going through. If I did you may be hunting me as the next Heartbreak Killer."

"Ha, could you imagine that twist? The media would be out of their minds with that story. But you could never do it."

"Why do you say that?"

"Because deep down, no matter how messed up your world is, you want to help people not hurt them." Said Agent Price with a pause. "That's what I see, anyways."

"Hmm, who can really say? I do know I've felt better since you have been here. Surprising, since I nearly retired again after hearing that you were coming. You have been good for me though. So thanks for that Nina."

"You're welcome," Nina said with a smile, taking the bottle from Paul hand and pulling a swig. "I think that was the first time you've called me by my first name. Are you okay? You must be getting drunk."

"I'm fine Agent Price." Paul said. "What about you? Do you ever think about finding someone new? A new prince as you would say."

"I don't think anyone can handle my damaged soul. I'm so destroyed from my past that I don't think I can be with a normal human being anymore."

"Yeah me either." Paul said swiping the bottle back. *Maybe you and I would be perfect for each other. Dark, twisted, and alone.*

A buzzing sound vibrated the hood of the car and both Paul and Nina reached inside their pockets.

"Mine," Paul said grabbing his phone. "It's Alexis, give me a sec, okay?" Nina nodded her head and took the bottle back from Paul's hand.

Walking away from the car Paul took the call. "Hey hunny, what's going on?"

"Dad, what are you doing?" Alexis said.

"Oh me and Ni… Agent Price are out doing some casework."

"Oh, I see…" Alexis said with a sigh.

"Why, what's wrong?"

"I don't know Dad, relationship stuff I guess. Perry still hasn't spoken to me since that night. I'm upset and I could really use a cheer up. I know it's kind of weird, but I thought of you. I thought maybe we could hang out like we use to, you know before Mom."

"Yeah… Yeah of course Alexis, we can do that. Let me finish up here with Agent Price and you can meet me at home in an hour."

"Okay Dad… Thanks. I'll see you in a bit." Alexis said, hanging up the phone.

Paul turned his phone off and stood still for a moment. *That was unexpected.* He couldn't remember the last time Alexis had called him for advice or help. *Like she said, probably not since Mom was healthy. She must be really upset.* Whatever the reason for the call, Paul smiled. *It will be just like it used to be.*

Nina yelled out to Paul. "Are you going to leave me here to finish this alone?"

Shit Nina. What am I going to tell her? We were having such a good time.

Paul walked back to the car. "Hey… I guess Alexis is having some trouble so I think we are going to have to call it a night."

Nina's face became discouraged and she put the bottle down. Paul could see she was displeased by the news but she tried to mask her feelings. "Well who knew, Detective Paul Fisher, still close with his daughter after all these years."

"That's the thing, we have been drifting since… well you know. Honestly, I was surprised but I think I should go. I'm really sorry to ruin the night." Said Paul.

"No, you didn't. I asked to see the city and you showed me the city. There will be other nights." Nina said, jumping off the hood of the car. "Let's go Detective."

The car ride back was silent. *She is mad at me, we were having such a great time too,* thought Paul as he arrived at the hotel. Agent Price didn't look at Paul as she opened the door but before she exited spoke up.

"Paul…" Said Agent Price with a pause.

"What?" Paul replied with shame in his voice.

"I… I.."

"What is it?"

"Never mind Detective, have a good night with your daughter. See you tomorrow." Said Agent Price slamming the door behind her.

Damn it…, thought Paul, now wishing he hadn't left the scenic view.

Paul arrived to his house with Alexis's car waiting outside. She was already inside when Paul walked in.

"Hey Dad, I hope I didn't ruin your work." Alexis said, greeting Paul at the door. "I really needed this though."

"No of course not hunny. This is what dads are for anyways, right?" Said Paul with a smile

"I picked us out a movie to watch and I made some popcorn too."

"Sounds wonderful. Let me just change."

"Hey, are you wearing the shirt Mom bought you for your birthday?"

"Indeed I am."

"Wow Dad, things have changed since the last time we hung out. Good for you."

"Thanks sweetie."

Paul went up to his room to change, and when he came back, Alexis was sitting on the living room couch snuggled under a blanket with a large bowl of popcorn. Paul sat next to his daughter and she rested her head on his shoulder.

"Thanks for being here for me, Dad." Said Alexis. "It means a lot to me.

Paul smiled and directed his attention to the movie. A feeling of happiness resided in him as he sat with his Daughter and he forgot about the sudden disappointment with Agent Price. *Almost like old times again*, he thought taking a bit of popcorn out of the bowl. *Things are getting better*.

"Dad, was there ever a time with Mom where you didn't know if you would survive together." Alexis whispered.

"Many times," said Paul.

"What did you do to fix them?"

"I found a way to show her how much she meant to me. One way or another that's all we needed."

Alexis stayed quiet for a moment, watching the movie and eating popcorn. Paul looked down to her, seeing the resemblance of his wife in Alexis like he always had before. *What a beautiful creation you and I had,* Paul thought.

What did you expect, rippled the strange thought from earlier on.

"Are you okay sweet daughter of mine?" Paul said.

"I will be Dad, I will be."

Paul continued to watch the movie, but overtime he became weary from the alcohol he had consumed and drifted off to sleep. When Paul awoke, he was alone on the couch covered by a blanket. Outside the window, the dark night had turned to a bright morning with birds chirping outside.

Unaware of what had happened to his daughter, Paul walked by for some coffee in the kitchen. Before he reached the kitchen, Paul noticed a bright yellow posted note on the front door.

Thanks for everything Dad, the note read, *I didn't want to wake you before I left. You looked happy while dreaming away. Let's do this again sometime, it felt good to be a family again.*

The note left a smile on Paul's face for the rest of the morning as he prepared for work.

A now regular group of reporters bombarded Paul as he left his home, asking the same questions they had the night before when he picked up Nina. *Damn, when will they ever leave me in peace? My morning was going so wonderfully too,* Paul thought as he shoved his way through the swarm giving no answers.

Paul arrived to the police station with FBI agents packing equipment into boxes. *What's going on,* Paul thought, and headed straight for Nina's office for an answer. When Paul reached the office, Nina had almost completely cleared the room of her belongings, stacking them in neat piles or throwing them into a brown box.

"What's going on?" Paul inquired to a turned around Nina.

Agent Price whipped around. "Oh, Detective you nearly scared me to death." She said with a deep breath.

"Why is everyone packing?" Said Paul looking around the empty office. Nina hesitated to answer as she held a file in her hand. She placed the file in one of her neatly organized stacks before answering.

"Paul, I received a call this morning. I'm being reassigned from this case." Nina said with sorrow in her voice.

"What? Why?" Said Paul, his heart sinking inside him.

"My director said he wants someone else to come down and head the case. He said that I haven't made enough progress."

"What? They sent you down here just for this case. How could they change their mind in so little of time?"

"I don't know, but I have to go back now or I will risk losing my job."

"What does that mean for me? For us? For our case?" Demanded Paul.

"It means there is no more we, Paul. We have no more case together. But you know, maybe it's for the best. This case is dead cold and we are wasting our time just sitting around. Let someone else be hounded by the media and fail miserably. I think it's time to move on."

"How could you give up like this? After all we talked about? How we wanted to find out this persons story. How you wanted this case so badly because of it."

"Like I said Detective, I don't have a choice. My plane leaves in an hour though, so I have to get going." Said Nina. She walked to Paul and gave him a tight hug. "Thanks for being such a good host. I won't forget the little time we spent together."

Paul was left speechless and his arms remained by his side as Nina embraced him.

"For what it's worth, I think you're a great detective and an even better man. No matter what they say." Said Nina before letting go of Paul and heading for the door.

"Agent I… Nina…" But Paul had nothing more to say, fully sunk by the news.

"Take care of yourself Paul. If you need a change of scenery give me a call. I think you could be a great help to our agency." And with that farewell, FBI Agent Nina Price gave out a wave and was out of Paul's sight, leaving the Detective alone in the empty room.

Paul turned to the lone desk and saw a tabloid laying on the edge of Nina's desk. The front cover was of Nina and him driving off together from the night before, the headline read, *Heartbreak lost: Lovers Unite.*

The Detective grabbed the paper, crumbling it in his hands before throwing it to the wall.

People around station heard loud curses to the media from the cleared out office.

Chapter 29

Regression

Regression is what a therapist fears. Working so hard with our patients to make them a better model of themselves, but somehow, they cannot shake the ailments they've brought to us. Something comes in between them and their progression, an impediment of sorts, and they are left to make one of two choices. Regress to the state they were in or progress past it. Regression is inevitable for most of us. No one can completely change.

The fat man tries to exercise but finds it difficult to lose all that excess weight. The food is too lucrative for him and the progress is too slow. The fat man losses hope and regresses to an even higher weight. He only lives to be fifty-five, losing twenty plus years of his could be life because of a heart attack.

The depressed woman takes pills, exercises, does everything required to progress. She becomes happy for a while, but the cruelty of life is lurking around the every corner. The woman losses her job, her house, and her money. The dark cloud of depression creeps into her mind once more. She sees no hope of getting better, regressing to a darker state. *I am a loser,* she thinks, *I have no place in this world.* The woman reaches for the medication bottle that once helped her recover and proceeds to overdose, leaving the cold world behind her.

Perry Nelson finds his emotions. He finds a heart. He realizes that he loves Alexis Fisher. But love is a twisted game, never going as planned. As much as Perry wanted to change, the world did not care. Alexis went into the house with Barry. So he regressed back into the

Heartbreak Killer. *Life is not a fairytale for killers. Even the purest of women will betray.*

I reached for a single silver bladed knife on the broken glass floor of my room.

Blood, Blood, Blood, Barry will pay, raged the dark monster.

How could Alexis do this to me?

There was always a plan in place for me if I was on the verge of being caught. Tonight was that night. There was no coming back from what I planned to do, nor did I even want too. A man with a broken heart is dangerous, he feels there is nothing to lose. A killer with a broken heart? Well, he has nothing to stop him from being manic and insane.

Kill Barry, slice his throat and spill his guts.

Fog shrouded the inner city as I raced my car through the blackness of night. I clutched at the blade while chains rattled in the back seat. *Make him suffer, make him scream in pain just like you have. Kill Barry.*

My darkness built the more I stared onto the house where it all happened. *You fucking scumbag. You're a sickness that needs to be cleansed from this world,* I thought as I gritted my teeth.

The red sports car was parked in the driveway as I stood in the lawn breathing rage filled hate. I paced to the car, plunging my knife into each tire, and dragging the blade across the paint. Then, in a blink of an eye, I was in front of the door where I had seen Alexis enter only hours ago.

The image of Alexis betraying me filled my mind and fueled my darkness. *How could she have done this? She was pure, she made me feel. She was the one to save me.*

She felt Barry's body, screamed my dark monster. The image of her and Barry rolling naked in the sheets stained inside my head.

That was our special thing. She was with me!

Women are all the same. Kill him Perry, gouge out his eyes from their sockets. Be the Heartbreak Killer once more.

With all my mighty rage I kicked in the door. Pieces of wood and dry paint flew as the door busted open. "Barry," I screamed. "Show yourself you slimy fuck." I stood in the doorway waiting, but Barry did not present himself at my demand. *I have to subdue him before he calls the police... No, he is too cocky and proud, he will try to defend himself.*

"Face me like the real man you claim to be." I snarled, trying to provoke him as I scoured the dark home.

I heard the creaking of a door. *He's over there in that room,* I thought, but pretended not to hear the noise.

"Come out Barry, I know you're here somewhere." I said, creeping closer to the room. As I pressed my ear to the wall I could hear heavy breathing. *He's mine.* "Stop playing hide and seek. I thought we were real men." I yelled right by the doorway Barry stood behind.

A yell ensued my words followed by a flying wooden baseball bat. Barry's first swing missed, denting a wall. A nearby hanging picture fell from the vibrating force, crashing to the ground.

The house was pitch black, prohibiting my vision to see, but I managed to dodge a couple more of Barry's wild swings. He finally over swung enough so I could grab the bat as it connected with air. Latching onto the bat, I tried to rip it from Barry's grasp, but as I pulled he threw a punch that connected to my face, knocking me down.

As I fell to the floor Barry swung down but I rolled out of the away just in time. I jolted up, noticing we had made our way into a large room with an assortment of furniture. Barry flipped a light switch on.

"You?" Barry said looking shocked and puzzled. "Why are you here?"

"You know why. You and Alexis. I followed you here earlier." I snarled.

"So you finally saw the reality of her and I and you think coming here is going to help you? What were you planning on doing, Perry? Aren't you in enough trouble from assaulting me in the street? Now you want to add breaking and entering? Well guess what, you're on my turf now you skinny fuck and ever since you threw that cheap shot at me I have been dreaming of inflicting my revenge. I'm going to beat you to a pulp."

Barry charged at me, swinging his bat and hitting a nearby lamp that shattered into tiny pieces.

"I loved knowing I was sticking it to you." Taunted Barry as I backed away from his advance. "You aren't anything compared to me, she needed something more. She needed a real man not some psychology pussy. Feelings are for the weak, for women."

He doesn't know who he is talking to. Show him, show him the true you, demanded the dark monster.

"You don't know me Barry." I said staring at him across the room. I reached for the silver blade stored inside my coat pocket.

"I don't need to know you. I see how weak you really are. I destroy men like you every day." Said Barry with a bellowing laugh.

"Have you heard of the Heartbreak Killer?" I said pulling my knife out to showcase for him. "You should have picked a different guy to fuck with, because frankly, I am fucking manic now." I began to laugh uncontrollably as Barry's face turned ghost white, realizing what I was here for.

"You…" Barry stuttered.

"Good, you realize why I'm here; your face says it all." I said still laughing. "I'm here to slice you piece by piece until you are begging me to kill you. I want you to feel my pain and when I am satisfied with your screaming and begging for death, I will kill you. Your blood will spill to the floor and you will be no more. The world will be a better place with one less lying slimy male around."

"You're insane, you're sick," said Barry cowering at my deafening threats.

"Wrong again Barry." I shouted. "I am quite sane, you see the world is filled with evils, I just embrace the role. I'm consumed by a darkness, a monster, and it only quiets when blood is spilled. What better way to silence it than to spill the blood of a man that lies and cheats his way through life. Steals things that aren't his to take."

Barry reached for his pocket, pulling out his phone. I charged forward and tackled him to the floor. The phone flew from his hand and onto the floor.

The bat swung at me, hitting me in the shoulder, and Barry managed to kick me off of him. Barry quickly sprung up and ran to the direction of his fallen phone. But I was too quick and tackled him again. This time from behind and shoved my steel blade into his shoulder as we tumbled. Barry let out a painful cry as we fell through a glass coffee table, shattering it to pieces.

The impact of the fall blurred my vision. I shook my head to empty the cobwebs while Barry lay face down groaning in pain. When my

vision came into focus I saw the knife sticking out of Barry's shoulder. I reached down to yank the blade from his flesh and it was followed by another cry of pain. Blood dribbled from the silver steel as I held it, staining to Barry's grey shirt.

Yessss, make him bleed, make him suffer, hissed the darkness at the sight of blood.

My head was aching for the impact of the fall and I stumbled backwards. *Barry's phone,* I remembered, and darted around the now messy room. Barry had started to stand up himself in my moment of search. I turned to him as I heard the sounds of stumbling around. *He is weary from the blood he had loss endured. He won't get far. His only hope is the phone now.*

I turned back to the glass shambles and spotted the phone seconds later on the ground among the mess. I stood over the cell phone, smashing it underneath the weight of my foot with a *crunch.* When I went to turn back around Barry had disappeared. *Hide and seek time.*

Deciding it best, I flipped the light switch off in the room so I could creep in complete darkness. While I searched, I carefully listened for the sound of heavy breathing while scanning for any little droplets of blood to lead me to Barry.

"Barry…" I said. "Were you not enjoying our play time? Running off and hiding like a scared boy. Tisk, tisk, I thought you were a man? Isn't that what you always claimed?"

I noticed something dark smeared on a white wall that lead to a multitude of doors. *Blood, he is weak,* I thought as I took a closer look.

"Barry, come out and play some more." I said dragging my silver knife against the wall as I taunted.

Make him fear you, terrorize him until his last breath.

Following the smear of blood, I made my way down the dark hall still listening for the slightest of sounds. Hard breathing made its way to my ears. *He is close. He is scared.* A lone door now stood in front of me. It had been opened ever so slightly and there seemed to be more blood droplets staining the painted wood. *His last resting point.*

"Baaaarrryyy… I hearrrrr you." I taunted. "I thought you would give me more of a challenge. Shame." I pressed my head against the open door just hard enough to hear. The breathing picked up as I listened, he knew I was close.

Kill him Perry. Blood, Blood, Blood. FINISH HIM.

"Hello Barry," I announced as I burst into the room. Barry's outlined shadow was lying on the floor next to a bed with something pointing out at me. *GUN,* I realized. The dark room lit up with a flash of bright light and then a loud *BANG.*

I dived to the floor, trying to avoid the shot but the scattered bullets pierced into my arm as I fell. I landed to the floor behind the other side of the bed with a *thud.* Barry couldn't see me nor could I see him now.

Clutching at my arm as warm blood soaked through my shirt I let out a yell. "Fuck," I said and took a deep breath, assessing the damage dealt to me. Seeing my own blood gush enraged me. "That's it Barry. No more fucking games." Adrenaline began to fill my body, taking the pain away from my wound. I regained my composure and with one swift motion, I shoved my fingers under the bed frame and lifted the entirety of it up from behind my back as I sat.

Barry had seen my movement, but was to slow to the draw, not expecting me to recover as fast as I had. He tried to fire another shot, but the surprise caught his aim, sailing it through the mattress several feet away from me. Untouched, I toppled the weight of the bed and frame onto Barry's lying body, crushing him with a sound of a grunt.

The gun dropped to the floor and I went to pick it up. Holding the gun by my side I lifted up the bed and Barry began to cry.

"No, please... She didn't want me, she wanted you." Barry whimpered.

"I don't like beggars or liars." I shouted.

"I'm not..."

But before Barry could say another word I took the butt of the gun and clunked him over the head. His head flopped to his chest and I dragged his unconscious body through the dark hallway.

"Barry... Wake up... Time to wake up." I said as I struck him over the face with my flat stiff hand. *Nothing.* "Well, you have done this the hard way up to this point." I picked up the blade from a resting counter and jammed it into his thigh.

Barry let out a piercing scream. "Where... Where am I? What are you doing to me?"

"This is your final scene Barry. Your last chapter. Your death." I said, ripping the blade from his thigh and placing it back onto the counter next to me.

I had chained Barry to a wooden chair I found in the house and placed him in the center of his kitchen with a single light illuminating over his beaten body.

"What... What are you going to do to me?" Barry cowered.

"I am going to make you suffer. Like you have done to me."

"I told you she didn't take me back. I tried but she wouldn't." Barry said as blood dribbled down his forehead

"And I told you that I hated liars." I snarled, grabbing the steel knife again.

"No, no, help." Barry screamed, trying to wiggle free.

I stuffed a dirty sock into his mouth to drown out the screaming. Fear induced in his eyes as I did.

Make him suffer. Make him bleed. He is scum. He took your love away, my dark monster raged.

I grabbed one of Barry's hands that was tied behind the chair and began to hack away at one of his fingers. Muffled screams came from him and tears flooded his eyes. After several hacks, the finger severed off and fell to the floor. Blood squirted from the wound and began to fester on the tiled kitchen floor.

"Now tell me the truth Barry, and I will end this quickly. Tell me you and Alexis came here." I said, removing the sock from his mouth while he sobbed in pain.

"Perry, she left, she didn't go through with it. I swear it. Just don't kill me. I won't say anything about this if you let me live." Barry pleaded.

Barry is a known liar. He is just trying to survive; he will say anything to get out. Make him suffer.

"You lie," I roared, stuffing the sock back into his mouth.

I slammed my blade into Barry's other thigh and twisted. He sobbed more and more from the pain.

Yes, make him suffer like you.

"Tell me the truth Barry." I demanded, pulling the sock out once more.

"I am. Please stop, I'm begging you. Let me go, I have learned my lesson."

"You would only learn my lesson from years of pain and suffering. Feeling nothing but cold darkness, wishing you could feel but never coming close. And you took all of that away from me."

"I didn't, she didn't want me, Perry. She left I swear. I was never able to get her back."

"You lie. No, you tricked her into thinking you had changed. You have always been a liar and you always will be." I said pulling the knife from his thigh and stuffing the sock back in his mouth.

I placed the blade across his cheek and sliced into both sides. Blood ran down his face and neck. Barry's head began to wane and his eyes rolled into the back of his head.

Stepping back, I marveled at my work of horrific art. *The scum of man.* Blood was dripping from every which way. Barry's clothes were drenched and stained with red, while the rest filled the tile floor in puddles. I glanced at my knife; it was painted red with my reflection.

Heartbreak Killer. Blood. Finish this.

I yanked out the dirty sock again. Barry was barely conscious, just hanging onto life as the last of his blood poured from his wounds.

"Just tell me the truth Barry and I will set you free of this pain." I whispered into his ear.

"I... I... I did whatever you think." He said slurring each word with blood as he spoke.

"What do you think I think?" I asked.

"She cheated... please let me..."

Hearing the words come out stung and I let out a wail before thrusting the blood soaked blade into Barry's heart. He let out a grunt but spoke no more.

She cheated. How could she do it to me? Why? I thought, disgusted by Barry's mutilated corpse

Because women and love are evil, said the dark monster of my mind. *Now, make her pay, just like you have for all those others. Let the Heartbreak Killer be reborn once and for all.*

I limped to my car in a thick and shrouding mist, still clutching my wounded arm. My clothes and face were soaked in both Barry's blood and mine as I glanced into a car mirror. Sounds of sirens began to ring in the air, becoming more distinct with each moment I wasted. *Surely they are coming here.*

Starting my car, I raced off into the darkness of night again. I had not decided the next move, but my mind filled with more and more hate, more and more darkness. All of it clouded my mind with evil. *Kill her,* the monster demanded. I was losing my mind to the monster, but my shattered heart was still with Alexis, even if she had cheated and betrayed. *What to do, who am I,* I thought in silence.

My phone rang, breaking the silence of dark thought in the car. I looked down to see Alexis's name and picture on the screen calling me. Picking up the phone, I stared at her beauty and part of me wanted to answer and forgive her for everything.

No, I thought and set my phone beside me.

Another sound echoed. A voicemail left behind. I reached for my phone again, this time shutting it off and throwing it behind me.

No need to talk, I will be seeing you soon my love.

Chapter 30
The White and Black Room

…The phone rang.

"Pick up, pick up hunny." Said Paul as he chewed on the end of a pen.

The voicemail picked up. "You've reached Alexis."

"Damn it," said Paul dialing again. "Come on Alexis." Voicemail picked up again so Paul waited for the beep to leave his message.

"Alexis hunny, it's your Dad. Where are you? Something happened to Barry… A neighbor called the police after loud noises came from his house... They found him…. I'm worried please call me when you get this… I am going to come check on you, I just don't feel right about something. I'll be there soon. I love you…"

… I stood in front of the house I came to so many times before. *First time as a cold killer, second time as beating lover, third time a broken heart unknown. What will I do?*

Silence surrounding the house as I stood wait, thinking deeply. A single light was lit inside Alexis's home. *Top middle left window. The baby room. She is here.* The shrouding mist that had engulfed the city seemed to dissipate and clear a guiding path to her door. *What will I do once I am inside, who am I?* I walked the leading path to her door.

I turned the copper knob to a click. *Unlocked.* The door opened with no sound of force, so not to draw attention on myself. *I want to lay my eyes on her before I decide. What do I want? Who am I?*

Kill the bitch, she is a betrayer just like all before her, the dark monster howled.

I crept through the house and began to reminisce on past memories. I saw the couch where Alexis confessed her feelings to me on. *The couch where we finally gave ourselves to each other.*

She deserves to die, she is just like every other women who made you this way. Blood is the only acceptable payment. Heartbreak, the monster raged inside me.

After the memory of the couch faded, my attention drew to the place where I had laid under the table, ready to strike Alexis down and tear the heart from her chest. *But then the feelings came and a strange voice... Barry said she left, that she said no to him. I ignored her, she was confused,* beat my heart.

Barry would have said anything to end the pain. He is a liar. A scumbag. She went to him while you were being hauled off. Be strong, the Heartbreak Killer is. Kill her Perry, the monster debated back.

The two sides of good vs. evil, black vs. white, cold killer vs. emotional human battled. Raging as they always had inside my soul and mind. Each battle tearing me to unfixable fragments of myself. *When will the battle be over? I have fought for a lifetime. What do I want? Who am I?*

I saw the light of the room shine through a slit in the door. It drew me in like a hapless insect. *Alexis... Who am I? I can only be one.* My eyes peered into the slit into the room. *I can only be one.*

Alexis sat in the center of the baby room that was now covered by a large white tarp. Next to her side sat a bucket of paint and various tools. Her head was turned from me, looking down onto something in her hand.

The room I had once seen in the dark, cluttered with baby cribs and past memories had been cleared and fully lit. Now only white walls stood, covered in splotches of black molding rot.

The white and black room from my dreams, I thought as a shiver went down my spine.

Alexis stood up, revealing what had been in her hand. The ruby red heart necklace she was holding now dangled from her neck as she reached for a tool. Alexis walked to the black mold and began to scrap and pry, knocking it to the tarped white floor.

She looks so beautiful. Just as she did in the dreams.

Looks are never what they appear, kill her Perry. She will never be what you want or saw, only a lying woman.

The battle raged as I pushed the door, which creaked as it opened. Alexis stiffened and stopped her scrapping, slowly turning to the noise. "Hello?" She stuttered with wide eyes and a frightened gaze.

Taking a deep breath, I waited a moment to enter, preparing myself to face her. *It is time to decide,* I thought as I stepped halfhearted into the doorway, shielding my wounded side from Alexis in the dark hallway.

"Perry…" Alexis stumbled out. "Perry, where have you been? I have been trying to get ahold of you. I missed you so much."

I stood silent, gazing on the eerie dreamed reality before me. *I can only be one,* I thought as I continued to gaze.

"Perry are you alright? Talk to me… Things have gotten so out of hand, all I wanted to do was tell you…" Alexis stopped as blood dripped to the white tarp. "Is that blood? Perry you're hurt. What happened? Say something to me god damn it, you're scaring me to death." Alexis screamed with tears beginning to fill her ocean blue eyes.

Blood continued to drip from my flesh wound, making its way down my arm and hand onto the floor.

Kill the cheater Perry, like you should have months ago, demanded the dark monster.

I love her, she is the one, said the strange voice.

Then why was she with another man. You can only be one Perry.

Alexis made a frantic move to assist me.

"Stop," I said while I gazed into her ocean blue eyes, seeing her fearful concern stir. "I saw you."

"Saw me?" Alexis said.

"You went into his house; you went to him when I was being taken away. You never wanted me."

"Oh my god Perry, how did you… Perry, it wasn't what it looked like. That's why I called you. Check your phone, please."

She lies to your face Perry. She sees you a fool. KILL HER. I felt the power of darkness swirling inside me, taking over my mind and soul with each poisoning word.

"Shut up," I screamed, pulling back on my sweat filled hair. "How could you…. You're a liar, you tricked me, and you used me. You're just like the others."

Alexis inched closer to me. "Perry no, I swear to you. Look at your phone. I didn't do what you think I did."

I could barely hear Alexis's words as the darkness cackled, trying to take control of me. But the goodness of my shambled heart still fought the dark monster, trying to gain its own control. "Ahhhhh." I shrieked, dropping to one knee and grasping my head with both hands.

"Perry you're hurt." Alexis said running to me and putting her hand on my shoulder.

"Get you're fucking hands off me you cheater." I roared, slapping her away. "You were supposed to be different. You were pure, innocent. You made me feel again."

"Pe… Pe… Perry I… I didn't… I want you… I L…." Alexis said trembling.

"I don't know what to believe anymore. I don't know who I am anymore." I said getting off my knee.

"Perry you're scaring me…"

Alexis took a step back with tears dribbling down her cheeks.

Look at her fear you. All the power you have when you let me free. She made you weak, vulnerable, kill her.

"You should fear me Alexis. I am a monster. You witnessed what I truly am the night I beat Barry to a pulp."

"No Perry, you're sweet and kind, I have seen it in you. You're just hurt inside right now. You saw something that hurt you, but it wasn't what you think. That's what I need to tell you. Just listen to me."

Listen Perry, remember the dream. You don't have to give into the monster, the strange voice whispered in my mind.

"You're right I am hurt. I have been hurt for so long… Women, just like you, have broken me for so long. I thought you were different… but you did what everyone else has done. Break my heart, tearing it to fucking pieces. Its women like you who created me. Created this dark monster you see in front of you now."

More of my blood ran down to the white tarp and I became dizzy.

"Perry stop, just listen to me… I thought you hated me, you wouldn't return my calls or texts for weeks after that night. I was confused and scared and sad, I didn't know what to do. I became vulnerable because of how you made me feel and then all that horrible stuff happened with you and Barry and it scared me when all I meant to do was tell you how you made me really feel."

"So you ran to Barry? You cheated while we were supposed to be together? You ran to him Alexis, when I was being carried off that night. And you ran to him again when I was angry. He was right, you used me. You never wanted me."

"I didn't Perry… I only wanted you."

"Lies, you're just like him. You deserved each other."

"Perry you're not thinking straight… you're not listening."

I reached for the blade inside my jacket's pocket.

Yesssss, hissed the dark monster as the steel touched my skin.

Alexis began to sob. "Perry, please listen to me. Hear me. Believe me. You see all this." Alexis pointed around the room. "This use to be mine and Barry's room when we were together. I left it here for so long because I couldn't let go of the memories of him and I. It just sat in the darkness and gathered clutter and mold. It was a rotting old memory. But you made me strong enough to change. So I cleared it out for you, for us. I was going to surprise you with a room to do with whatever you liked with it so you could feel at home when you came here. I cleaned it out just for you. I don't give a shit about Barry, he's a pig. Look, I am even wearing the necklace you gave me." Alexis held it up to me and the red rubies sparkled.

I became entranced into the red glow. *Isn't that what you wanted, a heart? She gave that to you, and you gave her your heart Perry. Don't listen to it Perry, the monster lies. You can never see clearly in darkness.*

I let go of the blade in my coat pocket. *Who am I? What do I want?* I looked at Alexis, she seemed to glow to me just as the necklace had. She was so beautiful, she was everything I wanted…

"Alexis, I love you… But I'm not who you think I am." I said.

"Perry I…" Alexis said, beginning to walk toward me.

…But some things couldn't change. I had made my path. I had slaughtered Barry. Regardless of Alexis cheating or not, she was still there at his house and broke my loving heart. I couldn't come back, even if I wanted. I could never be with her. My darkness grabbed hold of me once more.

Kill her Perry, kill her now, the dark monster demanded, showing me images of the two cheating loves rolling naked in sheets. After the images, I lost myself in the blackness. My mind and body were being controlled by an unknown captor as it had for so many years. The ooze of black tar filled my body and ripped the rest of my decimated heart away. I was consumed and drowning in my own self.

"I am the Heartbreak Killer." I said grabbing my blade.

I stuck the steel into Alexis's gut as she came to me to my wounded arm. The silver blade pierced though her soft pale skin and her vibrant ocean blue eyes dimmed.

I tried to hold Alexis up but the impact of the wound made her heavy. I reached out trying to grab hold as she fell but I only managed to grasp onto the ruby red heart necklace. Breaking it off in my hand as she thumped to the floor of the white and black room.

I stood stunned holding the necklace in my hand as Alexis's blood filled the white tarp floor, slowly running into mine.

"Perry," Alexis whispered, dying on the floor.

I went to my knees realizing what I had just done. I ripped my jacket off, stuffing into the bleeding wound. *No what have I done. NO, NO, NO... Alexis....*

Alexis reached out and touched my face with her soft fingertips. "I am so sorry. I understand everything now... I... I... just wanted you to know... I love you." She mustered out with her last breath.

Alexis hand went limp and fell to the floor.

Tears filled my eyes and gushed out, spilling to the blood soaked floor. I fell to her body, wailing uncontrollably. *What have I done? Alexis... My love...What have I done.*

... Paul Fisher reached his daughters house. Running inside as he saw the front door already opened.

"Alexis," Paul yelled out in the dark house.

He heard a rustling noise from down the hall. Paul Fisher pulled out his gun and ran to the sound. He spotted a light in a dark hallway from an opened door.

Paul came to the door, carefully positioning his back to the wall. *One, Two, Three.*

Jumping around the corner of the door and into the light Paul saw Alexis's body lying lifeless on the white floor. Bloody and pale.

"Alexis no," Paul screamed. "Not you, this can't be happening."

Paul dived to the floor, checking for a pulse. He put his hand on her wound but the blood had already spilled, staining his hands and soaking his clothes. "No, Alexis stay with me. I am getting help. Stay with me baby girl."

Paul reached for his phone in desperation. "You're not going to leave me here alone, daddy is going to save you." But before he could dial, things went dark for Paul Fisher and he fell into a pool of blood next to his daughter.

The Heartbreak Killer stood above the Fisher family. His tears dripped to their lifeless bodies as he looked around the room of his dreams. The white and black walls with the red blood drenched floor, all blurred together in his teary eyes.

He dropped a large metal rod held in one hand and pressed the ruby red necklace to his chest with his other hand. *Things were never just white and black,* he now realized. *What have I done, I am a monster.*

Chapter 31
The Heartbreak Killer

Paul Fishers was met by complete darkness as he came to a hazy consciousness, unaware of the events that had transpired. One moment he was lying on his daughter, the next Paul was in a depth of emptiness.

Trying to move Paul noticed his arms were tied above his head. Retained in what felt like cold steel chains, while the rest of his body was slumped on a hard surface. The haze in Paul's mind began to clear and he realized, *Alexis.* He tried to move and break free from the chains, shaking his arms violently as he did. But the steel proved strong and durable, not to budge from mortal attempts. Paul became tired and rested his energy. *Alexis, where are you, what has happened?*

"Alexis," Paul wailed into the darkness. "Why, my baby girl. She can't be. I can't lose her too."

Regaining his strength again, Paul tried to break free of his imprisonment, but the steel chains would not break no matter the pull. He screamed out in agony for help, for his daughter, for anyone. *Where am I? Why is this happening? My baby girl.*

Time passed between Paul's struggles and pleas for help but no one came to his rescue, he was left alone to think of his dying daughter's body. The thought cracked Paul's psyche and he began to cry. *I want to die*, he thought. *I have nothing to live for anymore. I am alone and empty, there is nothing left for me here.* Slowly Paul's heart began to

crack inside his chest. *No Alexis, sweetheart. I couldn't protect you. I'm a failure as a husband and father.*

"Come on, kill me you son of a bitch." Paul yelled out to his unknown captor. "You win… You fucking win. You took the last thing I had left you monster. I want to die so finish me off, don't make me suffer." Paul's voice was fading, and his roar turned into no more than a whimper. "Kill me… Please… The pain is too much to bare."

There was a moment of silence before Paul heard the creaking of the floorboards above. *He is coming. My final moments on this planet.* Paul took a deep breath and waited for his maker…

…I heard the chains, *ratatattat* they spoke, Paul Fisher had become conscious.

With cautious steps, I crept down the stairs where I was keeping Detective Fisher. I had dragged his unconscious body down the stairs of Alexis's home into the basement were I restrained him. Detective Fisher now hung from a metal bar shackled in chains.

As I reached the half way mark of the stairs, I heard Detective Fisher's screams and with each step closer, the screaming became more definite. He pleaded to be killed, that he was ready for death. The sight of his daughter lying on the floor must have broken him. *It would break any man, to lose the ones he loved,* I thought, knowing the pain of lost love.

I reached the door to the basement and gently pushed it open. Paul took notice too me standing in the dark entrance and moved around in his chains, calling out to me.

"I know you're there, I could hear you walking down the stairs. Show yourself and get this over with. I have no fight left."

With hesitation, I flicked the light on.

For the first time I stood face to face with the man who sought to bring me down without my mask. Finally, Detective Paul Fisher could see my true colors as the Heartbreak Killer. The monster who took his daughter away.

Paul let out a gasp as he sat chained to the back of the basement wall. His eyes puffy, his hair scruffy, and blood from the head wound had dribbled on his left cheek. "You... You did this... You're the..." Stuttered Paul.

"Yes Detective Fisher, I am." I said with tears filled in my eyes. I was ashamed of what I had done. Hating what I was inside. *I am a monstrous villain.*

"You cared about her... How could you... Why... I don't understand." Said Paul. "You monster, you killed my baby girl. She loved you and you betrayed her."

"I loved her too Detective, but she betrayed me. Running back to Barry when I was in need. I couldn't handle the pain and the monster you speak of came out. No matter how hard I tried to bury it in the depths of my soul, it always dug its way out again."

The Detective wept at my words. I could see the pain in his eyes as he had realized all the chances he had to capture me. All the heartbreak that had come with his miscues. Then his eyes sharpened on me. *He wants to kill me, get his revenge.*

Detective Fisher tried to stand and break free of his chains. All the time he was glaring at me and screaming like a wild animal but he could not break free. Each push for freedom zapped him and the fight and rage left him on the floor once more.

He is me, I thought while I stared at the defeated Detective, slumping his head to his chest. Thoughts of me in my room crying and

yelling alone during my own countless heartbreaks surfaces. *He is becoming me, I have created a monster.* I saw the darkness fill in Paul's eyes while he glared at me. The hate and evil was growing as the heart was breaking.

"You took away the last thing I had left Perry. A person who loved us both unconditionally. I may not know much but I do know she would have never left you for Barry. It's all in your fucking head." Said Paul stopping to sniffle. "I hope there is a hell just for you so you can burn for all that you've done. Once they find out what you've done to me there won't be a dark enough corner to hide away in. You will never get away with this." Paul paused a moment, staring into my eyes as darkness filled inside his irises. "Just kill me, I don't want to look at you anymore, you disgust me. I am done with this fucked up world."

I inched closer as Detective Fisher finished his speech. The image of the Detective in chains, beaten, defeated, and alone mirrored the image of my inner self all those years back. *The creation has become the creator. I have become the thing I vowed to rid the world off. I am no better than those women who hurt me.* I stopped myself just inches away from Detective Fisher's face as he still slouched on the floor. The fight in him had receded to almost nothing.

"Kill me Perry. It should be easy for you after all of the others. Please do one decent thing in your life and stop the suffering of a hopeless man." Whispered Paul to the floor.

"Detective," I said with stern conviction as I looked down on him. "I'm sorry, for everything. I never wanted to hurt your daughter. I loved her. I tried so hard to be better and rid myself of this cursed darkness and Alexis helped me through it all. She showed me I could become a normal human being. That's all I ever wanted, to feel again. But when I was faced with adversity and pain my monster surfaced, just when I thought I was free of him. I never wanted to be this way. I wanted to be with her forever."

"But you are, and you did. Do you think your words will change anything? What you have done? You are a serial killer and you killed innocent women no matter what you think your rational reason was." Said Paul. "While on the case, I wondered why you did what you did. I could see the darkness that fills you now when my wife died and part of me understood. Hell, I even could see a bit of you in myself. But now that I see you and what you are, we are nothing alike. I pity you and your illogical thinking. Nothing you say matters to me anymore, you murdered my daughter. She was so sweet and innocent. All you deserve now is to die."

"I think you're mistaken Paul. The death of your wife was tragic, I heard the stories, but that wasn't enough to break you. No, you are becoming me now. I can see it in your eyes as you speak. The darkness is consuming you in this very moment; inside you seek to get revenge on those who have broken your heart."

"Maybe you're right Perry, as I see you standing here I want to make you suffer for what you have done. I wouldn't have a single regret about torturing you and throwing your dead body to the sea. But I can't, you have me beat. You always did, always one step ahead of me. So finish the game and let someone else play, I am tired of the struggle of the Heartbreak Killer."

"Do you think killing me would help your pain, Detective?" I asked. The Detective looked up at me, thinking of my question but did not answer so I went on. "All the killing I have done and I still suffer.

The darkness lives the more I kill, exacting my vengeance on those I think have wronged me but never becomes full."

Detective Fisher hung his head. He couldn't bear to look upon my face anymore. "Our world is full of darkness. We have both seen it and that is how we are the same. If you truly believe that I am destined to become a heartless monster like you, set me free. Send me to a better place with my loved ones. End the cycle with you, Perry. Don't let me become you and suffer."

Kill him Perry, he begs for it, whispered my dark monster. *He has seen your face now, you must kill him to survive.*

I don't want to survive. I want to die just like Alexis. I loved her but instead I listened to you. I deserve to die as Detective Fisher said. At least that way you would finally be put to rest. You are a curse.

Putting my hand to Paul's chin, I lifted his face to mine. I stared into his eyes. *The darkness is waging in his mind just like in mine.* I let go, stepping away.

"I've killed five women listening to my darkness. I killed the woman I loved, the woman who could have saved me because of my darkness. It whispers to me now to kill you so we may have a chance to survive. I don't want to survive, you're right, I deserve to die. I am a monster. But even a monster like me can do something good with their miserable lives. Detective Paul Fisher I will not kill you."

I turned my back to Paul and walked away. He began roaring at me as I made my departure. "Kill me, kill me, kill me. You coward, kill me. I'll find you Perry, you will never get away."

He will never stop. Your face will be plastered across ever news outlet. You won't survive, screamed the monster.

That's the plan. He needs to use his darkness for good.

His darkness will consume him to evil just like it did to you. He will never use it for good, he is destroyed.

As I reached the doorway of the house, I paused. I felt the pain in his words, his calls to death, and his threats to find me. Detective Fisher raged in his chains, fighting the monster inside. But he was trapped like me and there was no escape for his broken soul. The heartbreak of his life was consuming him.

You're right he needs an escape so his darkness doesn't consume him.

Instead of leaving to make my escape I raced to the white and black dream room.

Alexis lay cold and lifeless on the floor. Blood and tears stained her clothing and the white tarp on the floor. "I am sorry, you deserved better than me." I said with tears in my eyes. "I wish I could have controlled my monster but it is who I am, I am cursed. I love you, please forgive me."

I kneeled down to her body, giving her a kiss on her lips and held her cold pale skin in my arms one last time. A final tear came dripping down as I clutched her. I wiped the tear off my cheek and picked up Detective Fishers phone that was lying on the ground in a pool of his daughter's blood.

With haste, I ran back downstairs to Detective Fisher. The screaming had stopped and only the sound of sniveling could be heard. I pulled the knife out of my coat. *He needs an escape from his darkness. I am that escape,* I thought as I advanced on him. *I can do one decent thing as a killer.*

Rushing into the door, I went to the Detective as he hung like a piece of butchered meat. He heard my footsteps and looked up from his sorrow to see the knife in my hand.

"Yes, do it, finish me. I am ready." Paul begged.

I used my knife to cut open his shirt, reveal his bare chest.

Yes, kill him, save us. Take his breaking heart and let the Heartbreak live on, said the dark monster.

"Do it quick, I have suffered enough." Said Paul with the fear of death in his eyes.

I glanced into Detective Fisher's eyes one last time as he stared at my knife, awaiting his death. I saw the blackened irises and knew his doom was emanate.

The blood laced silver blade dove into the Detectives left chest. He yelled out in pain, shaking in his chains as I carved. I carved and carved until the right deed was done and then dropped the knife to the floor.

Blood oozed down Detective Paul Fishers body from the wounds as I took a step back to view my work. A bloody broken and twisted heart now resided, permanently carved on his chest. One side flipped upside down and broken.

My symbol. So he can always be reminded of who did this. Even if the darkness consumes him he will never stop until he finds me. He will use dark monster for good. At least I can hope and maybe just maybe his darkness will end with me. Giving all of us dark souls hope for redemption and revival.

You fool, kill him, demanded my darkness as it witnessed what I had done.

No, I will not be a creator of evil we have done enough.

"What are you doing?" Said Paul wincing in pain, now realizing he was still alive. "Why did you stop?"

"Because… I need to know that someone who has endured darkness can make it past and do something good. Now you will always be reminded who did this to you. Who broke the final piece of your heart. Who killed your daughter. Even in your darkest moments, when the monster calls to you, this will be a reminder of me and what we both feel, heartbreak. Come find me Paul, I'll be waiting for you. I won't stop killing innocent people until you do. The Heartbreak Killer to you as Detective Fisher you are to me. A worthy advisory. Avenge your daughter Paul. Save the world from the dark monster."

"Why?" Said Paul. "Why make me suffer?"

"Doesn't everyone suffer in one way or another? There is still a part of me though, that wants to believe that even in the darkest moments we can make it through without being consumed. It is too late for me Paul, I see that now, but you can endure yours. Start with me, put me where I deserve to be. The world needs people who have seen the darkness but chose to do good so others don't have to endure the curses I have been shouldered with."

"You will never get away. I won't let you if you let me live." Yelled Paul.

"I don't want to get away. I have done enough damage in this world. I deserve to die." I said with seriousness. Quickly I wiped the blood from the Detectives phone and dialed a number.

"What are you doing?" Said Paul.

"Getting you out of here."

"Hello," answered a woman on the other line.

"Agent Price?" I said into the phone.

"Yes? This isn't Paul. Who is this?"

"This is the Heartbreak Killer and I have Paul Fisher in chains clinging to his life at his daughter's house. You better hurry." I clicked the phone off and threw it to Paul's feet. "Now we part." I said walking away.

"Wait," Yelled Paul.

"What?" I said without turning around.

"Tell me."

"Tell you what?"

"Your story, your story of darkness, of heartbreak. The Heartbreak Killer story."

"Maybe next time Paul. Come find me." I said with a villainous smirk to myself.

Paul pleaded and cursed out to me as I ventured into the darkness, clutching my wounded arm and dangling the ruby red heart necklace I had bought for Alexis. *The lasting memory of my love to you.* My mind raced as I thought of Alexis, of the Detective, of my plan to escape. There was no definite step for what the future held for me but I finally had the answer I was looking for all along. *Who am I?*

Was I a heartless killer or an emotional good willed human being? *Neither.* I went into the future as a mortal man, one who had seen too much, been broken too many times, and finally turned to the darkness. *Who am I? I am the villain.*

The world was not black and white, clear and cut, and neither was I. Life was like the floor of the room where Alexis lay slain, bloody with salty tears. Confusing and Grey. The pop fiction I had read and seen lied to me. Always portraying the villain as evil. *No, I am a villain with good in him just as I am a villain with dark flaws and monsters.* And like villains in the story, heroes like Paul Fisher were never as pure as they seemed. In real life they can be dark and shrouded with evils. *I have seen it in him now. The difference is the Detective sees the darkness and repels it while I embrace it. But how long can he hold on before he breaks like I have.*

I didn't know where I was going as I scoured the American city I had called my home for many years. But I knew I would be gone long before the police plastered my face on every corner block and on every TV station. I had a plan in case this day came.

Where shall I go next, I thought as the sun began to rise and the sirens screeched on a mild February morning. *Maybe I will go to your city next, lurking the corners of the street, waiting for my next victim. Maybe I have already found my next victim and am in their room now as they sit and read. Ever so ready to extract my next piece of heart. Maybe I never kill again and instead hide forever. Awaiting the looming wrath of Detective Paul Fisher alone in the darkness.*

I stood on the horizon thinking of my next move. In one hand I held a heavy silver briefcase, in the other the red ruby heart necklace. I dangled it in front of my face full of tears. The light from the sun reflected the red of the ruby onto me. *Who are you,* she whispered from above.

I am Perry Nelson, The Heartbreak Killer.

Epilogue
The Call

A handsome TV anchor broadcasted in front of a national audience.

"A country wide man-hunt has begun for the Heartbreak Killer. Perry Nelson, who slain the daughter of Detective Paul Fisher as well as Terry Connor and countless others, is the man police have identified as the killer. Nelson is now at large after what many are calling the Heartbreak Massacre as the horrific events accrued just hours before February 14th, otherwise known as Valentine's Day. "

A newspaper read.

Alexis Fishers body was found at the scene of the crime. Dead inside her home from a single stab wound. Detective Fisher was also found inside the home, chained, beaten, and cut. The cuts revealed the infamous Heartbreak Killer symbol (A broken heart with one side flipped upside down) knifed into the detectives left chest. Later the Detective identified the killer as Perry Nelson. Nelson was a renowned psychologist in the city he resided in and is now at large. Detective Fisher was quoted,

"I will not rest until the man that killed my daughter is put to justice. He is a monster that must be put away, before more innocent people are harmed."

For now, it's uncertain how these events came to fruition as much speculation is building about the relationship between the killer and Alexis Fisher.

A radio talk show voiced with a guest panel.

"I heard that this Heartbreak Killer was in love with the detectives' daughter but she didn't want him and he went on a rampage. He couldn't handle the rejection of her going back to the ex-boyfriend so he killed them both." Said the radio host.

"It's quite sickening that someone would try to take true love away from those two. What's the ex's name? Barry something? I heard he was an amazing lawyer and a real standup guy. The killer must have been jealous of all he had." Said one of the women on the panel.

"I couldn't agree more. On the eve of Valentine's Day no less, a day dedicated to love. The killer really lives up to his title." Said another man on the panel.

"Prayers go out to Detective Fisher. He has lost both his wife and daughter in the same year now. I can't imagine what he is going through." Said the woman.

"If anyone has any information on the whereabouts of this man Perry Nelson please contact the local authorities. Let's get this soulless monster put away for good." Said the radio host.

The internet boomed with trends and buzz on the story of the Heartbreak Killer.

True love cannot be broken. Rest in peace Alexis and Barry, posted a youthful teen.

Prayer for the victims loved ones in these dark times. Hopefully this man is brought to justice quickly, posted a concerned mother.

You're the truth Heartbreak, posted an unknown user.

You're sick and need help. You know nothing of our world or the situation, and should be put in jail with him. Sickening trolls, replied another, to the unknown user.

Around the country, the news swirled and swirled as the Heartbreak Killer roamed free. Everyone making up their own stories about what happened and why. The media cared little of the validity of the truth, and soon people around the world grew fearful of the Heartbreak Killer. *I could be next*, the public thought as they gobbled up news on the killer to feel safe. All the while the evil and greedy sold the fear becoming rich because of a serial killer story. *Who cares about the effect this story has on the innocent people,* the evil and greedy thought. *As long as the story sells…*

Two young teenage boys were playing around in the neighborhood where Alexis Fishers murder occurred. Police had marked the door of the Fisher house with tape presenting ***do not cross***. The boys saw the tape as they passed the house.

"Why do you think he did it?" Said one boy to the other.

"Who knows, love has always seemed complicated to me. I can't imagine me ever caring about a girl that much to go crazy." Said the other.

"Me either, it seems like once you get older things get more complicated than they should. I mean my parents fight all the time but say they are in love. It makes no sense."

"Mine too. Love is strange. For all I know the killer could have been right."

"Ha shut up, he was a serial killer."

"I guess you're right, but still he had some reason to do what he did."

"Or he was crazy."

"It seems like anyone in love is crazy to me anyways."

"Hey do you see that?" Said one of the boys pointing in the direction of a lone car parked on the street.

"Kind of, let's go check it out."

The two boys ran over to the car.

"It looks like blood." Said one of the boys peeking into the window.

"Yeah on the door handle too." Said the other pointing to the driver side door handle.

Together the boys examined the inside of the car to see if anyone was inside. They spotted a black phone in the back seat but there was no source that the blood could have come from. The boys turned to each other at the same time as they spotted a phone.

"You don't think?" They said to each other.

"The Heartbreak Killer's car?" Said one of the boys.

"Yeah, the news people said he was injured." Said the other boy.

"Should we go get someone?"

"In a sec, let's see if the cars unlocked. That phone could be his. I wanna see what's on a killer's phone, don't you?"

The boy reached for the door handle with blood on it. As he pulled the door, the handle revealed it was unlocked, and the boys began to search the inside of the car.

"Whoa, look at all that blood in the seat." Said the boy who opened the door.

"And on the side of the door." Said the other boy now in the front seat.

One of the boys clicked the switch to unlock the rest of the doors. He went to the back seat and got the phone. When the boy pressed the

single button on the black cell phone, the screen remained black, reflecting his face back on the glass.

"I think it's dead." Said the boy looking at the phone.

"Try holding the button, it may be turned off." Said the other boy, still examining the driver seat area.

"You're right."

The boy held the button. After a second, the phone lit up to a white screen. "It's turning on!"

"Really, let me see that." Said the other boy going to the back seat and snatching the phone from the other. "You think he has anything on here."

"Maybe he has pictures of his victims. Or what if he has texts from that Alexis Fisher woman he loved."

The phone turned to the main screen and both boys attention turned from talking.

"Look two missed calls." Said one as he examined.

"Click on it." Said the other.

"Alexis Fisher." Said the two boys in unison as they saw the red missed call.

"Look, she left a voice mail too."

"Should we listen?"

"I don't know. Maybe we should tell our parents, it could be police evidence or something." Said one boy stepping back from the phone.

"Don't be a puss. It be way too cool to be the first ones to hear this. We could be on the news and everything."

"Fine. But we have to take this to someone after. Deal?"

"Deal. Come listen, I'll put it on speaker."

The two boys huddled over the phone.

Alexis's voice spoke through the phone speaker in a soft manner. "Perry…" She said.

"That's the killer's real name." Said one of the boys.

"I know. Shut up and listen." Said the other giving a nudge.

"It's Alexis. I know you're not talking to me… but I had to call you and talk or vent. I need to get some things off my chest. I know why you're not talking to me and I understand but I wish you would, I miss you. I want to explain everything to you. So I hope you listen to this even if you won't talk to me."

The recording voice paused and deep breath could be heard over the speaker.

"Well here it goes, I hope you understand." Alexis paused again. "I went to go see Barry yesterday. I don't know what I was doing. I was really upset about us and how you were ignoring me. So I felt like maybe I should go back to Barry if I couldn't be with you. It was a huge mistake though. I know how bad that sounds after what you saw the night you got arrested, but I was vulnerable and he took advantage of that. He even said that if I went out with him to talk he would drop the charges on you, so I went. I don't even know why I went now. He offered for me to come over after and I decided to go. I was so lost, my mind was scrambled, but at the very least, I thought the more I went with things the more likely he would forgive you for the fight. Anyways, Perry, I went inside his house without thinking. He promised he would be civil and a gentleman. He wasn't.

Alexis started to cry on the phone.

"He started kissing me and tried to take my clothes off. But I stopped him. I knew that it wasn't right and my heart was with you. I slapped him and told him I wouldn't ever go back. I… I told him I love you Perry. I wish I would have told you before that night happened, I wanted to so bad. It was all I could think about on the drive home from the park. But Perry, I was nervous. It doesn't matter anymore with the way things are but you should know how much I care about you and how you make me feel. I truly love you and I want to spend the rest of my life with you, if you can forgive me for this whole thing. I was stupid, so stupid, but I didn't let anything happen, I promise."

Alexis paused again sniffling.

"I'm here at my house now. I'm cleaning out this old room that use to be Barry's personal room when we lived together. I finally know it's time to move on from him and never look back. You are so much better than he is or ever was. I was stupid to ever debate or even try to go back. So I'm making the room nice and clean for you. If you can ever forgive me it can be your little study for work or whatever you want. Perry I'm so sorry and I hope you can find it in yourself to forgive me and believe my words. I love you and no one else. I guess I hope to see you or hear from you soon. Goodbye Perry Nelson."

The message stopped and the two boys glanced wide eyed at each other, shocked and scared.

"Let's go get our parents. Someone needs to hear this." They said and ran.

The Heartbreak Killer

Book One

<u>Acknowledgments</u>

I would like to share special thanks to the people who helped make this book possible.

First and foremost, my editor Darlie Keizer, who helped to point out my many errors within these pages. Without you, this book would have been an utter mess. So thank you for improving the weakest parts of my writing along the way.

Second, I would like to thank Ana Grigoriu, who made the beautiful and elegant cover you have before you now. Art come in many different forms and you have a true talent for yours.

Third, I would like to thank Jordan Mendoza, who took countless author photos of me. They turned out wonderfully. I will not soon forget the incident under the bridge with the questionable people around us.

Lastly, I would like to thank my beta readers, who helped further the improvement of this book. Without your advice and voices I wouldn't have made this book what it is now.

Thank you all.

Copyright © <u>DapperBandit Photography</u>

<u>About the Author</u>

Majoring in psychology and having a passion for storytelling, Maddison L. Beckley created the Heartbreak Killer while on a long bus ride to Eastern Washington University.

Residing in Spokane Washington, Maddison now writes books and roots for his favorite sports teams, the Boston Celtics & Tennessee Titans.

Find out more about Maddison L. Beckley at

<u>Facebook- Author Maddison L. Beckley, The Heartbreak</u>

THE
⊘HEARTBREAK

For more of Maddison L. Beckley's work and upcoming titles visit:

WWW.ATALEOFTWISTEDLOVE.COM